BEAUTY WITH A GUN . . .

"Please don't move. I have a big gun aimed at your head, and I shoot well."

"Okay. I won't move." Beckett Snow was still sitting behind the steering wheel of his van. "So what do you want me to do?"

"Slide to the center of the seat." He started to move and she yelled, "Slowly, slowly!"

"Okay, okay."

The van vibrated and he heard the boxes in the rear rattle as whoever was holding the gun climbed toward the front. He smelled the faintest whiff of perfume mingled with perspiration, and then flinched as the cold that can only come with the muzzle of a gun was thrust in the back of his neck.

"This is a .44 magnum. It—"

"Yeah, I know, lady. It can blow my head off. Don't worry, I won't argue with you."

THE DELPHI BETRAYAL

LEWIS PERDUE

PINNACLE BOOKS   NEW YORK

The Delphi Betrayal

Copyright © 1981 by W. Lewis Purdue

An original Pinnacle Books edition, published for the first time anywhere.

First printing, June 1981

ISBN: 0-523-41139-1

Cover illustration by Brian Leng

Printed in the United States of America

PINNACLE BOOKS, INC.
1430 Broadway
New York, New York 10018

To Megan

The Delphi Betrayal

Part I

Chapter One

There was no body. Which was ridiculous, there *had* to be a body. It was just a matter of finding it.

Snow had seen the flashing lights just as he got halfway down the ramp leading onto the Pasadena Freeway at Avenue 60. He knew he'd made a mistake. There were no police flashers then, but the emergency flashers of half a dozen private vehicles winked and stuttered among the brake lights as car after car halted on the pavement.

He'd been some distance from the scene, but he parked his van off the shoulder next to the guardrail and got out to see if he could help.

He hadn't wanted to stop. Beckett Snow knew what he'd find ahead. He'd had too many nights as a cop, getting out of bed to face a nightmare of mutilated people. But he stopped anyway. He was a man who knew responsibilities and how to respond to them even when they made him sick.

Someone looking at his eyes as he got closer to the scene would have noticed them turn slowly cold, flat. Lines grew between his eyebrows, from his mouth, into a frown that wrinkled his forehead and made him look more than his 31 years.

He was not a large man, five-foot-nine. But he was compact and powerful. Many people would have looked overweight at his 170 pounds, but Snow was a mass of muscle. His shoulders were wider than those of men a head taller than he, but his compact muscularity was tempered by the litheness of a dancer—powerful and chain explosive.

Snow walked toward the scene, saw reflections of flashing lights, and turned to see two police cruisers threading their way through stalled traffic.

Damn Valerie! Snow thought. Why in hell did she have to change that way! Why couldn't she have been . . . Snow put the thoughts in a locker and closed it firmly. They could wait for later; *this* had to be dealt with *now*.

Snow realized what he did and did it gladly. Every cop, every person who came in contact with the destruction of human beings, developed the mindset: switch off the old thoughts, climb into the armor.

It was effective, Snow knew. He remembered times when the mindset allowed him to function professionally at the scene of hideous carnage, and when it was all over, he'd go back to the station house and throw up in the john. The first time he didn't feel like throwing up when it was over was the day he resigned and applied to law school.

Snow reached the car. The roof was bashed in so badly he figured there was almost no way anyone could have come out of it alive.

But there was no body, and no indication of a body being thrown from the wreck. He stayed out of the way while the policemen arrived and conferred. He watched as they became more and more perplexed. It was then that he introduced himself.

The cops and ambulance attendants searched for the body, certain it had been thrown from the wreckage.

"Hey, check the other lanes," one called to his buddies.

They did. Still no body.

"Ah, ain't got no body," Snow softly hummed to

2

himself and walked back to the wreckage. It was upright, backwards, and the undercarriage was impaled on the guardrail. The trunk was open. Something about it bothered him. He peered through the passenger side window. There was dirt caked on the side and roof. The air hung with the menthol from a eucalyptus tree branch that had been severed. The driver's side of the compartment seemed to be intact.

Snow looked back at a plowed swath running up the embankment in a fuzzy parabola, one end anchored at the guardrail edge and the other planted with the car, a late-model Buick. What had made it go off the road? Drunk driver? Suicide attempt? An attempt to avoid a collision?

"Well, what do you make of it?" one of the troopers asked him as he walked away from the car.

"Nothing," Beckett said. "I can't make any sense out of it."

The trooper at Beckett's left suddenly screamed toward the car's wreckage, "Hey you, get the hell away from there!"

Beckett turned to see a man with a grey sweater and a small camera walking away from the car.

"Goddamned reporters," the trooper muttered. "Don't see how in hell they get to places so fuckin' fast."

Beckett left his card, said his goodbyes, and pulled into traffic to head home. He looked at his watch and noted it was now 3:44 AM.

He felt cheated, frustrated, and angry in the same way that parents get angry when an overdue child they've been worrying about finally returns. His crisis armor had been unnecessary. But there was, to be sure, something of a mystery. What happened to the body?

Frustration and anger led his thoughts back to the things that were making him frustrated and angry before he reached the accident scene.

3

Over and over again he'd gone through it. It would never end—getting to know someone only to discover they're not what you thought they were to begin with. Honesty, he seldom ever found it. Sympathy for sure, maybe even security, but honesty? Never. And the little nibbles of compromise and accommodation, acceptable forms of dishonesty, nipped and gnawed until he could stand it no longer.

Valerie. He'd just dropped her off at her house. She was the sort who might have tried to be a model if she hadn't had such a sound mind. There was the natural blond hair, green eyes, and attractive face, but the square jaw was a little too square and the cheekbones not quite high enough. Her breasts were average size, maybe a little larger, and there was too much muscle from a love of athletics.

But the imperfections were what made her distinctly her. She was an athletic woman; a strong, assertive woman whose mind was every bit as facile and strong as her body. Even the name—Valerie—so like Valkyrie, which conjured up images of strength and power.

He liked that, liked someone who was at least his equal, who could fence with him intellectually, call his bluff, and be able to tell him to shove it and make it stick. She had a career as a reporter for the Los Angeles *Times*, and she had a vision of her future.

He'd loved her for all of it. He'd loved her for being a whole living breathing person. They'd fallen deeply in love. Very quickly.

Then things changed.

She started to defer to him, to act helpless in situations that months before she could have handled herself. She started to depend on him for things. She started, Beckett thought wryly, to act like a wife.

He hadn't a thing against marriage—thought it was a nifty institution—but he knew he'd never be married to a "wife."

4

He'd tried to figure it out, tried to talk things over with Valerie, tried to reverse her slide, and it had been hopeless.

They'd broken up that night. Both had cried for hours. It was inevitable, Snow thought bitterly. He was beginning to doubt that a man and a woman could have a relationship without one or the other being destroyed. It wasn't like he was asking for the impossible, he assured himself. He wasn't looking for Superwoman. He just wanted someone who knew who she was and stayed who she was even when she was with a man. Christ! Why couldn't he just like some beautiful flake whose ambition it was to get a guy to buy her a dishwasher, a Datsun Z, and lots of new clothes? All it took, he knew, was compromise. Just a little lie. It wouldn't hurt anybody and he'd be alone a lot less, and frustrated a lot less.

But he'd always been this way. Fuck compromise! He'd put himself through college in the late sixties by working as a newspaper reporter while he studied at Cornell. He'd covered riots and demonstrations. He sympathized with the students, but he had to get along with the police to get information for his stories. And he was fascinated by them and horrified at the same time. For violence was disorder and he liked order. So he joined the very people he disliked. When he graduated, he joined the New York State Police—as professional an organization as existed outside the FBI. He spent three years at the job, excelling at every assignment, finally being assigned to the Bureau of Criminal Investigation as an undercover narcotics agent for a year and a half. They were strange and rewarding years.

But though he loved the chance to make order out of chaos, he enjoyed more being the avenging angel, the sword of justice. He found himself staying callous long after his hours of work had ceased. So he quit.

Cornell Law School was happy to take an alumnus with his cum laude grades and outstanding scores on the law boards. He got through in two and a half years and went to work as an assistant U.S. attorney, a federal prosecutor. He worked four years in Washington. Those years had paid off, he thought now. He was the second in command of the U.S. Attorney's office for the Southern District of California. No mean feat: He was the youngest of his kind in the United States.

Lots of good that did him now, he thought, as he reached the Fourth Street exit of the Santa Monica Freeway. The job went just so far in satisfying his frame of mind. His personal life, he knew, was a cold pile of dog shit. Nothing, he was sure, could be worse.

"Did you find her?"

"She survived the crash."

"Was she hurt badly?"

"No. She wasn't around."

"Shit. Where did she go?"

"From what I could tell, she crawled into the bushes. She hurt her leg, though."

"How could you tell?"

"There was blood on the driver's side door. And about 30 yards from the car, there were drops of fresh blood leading up to a van."

"Why didn't . . ." The phone connection bounced off a satellite, faded, and lost the sound for a moment.

"I'm sorry, bad connection. I didn't get that."

"I said, why didn't you take her?"

"The van's driver returned before I had a chance."

"She's a crafty bitch, all right. You can bet that was no accident."

"I know."

"I presume you got the license number of the van?"

"Right."

"Did you follow it?"

"I couldn't. Our car was up on a side road where we parked it."

"But you will track it?"

"It's being done right now."

"And you're sure she has the dossier."

"It wasn't in the car. And if she doesn't have it I think we're . . ."

"You're not paid to think, so don't. Understand?"

"Yes, sir."

"I want her dead. Make her disappear; we're too close. Do you understand?"

"Yes sir, but . . ."

"And I want the Prometheus dossier as proof."

"But if she's dead . . ."

"I want two things. I want her dead and I want the file. And I get what I want or you're dead too. Understand?"

"Yes, sir."

"Good. Goodbye," he said. The long distance satellite connection echoed.

"But of course a group like this has to exist. It's the only logical progression; it's inevitable."

The young man was exasperated. He'd had enough of trying to explain the obvious to people who wouldn't listen.

"Are you *sure*, Peter? Are you quite convinced of the benefits of such a group, of the life that such a group would inevitably dictate?"

"There you go again. Even your word choice shows your prejudices! 'Dictate' indeed! True, it would be assertive rule, but logical, fair, efficient, and peaceful."

The older man said nothing more for the moment. He and the younger man, younger by more than a generation, regarded each other with a countenance of frustration and pity melded with respect and genuine fondness.

7

The younger man was Peter Gilbert, at 29 a White House aide and top staff coordinator in North America for the Delphi Commission. Peter was tall, aristocratic; first with degrees from Groton, then Yale, and an M.B.A. from Harvard. He was Connecticut blue blood, overendowed with the ambition and intelligence that were raw materials of success.

He was a wunderkind, and though launched by the money, power, and ambition of his family, he was soaring under his own power, sought after now not because of his familial relationships, but for his ability to create, organize, execute, and achieve.

No other 29-year-old in North America—perhaps in the world—wielded the power in his grasp, yet few outside of a circumscribed circle of business acquaintances and an even smaller circle of friends knew more than the fact that he was a hot item.

The older man was Isaac Roth, who the week before had celebrated his seventy-third birthday. Few knew what he did. For, though he did much, he did it out of sight, through others, in darkness behind visible power.

Isaac Roth was an adviser. He had no title, he appeared on no government payrolls. He had never given a press conference, interview, or had an article written about him. It was his will. For Isaac Roth had been an adviser to every president from FDR to the present. He, too, was of the purest Yankee heritage, and like Peter Gilbert had prepped at the best schools, excelled at the best the Ivy League could offer, and had been one of the New Deal wunderkinds.

But Roth wielded power gracefully. He spoke judiciously when necessary and bluntly when he was forced.

Isaac Roth was continuity. Every government, every institution must have continuity, and for the White House it was Roth. He knew where the bodies were buried and who had held the shovel. He kept presidents out of trouble when they listened to his advice, and got them out of trouble when they'd had the foolishness to ignore him.

He could accept and circumvent fools who knew nothing, and wise men who knew everything. But it was people—like this young Peter Gilbert for whom he had so much fondness—that frustrated him. Frustrated him when they had the intelligence to understand, and would not.

Their silence filled the room, deep in the bowels of the Washington soil beneath the White House. It was an odd room, unlike all but one other in the presidential mansion. The President was not allowed into Peter Gilbert's inner office.

The walls were covered with maps of the world, special maps silkscreened onto Plexiglas and lit from behind wtih lights in a multitude of colors. These were the sort of maps that can be used to chart trajectories and paths of armies, positions of units and their progress. But instead of spaceship trajectories or the march of tanks and guns, the map charted the progress—and, some would say from looking at it, the future trajectories—of the Delphi Commission. Peter Gilbert was coordinator of the North American section of the Commission. His was not a policy position but an administrator's position. What the Commission desired was his to execute: to figure the logistics, the details, to cover pitfalls before they became traps.

He was more, but he didn't yet know it.

Chapter Two

"Please don't move. I have a big gun aimed at your head—and I shoot well."

Though the voice behind him was weary, it was laced with a determination that told Beckett Snow not to do anything foolish.

"Okay. I won't move." Snow was still sitting behind the steering wheel of his van. He'd just pulled into his driveway, and had been about to open the door. "So what do you want me to do?"

"Slide to the center of the seat." He started to move, and she yelled, "Slowly, slowly! Whatever I tell you to do, do it slowly."

"Okay, okay." Beckett inched slowly toward the center of the seat.

"Stop." He did. "Put your hands behind your head." He did that too. The van vibrated and he heard the boxes in the rear rattle as whoever was holding the gun climbed toward the front. He smelled the faintest whiff of perfume mingled with perspiration, and then flinched as the cold that can only come with the muzzle of a gun was thrust in the back of his neck.

"This is a .44 magnum. It—"

"Yeah, I know, lady. It can blow my head off. Don't worry, I won't argue with you."

"Good. Now, let's walk into the house. First, I want you to get out slowly. Stop when I tell you to. Okay?"

10

"Sure."

"Okay, now slide toward the passenger door."

"I gotta get my keys to get in the house, all right?"

"Yes."

He tugged the keys out of the ignition.

"Okay, now get out the passenger door."

She's no slouch, whoever she is, Beckett thought. The van blocks the view from the neighbors, and we get out unseen. Smart, he thought, and filed it away for whatever use it might have against this crafty lady.

"Stop." He did. He heard her slide out of the van behind him. "Okay now, let's walk inside."

The house wasn't much, but it was all a U.S. prosecutor could afford. Stucco, a small front porch with an arched doorway, the house had two bedrooms, a living room, kitchen, and pantry. It cost him $139,000, mainly because it was two blocks from the beach.

They walked into the living room. He turned on the light. "Stand with your face to the sofa." After he had obeyed her command she said, "Now turn around and sit down. *Slowly.*"

As he did he noticed that the pistol was indeed a .44 magnum and by the expert way she held it—two hands outstretched, left hand cradling the butt of the pistol grip, legs spread to absorb the substantial recoil—she was familiar with the gun and probably knew how to use it. This, too, he filed away for possible recall.

"Now, I want your help," she said. She was serious.

He looked her over. Despite the fact that she was an aggressor, he saw her as a woman as well as an opponent. A threat, most assuredly, and dangerous beyond a doubt. A person notably worth respect, who just happened to be a woman.

She was about five-foot-five and had long, sandy brown hair. She was facing the window, and the light had contracted her pupils until they were almost all iris, one brown and the other hazel. In the ensuing

11

silence he examined her face. Most of the lines seemed to be from worry, and not age. He gauged her to be about 30 years old.

She wore a navy-blue blazer and poplin slacks. Under the blazer was a pinstriped, button-down shirt with a silk scarf. Her navy blue pumps were covered with fresh earth. So were her slacks. Everything was creased and rumpled. An abstract pattern of dried blood decorated the cuff of her left pants leg. A leather briefcase sat beside the chair.

Freshly pressed, the effect would be that of a businesswoman, a successful executive or an attorney perhaps, dressed in a feminine, but altogether sexless fashion. But the rumples and creases and the vulnerability of her weariness gave her a faintly sexual attractiveness.

She was, Beckett decided, an attractive, albeit dangerous, woman.

"I said, I need your help. Didn't you hear me?"

"Ah, sure. But don't you think that somehow I might wonder how much help I can give to someone who's threatened to blow my head off?"

She was silent.

"Uh, I would offer you something but I wasn't expecting company. This is, ah, the maid's day off." He smiled.

She didn't. "You're not funny."

"Okay, let's be serious for a moment. What kind of help do you want, especially what kind with a pistol in my ear."

"I don't know," she said wearily. "I've gotten this far, and I'm not sure where to go. I need time to think." Holding the magnum with her right hand, she pulled an Eames chair over to her, where she could sit facing Beckett, well out of reach.

"Giving you time is something I could have done

12

without your having to take it at pistol point," Beckett said. "Time I can give you but . . ." He raised his left arm suddenly.

She sprang up, pistol ready. "Hold it!"

"Easy, lady, easy. Be cool. I was just going to look at my watch. I have a job, you know, and somebody's going to miss me if I don't show."

She relaxed. "Okay, but whatever you do, do it slowly."

Beckett nodded with a smile and a sideways bowing of his head. He looked at the heavy Omega Seamaster diving watch on his wrist and noted that it was quarter of eight.

"What time are you expected?"

"I usually arrive at about 9."

"When can you call to let them know you won't be coming in today?"

He hadn't thought of not coming in that day. Though it dawned on him that it was ridiculous to think of going to work while someone pointed a gun at him.

"Somebody will be there in 15 or 20 minutes."

"Call then."

"Anything you say." He nodded toward the pistol. "Look, I'm sorry to have to do this to you . . ."

"But you don't," he interrupted.

"I'm sorry to have to do this to you," she began again, ignoring his interruption, "but there are some people who want to kill me, and I'll do anything I have to do to survive."

"So tell me about it," he said.

"I have something that some very powerful men want," she said. "And they'll kill me to get it back."

"Right, sweetheart, just tell Sam Spade all about the black bird."

"Look, there's nothing humorous about this whole situation, and I wish you would stop making jokes."

13

"If I stop with the jokes, my dear, I'll wet my pants. Look, you put up with the lousy jokes and I'll put up with your rude form of introduction. Okay?"

She didn't react.

"I cased the accident you stopped at tonight," she continued. "I was the driver of the car." Beckett looked down at the bloodstain on her pants cuff. "They were chasing me and I couldn't shake them. They'd tried to run me off the road twice and I knew they'd succeed sooner or later. Their car was bigger and faster.

"So when I got to the ramp, and it had all the streetlights, and there was a decent amount of traffic, I crammed on the brakes. They ran into the backend of my car, and I think it damaged the steering or something. Anyway, I hit the guardrail. You know the rest."

"Didn't they stop and come back for you?"

"There was too much traffic. They stopped, but couldn't back up. I hid in the brush on the side of the road. That gave me time to stop the bleeding on my ankle." She looked down at the stain. "And then all sorts of cars started stopping to look at the wreckage."

"But you had time to get this—whatever it is they want so badly—out of the trunk before you hid in the bushes, right?" Beckett said. She looked puzzled.

"How did you know?"

Ah, shit in heaven's back pocket. Snow thought. All I need is for some criminal to know I'm a federal prosecutor, a former cop. But this one, she doesn't *seem* like a criminal, doesn't act like my telling her I was a cop would spook her. Snow weighed his feelings against the logic.

He usually had hunches about whether or not people were guilty, and much more often than not he was right. After considering all of the evidence and logic of a case, he would rely on his feelings in deciding whether or not to prosecute. This was a different case, though. He was on trial in a certain sense. Still, he decided he'd level with the woman.

"I'm a federal prosecutor," Snow told her and watched her pupils constrict. "I also used to be a cop." He watched for further reaction and found none. That, he thought, was good. "That's how I know you took something out of the trunk," Snow said. "When I looked the wreck over I saw the trunk was open, but it was opened by a key and not knocked open."

"Yeah," she continued, seemingly unfazed by Snow's revelations. "So anyway, after a while you arrived and got out of your van. Lots of people got out to gawk, but yours was the only van."

"So you decided to take a ride?"

"Right."

"Hey, you still haven't told me what you've got or who's trying to kill you."

"And I don't intend to."

"And you expect me to help you?"

"Yes."

"But who? Who *are* these people?"

Beckett leaned forward, palms open and arms outstretched to lend emphasis. He startled her with the sudden motion and she straightened up. It saved her life. At that moment, the window by the front door exploded. A glass ginger jar lamp just to her left shattered, and showered them with the fragments of shells that had filled it.

"Never mind. There's one of them now," he said.

Someone on the porch, Beckett told himself simply, was shooting at them. The woman snapped her head away from him and trained the muzzle of her pistol on the windows.

Beckett was frozen. He watched and wondered briefly if this wasn't the point when he was supposed to review his life.

15

But his reflexes paid no heed to his head. He catapulted from the sofa and tackled the woman. His left hand snatched the gun from her grip as his right shoulder plowed into her midriff. The momentum carried them sprawling into the hallway that led to the bedrooms.

Beckett's head was vaguely aware of the stemmed glassware over the bar exploding. His reflexes noted that they were shattered by silenced automatic weapons fire, and noted the characteristic phut-phut of an Ingram. That frightened him. Only professionals used the Ingram.

"Well, sweetheart, looks like we're in for a time of it now. Don't your friends know how to ring a doorbell?" Getting no reply, he looked down asd saw she was unconscious and her temple was bleeding from a collision with the edge of a marble-topped table. "Oh shit. You're gonna be a lot of help."

Beckett started to pick her up when the sound of splintering wood echoed through the living room.

He lay on his belly and peered around the corner of the hallway and watched as the hollow core door buckled and surrendered. It swayed against the wall on drunken hinges, and standing in the doorway was the man in the gray sweater. The camera had been replaced with a machine pistol. And it was definitely an Ingram.

Beckett braced his elbow on the carpet, holding the magnum in his left hand as he leaned around the doorway. He lined up the red of the nose indicator in the notch of the rear sight and squeezed the trigger. He didn't have to think. Reflexes did it for him.

For an instant he was afraid he'd missed. But then he saw the man in the gray sweater pirouette clockwise, slam into the wall between the door and the window and slide to the floor. The Ingram skittered under the sofa. Beckett was going to fire again when he saw that the man's right shoulder was missing.

Snow remained still and withdrew into the safety of the hallway's darkness. He reached over to the woman, grasped her wrist, and felt for a pulse. It was there and strong. He reached for her head and cradled it in his hands. Snow's fingers were supple, strong, gentle as he parted her hair near the wound. In the dim light he could see that the bleeding had stopped, and a goose egg had started to swell. He was relieved that the wound seemed superficial. He smoothed the fine hair back over the wound and looked at her face. The lines of worry were gone. He wondered if she was really unconscious now, or if she was sleeping away the fatigue and tension. She *was* beautiful. He thought that, when this was all over, he'd like to get to know her.

Suddenly he heard a shoe grind glass fragments into the living room floor. Laying down the magnum, Beckett wrestled the marble-topped table onto its side to provide a shield just before it was raked with slugs from another Ingram.

Snow peered through a space between the tabletop and the doorjamb. He saw no one.

"Against the wall," Snow muttered to himself. "The mother must be flattened against one of the walls." Another piece of glass snapped. The floor was covered with the ruins of his stemware.

To his right, Snow determined. He crouched and stuck the magnum around the doorjamb and fired blindly. The shot was repaid with another volley from the Ingram. Some of the shots chipped out pieces of the soft marble.

The intruder ran for the middle of the room. Snow peered over the top and saw the intruder reach for the briefcase. He fired again. He missed. The intruder, a woman about five-foot-ten and wearing a plaid shirt

17

and blue jeans wheeled for the door with the case in her left hand. With the Ingram in her right hand, she sprayed a covering volley at Beckett and ran for the front door.

Beckett fired again. At first he thought he'd missed again. But she dropped the case and ran across the porch and into the street. He leapt over the table in time to see her sprint to a dark-colored sedan and drive away. He surveyed the street: There were few cars. It was a working neighborhood and most people had probably left for work. If anyone had heard the shots, no one had reacted.

The room was a shambles. There were shards from the broken glasses and from the window; splinters from the front door; marble chips from the table; plaster dust from the bullet holes in the walls and ceiling; and, on the floor, a man's body that had stopped bleeding shortly after the trouble had begun.

Beckett walked over to the man lying on the floor and turned him over. No pulse. He reached down to the man's face, and with his right thumb, pulled open an eyelid. Even with the face in the bright sunlight, the pupils were so completely dilated it was impossible to tell the color of the iris.

He was very dead.

Beckett rolled him back over and searched his pockets. He found a room key from a motel along the Pacific Coast Highway, a wallet with some cash—he didn't stop to count it—and personal identity papers and credit cards. There was an ID card, with his picture, that identified him as J. Longstreet Hawkins, an employee of the Institute for Strategic Arms Limitations Studies in Washington, D.C.

A defense think tank. But why was one of its employees trying to kill a woman?

The briefcase, he thought, might have the answer. He walked over to it, and finding it locked, slashed it open with his Swiss Army knife, using the short sharp blade. He reached in and pulled out a cardboard box of microfilm. There were three boxes in all.

He opened one of the cardboard microfilm boxes and held it up to the light, but couldn't make out its contents.

There was a locked metal container and a small leather-covered box. He opened the leather box and found a seal used to emboss documents.

Intrigued, he took the metal box and seal into his office, got a sheet of white paper, slid it between the two halves of the seal, and gripped the handles firmly. He held the paper up to his desk lamp.

The words, "The Delphi Commission," occupied the upper crescent of writing and below that . . . below that was a name he recognized, and in recognizing it sat down on the floor in shock. T. Adam Carothers IV, the former Vice President and philanthropist who had died of a heart attack only four days before.

Snow knew the Delphi Commission, just called "the Commission" by Washington insiders, from the controversy it generated after one of its members had been elected President.

It had been named Delphi, Snow knew, after the mythical Greek Oracle at Delphi, the source of knowledge and wisdom. And that, he knew, supposedly signified the rarified intelligence of the Commission's members.

The extreme left wing and the extreme right wing found themselves in rare accord on the Commission. They both agreed that it appeared to be some sort of conspiracy of the powerful.

Just what the conspiracy was supposed to do, however, nobody could agree upon. The controversy heated up after the new President's appointment of six more Commission members to sensitive positions in the government, including one as National Security Advisor.

Snow flipped through the pages of color photographs of a recent issue of *Time* until his attention was arrested by a photo of Carothers and a group of his employees. The woman lying on the floor in Beckett Snow's hallway was one of them. She was identified as Tracy Reynolds, executive assistant.

Turning to the strange metal box, he took an old screwdriver and tried to pry it open. It didn't yield. Snow then brought out a ballpeen hammer and cold chisel, and then a succession of power tools—all to no avail.

He left it on the floor of the large walk-in closet and moved back to where the woman—now he knew her name—Tracy lay.

Dazed, knowing he should call the police and an ambulance for Tracy, he stumbled to the phone by his bed and grabbed the receiver. The line was dead; just as dead, he thought, as the body lying on his living-room floor.

Use a neighbor's phone, he thought. Only I don't know any of them and they all work.

Try, he thought.

He walked past Tracy, pausing long enough to kneel down and assure himself that she was all right.

He headed for the front door but the vision of the dead man suddenly overwhelmed him. He looked at the lifeless form and sank slowly to his knees.

His Fiat Spyder plunged first into one S-curve and then the next, and Peter Gilbert had a compulsion to check his watch to see how late he was. But doing so on this cowpath would mean nothing less than a serious accident.

He hated being late. Hated waiting in lines, hated time. There was never enough of it, at least not for him. And people who wasted his time by being late were inconsiderate; worse, it reflected an attitude that their time was more valuable than his. He'd broken up with the last two women he'd been serious about because they could never be on time.

He double-clutched from fifth gear to third, braked briefly, and slammed the accelerator to the floor coming out of the curve. The tachometer hit 7,500. Gilbert shifted into fourth, and shortly afterwards into fifth.

The Traveler's Inne was a stone roadside inn, built in the 1800s. It was an "ordinary" then, a tavern with rooms upstairs to rent. More than a hundred years ago it had been a resting place for adventurous travelers. Today, it was a popular trysting place for Washington's elite.

Peter had been here before with the wife of a California congressman. It had been a brief thrill but the affair was risky. He knew it could damage his advancement should it become public. So he ended it.

But Isaac knew. Isaac, Peter thought as he rounded the last curve, was like a father. Where his own father had been a molder, a mentor, a coach and patron, Isaac was like a father. He liked Isaac, confided in him and respected him.

And thus it was Isaac, rather than a woman, for whom Peter was now in such a hurry to be punctual.

But in the past six months, his friendship with Isaac Roth had begun to bother him. Peter felt that perhaps he was confiding too much to the old man. What, Peter's finely tuned paranoia asked, if the old man were reporting the security breaches to Sherbok, or even the Commission itself? With Roth, Peter had trusted someone else for the first time in his life and he did not feel comfortable about it.

Also bothering him was Roth's attitude toward the Commission and toward global corporations. The arguments had gotten sharper and the words had cut deeper and more painfully in the past two months. The problem, Peter knew, was that Isaac was too persuasive. He was convincing. He'd come from the same background as Peter. In fact, he lived from his investments. The reason, Isaac had confided in him, that he didn't draw a government salary was that he was a millionaire, the founder of what had itself become a global corporation that parked cars, made telephones, baked bread, sold hotel rooms, and emptied the refuse of cities.

Lately Peter had begun to think that either Isaac Roth was suffering from the guilt pangs of an elderly robber baron, or the old man knew something he didn't. The first was understandable; the second, frightening.

For the multinational corporation was Peter Gilbert's womb, his spaceship that carried him above the great masses of people. It had given wing to his aspirations.

And his success in the corporation had given him a continuous "fix" of achievements to stave off that scar of inadequacy that drove him—and many like him—to overachievement. For, like others who matured among the accomplishments of forebears, his life was a continuous battle against failure; failure was death.

But his success defeated failure and gave him life. And he believed that the institution that gave him life could save the world.

Peter had jumped at the opportunity to be a management coordinator for the Commission; the Commission was actually a corporation of global corporations. Every large company, every major bank, every major investor, every major manufacturer was represented. Peter Gilbert was a world manager in that company. Rationalism was his religion.

He'd been shocked, especially during their first conversations, to find that Isaac Roth didn't think as he did. Roth's humanism, Peter had decided, would be the old man's downfall, for he would lack the decisiveness, the cold rationality, to make those decisions that would do the most human good. Peter parked his Fiat next to Roth's limo and walked into the lobby.

As he walked toward the older man's table, Peter thought of some of their past conversations with their white-hot intensity. The thought troubled him.

The arguments were nearly always the same, and the outcome was nearly always the same. Lately, though, Peter admitted, the old man had been more persuasive—and more persistent.

Just a couple of weeks ago, as they sat sipping Scotch in Peter's office after hours one evening, they had gotten into it again.

"The problem is nationalism, Isaac," Peter remembered saying exasperatedly. "The world's crying for global integration and good management. But politicians are tied to their own silly power structures, to an outmoded patriotism."

Isaac raised his hand as if he were about to speak, but Peter pretended not to notice. He went on. "National pride and prestige, patriotism and power, are inefficient and uneconomic. Look, Clausen, the president of Bank of America, said it best: 'The expansion of business' consciousness to the global level offers mankind perhaps the last real chance to build a world order that is less coercive than that offered by the nation-state.' And—"

"You think Bank of America is not coercive?" Isaac interrupted. "Just try selling that to some poor blue-collar worker who's a couple of months late on his car payments."

"You're being facetious," Peter charged, leaning back in his chair to regard the older man.

"No, not at all. You'd really put the management of the world into the hands of people whose biggest talent is the VISA card?"

23

"You're damn right I would, and it'd be a better place," Peter continued. "Look, there's nothing wrong with the profit motive. Nothing. The—"

"May I interrupt?" Isaac said, gently.

"Certainly."

"Now, you know I've been involved in corporations —some of them multinational—most of my life. And sometimes I think we're talking about two different worlds.

"You talk about social needs, human needs, and about how the global corporations are going to solve all those. But you seem to have a convenient amnesia when it comes to the horrible abuses that stem from the global corporations, and for which there is no market balance," Roth said.

"What about Dow Chemical going to court to fight for their right to sell Agent Orange, a chemical that causes cancer?" Roth continued.

"But that's—"

"Wait, let me finish, please."

Peter skimmed the condensation off his Scotch glass with the tip of one finger. "All right."

"Take Nestle's, for instance," Roth said. "Its executives know that the way they market their baby formula over mother's milk in the Third World promotes malnutrition and starvation among children there."

"I hadn't realized that. But still—" Peter spoke rapidly now to cover his uncertainty. "Those sorts of abuses pale in comparison to the invention of nuclear weapons to protect a nation-state."

"Don't forget, Peter, that there are huge corporations that make big profits from things that kill people," Isaac said. "Vietnam was a pretty good piece of change for a lot of companies."

"But that was because of the nation-state; the demand was there."

24

"So why didn't these good corporations exercise their good sense?"

"Because those were *American* companies," Peter said. "What we're talking about is global companies with no allegiance to any country at all. We're talking about companies—businessmen and managers—who are the first people in history with the power, the organization, the technology, and the money to make a credible try at managing the world as an integrated unit, not just a collection of Mickey Mouse countries interested in protecting their language, their culture, their price. They're obsolete. The sooner we can wipe out those lines between nations, the sooner people everywhere start wanting the same things, the more efficient business will become in supplying the needs." Peter's face was flushed.

"And you think the global corporations can do that?" the older man challenged him quietly.

"Do what?"

"Wipe out national boundaries, make people want the same things?"

"Not just one corporation, but the biggest ones working in concert. That's what the Commission is all about. We have to move beyond political boundaries. We have to subordinate countries to enterprise."

"And you think business can gain that power?" Isaac was baiting him now, and Peter knew it, but he plunged ahead anyway.

"Not *can*, Isaac. You know as well as I do, they already have the power. The annual sales of GM are bigger than the gross national product of Switzerland, Pakistan, and South Africa. Royal Dutch Shell is bigger than Iran, Venezuela, and Turkey; Goodyear outclasses Saudi Arabia. The decisions the managers of these companies make every day have more effect on people than the governments of the countries in which

25

the people live. Just think what something like the Delphi Commission can do if several hundred of these corporations get together and act in concert!"

"I can't wait," Roth said sarcastically. "You would turn the world into a giant corporation. You know corporations are controlled mostly by the management and by a few people who hold large blocks of stocks. The individual has no say, save what's based on money. I don't want a balance sheet to run my life. I want the freedom to do what I want—"

"Freedom! Blast your freedom!" Peter interrupted, aroused now. "Your damned freedom and the nation-state that goes along with it are responsible for more death and destruction than any other force. Because of your great nationalists—Hitler, Castro, Ho, Mao, the Roosevelts—our history pages are littered with millions of bloody corpses. And you think that business can do a worse job than that? Well, I don't."

"So you do away with individuals and their needs," said Roth deliberately, turning his chair to face the younger man head on. "You beat them into a mold and make every individual exactly the same so they'll want exactly the same things so the corporation will be more profitable. I don't think the corporation wants to meet human needs as much as it wants to make humans want to fill corporate needs." Roth's eyes held his captive.

Peter shifted uncomfortably in his chair. "That's unfair, Isaac—"

"Perhaps, but I want you to think about something: Is the maximization of profits really a step toward being so uniform and well adapted to a certain climate that we lose the cutting edge of individuality and adaptability? Does it mean that we'll pass away like dinosaurs if the climate changes? And are uniform people really human beings?"

Now, as Peter approached the table, he remembered

the conversation. Though he had no answer he did have a vague sense of anxiety, and that was something he resented.

"Hello, Peter. I was beginning to worry, what with your penchant for punctuality," Roth said, extending his hand in greeting.

Peter took the older man's hand and shook it warmly, with a firm grasp that conveyed his love and respect.

"I'm really sorry to be late, Isaac."

"Not to worry, Peter. I'm not upset at all. The interlude has given me an opportunity to . . . think."

"A dangerous activity. Positively subversive."

"Your humor is far closer to the truth than you may guess, my boy," Isaac said as he toyed with his drink.

What was it Peter saw in the older man's eyes? Sadness? Anger? Fear? Peter could only guess tonight that the old man was in a mood he'd never seen him in before, and that unnerved him. Peter ordered a double Chivas, and turned to Roth.

"So where do we go tonight?" Peter said, referring to their earlier discussions. "How about oil companies and—"

"Peter," Isaac's eyes implored. "I don't want to discuss these things tonight. I'm disturbed . . . by exactly what, I'm not sure. But it seems that some strange things are taking place at the White House. . . ."

"Like what?"

"It's undefinable, a break in patterns. I have an increasing anxiety about the men you work for." He gulped the rest of his drink and signaled the waiter for a refill.

"Oh, come on, Issac. Maybe you just need a vacation."

"I suppose. But, Peter, I . . . Have you heard anything unusual about the death of the former vice president?"

"Unusual?" Peter leaned back against the leather banquette. The waiter arrived with his drink, and Peter sipped it before continuing.

"Unusual? Well, nothing other than the news reports."

"No, not that. That it . . . it may not have been a real heart attack. That Adam was . . ."

"Murdered?"

"Yes."

"And you . . . you think the Commission had something to do with it?"

"I just heard. . . ."

"Isaac. Isaac, you've been letting your imagination run away from you. Why would the Commission want Adam dead? For that matter, why would they kill anyone? After all, this isn't the Mafia or a cheap bunch of street hoods."

"Why? I don't exactly know." He pinched the bridge of his nose between thumb and forefinger. "But I imagine if it happened it was because he opposed something they wanted to do."

"They're not that type of people," Peter declared flatly.

"But are you so sure? Let's suppose that some of them *were* those type of people." Isaac looked at Peter, asking for indulgence. "Just hypothetically. Okay?"

"Sure."

"Suppose that there was something so very important: an event, a program, a very import agenda they felt must surely be carried out. And suppose that Adam opposed it totally, and suppose that he had the means, the power to prevent it from happening. What would efficiency—their god, and yours—demand?"

"It would demand that Adam be opposed. But for God's sake, there are a hundred ways of doing that short of killing him."

"Suppose there wasn't. Suppose the alternatives failed?"

"I can't imagine that."

"Efficiency can."

Peter changed the subject. He'd been stunned by Isaac's emotions, the preposterous hypothecations. They passed the remainder of the evening discussing family, minutiae, Isaac's visits to his invalid sister in a suburban Maryland rest home.

Isaac placed his glass abruptly on the table. "It's time we left, Peter." He paused. "Peter," he said, his voice resigned, "I love you like the son I never had. May God bless you always. Goodbye."

As Peter drove home that night, he thought of Isaac's goodbye. It was so final. And the slight misting in his eyes . . . Was the old man getting senile? Peter hoped not. What Peter didn't realize was that Isaac had, indeed, said goodbye. Peter would never see him again.

Chapter Three

"And Ely?"

"He's dead."

"Shame."

"And you?"

"The doctor said nothing vital was hit."

"Shame."

Silence.

"Don't take it so seriously, Laura. Don't worry. We'll work something out."

"Your concern for my health is touching."

"My, my, aren't we cynical tonight?"

"It's my life."

"So it is. So it is."

"What should I do?"

"Go back to your room. You are much too valuable for us to lose you. Wait for me to call you."

"Okay, I'm really sorry. The guy she hooked up with was good. Really good."

"I understand completely. After all, who among us is perfect? Everyone is entitled to mistakes. Don't worry, my dear. Go to your room and get some sleep. Wait for me."

"Yes, I'll do that."

"Goodbye, dear."

"Goodbye, father."

Dial tone.

"Whitney?"

"Speaking."

"They botched it. Ely's dead, Laura is holed up at her hotel."

"I hear you."

"Kill her."

"Yes sir."

"Goodbye."

"Goodbye."

Dial tone.

"They fouled it up again."

"Have them killed."

"Ely is already dead."

"Good."

"Laura was wounded."

"Whitney will finish the job."

"What do we do with Carothers' girl?"

"And the dossier."

"True. We could have her arrested. Pin Ely's death on her."

"No. There's another complication. Ely was killed in the home of a federal prosecutor."

"Shit! Then we make them disappear?"

"They disappear."

"Good."

"Goodbye."

"Goodbye."

Beckett felt the coolness of her fingers on the back of his neck. He was seated on the floor, knees drawn to his chin, arms hugging his folded legs.

"You're nice."

The voice was Tracy's, but it now lacked the ragged edges it had had before.

"I don't feel so nice now," Beckett replied. He turned slowly and looked at her face. The goose egg was barely visible under her hair.

31

"You're all right now?" he asked. "I mean, you were unconscious for a long time."

"Not as long as you think. But yes, I'm fine. A brute of a headache, but fine otherwise."

"You mean . . . I mean, were you faking it?"

"No. Well, at least not the whole thing. The lights went out after you tackled me. Then I suppose I fell asleep, because I had a nightmare . . . and that woke me up. I was awake when you looked at my head. It felt good. Your touch, I mean." Her voice drifted as their eyes met.

Beckett turned to put his arm around her, and in turning, glimpsed the corpse.

"Jesus H. Christ." Beckett started and rose to his feet. "We've gotta do something about him!"

"What?"

"Well, hell, there's only one thing we can do," he replied. "Call the cops."

"No, then they'll arrest you and the Commission will know about me and they'll know where I am."

"And you think they already don't?"

"Hmmm. Uh, right."

"Look, these people—whoever they are—want you dead in the worst way. Right?"

"Uh-huh."

"And if they're connected with the Delphi Commission . . ."

"Oh!" she gasped, suddenly realizing. "You *know* about the Commission! How?" She stopped as her eyes landed on her briefcase with its slashed side. "Well, you didn't waste any time," she observed wryly.

Snow ignored her comment. "If they *are* connected with the Commission . . ."

"Which they are."

"Yes. Well, then I assume they want to keep your death quiet."

"Correct."

"So the best thing for you to do is get to the police, explain all of this—" Beckett's broad sweep of his right arm panned across the bullet holes and wreckage of the room, "—and tell them just how it all happened."

"But would they believe it?"

"I know a lot of them, even if I've only been here a few months. Besides, Mr. J. Longstreet Hawkins," he nodded toward the body, "is a pretty convincing corpse."

"Yes, I know. He's been a pain in my ass for more than three years."

"You *know* him?"

"Yes, he worked for one of the Commission's think-tank fronts, the Institute for . . ."

"Strategic Arms Limitation Studies," he finished her sentence.

"How did you know?" Beckett pulled out Hawkins' ID card. He displayed it between thumb and forefinger.

"My, you're just full of surprises, aren't you?" she said.

"Yeah, so are you. We make a great couple."

The silence lasted too long to be a conversational pause.

"So you want to call the police. Can you leave me out of it? I mean, not tell them about me?" she asked.

"Sure, I just tell the police that these two people I never saw just paid a social call and tried to kill me, and shot up my house, and I killed one of them with a gun I don't own, and I'm sorry but I can't tell them any more and would they please just help me get the body out of my living room, after all it doesn't match the drapes? No. If I were in their shoes, I wouldn't buy it."

"True. True. And the publicity might protect me.

After all, they couldn't really afford to kill me then."

"Right. And you've got the goods to lend credibility to whatever you say! The seal *and* the microfilm."

"Okay," she agreed. "For lack of a better alternative, and because you do seem to make sense, call the cops."

"Good. We'll have to use a neighbor's phone—if anyone's home—or a pay phone down on Ocean Park. They were real thorough and cut my line before they aired out the house."

"Let's go."

"No. First, I want you to tell me what we're up against. We could get some extra help if I know exactly what's going on and can figure out how to play the cops right."

Tracy Reynolds looked at Beckett Snow's face for a long time. She looked at his face; she looked at his eyes; she looked behind his eyes; and she looked at herself reflected in his pupils. He saw her face change a hundred times.

"I don't like to trust people, you know," she began. "Trusting means showing someone where they can hurt you. And you have to believe in them enough to trust that they won't. And you know, if you get stuck there too many times, trust becomes something you think other people should do."

"Yes, I know but . . ."

"That's happened to me. I didn't get to where I was by trusting people. I got where I was by *not* trusting people. I was close to Carothers. I wasn't his concubine. I let people think that because it made them vulnerable. They dismissed me as a stupid whore and turned their soft bellies right into my sharp edges.

"No," she continued, "I didn't get anywhere by trusting people. But I don't think that I'll get anywhere else without your trust, and without trusting you.

"Damn it!" she said, clenching her fists. "I don't want

34

to trust you, and I want to trust you. It scares me. But I have to; I need to trust somebody. I need to."

Tears appeared in her eyes suddenly, and then, just as suddenly, disappeared. She had regained control of herself.

"But wait," she said firmly. "Before I trust you, I want something from you."

"My trust?" Beckett's question was a statement.

"Yes."

Beckett looked at her. The absurdity of her request, of the entire episode with her, came crashing home to him.

"Trust you! Trust *you*?" His voice rose. "Trusting you has been a fucking disaster. Ever since I met you the sky's been falling in around my ears. You show up, and I get my house shot up, guns stuck in my face, and a body on my floor. Trust? You want *me* to trust *you*? Look, lady, I think you're beautiful, and I think I like you; but Jesus, you're dangerous as hell and I'm not about to start trusting you . . . not right now.

"But what I *am* going to do is call the cops," Beckett said. "Let's go."

He took her by the elbow and led her to the door. "Gonna use a pay phone," he mumbled. "What I've got to say I don't think I want my neighbors to hear." He turned to pull the door shut, and just as it was about to close, the top hinge gave way and the buckled hollow-core door crashed to the living-room floor.

"Shit," he said, looking at the wreckage. "Uh, hold on a minute." He released her arm and jumped over the door.

Snow grabbed the .44 magnum and the dead man's Ingram and started to pick up the briefcase when he heard the squealing of tires followed by Tracy's scream.

"What's happening?" He raced to the porch, the Ingram ready for trouble. Up the street the car, a teen-

35

ager's overdone Chevy, screamed around the corner in a blast of burned rubber and unrestrained exhaust.

"It's nothing," he said, putting his arm around her. "Just some asshole." He held her.

"I'm sorry I screamed," Tracy said. "I guess I'm just nervous."

"That's understandable. Let's go call the police now and get this straightened out."

Snow opened the door of the van for her and climbed in beside her and they drove off.

Chapter Four

Leslie Lewis noticed the snow when it started sprinkling on the White House lawn shortly before noon.

It was now 3 PM. A snow emergency had been declared and there were five inches of snow on the ground. The snow was coming down so hard she could hardly see the lights of the White House, barely 50 yards away.

"You know," she told Jacob Cohen, her assistant, "it feels normal—not being able to see the White House."

He looked at her quizzically. "Explain."

"More and more I feel that there's a blizzard between us and them." She was thinking aloud, unsure where the train of thought was leading her.

"Things we should be getting from Him." Everyone there spoke of the President with a capital "H" in the same manner that Protestant preachers spoke of Jesus Christ. "We should be getting reactions from Himself on some of the things we've sent him. Instead, all we get are vague notes from that iceman Sherbok. And what I'd like to know is why the fuck everything we deal with goes through him."

"Um . . . anything in particular?"

"Not really. It just looks like you and I have been more and more isolated the last few months."

37

"You mean about meetings and things? Not getting invited to some of them?"

"That's part of it. I feel there's a pattern, but I just can't put my finger on it."

"Hmm. I don't know," Jacob began. "I thought it was all connected somehow with the changes he was making to do something about his ratings in the polls."

"Yeah. Or maybe they're trying to tell me something?"

"Like what?"

"Like I ought to start looking for another job."

They looked at each other, and then back to the window. The blizzard had cleared momentarily, and to the left, they could see Pennsylvania Avenue, choked with cars and snow. Stalled cars, stalled buses.

But people weren't idle. Stranded pedestrians were helping to push cars stuck in the snow. A lone man dressed in a tan coat with a dark collar was directing traffic. It was an amazing situation, Leslie thought. Harsh weather descends and softens people, opens them up by making them dependent on others. Deplorable that the same human qualities couldn't work every day. Here were people acting in their own best self-interest by helping others.

Jacob cut into her thoughts. "Where would you look?"

"What?"

"For a job. Look for a job."

"Oh, yes, sorry." She turned to him. "I was daydreaming." She paused. "Oh, I don't know. I haven't really thought about it until now. I suppose I could look among the various organizations."

Jacob nodded. For two years the two of them had done nothing but correspond with the many groups and commissions and fraternal organizations of which the President either had been a member before he was elected, or had been made an honorary member since.

38

The task was staggering. The groups numbered in the hundreds.

"Not a bad idea, boss."

"Well, maybe I'll start this afternoon. Why don't you go on home now?"

"Check."

She watched him as he walked out the door. "Nice ass," she thought to herself.

Leslie stood at the window for another 15 minutes, until Sarah, her secretary, had said goodnight. She then walked into the other office, locked the door, and sat down in front of a black enamel four-drawer filing cabinet. She opened the top drawer and started at "A."

"Okay, Snow, what is it you want now?" The voice on the telephone was mock gruff, though Beckett knew that Inspector Jack "Iron Ass" Nelson, LAPD, was capable of being as tough as they came. "C'mon, whadda ya want? The drink I owe you, or are you having a hard time finding a racquetball partner? Prosecutors always have a lack of good friends."

"Jack, I've killed someone."

"Uhhh . . . run that by me again. I don't think I heard you."

"No, you heard me. I've killed someone."

"How?"

"With a .44 magnum."

"You don't mess around, do you. Where?"

"In my living room."

"Why?"

"He was shooting at me."

"You know him?"

"No."

"Why was he shooting at you?"

"I don't know. Well, I think I know but I'm not sure. He was a contract man who was trying to kill a

39

woman who was in my house. It's not what it sounds like . . ."

"Don't worry. Who stays at your house is your business."

"Well, they wanted a briefcase she was carrying and—"

"Three minutes are up," the operator interrupted.

"Where are you, Beck?"

"At a pay phone at Lincoln and Ocean Park in Santa Monica. They cut the lines to my phone."

Nelson whistled.

"Well, look, I'll meet you at your place. I'll have to call the SMPD, since it's in their area, but I know the chief and he'll meet us there."

"That's great, Jack."

"Get on back and I'll see you soon."

Snow hung up and they returned to his house.

Tracy was the first inside and what she didn't see scared her.

"He's gone! He's gone!"

Beckett looked where she was pointing. The body was missing. In the midst of the rubble and broken glass, the hot-waxed terracotta tile floor shone; it was clear of blood.

"Jesus Christ, Joseph and Mary!" Beckett held her tightly. She wrapped her arms around his waist. "Oh, this is too much. This is *too* much. In half an hour this place is going to be crawling with cops, and . . . and this is too much." She looked up at his face. "They're never going to believe this."

They didn't. Luckily Inspector Nelson got there first. He calmed down the chief and sent him back to the station.

"Okay, Beck." Nelson put his arm around Snow's shoulder and led him away from the chair Tracy was sitting in. "What's it all about? You all right? Did the lady feed you something?

"Jack." Beckett pulled away from the tall policeman's grasp. "It's just as I told you. Honest to God! She stowed away in the van at the accident, came in, and asked me for help," he said, omitting mention of the gun, "and these guys broke in and shot at us. I killed one of them. He was lying there." Snow pointed. "There, by the window, and he was unmistakably dead. Here, here's his ID card." Beckett produced the plastic laminated chip. "Look, do me a favor, will you? Get a rundown on this guy. Call up the place he works and ask for him. Then maybe you'll believe me."

"I don't know, Beck." The potbellied inspector mused, looking around at the bullet-pocked walls. "It all looks crazy to me."

"C'mon, Jack. We've been through a lot. Just a little unofficial favor, okay?" Beckett and Nelson looked at each other.

"Okay, Beck." The inspector pocketed the ID card and started to leave.

"Wait," Tracy said and grabbed the inspector's forearm. "Aren't you going to do something?"

"What do you expect me to do?" Nelson's words were white around the edges with frost.

"Well, there's been a murder."

"Not that I can tell. You find me a body, and I'll believe there's been a murder."

"But look at all the bullet holes."

"Lady, there's no law against a guy shooting up his own home . . . just so long as his gun's legal." Nelson looked at Beckett. "And because this man is a good friend of mine, I'm not even going to ask whether it was or not. And I don't like whatever you've gotten by my good friend. Good," he snatched his arm out of her grasp, "day!"

Tracy watched the inspector's car disappear up the street, and then lowered her head. Her shoulders quivered as she stood alone by the door. Beckett went to her, wrapped her in his arms. Tracy clung to him and wept.

"*He* didn't believe me. *You* don't believe me," she cried, her voice rising. "*Nobody's* going to believe me, but I've got to . . ." Tracy shoved Snow away and frantically searched the room. She spun in circles, dazed. "Now it's gone, they got it too. It's gone, gone . . ." She sank slowly into a chair. "There's no hope. It's all gone. All gone. A great man died for nothing."

Beckett looked and saw that the briefcase with its microfilm was, indeed, missing.

"You sure she's staying at the Sunray Motel?"

"That's the address Prometheus gave us. You getting cold feet about this?"

"Lay off, willya, Whitney? You know I don't have any compunctions about killing, but the whole thing stinks, you know?"

"Like how?"

"Well look, she's the guy's daughter. Sure she's a killer, but he orders us to kill his own kid? Shit! I've never done anything like that before."

"Maybe Prometheus is a better killer than you are."

"Whitney, you ever think just maybe he's a better killer than either one of us?"

"Don't worry. Do your job right and you won't end up like Laura."

"I'm not so sure anymore."

"That's why we've been following the two of 'em in case they screw up."

"Just don't screw up."

42

Chapter Five

"You're wrong, you know," Snow said as he grabbed two cans of beer from his refrigerator and handed one to her.

She looked in his eyes, her face perplexed.

"About me not believing you," Beckett said.

"Why now? Why *now* that I can't prove anything to you?" She sipped the beer, made a face, and set it down on the kitchen table.

"Too much has happened that I never dreamed could happen," he said. "I don't believe everything you've told me, because I don't think you've told me everything. But I'm a victim now and I want to know what the hell is going on."

"Thank you for believing me," she said. "But now, what are we going to do without the files?"

"We'll think of something, being the resourceful people that we are. For starters, let's pay a visit to the Sunray Motel," he said, producing the key he'd taken from the dead man's pocket.

They piled into his van and drove through downtown Santa Monica to the Pacific Coast Highway. The day was halcyon bright, and the sun burned his eyes.

Beckett stopped the van at a service station to fill up the tank with gasoline and to call his office. His sudden departure would cause chaos in the court scheduling. There would, he knew, be hell to pay when he returned.

And thinking of that, he wondered for yet another time, why he was doing what he was doing. He decided it just felt right.

"Carothers knew he was going to be murdered. He gave me the briefcase and told me that if anything happened to him, it had to get to the President."

"Hold on," Beckett said, not taking his eyes off the highway. "He died of a heart attack, right?"

"Maybe. No, not maybe, definitely not," she said. "You were a cop once, so you know there are drugs that can fake a heart attack, right?"

"I do seem to remember that from somewhere. I hadn't thought of that."

"Well, some people might. That's why his body was cremated so damned fast. Did you think of that either?"

"Ah, no. But who would have killed him? And why?"

"Well, I'm not sure. . . . I am sure the same people who are trying to kill me are behind it. He was going to explain the whole thing to me, but then he was dead." Tracy's face hardened. "Dead before he got a chance."

Snow nodded sympathetically. "The Commission?"

"Probably. In the past three or four months, he had some pretty hot arguments with a couple of the big names there."

"Arguments over what?"

"That was part of what he was going to explain to me. I think the answer is in the microfilm." She brought her fist down on the dashboard. "Ohhh, damn! How I wish we had the briefcase!"

"Yep. Me too. Do you remember anything at all about the arguments?"

"Very, very little, except that it had something to do wtih a project called Prometheus."

Snow took his eyes off the road to look at her. "Prometheus?" he repeated.

"Correct. According to the legend, Prometheus stole fire from the gods and gave it to man, and taught him many useful arts and sciences."

"Prometheus. The friend, the benefactor of mankind. Could this project be some sort of do-gooder campaign?"

"I wouldn't rule out anything," she replied. "But I'm sure that if it really was a 'do-gooder' project, as you call it, then he would have gone along with it."

"That's what the arguments were over? The Commission wanted to do something and Carothers didn't?"

"As far as I can tell."

"It must have been . . . must be some kind of big deal for them to kill him over it."

Tracy sighed. "We don't know for sure they killed him."

"Or that he was killed at all. Did you ever think, Tracy, that all we've got to go on is a suspicion, a fear that he expressed?"

"But he wasn't paranoid about things like that."

"Sure. But remember that a guy like that also has a lot of enemies. Even if he *was* killed, there's lots of adversaries out there who would be better suspects than his own Commission."

Snow skillfully threaded the van through traffic. Silence overtook them as they tried to assimilate what had happened. It seemed like a year since the gun battle in his house, Snow thought, yet here it was, only 1:30 in the afternoon.

"How are you holding up?" she asked him. "You haven't had much sleep."

"Yeah. I'm starting to feel it," Beckett replied. "How about you? Ah, but I forgot, you caught forty winks while I was playing cowboy and Indians."

"Funny, very funny. Make that about six and a half winks. I wasn't out for too very long."

45

Little sparks danced in his eyes.

"You know," she said, "if your eyes weren't so bloodshot, they'd be very attractive."

"Yeah. But both of them are the same color; I don't quite have the variety you do."

"You noticed?"

"Couldn't help."

Out of the corner of his eye, he saw a smile. He grinned. Neither spoke the rest of the way to the motel.

A black Ford Granada pulled out of the motel parking lot as they pulled in. Across the road a jogger plodded through the beach parking area and two sunbathers were stranded trying to get across the steady stream of traffic pouring both ways along the highway. The sun had started to paint short stubby shadows on its way toward the horizon. It was, Beckett Snow reflected, the perfect day to bake on the beach.

The Sunray Motel had seen better days. Not that it was in terrible disrepair, but Snow noted windows that had been sloppily painted one too many times, stucco that had been patched repeatedly. Snow pulled into a parking space beside a U-Haul trailer with Alabama plates.

They got out without talking and walked through the portico and up a broad set of steps.

"What number are we looking for?" Tracy whispered.

Snow took the key out of his pants pocket and held it up. "Number 10."

They mounted a short flight of four steps. Number ten was straight ahead.

Snow walked ahead briskly and motioned her back with a wave of his right hand. Tracy shook her head and walked over to him. Snow grinned ruefully.

He walked over to the partially opened, but barred frosted glass of what he assumed was the bathroom. He listened and heard nothing. Tracy likewise bent her ear to the door and detected nothing. Simultaneously they looked at each other with raised eyebrows to silently ask, "Did you hear anything?" Each shook his head.

"Here goes." The key grumbled as it slid into the knob. He kicked the door open and swiftly flattened himself against the outside wall. Hearing nothing, he peered around the corner. Straight ahead on the bed was a woman's figure, nude, spread-eagled, wrists and ankles bound to the bed frame with ripped portions of the sheets. Near the foot of the bed were blue jeans and a plaid shirt he recognized from that morning. She was the intruder that he'd wounded.

The woman had been disemboweled.

The sheets of the bed were crimson with fresh blood which still oozed from her abdominal cavity. A loop of her small intestine fell out of the slashed muscle wall and spilled a sour chum onto the floor from a long gash. The air hung nauseous with the sticky sweet smell of blood and spilled stomach contents.

Beckett and Tracy recoiled, and then were inexorably drawn to the bedside by a horror too terrible to turn away from. Snow motioned Tracy against the wall as he opened both closet doors wtih the Ingram, and then checked out the bathroom, the shower, and the terrace to make sure this wasn't a trap. Satisfied, he shut the door. Tracy had moved closer.

"Oh God, Beck! She's still alive."

Snow walked to Tracy's side, and saw a faint crimson froth moving on the girl's lips.

Snow tried not to look at the piece of living—dying—meat strapped on the bed.

Tracy started to untie the girl's left wrist.

"Don't touch anything," Snow barked. Tracy snatched her hand away.

"Can you hear me?" Snow leaned over the girl's face. It was swollen and bore the marks of a razor blade and of repeated cigarette burns. Her breasts had been mutilated with something sharp. "Can you hear me?"

The eyelids fluttered and failed to open. The lips moved. The girl's breathing became troubled, anxious as she tried to speak.

"What'd she say?" Tracy asked.

"I don't know," Snow said. "But let's get out of here quick."

"We can't leave her."

"Sweetheart, she's going to die."

"Shhh, not so loud, she might hear you."

"C'mon. She's a dead lady. Let's go."

"But we can call an ambulance then, can't we?"

"Yeah. Yeah, sure. We'll do that."

They walked quickly to the van and drove away.

Chapter Six

"We shouldn't have done that." The older man's voice was reproachful.

"Jesus! I'm tired of your chicken shit. You wanna get out? Then get out! Sell encyclopedias or something. You're like an ole lady with your bitchin'." The younger man glared angrily, as he steered their black Granada down Pacific Coast Highway.

"It was his daughter. . . ."

"She was a fuckup and he knew it."

"But did you have to do . . ."

"Do what?"

"Well, do all . . . all . . . that?"

"We had to know if she had the dossier. It wasn't at the guy's house. That means that either they've got it somewhere or she had it."

"Are you convinced?"

"Sure. I'm convinced now that she didn't have it."

"But—"

"Don't but. That wouldn't have saved her. She had to be snuffed anyway."

"But it could've been quicker."

"Yeah, it could've been quicker," Whitney mimicked the older man wtih a sneer. "So what's the difference, pop? She's dead, and that's half our job done."

"I just don't like *how* it was done." The older man remained silent for another five minutes. "You planning the same thing for those two?" the older man asked finally, as they merged onto the Santa Monica Freeway.

"Unless they cough up the dossier pronto."

"Which you hope they don't."

"What do you mean by that?"

"What do you think? Because you like cutting people open. You don't just like to kill people; you like to make people suffer. I've always done it swiftly and painlessly. . . ."

The young man jerked the steering wheel to the right and slammed on the brakes of the rented sedan. The car skidded to a halt in the loose soil at the shoulder.

"Look, pops," he said, grabbing the older man's necktie with his right hand. "Just don't lose your nerve on me now. My life depends on you, and that doesn't make me feel none too secure. If you start to drag me down, I'm gonna cut you loose. You got that?"

The older man nodded and gagged. His face flushed while the other man choked him, and then he gasped as he felt himself slammed into the car door and released.

Leslie Lewis was depressed.

She was also frustrated, angry, suspicious, and confused; but most of all, she was depressed. Her depression would have been worse had it not been for the snow. But to a woman raised in Florida, snow would always be a kid's treat.

Her apartment in Foggy Bottom was normally a brisk 15-minute walk, but tonight's drifted snow would double that time. She didn't mind. There was no great hurry to get back to an empty apartment. Even though David had moved out four months before, he was still there. And as long as he stayed, she would have the void that destroyed her concentration; that sent her

50

out at nights to avoid being alone; that trapped her in beds she didn't belong in and didn't want to be in.

That was bad enough, she thought as she shoved one leg after the other in another pedestrian's fresh tracks through the snow. Through the white curtain before her, not a glimpse of her destination was visible. She could barely see half a block ahead.

That was bad enough, she repeated to herself, without having that Goddamned Russian on her back. Sherbok! What was he after; what game was he playing?

It was nearly nine o'clock. Leslie Lewis, Special Assistant to the Council of Domestic Advisors for Organizational Liaison, had spent the past five hours thumbing through her files. When she got to the Delphi Commission's folder, and found that it contained nothing more recent than six months before, she had started to wonder.

First she looked on Jacob's desk, thinking that there was a second folder. She looked on her secretary's desk. She looked on Jacob's secretary's desk. She made herself a note to ask them all about it the next day.

But then she went to her personal file and pulled the desk calendar for the previous year. Every three weeks, she'd had a meeting with the Commission liaison. Then, after November of last year, there were no meetings scheduled. Could the National Security Advisor—that damned Cossack—have taken that over? He, too, was a member. Perhaps he was trying to consolidate some sort of hold by funneling Commission information away from her.

Before leaving the office, she'd made a note to confront Sherbok.

But now, as she trudged home in the snow, she felt differently. "Why get somebody upset? I'll just resign quietly."

Before she did, though, she resolved to talk to Himself personally. After all, he had brought her here, along with dozens of others of his youthful gubernatorial staff. She owed him that. He owed her just as much.

"Christ," she muttered. "Why this too? Why is it that every time things seem to straighten out, somebody leaves; something breaks; some . . ." Her voice trailed off, and she drifted into a black hole that even the snow couldn't lift her out of.

A passerby walking toward her would have seen a woman with medium-length, dull brown hair tucked underneath a loosely woven wool cap. Her dark brown eyes were coal black, all pupil from the darkness. She had the high cheekbones that other women tried to paint on with makeup, and an angular jaw anchoring an oval face. The corners of her mouth almost turned up so that she always looked like she was on the verge of smiling. But she was 15 pounds overweight, and the excess adipose blurred the classic lines of her face and dragged her one step closer to mediocrity.

She didn't recognize them as such, but the weight, the blemishes, the dullness that abounded in her hair and clouded her eyes were reflections of her emotions. Leslie Lewis knew she was a very unhappy woman, but she didn't know what to do about it.

"You need to get laid," said one group of her friends. She'd taken the advice, and found it a quick fix and a long-range fizz. Sport fucking, she decided, was the Chinese dinner of emotions.

"You need a husband," said another group of friends, and she almost had that once. She decided her problem was being alone. It hadn't been so bad when the job at the White House was commanding virtually every thought of the day and left her too tired at night to feel lonely. But now the job was demanding less because somebody was playing games with her, and the time it left opened holes in her emotions.

Leslie began to cry when she got to the corner of

23rd and G streets, and she wept softly to herself the rest of the way home. She walked through the brightly lit lobby of her yellow brick apartment building, took the stairs to the fourth floor, unlocked the door, and went to bed.

"Tomorrow," she told the clock radio as she set it for 6:30 AM. "Perhaps tomorrow will be my day." And she went to sleep, knowing full well that it wouldn't be.

Tracy and Beckett rode back to his house in Santa Monica, stopping only to call an ambulance.

"I'll just get a few things and nail the front door shut," Beckett told her, when they arrived. "Why don't you rest a bit?"

He ignored the clutter and wreckage of the gun battle, moving directly to his bedroom where he threw a change of clothes into a soft-sided Gucci overnighter.

He walked into his office. There he gathered the strange grey metal box that was still sitting on the floor of his closet where he'd left it, Carothers's Commission seal, and an assortment of personal papers, all of which he stuffed into a side pocket of the suitcase. He zipped up the suitcase.

"Okay, let's get the hell out of here to some place where we can think for a while and get a little rest without having to worry about people putting holes in our bodies." Tracy nodded her consent.

Snow stowed the bag in the back of his van and they drove away. Halfway to Lincoln Boulevard, he slowed down.

"What's wrong?" Tracy's voice was edged with alarm.

"Nothing. Calm down. I was just thinking about things. . . . Like maybe we ought to leave the van and take a cab so we won't be so easy to trace."

"Uhmmmm, yeah. We could rent a car."

"Uh, I've got my credit cards, but I'm not made of money."

"Beck, did you read that *Time* story on me?"

"No. But then I didn't know it was you. I mean, I didn't know you then and I didn't pay much attention. If I'd known we'd be potential gravemates, I would've memorized it word for word."

"Well, if you'd read the story, you would have learned that I had $60,000 per year expense account."

Snow whistled. "From the Commission?"

"No, from Adam."

"Uhm . . . that could be one reason everybody thought you were his . . ."

"Mistress."

"Right. So where was the money kept?"

"In a checking account."

"And where is the money now?"

She opened her shoulder purse and pulled out a wad of travelers' checks the thickness of a paperback novel.

"No shit?" Snow's eyebrows were arched halfway to his hairline.

"No shit."

"How much?"

"Nearly fifty-eight thousand dollars."

"Wow!"

Snow parked and used the same phone he'd used earlier in the day to call a cab. "Too late to rent a car today," he remarked as he got behind the van's wheel. "Tomorrow we'll get one, a fast one."

The cab arrived 15 minutes later. Snow threw the bag in the back seat, held the door for Tracy, and then followed her in.

"Beverly Hilton," he told the driver, and they took off.

Tracy paid and tipped the driver when he delivered them to the lobby of the hotel. Snow snatched his bag from the seat beside him, and strode through the lobby, past the registration desk, with Tracy in tow. Together they picked their way through a throng of science fiction movie conventioneers, past the convention rooms, and out a glass door at the other end of the hotel. Satisfied that no one had followed them, Snow hailed another taxi to take them to the Ramada Inn near Los Angeles International Airport.

"Airport's closed, mister," the hack driver said. "Look at the fog. Gets so you can't see at all at the airport. Dumbest thing they ever did, puttin' it next to the ocean where the fog'll cover it up whenever it pleases."

Snow mumbled an acknowledgment and gazed out the cab window at the mist that had painted halos around the street lights.

They checked into two adjoining rooms using two false names. Upstairs Snow opened the doors that joined the two rooms, and moved furniture to barricade the entryways. They were on the ninth floor with windows facing the airport.

Waves of fatigue swept Beckett to sleep. He was balanced on a rail somewhere in his mind that divided an unconscious alertness from deep sleep when he became aware of her presence.

"Beck, it's me." It was Tracy's voice. He sat up when she seated herself on the edge of the bed. "Beck, I'm afraid. I'm never afraid, but I am tonight."

"Hey, lady, I'm scared shitless if that's any consolation."

"I don't like to be scared," she continued in a plaintive voice, nervously plucking at the bedspread. "Because being scared makes me realize that I'm vulnerable. I could die, and I don't like being aware of that."

"Nobody gets out of this life alive, you know."

"That's funny, but I can't laugh right now. Do you

know what's happened to me?" She didn't wait for an answer. "Do you know that for the first time in my adult life I am aware, very aware, that I could die? Not next month or next week, but tomorrow or even tonight. And you know what else has come home? If it didn't come swiftly and I had time to think about things, I'd regret a lot of the past five years.

"Oh, not the achievements of the last five years," she continued. "But what I did to get myself there."

Beckett watched her eyes in the semi-darkness. The room was dimly lit by an exterior floodlight that filtered through nylon cheesecloth curtains. In the soft light, Tracy's eyes focused toward infinity. They weren't looking at him; they weren't looking at the windows. She was looking beyond at some landscape of her mind.

"I got there by armoring myself. I trusted no one, and in doing so, ended up not trusting myself. I shielded myself so that no one could hurt me, and I succeeded. But it's funny. I've just realized that all of the armor, all of the walls and guards are my own prison. They do more to keep me in than they do to keep others out. I've got to escape from it; I've got to trust you, and there are no conditions on that. I'm not going to ask you to trust me. That'll have to grow by itself. I want to trust you. But something else, Bec . . ." She shifted her gaze and held his eyes with her own. "Something else I want . . . is I want . . . I want to love you."

She saw the surprise register in his eyes. "That's dumb. You think that's dumb don't you? You . . ."

"Hey look, I don't think it's dumb," Beckett said and placed his hand on top of hers. He felt their cold perspiration. "I think that what you said was beautiful, really beautiful. And it took a lot of chutzpah to say it. It's just I'm a little surprised. I'm glad. What I mean is that I'm glad you said that because I was thinking it, well some of what you said, anyway. And I . . ." She placed the index finger of her right hand on his lips.

"Shhh, don't talk. You're going to spoil a magic moment."

And for just an instant, he saw a thousand miles through her eyes, and then she closed them and they kissed.

Chapter Seven

Morning came to Los Angeles International Airport wrapped in a blanket of fog. Inside the terminal stranded travelers flopped on benches, camped on the floor, lounged and loitered at the coffee shop drinking coffee that was too bitter, too hot, and too expensive. They weren't going anywhere very soon.

Less than a mile away, morning came also to Tracy Reynolds. She awoke and looked at the man sleeping beside her. Part of her told her to run, and another part wouldn't let her. She didn't know what was happening to her—she had been spinning since Carothers died—but she thought events of late, of the past ten hours, had been a definite improvement. She watched how he moved his mouth when he slept, and she watched as his eyes looked from side-to-side under closed lids, following life in a world of dreams. She found herself hoping they were good dreams.

She liked what she saw: his tousled hair, the thin lines at the corners of his eyes, the chin that was almost cleft, what little she could see beneath his beard. The dark brown of his beard was slated with grey and red strands, giving it a distinguished cast.

She slowly disengaged herself from his sleeping hug and stepped out of bed to dress. Then she slipped out of the room and went to the lobby, where she purchased a Los Angeles *Times*. Tucking the paper under her arm,

58

she continued on to the coffee shop. She glanced briefly at the menu.

"Orange juice, an egg over medium, wheat toast, and coffee," she told the waitress.

Orange juice and coffee arrived, and Tracy sipped them and gazed at the people gathering in the restaurant. There was talk of the planes grounded and connections missed; of the weather and how they were angry the airlines weren't paying for the rooms and food; and wasn't that murder ghastly and who'd ever think that a federal prosecutor would go berserk.

The last remark turned the coffee to ice in her throat. She snatched the *Times* from the bench beside her and looked at the headlines. Nothing. Then she turned the paper over, and there at the bottom of the first page was Beckett's picture, and the headline, "Federal Prosecutor Wanted as Suspect in Mutilation Death."

Los Angeles Police and California law enforcement officers are searching for Beckett Snow, U.S. Attorney for the Southern District of California, who witnesses say was seen fleeing a Santa Monica motel following the brutal mutilation murder of an unidentified woman there.

Police say that the manager of the motel observed a tan van, later identified by police as Snow's—screeching from the motel parking lot Friday afternoon.

The story continued, but Tracy Reynolds's eyes were swimming.

She panted up the stairs and sprinted to the room where Beckett lay still asleep.

"Beck, Beck . . . !" she cried and crossed the room quickly. He looked at her, propped on an elbow in surprise.

"Whoa, whoa. What's up? Who's chasing you?" He

looked to the door to be sure it had closed after her.

"*You!* They're chasing *you!*" She thrust the newspaper into his hand.

"No," he said. Calmly Beckett sat up in bed and read the story. The expression on his face remained unchanged until his eyes narrowed and started to burn.

"Bastards. Slimy, slimy bastards," he muttered. "And smart. Whoever said that nice guys don't have a corner on talent had these people in mind."

"You think they . . . they did this on purpose? But yesterday, you said the police thing would be protection. . . ."

"That was yesterday, sweetheart. Yesterday we had the key to this whole thing in the bag, your bag that is, and that bag was our ticket for safe keeping. But this—" He held the paper straight-armed in his left hand and slapped it with his fist. "This cuts off one of my arms. I can't use half of my contacts now."

"Why don't you just call up your friend, you know . . ."

"Nelson."

"Yes."

"Because he thinks I'm crazy anyway. The body disappearing and the bullet holes in the walls—that was too much. Now, I'll bet anything that if I show up, I'll be put in the looney bin somewhere for the shrinks to poke around my head. No, the best thing for me to do is find the rest of that damned briefcase." He swung his legs out of the bed. "But the first thing we've got to do is disappear."

"How?"

"Give me a few minutes and I'll tell you how." Snow went into the bathroom. When he'd washed his face and inserted his contact lenses, he sat down at the dresser and rummaged through the drawers. He found a sheet of Ramada stationery and started to write. Tracy waited. She paced the floor; went to the door and chained it; walked to the window, parted the curtains, and gazed at the thinning fog.

Ten minutes later Beckett was finished.

"Here." He turned around and waved the paper at her.

It was a list of cosmetics: bleach for his hair; dye for hers; brushes for applying same to their eyebrows; makeup to change complexion hues; cotton balls and swabs.

"You've got to go alone. I can't be recognized. There's a drugstore on Lincoln Boulevard about a mile from here. Take a cab and have the cabbie wait for you. Okay?"

"Okay." She started for the door, and then returned to his chair. Snow got up and kissed her.

As soon as she had gone, Beckett walked into the bathroom, took out a pair of scissors and snipped away at his beard, then took a steaming shower to soften the beard. Afterward, he stood dripping nude on the tile floor as he lathered and shaved off the remainder of his whiskers. Finally, he took his contact lenses out and put on his glasses. The contrast was striking. It had been nearly two years since he'd grown the beard, and he almost didn't recognize himself.

Taking out his contacts, he noticed, didn't change his appearance radically since his glasses were rimless. He decided to get a pair of heavy-rimmed glasses.

Snow was sitting on the edge of the bed watching a purple-faced housewife holding up puce underwear and proclaiming its whiteness when Tracy burst in and closed the door.

She gasped and started to run when she recognized him.

"Jesus, you scared me." She walked over and sat down beside him. She looked at Snow and ran her hand across his cheek.

"Not bad," she smiled. "The chin's nice and you

can't see that with the beard. You know, a lot of men grow beards to hide a weak chin. But yours is angular, strong. Why'd you grow it?"

"Lazy. And for a change. I don't know, it just felt right at the time. But what's right for this time," he continued, "is an even bigger change."

And a change they made. Tracy used the Clairol to turn Beckett's hair to a light blond and he dyed her to a bluish jet black.

"Better," he said, and took the makeup from the bed and used it to cover his cheeks, under his chin and along his sideburns where the beard had shielded them from the sun for two years. "Even better," he pronounced. "Now we check out, get us a car, a new haircut, and a new identity."

They settled their bills separately. The day clerk leered at Tracy when he noticed her lack of luggage. Out of sight of the clerk, they boarded a cab for the ride into Los Angeles.

"L. A. Times Building," Snow told the cab driver, and then leaned back against the rear seat next to Tracy. They rode in silence until the cab merged into the traffic of the northbound San Diego Freeway, and the noise of the wind and traffic gave them some privacy.

"You know, Beck," Tracy began, "we hardly know each other, and yet, we know each other pretty well."

He looked at her curiously. "Like how?"

"Well, you know . . . we haven't known each other long, yet we've been through a lot together. Isn't that what getting to know someone is about? Going through things together?"

"I suppose you're right. I . . ."

"Sure, getting to know somebody is more than listening to them tell you things. It's watching how they react to situations, and watching how they react to you; how they feel. That's what getting to know some-body means."

"And we've been through a lot in the past couple of days. That what you're saying?"

"What do you think?"

"I think you're right. It's just that I've never thought about it quite that way before. Sure, it *has* been tense; no, intense. But you know, I was attracted to you even from the first time I saw you."

"Come on! You were attracted to me when I was pointing a gun at you?"

"Well, yes. I was scared shitless, but I was attracted to you too. It was the way you handled yourself. That says a lot about someone. You know, lots of people scoff at the idea that visual attraction can be based on more than purely sexual or physical attraction . . ."

"Um-hum, go on."

"But that's not true. How a person walks, how they gesture, how they dress, the timbre of their voice, how they look at you . . ."

"Body language," she supplied, smiling.

"Yes, though I think it's more. But all of that can tell you a lot about the person before you've said the first word to them."

Her eyes opened wide, mocking him. "And that's why you liked me when I was going to shoot you."

"You weren't going to shoot me."

"I would've, if you'd given me reason."

"I know. I wasn't going to give you a reason. You are a very credible danger. Besides, I didn't say I *liked* you the first time I saw you. I said I was *attracted* to you."

"Oh, now the truth comes out," Tracy said coyly.

"Yeah, now it comes out. It always comes out the morning after."

"Oh, I wouldn't know," she continued. "I haven't

had much experience in that department." Tracy smiled. They both laughed.

They rode in silence until Tracy again spoke first.

"Last night was beautiful." It was a statement for her; a question for him.

"It was. It surely was," he confirmed.

"You sound a little hesitant."

"Well, it's just that . . . I don't want to come on too strong, but I wonder if maybe it's not real."

"What's not real?" Tracy asked.

"Us. I mean, two people thrown together in our situation. That we could both die anytime . . ."

"And we're just getting one last fuck? One last affair?"

"Uh-huh."

"I suppose you could be right, but . . ." Her voice trailed off. She stared out the window.

"Yeah, I could be, but I don't think so," he said.

Tracy turned back to him. "Then why bring it up at all?"

"Because I want to believe that you and I are real," he said. "Not just manufactured by events, but, you know, real."

Tracy nodded and took his hand in hers.

"Beck, why do you like me? I mean, I usually scare men."

"Oh, I dunno. I've always liked strong women. My mother was a strong woman. I grew up with the only authority figure in my life being my mother."

"Where was your father?"

"He disappeared when I was about five."

"What do you mean, 'disappeared'?"

"Just that. One day he was there, and the next day no one saw him again."

"Have you ever seen him since?"

"Nope. And you know the funny thing? His father did the same thing."

"You planning to carry on the tradition?"

"Not if I can help it."

"So go on. You like strong women because of your mother?"

"I guess that's a lot of the reason."

"So what's the rest of it?"

"People. Dignity. The right for someone to be whatever they can be . . ."

"That sounds pretty heavy, pious, very high-minded."

"So maybe I shouldn't talk about it."

"No. I want to hear."

They were barely conscious of having stopped when the taxi driver shut off the meter.

"Here we go," the cabbie said.

Tracy paid the driver and they stepped to the sidewalk beside the old Times Building. Inside, the uniformed guard gave them directions to the newspaper's microfilm section.

"What are you looking for?" Tracy asked as they started off down the hall. "I suppose we should have been talking about *that* in the cab rather than us."

"Nah. Anyway, what we're looking for is somebody with your birthday who died shortly afterward."

"Why?"

"So we can go to the office of vital statistics and get a copy of the birth certificate."

"Which does what?" she said, taking his arm.

"It gets us a driver's license, Social Security card, passport, whatever. That person gets resurrected, but you play the role. And since the person's dead, nobody's going to show up and question your identity."

"Sharp. Does it have to be the exact day?"

"No. Just sometime within about six months."

They checked in with the newspaper's librarian and filled out forms to give them all of the microfilm from 1947 and 1948.

It took less than half an hour.

"Mary Louise Fletcher, born June 17, 1947, died August 3, 1947. Infant daughter of Lorraine and Jackson Fletcher," Becket read. "Well, it's nice to know you. Do you go by Mary or Louise?"

"What hideous names. Oh, Mary, I suppose."

"We'll turn you back to Tracy soon, though."

"Have you found one?"

"Yep. Just a minute ago. May I introduce myself? I'm Elliot Greenleaf Stegner. Born February 29, 1948, died March 23, 1948."

"A leap-year baby, and what a name!"

"Yeah. Come to think of it, a little too distinctive. People might remember it."

"Is that a bad thing? As long as they remember the fake name, that could draw attention away from your real identity."

"Not a bad thought. Have you ever thought of becoming a thief?"

"You forget. I already am."

It was a short cab ride to the Bureau of Vital Statistics. The line was short and less than an hour later they had notarized copies of their birth certificates.

They took another taxi to Fairfax Avenue, just above Melrose, to an optician's shop. Beckett selected a pair of horn rims and Tracy a heavy, steel-rimmed aviator style. Both had plain, non-optical lenses inserted in them. They paid with cash and caught a cab to Beverly Hills.

Mary Fletcher and Elliot Stegner then had their hair styled in styles radically different from those worn by Beckett Snow and Tracy Reynolds. Both were shorter. Tracy wore a page boy; Beckett, a short style that he seemed to remember was in vogue in the gay community. By the time they walked out of the haircutters it was 4 PM. They had just enough time to get a cab to the Department of Motor Vehicles and take driver's license exams before the office closed.

66

"The girl is dead."

"I know. Why so brutally?"

"She was holding out on where the briefcase was. She claims it was left at the man's house."

"Was it?"

"No. I checked. And Hawkins's body was gone. Did you have it removed?"

"No. There's no one else in the area."

"So Reynolds and her prosecutor friend must have the file."

"Perhaps. But could they have removed and hidden the body?"

"It's possible. Or it's possible that—"

"That somebody else is operating in the same territory."

"But who?"

"That's my business. Yours is to kill Reynolds and recover the briefcase."

"She's pretty well immobilized, she and her beau."

"What do you mean?"

"The police want them for the murder."

"Ah yes. I heard."

"I engineered the frame-up."

"You what!"

"The frame-up. I engineered it. I pinned the murder on the prosecutor."

"You're a goddamned fool, Whitney! I'm not paying for you to 'engineer' anything at all. I'm paying for you to kill somebody and recover a briefcase. Do you understand?"

"Yes, but—"

"No buts. You have no idea how things like that could backfire on us all. You don't have the whole game plan. Don't second-guess me or anyone else. Do you understand me quite clearly?"

"Yes, sir."

"Good. Get your ass moving. I want those files and I want them next week. Understand?"

"I understand."

"Goodbye."

"Goodbye."

On the third floor of the white brick townhouse on Capitol Hill in Washington, D.C., a tanned, middle-aged man replaced the receiver of his telephone. His tan, from frequent vacations in Palm Springs where he played golf with people whose names appear in the gossip magazines almost weekly, was a contrast to the white hair of his temples that faded into salt-and-pepper black.

He was a trim man, and this day he was wearing a navy-blue pinstriped three-piece suit. He looked like a banker. Which he was.

The man's office was sparsely furnished, with natural wood, glass, chrome. There were no plants. It was sterile. There were no momentos hung on the light brown walls, and little on the drawerless desk. It was as if life was not allowed to intrude: Decisions had to be made here that were best made without an awareness of humanity. The man in the navy-blue three-piece suit liked that environment.

He hesitated briefly and then stabbed the button to a line that did not go through his assistant's console.

He punched one, then two, zero, three, and seven more digits. The earpiece buzzed but twice before it was answered.

"My daughter is dead," said the man in the navy-blue pin-striped suit.

"I suspected. Have we recovered the dossier?"

"No. She didn't have it."

"No? Then who?"

"I don't know."

"Please explain."

"There appears to be a third party operating in the territory."

"A third party. You mean in addition to us and Carothers's girl?"

"Exactly. I fear it may be Cranch's faction."

"But that would be suicide at this point. He's too smart."

"I thought the same. But if not Cranch, who?"

"I don't know. I hope it's Cranch because if it's not, then someone outside the Commission knows of Prometheus."

"Unlikely."

"Not as unlikely as you think. We're doing much now; it's hard to hide every track. Besides, the prosecutor, the girl's friend, must know."

"He only knows what she tells him. That may not be as much as we suspect."

"We can only hope—"

"No, we must do more than hope. We must act. We've come too far to have things fall apart now. We're too close. Too close."

The man on the other end of the line sat in a similar room. His hair was completely white, and though he was still muscular and powerful for a man of 73, he moved more slowly these days, as his joints and connective tissue gradually succumbed to the relentless assault of arthritis. Today had been a good day for him. The pain had passed with the previous night's sleep. But he knew the respite was not permanent. The pain would return.

Still, he spent the times of pain in the greatest of comfort, all of the comfort that fabulous wealth could purchase. And he made sure that the pain did not reach his reasoning capacity. For if it did, he would have to pass the command of Prometheus to another. He *was* Prometheus; he dreamed of the good their actions would bring.

There was silence on the phone line.

"Prometheus?"

"Yes?"

"Have you a suggestion?"

"No. But I will. I must think. We must both of us think of who this third person is and how to . . . neutralize him."

"Think."

"Yes."

"Goodbye."

"Goodbye."

Normalcy, or what passed for it in the nation's capital, had returned to Pennsylvania Avenue. The streets were salty, dusty-dry, and lined with embankments of snow, wet around the edges, black with dirt spread for traction, and punctuated by the stares of yellow eyes drilled by passing dogs.

Clouds had gone and the sky was beginning to color itself deep azure-black when Leslie Lewis showed her pass to the Secret Service Guard at the 16th Street entrance to the old Executive Office Building. The old building, with its grotesque Victorian architecture, was her favorite. It had character. It also housed lots of characters, she thought ruefully.

"Hello, Larry," she greeted the young Secret Service man at the desk as she flashed her pass.

"Morning, Leslie. You look happier today than I've seen you for a while."

"Really?" She was genuinely surprised. "I hadn't noticed."

"Must have been a nice night last night." He winked and smiled.

She didn't mind. They had an understanding that made the sexual repartee harmless, fun. They were both honest with each other. "No, it wasn't last night. That was a loser."

"Too bad. The men of Washington don't know what they're missing."

"I do."

"I wish I did."

They laughed. Six years before, Leslie used her influence with the governor to have him hired as a bodyguard in the state house. Larry Murchison had been one of her younger sister's boyfriends. Just home from Vietnam, he had been out of work for more than a year. It was Leslie's word that turned him from a statistic into a bodyguard. When the governor became President, Larry was brought along with him. He was bright and easily made the grade as a Secret Service agent. But his seniority was not such that he made any trips with the President. Like most of those low on the pole, he was guarding entrances and checking White House passes.

"So when are you going to start traveling with Himself?"

"Well, not soon," he said. "But my supervisor—"

"Sullivan?"

"Yeah, him. I don't think he likes me. But anyway, he said that I might take my first trip before the summer."

"Super. But you be careful. It's a lot safer here."

"And a helluva lot more boring."

It was a quarter of seven in the morning when Leslie arrived in her office. She was no exception in the world of White House, indeed Washington, workaholics. The disease was endemic; many top White House staffers regularly arrived at 6 AM and didn't leave before nine or ten in the evening.

The day before, she'd asked Jacob and the other personnel in the office to gather all they had on the Commission. Missing files, she told them; there must be missing files somewhere.

Leslie Lewis thought of what she had hoped to find;

a memo, a file, something that would indicate that she had not fallen out of favor with the man in the Oval Office. Why hadn't he talked to her? What could she have done? What could those leeches around him have told him about her? What imagined insults to the administration had been attributed to her? The questions had kept her awake for the last three nights. Something else was keeping her awake, but she couldn't put her finger on it. It was something in the files, or something that was missing from the files. She didn't know. She only hoped that some key would be on her desk in the morning.

But the answer wasn't on her desk. It was sitting in a chair. And it was less an answer than a complication.

Leslie Lewis jiggled her key in her office door, opened it, and reached for the light switch as the door closed itself.

"Stop! Please don't turn on the light yet, Ms. Lewis." She whirled toward the voice but saw only the grey shadows of early morning. As she reached for the doorknob to flee, the voice spoke again.

"Don't leave and don't call Security. They know me well."

She hesitated. "You work here?"

"Yes, but not in this building. I work across the lawn." She realized that he meant the White House. "And what I have to say comes more from my superior, whom I can't mention, than it does from the President."

"What's the message and why is everything so secretive?" She started to walk toward the bank of filing cabinets, behind which the man's voice was coming. It was, she thought, a mellow, not unfriendly voice. And it contained a hint of reservation. About her? About what he had to say? About who commanded him to deliver the message?

"Don't come any closer! I don't want you to know

who I am because it won't do either of us any good, and it might even be . . . inopportune."

"Very well. Do tell me." Leslie stopped short of the filing cabinets. She rolled her secretary's chair across the clear Plexiglas floor mat and sat down.

"It's about the Delphi Commission."

"What about it?"

"Leave it alone."

"Leave it alone? That's my territory. Why should I leave it alone now? What's so damned sacrosanct about it?"

"Leave it alone. Things have changed. Stick with it and you'll do yourself no good."

"Do myself no good? Is that a threat?"

"I don't know——"

"What do you mean, you don't know? You're threatening me and you don't know?"

Leslie wanted to rush behind the cabinets, but fear held her in her seat. Anger and fear.

"You are doing your job a little too well for some people."

"For some people, huh? Who? Would you mind telling me just who thinks I'm doing my job too well? You work for Sherbok, don't you? You're his henchman. He's too goddamned arrogant to do his own backstabbing, so you do it for him!"

The man behind the filing cabinets said nothing for several moments. Outside, Leslie could hear the sounds of Washington. Horns, traffic, buses gasping and wheezing; somewhere a policeman's impatient whistle; far away a siren urging all out of the way; the faint whisper of jets barnstorming low over the Potomac to touch down at National Airport. It was quiet. She heard her own heart and the rush of blood in her ears.

"I think I've said enough," he finally resumed. "Perhaps I've said too much. What is important is this conversation, because it could make a definite difference for your future. Remember your future.

"Now, go into your office and shut the door. It's time for me to go to work."

Chapter Eight

Snow jogged across the beach, its sand dark with early morning dew. As he labored across to the firm surface beside the waves, he left white prints on the damp-dark beach.

The waves were kinetic sculptures, graceful and beautiful, but in motion. Try to capture one, and all you get is seawater, he thought as he ran. Love, he reflected, was like that too: Try to hold on and you destroy it; let it go, and it knows the right beach to call home.

His head knew that, but he always wondered if his heart would let him live it.

Snow saw the waves rise from the still water and curl until one end broke and finally spilled cotton-water on the sand.

Snow ran up and down the edge of the water as it ebbed and ran, keeping just on the dryside, playing a game with the ocean. Catch me if you can. But now, he was running at the edge of something that was a lot more serious than getting wet.

He'd fallen in love.

Snow wanted Tracy. Wanted her. But he wondered if he could have her without destroying her.

And he knew that he was running up and down the edge of disaster with people out there who wanted both of them—some for a crime they hadn't committed; others, who just wanted them dead.

In the weeks he'd been in Los Angeles, Beckett had grown addicted to the hour of meditation gained by running along the beach. There was something compelling that drew him here. Perhaps, he mused, it was a primeval thought, lodged deep behind the reptilian, preprimate midbrain, unconscious but powerful. It was an unremembered memory passed through genes for countless generations, back to the times before creatures moved with legs and wings, when the sea was the womb and the crash of breakers on the shore was the pulsebeat of life: The ocean was a source that demanded a pilgrimage by its sons and daughters.

And so it was this morning that he could not deny the call. The evening before, after returning from errands, he and Tracy had checked into the Miramar, a hotel perched on top of the palisades of Santa Monica, looking down at the beach and the Pacific Ocean. It was his theory that people don't expect fugitives—which they were now, he recognized—to hide at the scene of the crime. He'd be safer the closer he was to the murders.

With his warm-up suit to insulate him from the early morning chill, Snow had kissed Tracy on her still-sleeping lips and headed out for a run, for his mind and for reconnaissance.

He ran along the palisades and south along Ocean Boulevard until he reached Ocean Park. He ran past his house. He reasoned that the hood on his sweatshirt, along with his new glasses, new-colored hair, and lack of beard assured him anonymity. Along the street he noticed a Ford Granada, with a rental agency sticker on the windshield, parked at the corner near Third Street. Snow also noted that the "For Rent" sign that decorated the window of the shabby stucco house on the other side of the street from his was gone. He ran on, back to Ocean Park, and west along it until he hit the beach.

It would have been impossible to follow him except on foot, and Snow took a circuitous route that assured him that any tracker would be seen.

"Hello, love." Tracy was up. Snow smelled fresh cologne, felt the humidity from a shower. "Are you hungry?"

"For food or you?" he smiled.

"Oh, I don't know. You tell me."

"Do I have to make a choice?"

"Not unless you want to."

"Then the answer is 'yes'."

"Yes to what?"

"Just yes." He sat down on the bed next to her and kissed her lightly on the lips. "Not too close right now, I'm dripping with sweat."

"I noticed."

Snow kissed her again and got up to shower.

"Hurry?"

"I will," he replied.

When he'd toweled dry and combed his hair, he walked into the bedroom, wearing a towel around his waist.

"Now," she said as he lay down beside her. "Don't hurry."

"So what'd you see?" The younger man rubbed his eyes.

"Nothing. A jogger. People going to work." The older man had been awake since midnight, watching the house across the street for any sign of its former occupant.

"I don't like this," the younger man said.

"Don't like what, Whitney, my boy?"

"Sitting here. Doing nothing. We ought to be *doing* something."

"Like what? As soon as you come up with better ideas, I'll *do* something. Okay?"

Whitney grunted and walked into the kitchen. He flicked on the light. "Coffee?"

"No. I'm going to sleep now. Patience wears heavy on an old man."

"And on a young one too," Whitney mumbled from the kitchen.

"What?"

"Nothing. Go to sleep."

"I love you," Tracy said. She kissed the back of his left ear. They were lying on their sides, limbs entwined. He kissed her lightly on her lips, on both cheeks, on her forehead.

"You don't have to say that, you know," Snow replied.

"I know I don't have to say it. That's why it feels so good . . . to *say* that, I mean."

"Well, I love you too."

She tilted her head back and looked at him. "How does that make you feel, telling me that?"

"Good. Scared. Apprehensive. Hopeful. I don't know, a lot of other things I can't put my finger on," Snow replied. "You?"

"The same. And wonderment—that this whole incredible thing's happened. It's been so much chance."

"There are no accidents in the universe," Snow stated solemnly.

"That's pretty heavy. You really believe that?" she asked skeptically.

"Yes. I don't believe in chance."

"You'd make a pretty good Presbyterian. I'm not sure I go for all of that. Chance is a big part of everything. Look. Maybe you read in a newspaper that a drunk driver ran a stoplight and broadsided a car and killed the driver. You look at it and realize you went through that intersection three minutes before it happened. The drunk could have hit your car! That's chance. Pure chance, luck." Tracy looked for his reaction.

"Oh, I don't know. Holmes—Oliver Wendell—once said something like 'while sleeping or awake we never hear the sounds of things that almost happen'. That's not a direct quote. I'm never good at them, but the thought's there."

"So you think that all this—you and me . . ." Tracy searched for the right words. "Me stowing away in your van—"

"Right," Snow interrupted. "And just the mere fact I have a van—I hate the mothers—but I needed it on the move out here. All of that was no accident."

"Fate works in mysterious ways . . ." Tracy began.

"Its miracles to perform? Yes," Snow said. "I believe that. Just as I'm believing now that you and I are real, that it's not just the situation that's brought us together."

"I hope so. I pray you're right. I really do."

They held each other, feeling the warmth, feeling so secure. And they made love: tender, compassionate, without the urgency that was crowding their lives.

After a shower, they ate silently from a breakfast tray ordered from room service, and looked at the ocean. Finally, with the spell broken, Snow mentioned that room service was sending up a typewriter.

"What's the typewriter for?" she asked.

"I think it's the way to locate our friends with the rest of your file. Whoever is trying to kill you—us—has the microfilm and they realize by this time we've got the box and Carothers's seal—"

"Which we've got to put in a safe place."

"Right. Anyway, when I jogged by my house this morn—"

"You went by there?!" She leaned over and grabbed his arm. "They could've seen you. Why did you do something dumb like that?"

"Relax. I had the hood pulled up, and the hair and lack of beard are enough to hide me. Anyway, I went by there, and I think they're renting the house across the street from mine. So what I'm gambling on is that they're watching things very carefully, including the mail. What we're going to do," he continued, "is mail me a letter to set up a meeting. I'm banking on them opening the mail and coming to the meeting."

"Would they think you're really going to go to a meeting? Especially with the murder charge and all?"

"I think so. They don't really have anything else to go on. They won't pass up the chance: They're professionals."

"Why do you think that?" Tracy asked.

"The way they cut up the girl." Tracy grimaced. "They had to know what they were doing to cut her up that badly without killing her quickly."

"Ugh. Do we have to talk about that at breakfast?"

"No. Anyway, I want to mail the letter today and set up a meeting for the day after tomorrow."

"If they're there, why not just go by your place and let them follow us? We could make contact that way."

"Not smart, lady. First of all, the police may be watching too. Second, we don't want to lead them back here. And, third, we want to meet them on our own ground. I choose the time and place of meeting and that gives us the advantage."

"Sorry. I'm new to this game."

"Apology accepted," he said.

"Thank you," Tracy replied, mock gratitude in her voice. "Now come here."

80

"Why?" Snow looked at her.

"I want you."

"Again?"

"Again."

Chapter Nine

Beckett Snow drove the rented Plymouth down Washington Boulevard, accompanied by three strangers.

In the passenger seat was a hefty man who vaguely resembled Snow. In the back were two other people.

The person on the left had sandy brown hair and blue eyes. All considered, the person looked remarkably like the Tracy Reynolds of the previous week, which, not coincidentally, was exactly what the person was being paid for.

But it was there the resemblance ended, for the remarkably attractive woman was not a woman at all, but a man.

And also not by accident, the man sitting by the door on the passenger side looked to be a dead ringer for the Beckett Snow of the past week. All were out-of-work actors who had turned to male prostitution. Snow figured they would be unlikely to reveal their role in whatever might become public about this morning.

It was now 10:30 AM Sunday. Beckett looked away. In the rearview mirror, he saw Tracy's face as she followed his rented sedan with a Mercedes 450 SLC they had rented Friday from a Beverly Hills dealer. Beckett's Plymouth had been rented at the airport.

Also on Friday, Beckett had typed and posted the

letter. He was banking on its delivery on Saturday and its interception by whomever was after them.

The letter was a fictitious note to a fictitious person about a fictitious brunch date at a sidewalk cafe on the boardwalk in Venice, which was where they were presently heading.

Beach traffic was still light, and they found space for their two vehicles on Pacific Avenue. The actor who looked like the old Beckett Snow and the transvestite who resembled the old Tracy Reynolds walked arm in arm along the boardwalk, carefully dodging the joggers, bikers, and roller skaters. They took a table for two at the Fisherman's Wharf restaurant and sat gazing into each other's eyes, holding hands, and waiting for the visitor to whom they'd utter a single sentence that would be their entire day's work for the $150 apiece they'd been paid.

Tracy took the arm of the other actor, and headed another 200 yards up the boardwalk to the Sea Catch where they took a table for two outside, but in the tier of tables next to the building and not on the extreme outside row.

Wearing a blond wig made suitably scraggly by wiping the dirt off a parked car, sporting decrepit blue jeans and a tee-shirt with an obscene slogan, Snow sat cross-legged on the lawn midway between the two restaurants and plucked abstractedly at an out-of-tune guitar. What he *was* concentrating on was anyone who was out of place, someone who was too wary, too aware.

An unsteady old man huddled at the base of a palm tree dressed in a woolen greatcoat that had once known elegance. Despite the sunshine that brought beads of perspiration to Snow's forehead, the old man's coat was fastened from his knees to his neck as he swigged wine from a paper sack and chased it with a bottle of

Perrier. Venice! Snow thought: the comfortable accommodation of extremes.

Someone besides Snow also took notice of the old man with the wine bottle. The observer was a muscular young man just under six feet tall. His well-defined muscles were exposed by the tank-top tee-shirt and the pair of cutoff Levi's he wore. His feet sported new running shoes and he was trying to master a skateboard. The red rucksack on his back was new. The young man was having trouble with the skateboard, fell frequently, and cursed profusely. Inside the new pack was a well-used 9mm Mauser automatic pistol with its sausage-shaped silencer attached. Resting beside it was a leather box housing an assortment of surgical instruments.

A Chicano busboy finished the task of clearing off the table's soiled dishes and flatware, spread two paper place mats in front of Tracy and her escort, and replenished the settings. Tracy ordered a Margarita; her companion ordered a Dewar's on the rocks.

They sat in silence. Tracy hid the menu, which she scanned without interest. She caught a glimpse of Beckett's head, framed between the bodies of two diners sitting next to the boardwalk.

She could see Beckett and next to him, a derelict. She also saw a skateboarder whose appearance bothered her for some reason she couldn't touch upon. She put it down to nerves and sipped the Margarita.

It all seemed so peaceful, the sailboats sliding smoothly across the water; the freaks and gawkers; the sunbathers and diners; all come to have a good time. Violence and mayhem and conspiracies were unlikely intruders to this world.

How wrong she was would be apparent in moments.

The young man with the skateboard eyed first the old man and then the couple seated at the sidewalk cafe. There was, he decided, no mistaking the pair. After the couple had been seated, he waited ten minutes, and then unharnessed his rucksack, retrieved from it an object, and slung the pack over his right elbow. He took the skateboard under one arm and approached the couple. The old man in the wool great-coat watched, keenly interested.

"Please don't do anything foolish," the young skate-boarder said as he pulled a chair up to the table. "I have a gun and I'll kill you if you give me any trouble." The fake Tracy Reynolds choked on his drink, coughed, and grabbed for his napkin to blot the dribbles of liquor that ran across his chin.

"The party you seek, sir, is sitting at the next res-taurant down. You won't recognize them." The fake Beckett Snow had summoned his best stage courage and spoke clearly and without trembling. "Go to the Sea Catch and ask the hostess for Mr. and Mrs. Provenzano." The young man with the skateboard and arctic eyes looked coolly past him. Those eyes now searched the two people at the table like an anatomist slowly dissecting first this muscle, then that gland, and this tendon. When he'd finished comparing their fea-tures with those of the photographs he had studied so thoroughly, he was satisfied that these were, indeed, imposters.

"Clever, very clever," the man muttered aloud. He looked at the fake Tracy Reynolds, slowly raised his right foot and plunged it into the actor's groin. The actor's eyes grew wide. The young man with the skate-board looked back as he walked toward the Sea Catch and sneered as he saw the "woman" doubled over the table, her friend with a comforting arm about her shoulder.

The old derelict watched and silently took another swig from the brown paper bag.

Another group of people also observed the scene at the restaurant. They were members of the Los Angeles Police Department who, along with Inspector Jack

Nelson, scanned the restaurant through excellent optical devices from a table by the Venice Pavilion. Venice was patrolled by the LAPD, and Nelson and his men now had the home court advantage. They, too, had been reading Beckett Snow's mail. In fact, Beckett Snow's mail for the past week had been read by so many people, he might as well have had it published in the L.A. *Times.*

"Now, Inspector?" asked one of the men in the van.

"No, just keep an eye on him. Don't let him out of your sight. The rest of you, follow me, about 10 yards behind."

Inspector Nelson barked orders into his radio, and then set off toward the restaurant alone. Unlike his backup men, members of LAPD's famed SWAT team who were dressed like beach people, Nelson was attired in the sartorial cliche that had become his style: beat-up brown wing tips, a baggy dark-brown summerweight wool suit, a cheap short-sleeved shirt, and $1.98 tie that claimed no family relationship to the rest of the outfit.

Ten feet from the table, Nelson knew something was wrong. The man, although he resembled Beckett Snow, was not him. There are a thousand unspoken and unthought and undescribed characteristics that distinguish an individual. Physical appearance—hair color, facial features, height, weight, color of eyes—is but a fraction. All of these matched in Nelson's mind, but what didn't was the manner in which the man carried himself, the way he moved his arms, the way he spoke, the way he moved. Nelson's instinct made him hesitate; but, knowing he was committed, he continued toward the couple.

"I know you're not Beckett Snow, so why don't you tell me where he is?"

The man who looked like Beckett Snow stared at him blankly. They had been told that only one person would come to them, and they would be free to leave.

"I don't know a Beckett Snow." This was true, since Snow had given them no names. "I don't know a Beckett Snow," he repeated to the man in the brown suit.

"Here, maybe this will refresh your memory," Nelson displayed his LAPD identification.

"I still don't know a Beckett Snow. Look, officer ... sir, I was paid by a man to sit here and tell a person that the people for whom he was looking were at the Sea Catch and to ask for Mr. and Mrs. Provenzano. That's all. I'm just an act—" He stopped as Nelson strode away toward the Sea Catch.

"My name is Whitney, and you had better tell me what the hell is going on, unless you want to get badly hurt," said the young man with the skateboard.

Whitney's abruptness shattered Tracy's concentration, and drew her thoughts back from the Pacific's horizon, back past the sailboats, through the surf, across the beach and its well-slathered sunbathers, like a camera zooming. The focus slowly passed by the skaters and the skateboarders and the strollers and joggers and freaks until it centered on the face of the young man with the skateboard, who had suddenly snatched a chair from an adjacent table and sat on it, squarely in front of Tracy.

She started, uttered a barely audible gasp, and reflexively pushed her chair away from the table.

"Hold it," Whitney ordered, and revealed the Mauser pointed at her. He skillfully shielded it from public view with the rucksack hanging from his arm. "Don't try to run, because you'll be dead and I'll be gone before you hit the floor."

Tracy glanced around, and noticed that none of the other diners was paying attention. She wanted to look and see if Beckett had noticed, but dared not glance in his direction, for fear of betraying his presence. Surprise, he'd told her, would be the key.

As soon as he saw the young man with the skateboard sit down next to Tracy, Beckett put down his guitar and slid his hand into the beat-up plastic flight bag containing the Ingram. Feeling its reassurance, he shouldered the bag, grabbed the guitar by its neck, and started toward the Sea Catch when he saw Nelson half-walking, half-running down the boardwalk.

Christ! he thought. Of course, the police had been reading his mail too! Nelson had found the actors and they'd given him the same information they'd given the fellow with the skateboard. Snow glanced up the boardwalk and saw the two actors hurrying up the tarmacadam strip. Between them and Nelson was a group of men: a little too old, a little too clean, a little too cohesive, and just a little too aware to be average boardwalkers. They, he knew, would be Nelson's back-up team, probably SWAT.

Snow knew Nelson would try to approach him and talk him into surrendering. The gesture would be as much from curiosity as friendship. But what to do? Snow had no intention of shooting his friend, nor could he rush to Tracy's side, for then they would all be arrested for sure.

Wait. Be cool. Look for their mistake.

But he couldn't wait long. If they had to shoot their way through Nelson's backup men, they would have to open fire while the men were together. After that, they'd have no chance.

Snow watched as Nelson walked up to the hostess station, scanned the diners and stood perplexed, having failed to spot Beckett Snow.

Nelson's small army grew closer.

Snow saw Nelson approach the hostess, and he knew the policeman was asking for the table of the Provenzanos. He was soon seated next to Tracy. It was obvious

Nelson still failed to recognize her. He pulled from his brown coat a tattered case containing his inspector's badge and his identification. It was the last thing that Inspector Jack Nelson, LAPD would ever do.

The inspector's shoulders jerked backward, his head snapped forward and down, looking like a man who had been slugged in the solar plexus—which was what happened. Only the impact was made not with a fist, but with a mercury-filled explosive bullet from a 9-millimeter silenced Mauser. The young man with the skateboard had fired the pistol from under the table, and it entered Inspector Nelson's abdomen through a clean puncture just above his navel. The impact slowed the slug. But the head of mercury sealed inside the hollow core of the slug did not slow down. Its momentum carried it racing into the closed end of the slug. The impact shattered the slug. A mass of fragments jerked and arced through the breakfast Inspector Nelson had eaten three hours before, obliterated his right kidney, and spewed lead and protoplasm across the table behind him.

The two elderly ladies sitting at the table were instantly speechless. There was no experience within memory that could account for the sudden appearance on their white table cloth of the spaghetti sauce material. No one else was looking; no one had paid attention to the cough of the silenced small caliber pistol.

Horrified, Snow moved more quickly toward the restaurant as he saw Nelson jerk. The movement was unmistakable, its cause beyond doubt.

It was but a split instant before Snow saw the actor at Tracy's side imitate the inspector.

As the inspector's large bulk crashed face-first into the glasses of water and silverware on the table. the two women behind him saw the raw hole in his back, connected it to their tablecloth, and screamed. One of them did. The other fainted.

The actor's slight body, unable to absorb the impact of the slug as well as the inspector's large bulk, was blown out of his chair and fell against the back of another diner's chair.

The smell was immediately nauseating. The slug passing through the actor had severed the involuntary nerves controlling his bowel functions, and was soon awash with his own waste.

Inspector Nelson had fallen on the table in a crucifix position, his arms outstretched as if to embrace the table. As Tracy and the young man fled, the inspector's body slowly rolled to the right, on top of the actor, bringing down on top of both of them the table cloth and its contents of dishes and trays and menus and condiment containers.

Snow saw Tracy and the young man push their way through the crowd of screaming diners who had started a stampede out of the restaurant, while waiters and restaurant workers elbowed their way toward the table.

Snow was running toward the restaurant when he heard the thudding of heavy men also running in the same direction. He looked to his right and saw Nelson's SWAT members heading toward the scene, too late to give any assistance to their fallen leader. They abandoned any pretenses of being anything other than policemen, and all advanced with their weapons at the ready, safety catches, Snow knew, disengaged.

It was a fortunate set of circumstances, Snow thought quickly, that the scene took place in Venice rather than East Los Angeles. Here, the bystanders were Caucasian; in East L.A. they'd be black or Chicano. He knew that if the people were not Caucasian, the LAPD were more likely to blast the hell out of them first and ask questions later. By now a dozen people would be dead or wounded if they had been anything but white.

Snow froze as the policemen approached. He watched as Tracy was shoved by the young man not toward the sidewalk, but back into the restaurant, probably to exit through the kitchen. The same thought must have occurred to two of the SWAT members, as they broke from the main group and headed down an alley toward the rear of the building.

Snow intended to follow them as soon as the main group passed. But then one of them tripped and fell. Fell to the pavement and didn't move. His partner stopped, turned around, and then collapsed on top of his buddy. A crooked line of red splotches materialized on his torso and head.

No sound had preceded the slugs before they tore into the two policemen; Snow deduced they were from a silenced weapon, and hit the pavement. He rolled toward the shelter of a group of palm trees at the edge of the boardwalk, and took cover as one of the four survivors sighted him, assumed he was the killer and squeezed off a round from a .44 magnum. It passed harmlessly through the trunk of the palm.

And then Snow thought he was hallucinating. To his right, the old derelict had thrown off his shabby great-coat and stood crouched behind a concrete refuse barrell, spraying the SWAT team with slugs from a silenced Uzi machine gun. The man who had fired at Snow quickly hit the pavement, as did another at his side. The remaining two had taken cover around the corner of the building and were out of the line of fire from the old man's Uzi. They were in Snow's sight.

Time passed quickly. He hadn't any idea whether there were other policemen waiting at the rear of the restaurant to pick up Tracy and the young man. Worse, he worried about the young man forcing Tracy into a vehicle and escaping. The old man, he determined, was the young man's accomplice.

First, Snow decided, he'd take care of the two cops, and then the old man. While the two policemen radioed for reinforcements, which would arrive in moments,

91

Snow retrieved his Ingram machine pistol from his knapsack. The old man continued to pick away at the corner of the building. He had moved from his original position and now concealed himself behind a rise of sand, trying to get a better angle at the men, trying to hold them down long enough for his accomplice to make good his escape.

The two policemen pinned down by the old man were oblivious to Snow as he braced his arms on the ground and sighted carefully. He checked one last time to make sure the Ingram was in full auto position, and then raked their position with bullets.

Snow sprinted for the alley in which lay two slain policemen. Two strides into his sprint, Snow whirled and fired at the old man, hoping to pin him down long enough to get out of his gunsight. Snow emptied the Ingram's magazine in the old man's direction, turned and made for the safety of the alley.

The last thing he remembered as something hot and painful shafted through his neck was wondering if he was going to break his nose on the pavement when he hit.

Chapter Ten

Sunday was the shits.

Leslie rolled over, and the slats of sunlight, chopped by the unfashionably thick venetian blinds, turned her closed eyelids red.

There had been a time when Sundays were days to be looked forward to: days when the family was home, went to church, fought over who got the comics first, and gorged on something special for Sunday dinner.

But Sundays, like Sunday's children, were no longer full of grace. Sundays in Washington meant a day for single people to sleep late, a day for wandering to a pub to have brunch and watch the beginnings of whatever sports event had started at noon, to try to crowd into the Smithsonian, or ride a bike down the Mall and look at all the other people alone and covet those who weren't, and begin—as every Sunday—to dread how lonely the evening was going to be.

But this Sunday felt different. She didn't know why, but she knew she was going to *do* something. What? She wasn't sure any more that she knew why.

She didn't know what or why and didn't care.

She got up at 11:17 AM, according to her bedside clock.

The refrigerator was empty save for a container of cottage cheese in which grew a colorful swamp of fuzzy mold.

Leslie dressed and ate breakfast at a greasy spoon on 18th Street and walked down to the Mall and across to the Jefferson Memorial. If she had been a man, she thought, looking at Thomas Jefferson's statue, she'd have liked to have been Jefferson.

If she had been a man. The thought stayed with her as she walked around the Tidal Basin. If I'd been a man, she mused, would I have reacted the way I did last Friday?

The question nagged at her.

No, she decided. She would have acted. Her reaction on Friday to the strange visitor had been a nonreaction. She had been frightened. And angry; but not motivated to action. She had done what she had been told. She had acquiesced to a stranger. Because he was a man? Partly.

That shit, she concluded, had to stop. Today.

She knew that if she did nothing, she'd keep her ass intact, and watch her job slide down the tubes. On the other hand, if she tried to resist, she'd probably see her job and her ass go down the tubes at a highly accelerated rate.

Leslie was tired of being bullied by the whole fucking world. If it meant losing her job, maybe, just maybe she'd find herself. And finding herself was worth the risk.

Now, as Leslie drove her Starfire north along Route 29-211 just south of its intersection with the Beltway, she felt like she'd taken a decisive step toward charting a different path for herself.

If I were a man, Leslie thought, I'd probably do *exactly* what I did today. If I were a man, I wouldn't take any shit from a threatening voice from behind a filing cabinet. I'd be fucking mad. I'd fight back.

Which, Leslie decided, was precisely what she was going to do. The depression was turning to rage.

The drive into the Virginia countryside had been a

pleasing one, satisfying. Leslie looked at the bag on the seat beside her. It had come from Clark Brothers, a roadside gun-nut establishment near Warrenton, Virginia. Inside the bag were a .44 magnum and four boxes of ammunition; a purse-sized, pearl-handled .38-caliber, two-shot derringer; and an equally purse-sized .32-caliber automatic pistol, so compact it fit into her small palm.

When the nondescript panel truck pulled out of the garage of the Victorian brick townhouse on 18th Street just north of E Street Northwest, none of the passersby had any idea the truck and the house were owned by an elite intelligence operation reporting solely and directly to the President's National Security Advisor. Nor did they realize that the van's occupants had arrived at the house by way of an underground passageway that had been built as an escape from the White House. And finally, none of the passersby—even if they had taken note of the van, which none had—would be able to discern that the van's premier occupant was the President of the United States.

Relaxing inside the rear of the van as it plied its way through the darkening Sunday evening streets of the nation's capital was the President, his National Security Advisor, Stefan Sherbok, Sherbok's assistant, Peter Gilbert, and four Secret Service protectors.

"I don't like this," the President told Sherbok. "The man is pushing too hard, accelerating things much too quickly. It's not time yet. We have to have more time."

The National Security Advisor looked at the President of the United States of America and failed to respond. This irritated the President.

"Besides, it shows a lack of respect for the office to call on such short notice and demand a meeting—a clandestine meeting, yet—with the President, with me."

"I'm *sure* you can restrain your anxiety," the Na-

95

tional Security Advisor said. The President, chastened by his tone of voice, remained quiet, examined the man who commanded the least-known and possibly most-effective intelligence organization in the world, the National Security Intelligence Agency. Sherbok looked Russian, which was what he was. His parents had come to the United States during World War I. He was a brilliant, cunning, creative man whose mind was in great demand. It was now demanded by the Delphi Commission, which also demanded—and received—a person's ultimate loyalty.

After a tortuous route, the van headed south into the Northern Virginia hunt country hamlet of Middleburg and turned left three miles later onto a gravel drive.

The drive led through three sets of gates with security fences that would have been suicidal to attempt to breach.

Sophisticated acoustical and chemical sensing devices were located every 25 yards around a perimeter of more than 17 miles. Nothing passed the fence without notice.

But if something *did* pass the fence, and if it weren't immediately killed by the guards who stood with the monitoring devices every 25 yards, then it was faced with two hardened chain-link fences each more than 30 feet tall, electrified and topped not with barbed wire, but with what could only be described as ribbon razor blades.

The space between the two fences was patrolled by members of the elite Navy SEAL team.

Units with surface-to-air missiles guarded the air space covetously.

It was through these barriers that the van passed, but only after all its occupants had placed their palms on a computer scan laser analyzer that examined and compared them to prints in storage, and after speaking into a voice-print analyzer that made a fail-safe identification.

As they rode toward the stone estate house that overlooked the land, they noted the blue lights of the runway and realized that Prometheus would be landing shortly. The runway lights were turned on only when a plane, which had received advance clearance, was about to land.

"I want to know what's happened. I want to know it all, and I want to know it right now!"

Silence crackled through the evening air. None of the eight men who listened seemed likely to end the silence. The table around which they sat could comfortably accommodate more than 50 people, and had frequently been used by meetings for the full Commission. But tonight, the men clustered around both sides of the table were a select slice of that select body. They were the brains of Prometheus: a Japanese industrialist whose company was in autos, electronics, armaments; a West German banker whose assets controlled a war industry greater than the Krupp family could have imagined; a British insurance magnate whose business infiltrated every major insurance company in the world; an American banker, his name and his bank a household word; another American, a businessman-financier whose investment advice was law to the largest pension funds and portfolios in the United States; yet a third American, the chairman of the board and chief stockholder in a company which held the communications system of his country and two dozen others in its grasp; a Swiss whose inroads into his country's banking system was mandatory for any such operation; and the National Security Advisor of the United States. The President, not cleared for this meeting, waited patiently outside.

The man who commanded the respect of this powerful assembly—a man just a little more equal among his equals—was not an American; he was Belgian. Flemish, actually. Few people knew this. Most thought him to be American, made obscenely wealthy in the insurance business. He was the perfect person for the position. Though older than any of the other members of the Prometheus council, his mind was clear, cold, hard, and analytical when it came to making hard decisions.

It had been his decision, and his decision had swayed the rest of the group, to assassinate Carothers. The arguments had been fierce, humanitarian.

"But you *can't* just murder a man like him," the gentleman from Great Britain had argued. "The enormity of it all! Good Lord, man, Prometheus is supposed to bring order, stability to the world, decrease bloodshed, and here we act like an immoral band of . . . of gangsters and hoodlums plotting to, ah . . . rub out one of our own."

"It's not a moral issue," Prometheus had argued persuasively. "We have a plan—Prometheus—which will do the world good. We've all agreed on that; correct, gentlemen?" The murmurs of consent had traveled around the table to a man, the same eight who now sat before Prometheus. "And we've also agreed that nothing must be allowed to stand in the way of that good, that greater good of mankind." The murmurs continued. "And for that, we have no moral question to consider. Either Prometheus is born and the good is done, or it isn't. And, gentlemen, I submit that the loss of Prometheus because of this man's interference and opposition is a much greater loss to the world than his own life, or the lives of anyone in this room. Do you agree?" The murmurs were more affirmative, aware of the thinly veiled threat implicit in the man's statement.

98

There had been no further opposition.

The eight in that room were the only members of the Commission who knew fully the details of Prometheus. To reveal the entire operation to every member would have been infeasible, creating unacceptable risks of exposure. The other members had been told just enough to obtain their agreement to cooperate when the time came, and to place further planning in the hands of the Prometheus Council. These decisions were not based wholly on trust. The Council also provided them with deniability in the unlikely event that the operation failed and the Commission had to account publicly for its dead.

Tonight, the eight men with their eight blotters and eight pitchers of water and eight cut-crystal tumblers avoided eye contact with the man called Prometheus and with each other.

"Well, since none of you seems capable of speaking for himself," the man called Prometheus began, "let me state what I know, and the questions I have. Then, gentlemen, you may answer them. First: Why is the China phase taking so long? I expected tangible results by now."

Sherbok found his voice. "You . . . we *have* tangible results, sir. The Secretary of the Treasury, as you are aware, is now in China. He tells me agreements will be signed within a month, both with our companies for goods and services, and with our banks to finance those."

"Yes, yes, I know that," the man called Prometheus said impatiently. "That is all well and good; but the war is not widening. Why?"

"It's hard to say," Sherbok replied. "Of course, conditions are difficult these days. But . . . I believe we're pretty much on schedule, aren't we?"

"We are, on the *old* schedule. But the situation with

those religious hoodlums in Iran has thrown another change into our plans. The schedule must be moved up."

"But that's hardly possible," the businessman from Japan protested. "We're pressed to the wire with preparations now. We've already moved things up once and that's meant starting this . . . this distasteful thing in Indochina, which made necessary the rather, uh, precipitous action we took."

The businessman placed his palms on the edge of the table and waited for a response. Before Prometheus could answer, the American communications industrialist spoke. "We all share your discomfort at the death of Adam Carothers, my dear colleague, but as you know, his opposition to fueling the border war between Vietnam and China made it unfortunately necessary. There was really no alternative." To this, the Oriental nodded his unhappy assent and looked expectantly at Prometheus.

On one point the entire body of the Commission was in undisputed agreement: the arrival of the corporate global state must be hastened. Indeed, the Commission had its origins in a deep-rooted conviction that nationalism was bad for business. High-ranking corporate executives feared, quite simply, that nations would wreck their corporations' economics.

So they approached nationalism like they'd approach any other corporate headache: They reached into their managerial bag of tricks and brought out one called the Delphi Technique. In a corporation, this involves summoning the best minds to meet and develop an answer to a problem. They just did it on a bigger scale and drew together what they considered the best corporate-oriented minds in the world, calling it the Delphi Commission.

Capital, they understood, knew no ideology or nationality; it moved to where it got the best treatment.

If that meant a flow from the Third World to the superpowers, then that was a law of economics.

But increasingly, Third World politicians demanded a voice in the flow of capital: They had nationalized corporations, taken control of oil fields, of reserves of bauxite, and other mineral deposits.

In the process, they had taken from the corporations.

The Commission was the corporations' way to fight back. Build a car whose parts are made in 12 different countries. Then if one country nationalizes a plant, production shifted to another country. These disruptions, however, are still costly. To minimize them, the world economy must be dominated by the global corporations.

Thus the plan for Prometheus evolved. Global corporations, the Commission members agreed, had the combined economic might to control the world. Thus far, they had been prevented from doing so because they had not worked in consort. The Commission gave them their framework for cooperation, and Prometheus became the method by which it could be accomplished.

Only the few people in that boardroom that night knew every detail of the plan.

The plan was ridiculously simple in concept, enormously complicated in its execution. The plan was to flood every securities and commodities market in the world at once. Simultaneously, the Commission members would withdraw all of their billions in foreign currency from all nonmember banks.

On a single day, when the world economy was at its most vulnerable, the word would go out through three people—one of whom was Sherbok, and another, his assistant Peter Gilbert.

"Imagine," the man called Prometheus had enjoined them in 1974 when the plan was first devised. "Just visualize the effects of Prometheus. It will make the Great Depression look like a lull on the Dow Jones

Index. Stock will be worthless; banks will close; money will have no value; the transport of goods will cease as barter becomes the medium of survival. Commerce will grind to a halt. And within a month power companies will be out of fuel; freeways will be deserted; the shelves in supermarkets will be bare. Civilization as we all know it will cease to exist!

"It will cease to exist and we, the Delphi Commission, will begin to remake it in a better image, in a better shape than even our namesake, the Oracle at Delphi, could have imagined in its wisdom.

"For the Oracle's wisdom was mythical; ours is real!

"Can't you see it?" Prometheus had demanded rhetorically. "Every politician from banana dictators and oil despots to the President of the United States will be cowering in their offices, their countries, their political bases, falling in around their ears. We'll give them enough time to let the situation soak in, and then give them our ultimatum: Either we call the shots, or the country collapses. Let us run things, and we'll buy back the stock, reopen the banks, give people back their jobs, and put things back together in a helluva lot better shape than it was before!"

Most of the early discussion among the Prometheus Council had centered on the communist countries—Russia and China. Less dependent on the Western economic system, they could be expected to move aggressively when the Western world was brought to its knees. From these discussions grew a strategy.

Early results of the program were apparent in the Soviet Union. That country was the first to become entangled in the web of Western finance, buying everything from computers and wheat to Fiats and Pepsi Cola.

China was another story. It was obstinate, proud; and its people still lived in another century. Though Richard Nixon had taken the first steps toward normalizing relations with China, he had done so for his own reasons.

Only when the Commission gained a President who was one of their own did it have a firm hand in guiding the American incursion into China. By the end of the 1970s, the Western presence in China was the economic equivalent of D-Day.

But events in the Middle East, Turkey, and on the African continent caused deep concern among the Commission members. A decision was made to accelerate China's entanglement.

The plan was to initiate a border war between China and Vietnam, hoping to drag China into a protracted war in Indochina much like the Tar Baby that the United States had finally pulled away from. The Chinese economy would be unable to accommodate a major land war without Western economic loans and technology. Its dependence on the West would be assured.

T. Adam Carothers IV was in agreement with the goals of Prometheus. But he was violently opposed to the bloodshed that would accompany such a war. If the Commission carried through with the plan to initiate it, using mercenary soldiers as the provocation, Carothers promised to "go public" with the Prometheus operation.

That, all members realized, would be a disaster. The Commission might then be neutralized, disbanded, even outlawed. The result would surely be further nationalizations and government control.

And there was another threat, vague and understood fully only by Prometheus himself; a threat that Prometheus declined to elaborate upon but obviously considered serious.

"Just how are we going to accelerate an already accelerated schedule?" the Britisher asked tonight, echoing the Japanese businessman's objection in perfect BBC English.

"That, gentlemen, is a problem for us to consider,"

Prometheus said. "I believe the National Security Advisor has some thoughts about it."

Sherbok cleared his throat. "You are all aware," he began, "that the Chinese showed a bit more foresight in this instance than the United States did in Vietnam. They invaded, got stuck, declared victory, and left. This was not our expectation.

"Our intelligence reports indicate that it would take a major initiative on the part of the Vietnamese—one the Vietnamese are unwilling to assert—to get China involved again. There is, however, one situation to which the Chinese would respond in force: a nuclear attack by the Vietnamese."

Silence. The Commission members held their breath. Sherbok continued.

"As you know, the United States was totally unprepared for the onslaught that finally drove us from Vietnam." The men paused, picturing in their minds the news photos of helicopters hurriedly evacuating American personnel from the embassy in Saigon; the pictures of sophisticated fighter bombers lined up row on row at air bases, helicopters, munitions weapons and stockpiles. "And when we departed, more than fifty tactical nuclear weapons remained in the hands of the Vietnamese. Yes, the Vietnamese have those bombs and they know how to use them.

"What I am suggesting," the National Security Advisor went on blandly, "is a flight of the Vietnamese-captured F-4 Phantom jets to drop nuclear weapons on selected Chinese targets. I have the contacts within the Vietnamese air force to execute this. Of course," he said, pausing to take in his rapt audience, "the damage wrought will require economic assistance, as will the subsequent war. A war that will end when we pull our strings."

Pandemonium erupted in the boardroom.

Chapter Eleven

Sailing through nothingness was forever captured in a second.

He was thirsty. His neck burned and throbbed. He heard the sounds of someone gagging and trying to scream. He wondered for a moment if the sounds came from his own body. No, he was sure, it was not him.

Beckett Snow slowly opened his eyes. He was face down on cheap acrylic shag carpeting. The odor of cigarette smoke permeated each painful breath. Gradually he became aware of a cramp in his shoulder, and he realized his hands were bound behind his back.

The toe of a well-aimed boot entered his peripheral vision and slammed into his ribs.

"Hey, looks like sleeping beauty here's waking up."

It was not a voice Snow had heard before. Snow twisted himself into a fetal position—as well as he could with his hands tied behind his back—in a futile attempt to protect himself. The next kick glanced off the top of his head but the blow was enough to reopen the wound in his neck. A wound, Beckett would later learn, made by a pellet from a compressed air gun, a pellet coated with a powerful anesthetic.

Snow heard a male voice order, "Stop! That will do, Whitney." And the pounding ceased.

The young man named Whitney stopped and manhandled Snow to a straightbacked chair facing Tracy.

She was tied to the chair, hands bound behind her, her ankles tied one to each of the front legs of the chair. She was naked. Their eyes met. Snow wanted to cry; then he wanted to kill.

"We've been waiting for you to join us, Mr. Snow, so we could continue with our business," the older man spoke. It was the old man, the derelict, with the Uzi machine gun. "Yesterday afternoon was a rather messy one, and you've been away from us for a while." Snow could see daylight through a thin gap in the curtains. It must be sometime Monday; morning or afternoon, he couldn't tell.

"Whether your stay here will be pleasurable or not is entirely up to you," said the young man, Whitney. "You, Mr. Snow, and no one else. You see, we have one portion of the contents of this beautiful woman's briefcase, and we want the other. Give it to us quickly, and you will go free. Resist, and I'm afraid I will have to ply my craft. You are—I'm sure—familiar with my work."

Snow nodded numbly.

"Please give me the location of the box and the seal, Mr. Snow—since the lady here refuses—and I'll let you go."

Tracy, who was gagged with a red rubber ball tapped in her mouth, shook her head violently side to side. Whitney slapped her with the back of his hand; a pinkie ring caught flesh and opened a gash on her chin. Snow strained at his bonds and succeeded only in overturning his chair. His captors left him lying sideways on the floor.

"That's not being a sensible man. I've had a lot of experience in . . . ah . . . persuading people. I was well trained by the American CIA. In fact, many would say I'm the best of my kind in the world. The CIA used to lend me to the Iranians. I taught SAVAK all it knew.

"What I am going to do—that is, if you don't give

106

me the location of the box and seal immediately—is to slowly, very slowly, destroy your friend here, right before your very eyes." Tracy shook her head again, despite the last blow fom Whitney. He raised his hand again; she cringed. But the blow never came.

"The anticipation sometimes is worse than the actual event," Whitney said, smiling at Tracy's bloodied face. A bruise was beginning to form around the gash on her chin.

"Knowing that, Mr. Snow, I'm going to give you a preview of our coming attractions." He reached behind the chair and withdrew a machine that resembled an electrocardiograph machine. "This is an ingenious device," he said, displaying the snake nest of electrodes. "The electrical currents and voltages and pulses are designed to provide the most painful experience possible, short of killing a person." Snow could see a tear slowly crawling from both of Tracy's eyes.

"Now," Whitney said to Snow, walking over to where Snow still lay on the floor. "Maybe we can do business, huh?" Whitney bent over to return Snow and the chair to an upright position.

Snow had said nothing in reply. His mind was racing, searching for a bargaining tool, searching for a way out.

"You're a very stubborn man, Mr. Snow," Whitney said as he secured Snow's ankles to the rear legs of the chair. The former federal prosecutor was now bowed in the chair, his hands tied to the back, his legs spread, his knees bent. "I'm sure you have no idea of the extreme pain which my persuasion can bring, so I'll have to give you a demonstration."

The older man sat passively, watching.

"Don't worry about your screams being heard. I selected this particular motel because it's nearly bankrupt. There's no more than two other rooms occupied, and none of them are on this wing," Whitney explained.

Producing a single-edged razor blade, he cut Snow's shirt open and slashed an opening in the front of his trousers. Snow stared in horror as the man attached one alligator clip to his right nipple. Then the man named Whitney grasped Snow's penis in his left hand and fondled it. Snow wondered if in addition to being a sadist the man was also a homosexual. To Snow's embarrassment, his penis began to get hard.

"It's the excitement, the adrenalin," Whitney explained as if he'd read Snow's mind. "It shows you how closely sexual drives and aggression are related." He smiled. Whitney then took a second alligator clip, and let it snap shut on the glans of Snow's now-erect penis.

Snow screamed as white jagged pain seared through his mind. He screamed again. Pinpoints of colors flooded his vision. Then the pain transformed itself from the honed cutting edges of two-edged daggers to the dull thudding agony of nerves overloaded with sensation.

Snow breathed heavily, breathless. He opened his eyes and saw Tracy was crying.

"Ah, but Mr. Snow, that is only the beginning." Whitney turned and to the old man said, "Plug in the unit." The old man complied. "Give it a few minutes to warm up," Whitney said, flicking a toggle switch. He adjusted two dials. When he tripped yet another switch, Snow's mind seemed to split. One part exploded in a paroxysm of torment that was agony carried to the edges of the universe. The other part gazed at the subhuman, suprahuman sounds of agony that escaped the body, amazed that pure guttural sounds were able to convey such perfect reflections of agony.

Whitney clicked the second toggle switch and Snow collapsed against the bonds which held him to his chair, his chin resting loosely against his chest.

"There, Mr. Snow, we've shown you a medium-sized dose of our first persuader." Snow raised his head slowly to look at his tormentor. "I can assure you that we'll *start* at this level on your friend here; and we'll get what we want. So give us the location of the box and seal now and spare yourself the agony of seeing this beautiful lady taken apart piece by piece."

"You're slime; the lowest order," Snow spat.

"Oh yes, I realize that," Whitney said pleasantly. "But I'm paid well and I get what I want. And I may be slime to you, but I *am* your superior." With that, he jerked the wires attached to Snow, tearing them from Beckett's body and with them small pieces of flesh to which the clips had been attached. Snow cried out again.

Whitney wheeled the electrical machine to Tracy's chair.

"I suppose I should have a little fun with your friend here before we continue," Whitney said, and leered first at Tracy and then at Beckett. Whitney untied one of her legs, and when she tried to kick him he slapped her again. "Bitch, behave yourself." He tied first one then the other ankle to the rear legs of the chair, in the same position as Snow, exposing her genitals. Snow struggled to find his voice as he watched the man probing Tracy, first with his fingers, then with a soft drink bottle. Tracy stiffened but could not resist. Her torturer was skilled at his work.

"Watch closely, Mr. Snow," Whitney said as he removed his pants and undershorts. "This is the way to do it." He grinned hideously at Snow and made a show of rubbing his erect penis with petroleum jelly. Snow was speechless as he watched the man enter the woman he loved.

It had been a hard time tailing the two men. They'd carried the two people in separate autos, taking two divergent routes. The man in the three-piece suit had

109

elected to follow the auto containing Snow. Hours ago, he had lost sight of the car. Respect, that was what he had for the people who had captured Beckett Snow and Tracy Reynolds.

It was a few minutes before 3 PM on that Monday afternoon when he drove through the parking lot of the Ventura Ocean Inn in Oxnard when he finally spotted the Mercedes 450 SLC which had eluded him Sunday afternoon. Since the time he'd lost the car, he had searched motel parking lot after motel parking lot, hoping they had not switched vehicles.

Relieved to finally pick up the trail again, the man in the three-piece suit steered his rented Camaro into a parking space next to the Mercedes and killed the ignition.

Rolling down the window to admit some of the stiff breeze that zipped past, he paused to compose his thoughts. From his inside coat pocket, he pulled a well-seasoned briar pipe, and carefully filled it with a fragrant tobacco blend. The man drew a sterling-silver pipe tool from his vest pocket and tamped the mixture before lighting it.

He drew deeply and turned to gaze at the windows of the motel rooms. On one wing, all the draperies visible to him were open. That, he surmised, meant the wing was not being used. A random pattern of open and closed curtains decorated the other wing.

The man walked to the motel office and checked in. Inside, he went to the window that overlooked the other side of the unused wing and noted that only one window had the draperies drawn. Probably an oversight by the housekeeper, he decided, but he would check after freshening up from his chase. He hadn't rested since the night before; he had been searching motel parking lots all night. The continuation of the search could wait for ten or fifteen more minutes.

* * *

It was like a scene from a pornographic movie. Beckett Snow watched, anger rising in his throat, as the man named Whitney raped Tracy. And like the typical cliche ending of each intercourse scene in porno movies, the man withdrew just before climax, and ejaculated in Tracy's face.

"You filthy bastard, you dirty filthy bastard," Snow screamed helplessly. "Don't you have a conscience? Don't you have any decency?" Whitney slapped his penis on Tracy's face, and turned to Snow.

"No, I don't have a conscience. I have a sense of pleasure and I have a sense of duty to people who pay me. You don't do either for me. What you'd better do is tell me where the box is. I'm going to give you ten minutes to think about it. After that, what you've just seen will be the least of what this lady will have to face."

Snow noticed Tracy had stopped crying, and once again shook her head.

The man buttoned up the vest of his three-piece suit, looked in the mirror, and adjusted his necktie. He had to bend down slightly, such was his height: taller than six feet five inches. His bulk was considerable. When he'd played professional football, he had pushed 280 pounds, but now he was slim at 235. He was a man few people forgot.

He made one last count of the windows and reassured himself the one with the closed draperies was the twelfth from the apex on the third floor.

As he neared the middle of the corridor, he heard shouting. With a grace remarkable for a man of his bulk, he ran the rest of the way to the twelfth room on his left, barely slowing as he pulled from his coat a short, fat, stubby pistol. He listened at the door, heard a woman shriek once, then again. Two angry voices rose above her cries.

111

"You fucking animal, stop it . . ."

"*You've* got the power to stop it all. Just tell me where the box is."

Tracy screamed again. The large man with the three-piece suit surveyed the construction of the door, stepped back five paces, and ran toward it.

The doorjamb splintered under the impact, but before the door had a chance to slam back against the wall the room was filled with the soft cough of the stubby pistol. The old man twitched and jerked as the projectiles slammed home.

Whitney had time to whirl and reach for his weapon. "You!" was the young man's last words as his body, choreographed by the same weapon, danced a grotesque solo that sent him sprawling over his persuasion device.

"Don't be frightened, I'm not going to hurt you people," the large man said. He went first to the old man, and next to Whitney. He looked for a pulse. Satisfied that there was none, he strode to the door of the room and closed it as best it would close.

"Are you all right?" he asked, turning to Beckett. Beckett nodded. The large man walked to Tracy, now unconscious from the last assault of electricity. He delicately took her wrist and searched for a pulse, his massive hands dwarfing hers. He detached the electrodes and turned to Beckett.

"She'll be all right. Her pulse is strong. Looks as if I got here just in time."

"Who are you? Police?"

"I'll tell you in a moment. But first, I want the microfilm." He searched the room, and quickly found Tracy's briefcase.

"Okay, let's get the fuck out of here before somebody comes." He cut through Beckett's bonds and handed the knife to him. "Cut her loose and follow me. Can you carry her?" Beckett nodded and obeyed. There was nothing to be gained, he figured, by bucking such a man, particularly when he had just saved their lives.

The man in the three-piece suit relieved the two dead men of their identification, rings, watches, and valuables, and led the way down the corridor, carrying the briefcase and the men's luggage.

"Pretty nasty place to get injured," the doctor smiled as he treated the wound on Snow's penis. But the physician asked no questions about how his injuries, or Tracy's, had been sustained. They were in the fashionable offices of a fashionable doctor in fashionable Beverly Hills, where many of the doctor's well-known fashionable clients frequently sustained very unfashionable and somewhat embarrassing illnesses and injuries about which they wished a minimum of curiosity.

The doctor was good, discreet, and expensive.

They paid the doctor and walked down Rodeo Drive to the Beverly Wilshire Hotel, where Snow took a room. After seeing Tracy to sleep, Snow and the large man—who had to that point identified himself only as Eric Simon, a financial consultant from Washington, D.C.—took a table at the hotel's coffee shop.

While he and Tracy were being treated by the doctor, the man had retrieved their suitcases from the rental cars, and had the autos returned to their owners. Neither Tracy nor Snow had been inclined to disagree with Simon, such was their fatigue, and such was Simon's persuasive nature.

"I still don't follow you exactly," Snow told Simon after the waiter had departed with their food order. "You used to work for a New York bond firm and you work as a freelancer now?" Simon nodded as he popped a chunk of buttered bread into his mouth. His eyes scanned the room without stopping. "And you heard of the large financial deal with a code named Prome-

113

theus? And you want us to exchange information so you can make a killing in the market when this Prometheus happens?" The large man nodded again, and signalled for the waiter to replenish the bread.

"But that doesn't explain your nifty little gun, or why you need whatever it is in the box I have, or why you risked your life for us, or why you happened to be following us, or a dozen other things. It just doesn't seem to square—all of this."

"It doesn't have to," Simon spoke. His voice was soft, measured; the voice of a man who had learned that his size alone threatened people and he need not aggravate that with aggressive speech. "Please try to accept something here: Both of us, for our separate reasons, want to know everything we can about Prometheus. I want to know because it can make me very, very rich. You want to know so you can stop it. . . ."

"Which is a reason," interrupted Snow, "why you *shouldn't* be cooperating with us; or us with you, for that matter."

"Yes . . . but let me finish. You have something I want. I have something you want. We both have something that the people involved with Prometheus desire to have returned to them, and they'll kill us to get it.

"What I am proposing, then, is a temporary alliance; I'm suggesting we team up for a while, so it's us against them. Once we've made our exchange, well, then it's time to go our separate ways for our own reasons. I don't think I could torture the location of your materials out of either of you, nor do I wish to. You and the woman may be a lot more useful as allies and living."

"Strictly pragmatic." Snow's statement was both a declaration of fact and a question. The other man nodded.

It just didn't make sense, Snow thought. There was something inconsistent about Simon, something that

114

made Snow doubt the veracity of his statements. Snow was also doubtful about continuing the search on his own. He was gambling his future on tracking down some elusive gang of powerful men. His training and better sense told him to turn the entire thing over to the police.

And then he thought of Tracy, and the people somewhere who had hired a man who liked to cut people open; a man who would rape a woman in front of someone who loved her. Because of that, he couldn't turn it over to someone else.

And the people involved: If they were as powerful as they seemed, then it was also likely, he reasoned, that they would have influence over a police investigation. And if they really wanted him dead, it would be an easy thing. No, he and Tracy would have to solve the mystery themselves—or die trying—for there would be no rest until one or the other happened.

And here, Snow mused, was this mysterious giant who had offered a piece of the puzzle they sought. A financial deal. Was Prometheus just the ultimate inside deal, a transaction so profitable they would kill anyone who got in their way, including one of their own?

It was all so alien, all so frightening. But he was in, and the only way out was through the maze to the other side.

"Okay," Snow said. "I need to depend on you, though God knows I don't want to. Let's talk."

"Fine. I thought you would be a realist," Simon replied. "A week from today, I'll place an advertisement in the announcements section of the *Washington Post* classifieds. It'll be in the 'I'm not responsible for debts other than my own' category. There will be an address in the ad. Convert the number into twenty-four-hour time, and go to the address at that time.

"Fine," Snow said. "But how will I know which ad is the correct one?"

"It'll use the name Damien. Hesse, remember the book?" Snow nodded.

While Tracy slept, the two men ate in silence, each trying to absorb the impact, the significance, of the events they were caught in.

"Eric," Snow said as they finished their final bites. "Just what makes you think that little people like us can tackle these men, these corporations?"

"Big institutions are prepared for big threats," Simon began. "They don't believe that something small has the power to hurt them. They're not prepared to deal with small.

"We're small," Simon concluded. "And small has to be bigger than big, or small is dead."

Early the next morning, Simon took Tracy and Beckett to the Los Angeles International Airport, and saw them to their gate.

When the final call was made for their plane's departure for Dulles Airport in Washington, Simon turned and walked back toward the parking area. He stopped before leaving the terminal and plugged a dime into a pay telephone.

"They're on their way now. Flight 712 arriving at 4:36 P.M., Dulles. Got that? Good. Listen, it's going to be easy now. They bought the whole story. They'll both be very useful, but only if we control them completely. Give them a day or two to start feeling secure, and then begin. In a week, Beckett Snow and Tracy Reynolds will be so confused and desperate they won't be able to think clearly. That's the way I want to use them."

Simon replaced the receiver and walked out of the airport.

PART II

Chapter Twelve

With a groaning shudder, the DC-10's landing gear rumbled into place. Beckett Snow slowly opened his eyes and stared out the window.

". . . and return your seatbacks and tray tables to their full upright and locked positions. We'll be on the ground shortly," the mechanically pleasant voice burbled.

Snow shook his head and turned to Tracy. "Hey, babe, what're we doing landing at National?" She leaned over the armrest, kissing him lightly on his lips.

"Something about one of the runways at Dulles being closed for repairs. They're diverting traffic to National. They announced it while you were asleep and I didn't think it was worth waking you up for."

"Thanks," he told her. "Did you get any rest?"

"Some. But mostly I thought a lot."

"About what?"

"This thing. You, me." She was silent. He wanted to ask more, he wanted to know more, but Tracy was obviously not in the mood to talk. He would hear when she was ready.

Meanwhile, they both leaned toward the window to watch the scenery passing by. Though it was a familiar sight, it never lost its fascination. The spires of Georgetown University passed below, and the DC-10 banked

119

sharply to the right to try and follow the course of the Potomac.

Generally the smaller, short-hop jets used National. But today, the wide-bodied DC-10 would land there. The aircraft leveled out and finally touched down.

They had brought only carry-on luggage, and when the plane pulled in to the terminal, they rushed through the crowd, mingled with the first passengers to disembark.

They headed for the subway. "I just want to get out of here as quickly as possible," Beckett explained. "A cab could take longer, and there's no telling who knows me and might be here."

"Yes, but would they recognize you?" Tracy asked.

Beckett started. He'd forgotten about the change in his appearance. That, along with his new name and identity, was something he resolved to keep in mind.

He was about to enter a forest that had once been his preserve, which was now a treacherous jungle whose rules took no heed of society. A jungle that required wariness and ruthlessness.

Now was the time he had to become as good as he'd been when he was a cop.

He had vowed never to do it again. And here it was once more, the alien which must become familiar, the senses that had to be better than his adversary's if he and Tracy were to survive.

They bought fare cards and boarded the Metro. After the train stopped at Crystal City, Snow motioned Tracy to get off at the next stop. They did.

"Hardly anybody uses this stop," he commented, motioning with his head at the nearly deserted platform. Only one person stood waiting, and he'd been there when we arrived. "It makes sure that we'd spot anyone following us. The only other person getting off the train," he said pointing at a man in a camel-colored coat, "is already riding up the escalator. We're okay."

They got on the next train that stopped at the station heading into Washington. What they hadn't seen was the man in the camel-colored coat pulling out a leather-encased radio transceiver after he'd reached the top of the escalator. They didn't see him speak into it, and they didn't hear the reply which was piped through an earplug.

While Beckett and Tracy rode the subway, Leslie Lewis paced in her office. Through the window she watched the snarled rush-hour traffic inching its way through the gray rainy evening.

But her mood was far from gray. It was white-hot. She had wrestled with herself about what action she should take about her job, the threat. She looked at her watch; it was 5:19 PM. But the White House would still be in full swing.

For the fifth time, she checked the White House directory. Then she strode to her office door.

"If anyone calls, I'll be back in half an hour or so," she told her secretary as she walked quickly out.

She turned left from her office and down the darkened shadow-ridden corridor.

Up, third floor. Which way? The sign on the wall opposite the elevator indicated to the right. She found the door with its seal: the National Security Advisor. She walked in.

"Yes," the receptionist looked up at her. "May I help you?"

"I want to see Mr. Sherbok."

"I'm sorry," the receptionist snapped. "But the National Security Advisor cannot see anyone without an appointment."

Leslie pushed past the woman and shoved open the massive mahogany door to the National Security Advisor's office. He *wasn't* there.

Peter Gilbert was.

121

"Where is he?" Leslie demanded.

"Who, Sherbok?"

"Yes, him. Where is he?"

"Obviously not here. And who are you?" Gilbert asked, even though he already knew her as the woman he had covertly threatened only the week before. He looked up as the receptionist motioned for him, asking in sign language if she should call Security. He shook his head and waved her away.

Peter felt constricted. Had Leslie found out about him? How had she deduced his identity? He swallowed. No, he thought, it was not he, but Sherbok she had come to see.

"Goddamnit!" she cursed. "I want to see him." She felt cheated, frustrated. She'd worked up her courage and it was all for nothing. Suddenly, the adrenalin drained and she started to grow afraid.

"I . . . I had something I wanted to discuss with him."

"I'm Peter Gilbert, his assistant in a lot of matters," Peter explained as he rose from the leather upholstered wing chair and walked around the side of the desk to her.

"Why don't you sit here?" He motioned to the Chippendale sofa next to the large bay window. "And let's talk about it."

"I'm sorry, but I don't want to talk to *you* about it," Leslie said, standing over the man where he'd seated himself on the sofa. "I want to talk to the National Security Advisor himself and not to someone who works for him. I want . . ." Suddenly embarrassment flooded over her, and with it uncertainty. What *was* it she wanted? She was afraid, ashamed. No, she quickly resolved: It was anger that she had entered with, and it was anger that she was justified in feeling.

"I'm mad as hell," she said, finally. "Over a threat I've received. And I have every reason to believe it came from this office." She looked at Peter's face, and thought she detected a change in those pale gray eyes. "I think it came from here; it's improper and I want it stopped."

She stood over him, breathing heavily from her tirade, unsure of what should happen next, afraid he wouldn't respond.

Peter Gilbert leaned back against the arm of the sofa, trying to look Leslie firmly in her eyes, to give her the impression that he was trustworthy, and yet not give away the panic that was welling up inside him.

"Look," he told her, "I don't know anything about this threat or anything. I don't normally work here. . . . My office is . . . located in another part of the White House. If you got a threat, why didn't you call Security? That would be the logical thing."

"Because the person who threatened me scared me— told me not to. I *should* have called Security," Leslie said, annoyed that she was being placed on the defensive. "I want you to tell your boss that Leslie Lewis wants some answers. And I want you to tell him that—"

"Look, I don't know anything about what you're talking about," Peter lied. He tried to lend credence to his lie by assuming all of the proper body language he'd tried to learn—knees uncrossed, arms outstretched, palms upward and open—the psychological picture of candor.

"I want you to tell him that I'm not going to be driven out of my job, and if he wants me out he can bloody well kill me!" Leslie continued, ignoring Peter's interruption. "I'm tired of people trying to push me around. I'm—"

"Maybe you ought to have some patience, go through chan—"

"Fuck channels and patience! Mister, I've had a lot of patience, and I've had a lot of understanding, and all it's gotten me is screwed—literally *and* figuratively!"

Leslie whirled on her heel and left the room, slamming the door behind her.

The thud of the door was accompanied by the slap of Peter's right fist as it smashed into the arm of the sofa.

The sleek aluminum and glass cars of the Washington Metro glided from the stop at Arlington cemetery after picking up two soaked tourists who'd come unprepared for the rain. The train gathered speed, and raindrops bent a sharper and tighter angle against the speed of the car until darkness swallowed the train in a tunnel of concrete. Two stops later, the train came to rest at the Foggy Bottom station.

"Go stand by the door," Beckett told Tracy as the car slowed. He followed her. "Don't act like you're going to leave. Look like you're going to get off at the next stop." The two of them stood silently by the Plexiglas divider as disembarking passengers jostled by them. New arrivals pushed their way past. When the flow stopped, chimes sounded, warning that the doors were about to close.

"Now!" He whispered in her ear, and gave her a shove. They barely cleared the doors as they shut. Snow quickly looked up and down the futuristic platform with its curved walls and tiled floors. No one else had jumped off at the last minute; no one was staring at them like quarry lost to the hunt.

Satisfied, Snow led them up the escalator, holding both their bags.

They walked toward the fare gates, silently aware that someone was looking for them.

He dropped the bags by a pay phone, dug in his pocket to find a dime and a nickel, and dropped them in.

"Hello. Congressional News Syndicate."

"Drachler, please." There was a pause.

"Drachler speaking, what can I do for you?"

"Steve, go to the bar at Mike Palms. Wait for a call there. I'll call back in exactly twenty minutes," Snow said and hung up. Then he turned to Tracy.

"Okay, let's go." Instead of moving, he suddenly turned, dropped the two pieces of luggage and embraced her. Departing passengers from a train that had just reached the station parted around them, eyes averted as the two kissed. When the crowd had passed, Snow picked up the luggage, and they headed outside, up the escalator, and into the weeping weather. The rain had slackened off, and it was now barely misty, but cold to the dew point. The mist swirled in whirls of orange fire lit by sodium vapor streetlights: Washington was burning in wet fire.

Tree limbs hung sadly under the orange of the street lights, their buds waiting for a warmer season. Snow looked at Tracy and wondered if a change of seasons was going to come to them.

Tracy and Beckett barged their way through a crowd of people streaming across the sidewalk, turned left, and headed toward Washington Circle. Neither of them noticed the rain-soaked tourist by the bus stop shelter who had gotten off the train before them and who was now speaking softly into a leather-encased radio.

"Who was that you phoned?" Tracy asked.

"Steve Drachler. He's a newspaperman, a damned good one. In fact, one of the best I've ever met. I met him about three years ago when he was digging into a case I had worked on. Turns out he uncovered more about the damn thing than the FBI did."

"What was the case about?"

"A weird one. Seems there's this writer—Robert Morgan—he wrote about a big Manhattan drug bust. Well, he got mixed up with a fellow in a tax-shelter swindle, and then he got entangled in some international intrigue with mercenary soldiers in South Africa. Anyway, the FBI could never get the goods on him and his cohorts. But Drachler did."

"You mean you got Robert Morgan?"

"No, he's pretty harmless. Unfortunately, the guys he dealt with weren't. Drachler sewed them up pretty well, and Morgan actually became a good friend of both of ours. We always get autographed copies of his new books when they come out.

"Anyway, Drachler's a friend. A damned close friend."

"Someone who'll help us?"

"You bet."

"Beck, what sort of person is this making you? So many things. You act naturally now, like this is something you're familiar with."

"Well, it is. Or it was, and now it is again."

"Like being a cop again?"

"Like being a particular kind of cop again."

"Do you want to talk about it?"

"Not now." How could he tell her? How could he describe what he had been through, how he had to learn the forest, its million unseen trails, its unseen hazards and hiding places. For once he'd seen, and he'd paid the price of nearly losing his feelings in order to buy that sight. And now, the trails were coming back into focus. He prayed that he'd see what he needed to protect them without losing his feelings again to the god of survival. Beckett propelled the two of them along, toward the circle.

They walked up to the statue of General Sheridan and sat on its granite base for an instant.

"Did you know there's a rumor that the position of the horse indicates the condition its rider wound up in after the battle?"

"No, smartie. Tell me." Tracy smiled. Beckett noticed that it was the first time he'd seen her smile since they left Los Angeles.

"Well, some people say it's true. If the horse has all four feet on the ground, then the rider wasn't even touched; one foot off the ground, he was wounded; and if three feet don't touch, he was killed in action."

"Uhmm," Tracy murmured as she kissed him. "Let's keep *all* our feet on the ground."

Beckett grinned. While rush hour surged about them, they kissed at the feet of a statue whose horse stood on a single foot.

Snow checked his watch.

"Hate to interrupt, but I've got a friend to call."

Tracy said nothing.

That, Tracy thought, was unusual for her. But then so much had been unusual the past two months that routine itself was the only nonroutine thing in her life. Where *was* she two months ago? She tried to think: in New York City, working for Carothers. Working in a field she had prepared herself for and had excelled in, an overachiever in a position that virtually guaranteed her even greater success. She'd studied economics at Yale as one of the first women admitted there as an undergraduate and then stayed on there to get her M.B.A.

She'd have been just another terribly bright woman with a business degree, sought after by corporations but not distinguished for a long while, had it not been for an encounter with Carothers during a speech he made to a group of Yale Phi Beta Kappas during her senior year.

While the others in her group asked smarty questions, trying to get an "in" with the great man, Tracy had zinged him with two sharp queries, one about his relationship to his brother's banking interests, and the other about the responsibility of wealth, something which she

127

opined had died two generations ago in the Carothers dynasty.

Tracy remembered now that Carothers had been unable to answer the questions; later, her companions had accused her of poor manners.

Tracy also recalled their consternation when, two weeks later, she got a call from Carothers himself, offering her a position on his personal staff, to, in his words, "Help me find the answers to the questions you posed."

Though she originally occupied a minor position in a cramped windowless office, Carothers gradually placed more and more responsibility on her shoulders, as well as more confidence in her opinions.

People who had worked for Carothers for years began to resent her power and influence as it swiftly developed. Then the rumors started to fly: vicious rumors that attributed to her combined attributes of Mata Hari, a 42nd Street whore, and a KGB brainwasher.

They had tried to destroy her but Carothers remained steadfast.

But with his death, came the death of her career in that organization, and now, now the possible—did she dare think probable?—death of her and the man she now loved.

Tracy was silent as they crossed the street once more, this time heading for a telephone booth outside a convenience grocery store. That she was silent, that she was allowing herself to be guided by a man—a stranger who was no longer a stranger—struck her as bizarre.

Beat-up green Metro buses and bright new red, white, and blue ones waited nose-to-tail in the jammed traffic just yards from the telephone where Tracy and Beckett now stood.

Snow fumbled in his pocket, found only a quarter and plugged it into the machine. The bartender answered. Snow asked for Drachler and listened to the busy babble of after-work barflies before Drachler finally picked up the receiver. As an investigative reporter, the man was used to accepting strange telephone calls.

"Hello?" The voice on the other end sounded impatient.

"Steve, this is Beck Snow."

"Jesus, I never expected to hear from you again. What the shit are you doing?"

"Listen, don't use my name and don't tell anyone you've talked to me, okay?"

"Hey, you don't have to tell me that. Got yourself in some deep shit, have you? Saw the piece in the *Post*. They did a real good job on you. Who framed, the Mafia? How about our good friend Morgan?"

"No, neither of them. I've got an idea and if it's true you're not going to believe it. I'm not sure I believe it yet myself."

"Sure. But . . ."

"Listen, what I do need right now is some help. . . ."

"Figures. Don't call me until you need help, right?"

"Damn. Look, I've got to have a place to stay, and I'm going to need some things that I can't do myself. But mostly, right now I need to have a place to stay temporarily."

"Okay, good buddy, the key's where it always is."

"Right. Thanks, Steve. Uh, why don't you stop by later and I'll fill you in on a few things?"

There was no way that Snow could have seen the two men who were working their way up Pennsylvania Avenue through the rush hour bus crowds. Dressed in khaki London Fog raincoats that were a uniform of the government bureaucracy, and carrying the newspapers and attache cases that were also part of the same uniform, each man wielded in his right hand an umbrella with a deadly nicotine acid hypodermic needle concealed in the metal tip. Just two ordinary bureaucrats with two extraordinary umbrellas.

"Sure," Drachler agreed.

There was no way that Snow could see the soaked tourist from the Metro station as he followed the two men with the poisoned umbrellas. The three men were now less than ten yards from where Beckett and Tracy stood.

"Look, let's talk about . . ."

Beckett's conversation was interrupted. Accounts in the *Washington Post* the next day would be contradictory—as all eyewitness reports are apt to be—but all were unified in the conviction that someone had gone crazy.

"All right, motherfucker, give me your wallet!"

Snow and Tracy wheeled toward the sounds, but the crowd blocked their view.

"Gotta go," Beckett said and slammed down the receiver. He grabbed their luggage and shoved Tracy in the opposite direction from the noise. Behind them he heard the booming report of a large-caliber weapon and a woman screamed. A second shot followed and more screams. Tracy and Beckett fled across the street and mounted the steps of an old Victorian corner house that was being restored. They ran inside the foyer and crouched by the walls, hidden by shadows but with a clear view of the street.

Snow was amazed when he saw the rain-sodden tourist from the subway. The tourist ran wildly and fired the weapon to keep his pursuers at bay. The man stopped beside the steps of the building where Tracy and Beckett hid. He looked directly at them and smiled.

"We're watching. Be more careful," he said.

Surprise shot through Snow's body like electricity, so certain had he been of eluding any pursuers.

"Who are you? Who're you with?" Snow cried out. But the man quickly raised the gun in their direction

130

and fired, not to hurt, but to put a punctuation mark on his statement. And just as quickly, he whirled and fired at the pursuers who'd been brave enough to creep out from behind their places of safety. One shot—an exclamation mark; two shots—end of paragraph; three shots—end of episode.

The man's footsteps were soon drowned in a flood of sirens.

Chapter Thirteen

Snow quietly forced the front door of the building open, waved Tracy through, and closed it just as carefully and silently as it had been opened.

The rear exit opened out onto an alley leading to New Hampshire Avenue, away from the commotion.

They raced down the garbage-strewn brick surface of the dark alley toward the lights of the main drag. But Beckett's mind had already raced far beyond. Who could have followed them? The fear that they were being followed took his breath away faster than the running. The rain-soaked tourist! What had he said? "We're watching." Who was watching? He couldn't have been the Commission's man because he hadn't hurt them. Simon! Simon was the only person who knew what flight they were on.

But how had Simon followed them? Their precautions to evade surveillance would require almost unlimited manpower to defeat—resources a freelance investment counselor was unlikely to have.

Nobody had that sort of manpower except the Commission, which he could exclude, or the government.

The government! But who? Not the Justice Department; not the FBI. Either would have arrested him or killed him trying to escape. Intelligence agencies might want whatever was in the box, or whatever they thought he and Tracy might know.

But spies stumbled all over each other in Washington. They could be from any number of agencies: the CIA, the Defense Intelligence agencies, Army, Air Force, Navy, maybe the Secret Service or even the Securities and Exchange Commission! No, Beckett reflected, the SEC's intelligence people were mostly accountants and did their battles on paper and through computers. The job was too small for the elite corps controlled by the National Security Advisor. And the military didn't have an interest. But why was the CIA interested in them, and how did it find them? And why in hell did the guy shoot the people at the bus stop?

They reached the street.

"Okay, just act normal."

"I think I'm beginning to forget what that means."

Beckett looked at her.

"It's all relative, I suppose. Just think, there are people who do this sort of thing for a living," he said.

"Like the tourist?"

"Like the tourist."

Beckett hailed a cab when they got to Dupont Circle and gave him directions to a corner in the Adams-Morgan section. Snow considered changing cabs on the way, but he decided that anyone with the resources to track him so far wouldn't be fooled by anything as ordinary as that.

The cab deposited them in front of the neighborhood liquor store where Drachler cashed his checks and bought his beer and wine. It was the sort of neighborhood institution that was dying along with the neighborhood. Tracy paid the driver and they walked toward Drachler's apartment.

"Wait a minute." Beckett stopped suddenly. The abruptness startled Tracy. "Come on back this way, into the store."

Tracy's eyes darted about her, fearful of what the night might bring again. She relaxed when she saw

Snow carrying two six-packs of a dark Dutch beer and a bottle of champagne with him to the counter. He paid for the purchases and they walked on.

"You scared me."

"Sorry, but I can be impulsive, you know."

"I've noticed that the past couple of days. Tell me, have you always been given to running off with women you don't know?"

"Not unless I fall in love first." He grinned.

Snow set the suitcases on the sidewalk, careful to avoid the ubiquitous dog feces, and retrieved the key to Steve Drachler's apartment. After opening the deadbolt on the outer door and walking up one flight, they paused on a dimly lit landing as Beckett fiddled with a cantankerous lock.

The balky tumblers finally surrendered to Beckett's jiggling and coaxing. Snow turned the old cut-glass doorknob and cracked the door open. The lights were out. He bent down to pick up the two suitcases.

If Snow could have slowed his life to a frame-action film he would first have seen a bulge begin in the middle of the door panel about five feet from the floor. The bulge would be followed by others. As the slugs passed through the wood of the old door, the bulges would begin to crack, showing the multiple colors of paint layered on year after year. The cracking bulges would then resemble small volcanoes, spewing forth chips of paint, splintered wood, and deadly masses of metal spat from a gun within the darkness.

Had Beckett been standing as the gun's operator had hoped, the slugs would then have passed in a dribble pattern through Beckett's upper torso and neck, before embedding themselves in the plaster wall of the hallway behind him. But the slugs met with no resistance as they slammed into the plaster, showering the two with dust and exposing the practiced irregularity of the lathe work.

134

The impact slammed the door. There was no further sound.

"Jesus, not again!" Beckett threw himself in the corner of the landing, pulling Tracy down with him. The gunman resumed firing and the pattern of holes in the door continued down to the floor, drumming into the wall just inches away.

Suddenly a single shot from the floor below ripped through the large pane of glass in the entranceway and slammed into Beckett's suitcase.

Tracy screamed. Another shot, this one a distinct cough from a silencer. Somewhere downstairs, outside. It was a hard angle to shoot upward; Beckett knew it was the only reason they were still alive.

Footsteps gritted on the concrete sidewalk outside. Unarmed! Beckett had nothing, save his bare hands, to protect them. He looked over and saw Tracy was bleeding from a scratch on her upper arm.

A naked 40-watt light bulb cast fuzzy shadows on the landing, and Snow knew they had little chance unless it were extinguished. He spotted the switch, but figured his chances as zero if he got up and exposed his full body to the gunman outside.

And how long would the gunman inside Drachler's apartment wait before coming to the door? How long had it been? It seemed like minutes, but he knew it was only a few seconds since the first shots had been fired.

Beckett removed a shoe and threw it at the light bulb. The shoe thudded impotently against the ceiling and clattered down the stairs. In reflex, the gunman downstairs shot at the moving object.

"Shit."

Beckett removed the other shoe, heaved it up at the light, and sighed when it connected with the bulb, glass tinkled, the filament flared white hot for an instant, and then plunged the stairway into darkness.

"Okay, upstairs, hurry," Beckett said. But they had

no time to move. A man in shallow silhouette, revealed by streetlights outside, was running up the stairs toward them with a gun in his hands.

In slow motion they saw the man just yards away raise the pistol and level it at their heads. But he seemed to hesitate in the darkness, stumbled, and smashed face-first into the steps. The gun skittered down the stairs and the gunman's body tumbled after it.

Another figure, this one dressed in a gentleman's camel-colored coat, leaped over the man's body and scaled the steps three by three.

"Downstairs. Get downstairs and get out of here," the man yelled at them. "Now! Move!" He shoved both of them toward the first floor landing.

As Snow reached the bottom of the landing, he heard the splintering of wood and a silenced exchange of rapid-fire weapons.

People strolled by outside, oblivious to the drama unfolding steps away. Snow wondered how long it would be before another resident of the building would call the police. It was an older building that had been converted into apartments, and that, Beckett assumed, meant it probably had a basement apartment with the entrance under the front steps.

He was right and shoved Tracy and the suitcase under the steps.

"How's your arm?"

"It hurts, but everything works."

"Let me see," he asked, and tenderly pried her hand away from the wound. It had stopped bleeding.

"It's a graze. Nothing got hit from the looks of it. You're lucky; we're lucky."

"How much longer can we continue to be lucky?"

"I don't know. But we've got to make some luck in case the freebies run out. Wait here." He started for the entrance.

"No, Beck! Don't go back in there. Don't leave me."

"I've got to. Somebody tried to kill us, and somebody else saved us. We've got an idea who tried to kill us, and no idea who the other guys are. The man up there and the tourist must be together; but who are they? If I can find out, maybe we can *make* some luck for ourselves."

Snow ran up the steps, pausing to retrieve the weapon the dead man had dropped. It was an Ingram, just like those used by the killers in California. A search of the man's pockets revealed five spare clips; Beckett pocketed them. He retrieved his right shoe, now adorned with a bullet hole, and put it on. He found the other one on the landing.

It was ominously quiet. Try as he might, Beckett couldn't walk silently because the pieces of glass from the light bulb popped and cracked under his feet.

The door was open. Beckett edged his way along the wall, peering around the edge of the doorjamb into the darkness. Flattening himself against the outer wall, Snow reached inside with his right hand and flipped on the ceiling light. Still no sounds; no noise made by an attacker moving into a better position to shield himself from the light.

That meant, Beckett knew, that either the man was already properly concealed; had fled through the rear door; or was dead.

Snow checked the clip in the Ingram, flicked the selector to full automatic, and prayed. The sight that greeted him when he lunged into the room was gutrending. The man in the camel coat lay on the sofa staring at the ceiling light, clutching a widening red splotch near the beltline of the coat. Another man's body lay sprawled over a pile of unread newspapers, with most of his face spread over page one of the top paper.

The man in the camel coat was still alive. Snow went

137

to him. "I'll call you an ambulance." Snow moved toward the telephone.

"No!" the man screamed, a frothy gurgle from deep in his chest. He lay back, drained from the exertion.

"Why not? Why shouldn't I call a doctor?" Snow knelt beside the man.

"No . . . no time . . . dying. Must tell you." The words were coming staccato, faster with his quickening breath. "Just listen." Snow nodded. "Use radio . . . must call . . . warn them . . . the Consortium . . . thē Consortium is . . . is violated."

"Who at the Consortium? Who is the Consortium? Who's violated the Consortium?"

"Commission . . . Cranch's people," the man gasped.

"The Consortium is Cranch's people?"

The man's eyes had come unfocused. With great difficulty he pulled them back, caught Beckett's face.

"Tell who? Who is the Consortium?" Snow realized he was yelling, and just as quickly knew that would do no good. But he was stunned at having to absorb the existence of yet another group which knew about him. "You're with Simon, aren't you? Simon's with the Consortium?" The man shook his head. There was a lack of recognition the source of which Snow was unable to discern. It could have been genuine or merely a result of the man's condition.

"Okay, if Simon's not involved, who is? This has got something to do with Prometheus, doesn't it?"

The man's eyes suddenly regained some vigor.

"Yes, yes, we must have the records. . . . We can use them best." He was like a music box winding down. Each word following the last with longer and longer pauses between.

"Tell me who I must contact."

"Can't . . . tell you. You . . . must use radio . . . use rad . . ." The man's eyes suddenly came unfocused.

His head took one short roll to the back and slumped forward, chin on chest.

He was dead.

Another dead body, another enigma wrapped around the riddle that started in L.A. Christ! Snow thought. But at least he and Tracy were still alive.

Snow pocketed the Ingram he'd retrieved from the dead man in the hall. He turned to the man in the camel-colored coat and quickly removed the contents of his pockets. He picked up the man's firearm: a garden-variety .38-caliber police special revolver outfitted with a silencer. The radio was smashed.

Just as quickly, he searched through the pockets of the other dead man inside the apartment. They were empty save five spare clips for his Ingram.

He looked around quickly at the apartment. Despite the gun battle, it was in about the same degree of shambles and disarray that Snow recalled Steve lived in. Snow turned out the light, closed what was left of the door, and ran downstairs. Still, no one had ventured outside; still there was no police car. He looked at his watch: It had been less than 15 minutes since they'd arrived.

A body still sprawled over the bottom four steps at the bottom of the landing, and Snow leaped it as he ran down.

Under the darkened stairs, Tracy sat holding her arm. Despite her wound, she was still clutching the champagne and beer.

"How's your arm?"

"Take a look." She moved her hand and showed it to Snow in the dim light. "I think it's fine."

Snow agreed. "Okay, let's get out of here. Steve should be driving over to meet us."

The pockets of his suitcoat bulging with armament and ammunition, Snow first offered a helping hand to

Tracy, which she waved away, and then picked up both suitcases. They'd walked only half a block when Steve's blue Pinto lurched around the corner, narrowly missing a parked car and an old woman on a bicycle. The Pinto weaved precariously between the two rows of parked cars on the one-way street and skidded to a locked-wheel halt when Snow flagged it down. Drachler had had a driver's license for only seven months. He had grown up in Manhattan, had always lived in cities, and never saw a reason to buy an automobile or learn to drive.

Despite the tension, Snow had to chuckle, the infamous Pinto and its exploding gas tank, and a driver behind the wheel with all the acumen of a sideshow daredevil wired up on something illegal.

"Jesus Christ, Joseph, Mary, and the donkey, I could have hit you, you crazy bastard," Drachler yelled. He looked at Snow, confused. Slowly he saw things as only close friends can. Through the disguise, he recognized Snow. "Couldn't wait, huh? Hadda lay down in the street in fronta me, you crazy guy." Drachler started to get out of the car to greet Snow, despite the line of cars behind him, and realized the car was still in gear as it started off with no one behind the wheel.

"Ah horseshit!" Drachler leaped back in the car and slammed the gearshift lever into park, stopping the car with a banshee grinding of transmission gears that locked the rear wheels, leaving black skid marks on the pavement visible under the streetlights.

"Haven't mastered that goddamned thing yet." He shook Snow's hand and shot a quick Anglo-Saxon salute to a frustrated motorist behind them who'd blown his horn. "You didn't tell me you'd be in the company of such a beautiful woman," he said turning to Tracy. "Since Beck's got no manners I'll introduce myself. I'm Steve Drachler, hack reporter—"

"This is Tracy Reynolds, and," Snow said turning

to her, "he's the best reporter in Washington, so don't pay attention to any of his deflated opinions of himself."

Several other cars joined in a cacophony of anger.

"If you don't mind, Steve, why don't we get out of here and let these people pass?"

"Sure thing, good buddy. I'll just park it and we'll get you settled."

"I don't think that's a good thing," Snow said. "Let's leave, and I'll explain why."

Snow and Tracy put the baggage in the rear seat and got in. Snow fumbled for the seat belt as the Pinto jerked and lunged into an alleyway.

"All right. Want to tell me why I can't go up to my own apartment?" Drachler said as he drove.

"Well, for starters, the place is a shambles."

"Fuck, that's nothing new. Place always did look like the Anacostia landfill anyway." Drachler laughed.

"Yeah, but this time there's three dead bodies up there."

Drachler drove on, unfazed, as if Snow had just given him the score of a nonconference basketball game.

"Well, go on, tell me more. How many of them did *you* kill?"

"None of them. We were attacked when we entered your building. Somebody came to our rescue and killed the two people trying to kill us, but was fatally wounded in the process."

"So is all this connected to that mess you got in in San Francisco?"

"Los Angeles," Snow corrected.

"Yeah, yeah. Los Angeles. All of California's the same to me anyhow. So is it connected?"

"Well, from what I can tell, I think it all ties in together." Snow started with the events of the previous week, bringing Drachler up to date from the time he met Tracy to the present.

Drachler was uncharacteristically silent.

"Man, you're trouble," Drachler said. "Okay, you've gotta go somewhere. Let's go to my girlfriend's house. We can't drive around like this all night."

"That's not a good idea. It might get you involved—"

"Hey, buddy, that's what friends are for."

"I know, but you might be more help if you're not connected."

"That's gotta be hard, man—what with those dead bodies in my apartment."

"Right. But just the same, why don't you take us to the Hilton or something? I don't want to fuck up your love life—uh, pardon the pun."

"I got a better idea. Carl Anderson—remember him, covers the Hill for AP?—well, he's on vacation, gone to Aruba or some shit, and I've been looking after the place. Anyway, why don't I take you there? He lives on the Hill just behind the Capitol Hill Club."

"We can call the police from there—that is, you can."

"So how am I going to explain it all?"

"Just like you would if you didn't know me and you stumbled home to find all of it. You've done some investigative reporting, made some enemies. . . . Right?"

Drachler grunted. Snow knew that it meant assent.

They arrived at the house on C Street S.E. Drachler helped carry the beer and their luggage into the apartment and then sat down at the hallway phone and dialed 911. Tracy and Snow walked in behind him and waited as he phoned the police.

"I want to report a murder . . . uh, three murders," Drachler said into the mouthpiece. And almost as soon as he did, his eyebrows shot up in perfect upside down vees.

"Really," Drachler told the person on the other end of the line. "And who gave you that information? . . . Really? Well, uh . . . just a minute, officer."

142

"Beck, Beck, come here." Drachler covered the mouthpiece of the receiver and whispered to Snow.

"Guy on duty here say they got at least six calls about the murders; says they sent cars to the scene and found that there was a movie crew, complete with cameras and the whole bit at the scene, that they were shooting a murder mystery."

"Hand me the phone," Snow said and grabbed the proffered receiver. Tracy sat down slowly in a chair next to the telephone.

"I'm sorry, but I . . ." Beckett started to explain and then hung up the phone.

Snow sat down on the floor, still holding the receiver in his right hand.

"I don't believe it. I don't believe it at all. There's nothing that somebody won't do to keep this quiet."

"Beck, are you all right?" Drachler asked.

"Sure, Steve, but something I didn't mention is that back at my house in Santa Monica, I killed somebody, and by the time the police arrived, the body was gone. Somebody wants to keep this very quiet, and I don't know whether it's the Commission or the Consortium. Problem is, I don't know who this Consortium is, or why either one of them would want to hush up the killings."

"Jesus, Snow, this is a helluva story." Drachler started walking toward the living room. Tracy and Beckett followed. "I've been sniffing around the edges of the Delphi Commission for nearly three years now, and I haven't been able to get anything I could write about."

"Whoa," Snow said as he and Tracy sat on the Queen Anne sofa, "when did you get interested in business? Ever since I've known you, you've been a political reporter—that is a troublemaker with all your investigative reporting. So why'd you get so

143

damned interested in the Commission and corporations?"

"Snow baby," Drachler settled down in a wing-back chair and threw one leg over its arm, "there ain't a reporter in town who don't think something's rotten as buffalo puke in the Delphi Commission," Drachler said. "And as you goddamned well know, the Commission is part corporate and part political. When I started following up on some political leads, I'll be damned if they didn't just turn right into corporate ones and back again. That's why I'm interested in the Commission, my ole buddy."

Snow whistled. "Tell me about it."

"Look, first of all the huge global corporations are cutting the balls off America," Drachler began. His voice suddenly lost the good-ole-boy flourishes, and Snow knew this was the cutting edge that had slit the political throats of dozens of people. Drachler sat up in the chair and leaned forward.

"It wasn't so bad for us—America, that is—when the corporations had an American orientation. But now that they've gotten so big, and since it could be hazardous to their balance sheets to appear too American, they're treating us just like any other country, to be exploited and disregarded.

"That sounds like a lot of rhetoric," Snow said, turning to face the reporter. "No wonder you've not got enough to publish."

"Hold on," Drachler held up an open palm. "That's just the preamble. Did you know that when the first Arab oil embargo hit us in 1973-74, the oil companies were working with the Arabs?"

"Everybody pretty well suspects that."

"Yes, but there are damn few facts. The companies kept things under wraps pretty well. But some of them slipped out," Drachler said as he leaned back in the chair. "For instance, did you know that Exxon refused to sell fuel oil to the U.S. Navy at the Subic Bay base in the Philippines because they said they were supporting the OPEC boycott?"

"No," Snow shook his head, stunned but not surprised. "I never heard that."

"You and most other Americans," Drachler said. "They've done a good PR job and I'll bet you'd have a hard time believing it all if somebody hadn't been shooting at you for the past week and a half. Right?"

Snow nodded.

"Anyway, to give you an idea of the mentality of these global managers, Frank uh . . . whatsisname . . . Zingara of the Caltex Corporation . . . he was one of their VPs, said that martial law in the Philippines had 'significantly improved the business climate.' If I remember the quote right. So what we've got is a bunch of financial Hitlers who don't care what government does to people as long as it allows them to make a profit."

"Okay, I understand that," Snow said quietly, "and I agree that it's a crime, morally reprehensible. But it all seems like good stuff for the American empire. Where's the support for the fact that they're screwing us as well?"

"Foreign investment."

"Huh?"

"*Surely* you've read about all of the companies going overseas," Drachler began pedantically.

"Sure, lower labor rates and such."

"Lower labor rates, and better ways around legislation, around antipollution requirements, fewer safety and health regulations. It's a lot better when you can pay your workers $30 a month, foul up their air and water, and not care too much if they lose an arm or leg at work. But what that's done is produce unemployment here at home, and inflation and a balance of trade problems."

145

"Some plants have been moved lock, stock, and barrel out of the U.S. to another country," Tracy interrupted. "The goods are manufactured there and shipped back here. So we now have to import what was once made here at home, which means it counts against us on the balance of trade deficit—that makes our money worth less, and money that buys less means inflation."

Snow looked first at Steve and then at Tracy, dumbfounded that they were so well versed in an area he was totally lacking in.

"More and more we're starting to resemble an underdeveloped country," Drachler slammed his fist on the chair arm. "We're dependent on exporting agricultural products and timber to produce the foreign exchange needed to import all those goods that were once produced here. And don't believe that foreign investment means jobs in the United States. When a corporation ships out, it leaves behind a lot of people who can't find jobs."

"So where's all the money going?" Snow asked. "If all the investment capital is leaving the United States and it's leaving the Third World countries, what's happening to the money?"

"It looks like somebody's taking it out of circulation."

"What good would that do?"

"It would give them tremendous leverage," Drachler said. "Right now the global corporations hold more currency, more gold, more bonds, and more stocks than ever before. Their inventories of money alone are bigger than the entire U.S. Treasury. If they played even five or ten percent of any one currency on the international monetary market, it would cause a collapse in the economy of that country."

"I wonder if that's got anything to do with project Prometheus," Tracy said. "After all, Simon did say that he thought it involved a big securities transaction."

"And after all, people have been trying to kill you two for the past few days," Drachler said. "I hope you two don't mind, but I'm going to stick pretty close. This could be my Pulitzer."

Snow smiled knowingly at him. "Stick as close as you like. But can I ask you a favor?"

"Depends, but probably yes."

"I need some directories: a White House one; one from the executive branch. And, could I have access to that huge black notebook of yours?"

"You got it. Lemme run down to the office and get them. It'll only take a few minutes." Without waiting for an answer, he bounded through the door and was gone.

"I don't know," Snow told Tracy. "It's all so boggling. Could Carothers have been tied up with this?"

"I'm *sure* he was," Tracy said. "We talked a lot about the actions the big corporations were taking in the Third World—"

"And could that be why they killed him? Because he wanted to block something that would make them a profit?"

"No. It would have to be a lot more than that. Carothers had blocked some of his brother's profit-making schemes with his own money, but that never did anything but provoke family arguments. No, it would take a lot more than that for them to kill him. It would take something really major. I'm sure it has something to do with Prometheus. If we only knew what it was."

"Well, we do know it's a financial transaction," Snow suggested.

"True. But it's got to be more. I *know* the answer must be in the microfilm—"

"Or in the box."

"Or the box. Beck." She looked at him softly.

"I'm afraid of this all. I feel so small. So insignificant."

Snow walked to her and they embraced. Tracy laid her cheek on his shoulder.

"I'm afraid too," Snow confessed. "But I wonder if being insignificant might be an advantage. . . ."

They're not prepared to deal with small. Snow remembered Simon's words.

Small has got to be bigger than big, or small is dead. Snow thought of the large man's words, thought about them and kept them to himself. He took Tracy in his arms and they held on to each other for a long time, taking solace in the sweet closeness.

They were still standing near the living-room's French windows when the sound of footsteps on the front walk jolted them back to reality. Snow motioned Tracy into the hallway and rushed to the front door, relieved to see Drachler's grin through the peephole. Snow unlocked the door.

"Here y'are my friend," Drachler's face beamed with excitement as he thrust the directories at Snow. "I'll see *you* day after tomorrow at lunch," Drachler said to Snow. " And I'll see you," he looked at Tracy, "in a dream. Cheers."

Drachler bounded down the walk as Snow closed the door. They smiled at each other as they heard the angry blast of an auto's horn as Drachler's Pinto plunged into traffic.

Snow's smile faded as he turned from Tracy and stared out the window after Steve's car. She walked to him and hugged him around his waist as he continued to gaze silently through the sheer curtains.

He was, to be sure, now engaged in something that ran directly counter to everything he had ever believed. All his life, Beckett Snow fought disorder. That had been explicit in his efforts as a policeman and in his role of public prosecutor, avenger against those who brought disorder to civilization.

And now he faced the most ordered, the most efficient creature the world had ever experienced: the global corporation, cum corporate government.

But the order and efficiency produced by the corporations produced sameness rather than protection for the individual; it sacrificed choice for efficiency; freedom was butchered in the name of manageability; and moral choices were rendered moot by the balance sheet.

The global corporation mentality had decidedly evolved to the totalitarian point of view. It saw itself as a benevolent dictator, but the fact that it was a dictator remained untouched.

The corporate managers had themselves ceased to be capable of independent thought and emotional sustenance outside the corporation. They had lost to a great degree the measure of humanness that separated them from the carpenter ants and simians, and they therefore assumed that everyone should also willingly trade their integrity for a loaf of chemical bread laced with air, a flush toilet, and light switch.

No, Snow thought, he wasn't going to be a part of it all. He'd apply the monkey wrench where he could and if it cost him his life, he would have his integrity, which was more than those who'd take his life from him would ever have.

Snow turned to Tracy and kissed her gently. She returned the kiss with her own, deeper and more penetrating. He let her lead him upstairs to bed.

Amid somber rooms lit with cut-glass chandeliers and paneling so dark it seemed to absorb light like a sponge, Eric Simon dined with the Assistant Director of the Central Intelligence Agency in charge of Covert Operations. Like Simon, Everett Lowell was a Yale man, class of '52, another cold warrior who'd never stopped fighting.

Simon was talking; Lowell was intent on his tournedos.

"I'm convinced that the information in the box will lead us to a larger body of information with which we can control some of the larger corporations," said Simon.

Lowell looked at him and washed down a bite of steak with a drink from the second bottle of St. Emilion.

"I can't confirm everything," Simon continued, "but I've got reason to believe the box contains directions that will lead us to dossiers on several of the top corporate officers or industrialists in the world."

Lowell stopped chewing. "What do the dossiers say?" he asked.

"I'm not sure, but I think it has something to do with assassinations."

"Here?"

"Maybe." Simon was about to continue when the maître d' appeared at his elbow, holding a telephone.

"Excuse me, Mr. Simon," the man said apologetically. "I know you left instructions not to be disturbed. But he says it's urgent. Will you take the call?"

"Very well." Simon scowled as the man in the tuxedo plugged the telephone into the jack behind Lowell's shoulder.

"Yes?" Simon growled into the phone. He listened and nodded. "Balls." His tanned, athletic face was a mass of frown lines. "Get it cleaned up, fast." He hung up.

"Trouble?" Lowell asked.

"Some. Looks like the Commission is really putting on the squeeze. They want the box, badly. Tried to get them Bulgarian-style at the bus stop in Washington Circle. My man picked up the killers and dispatched them. But they tried again. Tailed them to an apartment—I don't know whose yet; I'm having it traced—

and tried to kill them again. I don't know how, but one was already in the apartment when they arrived—"

"Lots of ways," Lowell answered. "You know that. Someone nearby eavesdropping; good optics and they can watch a person dial a phone and get the number; profiles of a person's—"

"Yeah, I know, I know. But I didn't think they were going all out. We must be right about the contents of that box!"

"*You* must be right," Lowell corrected. If anything went wrong, he wasn't going down with Simon's ship.

"Sure. Anyway, my man picked up the Commission operatives, got both of them, and then bought it himself. But it's not as serious as it could have been. Snow and the girl are all right."

"I don't completely understand," Lowell said. "Help me out."

"On what?"

"The girl and this Snow. How you're using them."

"Two ways. First of all, his being at large is keeping the Commission guys hopping. I know they're pretty well pissed off at their failure to catch him and the girl. Since Sherbok's in charge of intelligence and security in addition to his other duties, his continued failure is going to weaken his hand, and strengthen Cranch's. And the better those two Commission factions are balanced against each other, the closer we come to being the king maker."

"Uhmmm," Lowell nodded as he folded an entire asparagus spear into his mouth without cutting it. Simon made a mental note to make sure they got a table where people couldn't see Lowell's manners the next time they had to meet over a meal.

"And second," Simon continued, "this guy Beckett Snow is a helluva smart fellow. If we can keep him off balance enough, he'll see the advantage of working with us."

"If this guy's as smart as you say he is, how do we know he won't grasp the whole thing?"

"We don't. But if that starts to happen, we'll kill him. Dessert?"

Chapter Fourteen

Christ! Where is he, that obnoxious asshole. What was his name? Gilbert, Peter Gilbert. Sherbok's gopher —wouldn't even explain what he did. That, Leslie decided, meant he didn't do anything important; at least as she understood the rules status at the White House. Anybody who *did* do something he thought was important was always careful to flaunt it.

So here she was waiting for someone who didn't spend a lot of energy advertising his power, and she decided that it meant he either had no power or possessed something too awesome to fuck around with.

Oddly, Leslie wasn't annoyed yet at having to wait. She was enjoying the time to think. She'd learned something about herself yesterday when she walked out of Sherbok's office. She learned that being forceful didn't necessarily mean that people would hate you, or leave you. It wasn't like her father. She remembered him well—a standard American daddy. He wanted her to do certain things in a certain way and if she did them she was Daddy's angel, and if she didn't want to do things his way she was a slut. It was pure and simple.

But now it wasn't working any more.

She looked about her at the other diners at Dominique's, wondering if they'd learned any lessons like that lately.

Dominique's. It was a strange place to be angry,

Leslie thought. She'd always been happy, animated here, usually reliving a play or ballet over a late dinner after the Kennedy Center. Dominique's had always been delightful.

And so it was that she'd chosen this restaurant when Peter suggested lunch. She chose it because it was her turf, a place where she felt confident.

She was playing the game. Funny, she thought, she'd always known *how* to play the games. But now she was going to play to win. And if it meant some bent male egos, well, too fucking bad.

It was now 12:17 PM, Leslie noted. Gilbert was 17 minutes late. She was getting irritated. She detested tardiness and decided to tell Gilbert so.

Leslie glanced about her in the darkened room, sipping on a glass of Soave. The restaurant had a two-story ceiling that was half below sidewalk level and half above. One could look up at the passersby outside. The walls were covered with the usual pictures of political powers and celebrities, along with an unusual collection of kitsch from plastic animal heads to signs, mirrors, and other accoutrements that indicated that Dominique did not take himself as seriously as most of his compatriot restauranteurs did. She liked that.

Looking up toward the glass-enclosed entry hall and staircase, she saw Gilbert enter and pause while his eyes adjusted to the light.

He spotted her as she was coming down the stairs and waved a friendly hand. He spoke briefly to the maitre d', then strode purposefully toward her table.

It had been a long walk for Peter Gilbert, those three blocks up Pennsylvania Avenue from the White House to Dominique's. A walk that was at once too long and over too soon.

Yesterday afternoon had been purgatory. He thought about this Leslie Lewis, and he thought about her outrage. He thought, too, about his role in provoking that outrage. It had been necessary, he told himself repeatedly. But for some reason he still felt bad. Things were bothering him; they were piling up. He hadn't been able to get in touch with Isaac Roth since their meeting in Potomac. Isaac wasn't home; he hadn't been at work; and, oddly, he hadn't been to visit his sister. He rarely missed that. That something could have happened to the old gentleman troubled Gilbert sorely.

Roth's questions and doubts about the Delphi Commission nagged at him as much as did his role in trying to coerce Leslie Lewis. They hadn't expected such a reaction from her.

Sherbok was out of the city and Gilbert felt that since he'd been charged with dealing with the woman in the first place, he ought to see the assignment through. He would, he decided that morning, meet with her, reveal his role, and explain to her why it was all necessary.

But anxiety reigned. A car blew its horn. Gilbert was immersed in thought and failed to notice he was crossing against the light.

What was wrong with him! He was losing control of himself and that made him feel weak, made him feel soft and inefficient, too . . . human.

No, she would understand. He would convince her.

"Hello, Leslie. I'm sorry to be late. I really am." Leslie looked first at her watch and then at him in her most reproachful manner. In spite of it, she believed him.

"Of course, Peter. It's all right. Do sit down." Leslie surprised herself with her graciousness. She had intended to be harsh, abrasive.

A waiter arrived to take Peter's order for drinks almost as soon as he had seated himself. Leslie looked at him, saw what was, perhaps, the reason for her gentle reaction. The arrogant bravado of the day before had been replaced with a vague uncertainty. She was torn: her feelings told her to be kind, but her newly confirmed instincts said play to win.

Gilbert looked at her and quickly away, at the walls, at the windows.

"Certainly is a change from yesterday's weather," he said.

"I suppose," Leslie replied. "But did we meet here to discuss the weather?"

"Uh, no. I guess not."

"Well, this is your conversation and I would appreciate your moving it along."

"It's a hard thing to explain. . . . I—well, if I seem to be stumbling along sometimes, it's because I'm trying not to violate security cleara—"

"Don't pull national security on me. I want the truth without any waffling."

"That's not going to be easy," Gilbert hesitated. "But I'll try to do my best." He paused, hoping she would indicate her satisfaction with that. Leslie Lewis took another sip from her wine glass and looked at him. The look—he noticed to his increased discomfort —conveyed nothing that could be construed as acceptance.

"I suppose that the best way to start is also the hardest way. That person in your office last week . . ."

"Yes, the person who threatened me."

"That person was acting on Sherbok's orders. It's because the Delphi Commission is getting ready for something very important. Others—"

"Meaning Sherbok?"

"Well, yes, and others too—feel that the situation is sensitive enough that someone who is not part of the operation itself might accidentally . . . innocently . . .

uh, upset the balance, the negotiations. So it was decided that—"

"Who decided—Sherbok?"

"Yes. That any involvement on the part of those who are not directly involved in this . . . project should not deal with the Commission."

"So you decided on a meat axe approach?" Leslie asked. "You had to act like the fucking Gestapo to do it?"

"Well, it was originally decided that the approach would be more . . . expeditious than a formal procedure."

"What you didn't count on was a woman fighting back, right?"

Peter Gilbert took too long in responding.

"You seem to know a helluva lot about this whole thing for somebody I just stumbled across yesterday," Leslie said. "Did you have a chance to talk to your master, or have you been involved with this all along?"

"Yes—well, you see . . . I was the man in the room who threatened you last week." Peter Gilbert hadn't intended to say that, at least not in that manner. But it had slithered out. He knew immediately that he'd made a tactical error, perhaps a mistake of strategic importance. It was embarrassing, he thought during those few fragments of time before Leslie had time to react. But more than embarrassing, it was bothering. Time after time in the past few weeks it seemed that he was losing the control over himself that had been the sustaining impulse of his life and of his success. He had, to be sure, become more human. But he'd agonized that while being more human had made him feel somewhat better, there was certainly no marketability in it; and it most assuredly diminished one's chances to be not only a survivor, but a master.

"You!" It was a single word, but delivered with

sufficient amplitude to dominate every other string of words; every other conversation; indeed, every other activity in the restaurant.

An embarrassed silence swirled through the room.

Peter's panic was transparent. But Leslie continued her lambasting in a hushed tone. Diners returned to their truffles; the waiters to their trays; the busboys to stacks of glasses; and the maitre d', somewhat reluctantly, to a couple who had just gained the foot of the steps.

"You!" Leslie hissed. "I should throw something at you. I should scream and yell and stand up on my chair and announce to this room and to the world outside what Peter Gilbert, assistant to the President's National Security Advisor, has been doing with his spare time.

"I ought . . . ought . . . Why, for God's sake? That's despicable, cowardly. Did you stop to think of what you were doing? Did you have time to realize that you were playing with another human being?"

As a matter of point, Peter thought, he *had* thought about those things, and had decided that the importance of the project took precedence. He considered telling her that, but the melt-down temperature of her language indicated that she would take scant notice.

"I can explain—" Peter began.

"I'm sure you can. But would you waste it on a mere woman?"

"—I can explain and I will if you give me the chance."

"Why should I give you a chance? Why shouldn't I just report this whole affair and have it out with you in the presence of God and the President, mostly the President? But might I ask for whom this charming bit of fascism was performed, and why?" Leslie asked.

"Well, by my employers, the Delphi Commission."

"I thought you worked for Sherbok."

"I do, but I do work for them as well. Sherbok also works for them."

"But why? The members of the Delphi Commission are for the most part the big multinational operations that—"

"*Global* corporations," Peter corrected.

"All right, *global* corporations. That's my point. Why are you, an employee of the President of the United States, working for a bunch of global corporations?"

"A lot of people in government do. Look," Peter began, "the global corporations can do what governments can't. Our government hasn't been able to do a lot of things it should for the best efficiency because it's had its hands tied by the cumbersome process that—"

"Democracy is rather confining, I imagine, to corporate goals," Leslie interjected.

Peter ignored the interruption. "A cumbersome process that has made it necessary to assign some of the functions traditionally handled by government to the corporations," he went on.

"The purpose of which is what, Mr. Gilbert?"

"Yes. Well . . . it's hard to explain—"

"*Do* try."

Gilbert exhaled an exasperated sigh. "They can do what governments could never do because of their ideologies. The corporation isn't governed by national boundaries or nationalism or patriotism. It can govern the lives of people much better than creaking governments."

"By what right?"

"Pardon me?"

"By what right do your corporations intend to govern people's lives?"

"I don't quite follow you."

"I don't imagine you do," Leslie said. "What I mean is, what gives your global buddies the right to rule

159

people's lives? You know, the European kings ruled by divine right; military dictators rule by might; the U.S. is supposed to be governed by the consent of its people. What gives your corporation a right to rule?"

"Efficiency."

"I might have guessed."

"Don't scoff. The global corporations have set up the most efficient managerial system in the world . . ."

"Lockheed," Leslie interrupted.

"Huh?"

"Penn Central."

"But—"

"Equity Funding. Chrysler."

"But those are the—"

"The exceptions, Mr. Gilbert? I don't know. I'm not as *au courant* in the rarified world of corporate management as you are. But I do know that government is bailing out more and more of your 'efficient' businesses day after day. And that bailout money comes from a lot of people who don't earn a huge amount of money. Are they going to let someone rule their lives from the boardrooms?"

"I don't think anyone is going to have a choice," Gilbert replied.

"Because of your Commission?"

"Yes."

"And you believe in all this?"

"I do."

"Then I don't think we have much to discuss."

She shoved her chair back and tossed her napkin on the table.

"I'm going to think about things for a while." Without waiting for his reply, Leslie started for the stairs. She stopped, turned around, and walked back to the table.

"Here," she said, tossing two one-dollar bills in his

direction. "These should cover my wine. *Bon appetit!*"

Peter Gilbert watched as she scaled the steps two by two and then turned his attention to the dollar bills that lay on the floor, trying to decide if he could bring himself to pick them up.

"What do you mean they just 'dropped out of sight,' Mr. Sherbok? People don't disappear, they have to *go* somewhere."

"Well, Reynolds and Snow are very cunning, very—"

"And that's what *you* are supposed to be. You, the National Security Advisor, charged with the welfare of an entire country, can't manage to . . . deal . . . with two people whose resources are nearly nonexistent. I sug—"

"That's hardly fair," Sherbok insisted. He sat in the chair, facing Carothers's brother, Kincaid, world financier and member of the Delphi Commission, who had taken a leave of absence from his work to handle the final six-month stage of Prometheus. Next to Prometheus himself, Carothers was the most powerful man in the Commission.

"You *know* I was never in favor of the man's daughter being involved with this affair from the start." The flavor of Sherbok's accent grew thicker as his anger increased. It was now exceedingly prominent.

"The operation should have been handled professionally by my people from the very beginning," Sherbok continued. "But no, this woman, this offspring of Prometheus, had a grudge to settle that had to be set right, and he allowed it. That, Mr. Carothers, was not my fault." Sherbok leaned back in his chair, satisfied with his own answer.

"But the fact remains that now, even your 'professionals' can't seem to locate these people. Why?"

161

Sherbok squirmed uncomfortably in his chair. "I don't entirely know. Partly because they're getting help."

"From whom?"

"From the Consortium."

"But that can't be much help at all, can it? From what I understand of those people, they're just a ragtag handful of self-righteous fanatics. Am I correct?"

"My intelligence reports indicate that is the case."

"Oh, come on, Stefan, don't be so formal. Sure I'm upset, but it's because we're on the same side. We always have been even from the time my brother, my late brother, worked with . . . assisted you at Harvard. You and I have always been close. So tell me, are my assumptions correct about this Consortium?"

Sherbok ran his hand through his thick shock of long black hair. "I believe so. I think they have a few more people than we originally expected, but they're mostly harmless. They communicate with each other, exchange information, but seem unlikely to act on any of it, despite the fact they have as their spiritual leader a fellow named Eric Simon who was once with CIA covert operations before being assigned to the investigations unit of the SEC. His power dissolved when Nixon resigned, and from what I can tell, he's spent most of his time trying to make money in the securities market. That, I believe, is how he's come to get involved with Prometheus."

"You mean he wants to use it—us—to make money?"

"Yes."

Both laughed at what they considered a heroically comic effort.

"But that doesn't solve our problem," Carothers continued firmly. "This man Simon's got the microfilm, and the other two've got the box. By the way, Stefan, do you know what's in the box?"

"I have an inkling."

"Let's just say that my late brother was a cunning man. But he spent an enormous amount of time and money—all wasted—trying to assuage some sort of misguided guilt, instead of using his resources to increase his resources. It won him a lot of friends, but also got him into the ultimate trouble. A lot of good all those friends are going to do him now.

"No," Carothers continued, "I can't describe fully, precisely, what is in that box. But I can say that its contents could finally be worth more than all the combined assets of every member corporation of the Commission."

Sherbok's eyebrows arched.

"No, Stefan, I don't mean that it could be converted directly into monetary assets. But it *could* be so powerful as to make those existing assets nearly worthless . . . . That, my dear friend, is why recovering the box is so important. Can you tell me how you're going to do that? For unless it's done within the next two weeks at the outside, Prometheus will have to be told—"

"But that means—"

"Prometheus will have to know, and yes, I know that means the split between you and Secretary of State Cranch will widen, with him possibly gaining the upper hand. Since I have cast my bread upon your waters, I wouldn't like to see that happen. But should it threaten, I will have to take the most expedient course and put some distance between the two of us. And I wouldn't want that to happen to our long and . . . deep friendship."

"The woman and her companion have received assistance from Simon in Los Angeles and again here. We were tracking them until Consortium people interfered," Sherbok explained. "They will make contact again I'm sure, and we'll have them at that point. The matter is a rather straightforward one of keeping Simon and his closest associates under surveillance. I do not think Simon will trust the contact with the woman to any other, and will therefore make the contact himself."

"When that happens, we've got our two trouble-makers, the box, the microfilm, and the head of the Consortium."

"Hey, turkey, are you going to spend the whole night like that?" Tracy walked into the study.

Tracy's voice broke his concentration. Snow looked up from the directory he was examining.

"No, a few minutes more. Steve's gonna need these at work and I don't want to keep them from him." Snow was perusing a thick black notebook of the reporter's telephone numbers and two volumes, one a White House telephone directory and the other a guide to the Executive Branch.

He and Tracy had each spent the day fruitfully, in a final prelude to action. A quick purchase of a blond wig had transformed dark-haired "Mary Fletcher" back into the old Tracy Reynolds. Then, armed with her real identification, Tracy had gone from bank to bank to cash the remaining traveler's checks: $53,000 in all. Steve Drachler had driven her to each bank, waiting outside while she conducted the transactions. "Don't worry about it, it's great color for my Pulitzer story," he had assured her when she tried to thank him. Since Tracy was a fugitive, the operation entailed con-siderable risk, but she gambled that most people would not make the connection between a newspaper story they might have seen and the normal and pleasant-looking young woman who stood before them.

Even so, it had been an anxious and suspenseful day. Each time, she had to wonder if this teller would be the one to call for confirmation, would be the one to recognize the name and alert the police. Every question seemed an accusation, each query as to what denominations Tracy would like, an inquisition to reveal her criminality.

But it was not to be so. By the end of the day, she had cashed all of the traveler's checks. She and Steve had visited thirteen banks in the process.

While Drachler and Tracy exchanged the traveler's checks, Snow had contacted a professor of metallurgy at the University of Maryland to see about getting the strange metal box opened. Snow explained his situation over the telephone to the professor, a kindly gentleman who had remained grateful to Snow for help offered in an immigration case a few years earlier.

Professor Albertsen met with Snow in a working man's bar on Pennsylvania Avenue, where they discussed the past, the present, and the future for 45 minutes, while Snow's anxiety mounted. Finally they got to the box.

A quick look, and the professor, who had done considerable work for the military, thought he knew what it was. The box seemed to be fabricated of the same metal alloy used as armor for the newest generation of tanks. If so, it would be impervious to all but the greatest forces. Forces which, he added, would destroy the contents of the box before they weakened the box itself.

The locking mechanism was nothing he'd ever seen before. But since he was familiar with the metal alloy, he was optimistic that he could break its defenses chemically, or perhaps with the university's massive continuous wave laser, without damaging the contents. At any rate, they'd have an answer within the next two days.

Snow's thoughts returned to the directory in front of him. Like most things in Washington, information was available on just about every individual and every institution if a person but knew where to look. And reporters were probably the best people to call on when obscure facts had to be gleaned.

What Snow wanted was the name of someone at the White House who could be approached, obliquely, about the Delphi Commission. A person in a middle-level position. It couldn't be someone so high up that he would be alarmed at an approach—such as a person in the National Security Advisor's office, or anyone in the ruling cabal—but yet someone high enough to have knowledge of the Commission's relationship with the President. He could not forget that Carothers had implored Tracy to get the contents of the briefcase to the President.

That, he thought, made no sense. The President had been a member of the Commission before being elected, as were all his top appointees. So it stood to reason that anything they did, he would control.

But there were a lot of things that didn't stand to reason in the entire story, and that was just another for which an answer would have to wait.

"Are you *coming* to bed?" Tracy's voice was edged with exasperation.

"In a moment. I've only got three more pages left."

Investigative reporters and other resourceful and knowledgeable Washingtonians knew that much could be gleaned about an organization by the way in which its telephone and personnel directory was constructed. Subtle relationships and those not so subtle were transparent to people with experience in sorting out the players.

Snow had been an expert. One didn't survive as well as he had without knowing the roster.

"Here it is!" Snow cried, getting up from the desk. He walked to the canopied bed in which Tracy lay half propped up, the entrails of the *Washington Post* spread about her. "Special Assistant to the President for Organizational Liaison, Leslie Lewis."

"So what?"

"Wanna bet she's the person that the Commission goes through—along with a million other organizations he's a member of?"

"Nope."

"Nope what? I think she—"

"Nope, I don't want to bet you. I think you're probably right," Tracy said. "Are you going to come to bed now? I have something to talk to you about."

"Sure," Snow said as he walked back to the desk to organize his notes and prepare Drachler's materials to return to him. Snow was to visit the reporter at their favorite bar, the same one Snow had met the professor at, for lunch the next day.

He turned out the desk light and returned to the bed.

"Beckett, I'm worried about us."

"I know. . . . So am I if that helps any."

"More than anything else, I'm bothered by me," Tracy said. "The other night, Monday night, when we arrived here, I started to tell you some of it, but the time wasn't right. It's funny, but I've almost stopped being scared. It's like these things are normal, that they happen every day to everybody. It's almost as if they're not real except—" she touched her breast painfully, "except when there's physical evidence." Snow nodded but did not interrupt.

"When I tell you what's bothering me, it will sound trivial compared to the task of staying alive—"

"Go on," Snow said as he pulled up the desk chair. He sat straddling the back.

"You're absorbing me. I defer to you and I've never deferred to anyone before. Look at it this way. I'd survived the efforts of the Commission to kill me for more than a month without anybody's help at all. And now, I'm starting to turn over decisions to you; following your instructions without question; putting myself in the hands of your friends, people I don't know.

"I know that you *do* have experience in this world of violence and you *are* bigger than I am and you *are* expert with a variety of weapons and you *do* have reflexes from training I didn't have. All of that makes a lot of sense, and—" She saw the lines of bewilderment form between his eyebrows. "And I know you're not to blame. You are what you are. But that doesn't alter the fact that our relationship is changing—I'm changing—in a way that makes me uneasy."

"But this is an artificial situation," Snow began slowly searching for words. "It can't last much longer." They looked at each other, the gravity of their predicament implicit in his words. "Then when it's over, we can try and live a life where I won't be absorbing you. We can—"

"But do you think we *can*?" Tracy asked. "We're forming some kind of relationship here and it's moving more and more to you running things and me following. What happens when we get back to the real world, and I don't *have* to depend on you?"

"It'll be great," Snow said. "I wouldn't want to marry somebody that's dependent—"

"You never mentioned marriage before," she said.

"No, I guess I didn't. Well, I'm mentioning it now. Would you—?"

"Oh, Beck, I don't know. I can't say now. It all depends on how this all works itself out." Tracy looked intently into his eyes. "I have to be *me* and nobody else. I can't eradicate myself, I can't kill part of me to marry someone."

"But I wouldn't love you if you were somebody else," Snow protested. "You, Tracy Reynolds, are my equal, *at least,* if not more." He kissed her cheek gently.

"Am I?" she sighed. "I don't know. I thought I did. But now I'm not so sure. That's why I couldn't say yes to marrying you. I have to see whether I am strong enough to resist you; to avoid getting stuck somehow in your shadow—"

"But I wouldn't do that—"

"God! You're stubborn and for somebody so intelligent, you can be awfully stupid, you know. Look, you can't *do* a damn thing; would you get that through your fucking ego? You have an overwhelming personality and you absorb people—male and female—by just being yourself. I know you are sensitive," she added, more gently.

"But what *I* have to decide, what *I* have to see, is whether I am indeed your equal; whether I have a personality that, given the real world, is equally overwhelming as yours and can balance us as we have to be balanced. . . . Am I getting clearer?"

"Yeah. I understand," Beckett said dejectedly. "It's happened before. Instead of women, they turned out to be wives.

"But *I'm* frustrated also," Snow continued. "I'm not used to doing nothing. Savvy?"

"Sabe," Tracy corrected. "But that's me too, and I don't feel very much like I've had much of an influence on the past few days."

"Neither of us has, really," Snow said. "We've just been reacting, surviving. That's all going to stop."

"True. Maybe that's got more to do with my apprehension than I realize, but the future will tell . . ." She paused. "You do believe there will be a future, don't you?"

"I've had my doubts the past few days; I really don't know. But Tracy, whatever time we're together from now on, no matter what happens, that's a future. And I love you so much that two weeks or two months with you is a much brighter future than ten times without you."

"That's a very sweet thing to say," Tracy said, extending her arm to him. "Come here. I love you."

Chapter Fifteen

"Damn, damn, damn! *Goddamn.*" Peter Gilbert slammed his fist into a pile of loose papers that cluttered his desk, his curses unheard by anyone but himself. He looked at his watch: 6:17 AM and the date had changed. It was Wednesday morning.

He was pissed at Leslie; pissed at himself for letting her bother him this badly. He was angry because she had somehow touched that perpetual scar of his own inadequacy and now he was worthless.

He'd been up all night, had paced the floor of his office; had started to call Leslie at home several times, and always replaced the receiver before the number rang. He was most of all mad at himself, mad at letting her get to him.

Yet it was amorphous. He felt there was something inside that needed untying, that when he somehow changed his way of looking at something—what, he didn't know—the knot would be cut, the paralysis would lift. It was an enemy without a face, and that was the most dangerous type. But more than that, he knew the enemy was himself, and he had enough respect left to know that he was a formidable foe.

He got up, walked over to a map of North America, pressed a set of buttons, and immediately the map lit up with a series of alphanumeric codes. Simultaneously a teletype next to his desk clattered a stream of names and addresses and telephone numbers and itineraries that corresponded to the codes. Each code represented a member of the Delphi Commission.

Each person controlled hundreds of millions, in some cases billions, of dollars worth of currency, securities, stocks, bonds. It was Peter's job to know their exact locations at all times. Peter had been drawn out of private industry to design the system, to execute the plans, and to cut out all of the gremlins. His orderly mind and rigid discipline kept him from getting mired in the ambiguities that had tripped up two others before him.

Peter ripped off the teletype paper and looked at it without really reading the words. He walked back to his desk, sat down, rearranged the papers on his desk from one pile to another, looked at his watch again—6:29AM—got up, and walked over to make his third pot of coffee since midnight.

It had been like that all night. Bound by his discipline and duty, he had been unable to leave his office until he'd accomplished something. Yet, frozen by the free-floating anxiety, he had been unable to perform any useful tasks. He'd accomplished nothing. That very fact stimulated his feelings of worthlessness and propelled him even farther from being able to do anything worthwhile.

Peter spotted the winking light button on the telephone. Who could be calling him so early?

"Hello, Peter Gilbert here."

"Oh, yes, yes, good." The voice was brittle. "I'm so very happy to have found you. I'm Rosanna Roth . . ." she waited for Peter to recognize her name. "You know my brother—" her voice cracked. Peter thought; then instantly realized that the woman was Isaac Roth's sister. He remembered that she had suffered multiple sclerosis for nearly twenty years. She was sixty now, and could move about only with the greatest of pain.

Peter's heart tripped on itself. Had something happened to Isaac?

"I've been trying to get hold of you, Mr. Gilbert. You're the only person . . ." she paused. "The only one my brother really trusted. He said if anything should happen, I could call on you for—"

"Excuse me, Miss Roth," Peter interrupted, "but is something wrong?"

"Yes." Her voice cracked. "Isaac's dead."

Peter inhaled sharply; his head filled with white light. "Oh, my *God*." Peter whispered. Instantly the clammy glob of anxiety in his chest turned to burning molten steel.

"Mr. Gilbert? Mr. Gilbert, are you still there?"

"Yes, ma'am," Peter said quietly.

"Well, *listen* to me." The voice, Peter thought, might be aged and tired, but he heard strength behind it.

"Are you listening?"

"Certainly."

"Good. There's not much time, they'll be after me in a minute or so."

They? Peter thought.

"Isaac was murdered," the antique voice told him. "There was no way Isaac could have died in the manner they claim. He was murdered, Mr. Gilbert, and they'll get me, and unless you find out who they are, they'll get you too."

Murdered? They? Who? And why should they want to get him also?

"Because you were too close to him," she said as if she'd been reading his thoughts. "He knew too much about something you're working on."

What? Had Isaac gone mad and confided those ridiculous suspicions of his about the vice president's death to his sister?

"Listen to me. The answer went down on the sail-

172

boat. Isaac had a violent fear of the water. He'd never go on a sailboat willingly," she continued. "They had to force him on there; they had to kill him there and sink his body along with the boat."

"Who is they?"

"I don't know, Mr. Gilbert." There was a pause. I have to go. They're coming for me. I—"

Peter heard the receiver strike against something hard, presumably the wall, and then the call was disconnected as someone replaced the receiver.

Peter hung up, rested his head on his folded arms, and wept.

Kincaid Carothers leaned back against the leather upholstery and extinguished the reading light behind his seat. He'd have 15 or 20 minutes worth of thinking time before the limo reached the home of Prometheus in West Hartford. It was right, he thought, as he swept along silently through the winter darkness, that people such as he, such as Prometheus and the members of the Commission, should ultimately come to ultimate power, to give the world the benefit of their superior managerial ability.

Weak people! He despised them all. They existed for people like him to enjoy, to play with. To use in games among themselves.

And his brother, weak and compassionate—he loathed him. Loathed him because he had the chance to be strong, had all the opportunities, the education, the family. My God, the *family!* What if their father could see them now? He'd think that Adam had been a sniveling weakling, engaging in politics as an elected official! It wasn't a fit goal for one of them to be so obviously involved in politics.

And his brother had made his pitiful attempts at stopping them. Imagine. He almost laughed to himself.

Imagine his brother thinking that the men of Prometheus could be stopped by some sort of dossier. It was ludicrous!

So he dismissed the threat posed by Adam's little concubine and her new male friend. No matter what they had, these two were no match for the Commission.

The limo slowed for its exit from the interstate, banked smoothly around the ramp, and turned onto an unlit blacktop road. Carothers finished the rest of his whiskey and placed the used glass on top of the bar for the chauffeur to attend to. Minutes later the limo pulled into the circular drive of the most magnificent home on Stoner Drive.

Had it looked like Versailles or Buckingham Palace, Carothers thought he wouldn't be surprised. For Prometheus was a descendant of some European nobility or another.

But which king or queen, Carothers was never sure of. But Alec Baran, Prometheus, was certain. One had only to ask him. Baran had come to the United States in the 1930s, shortly before Hitler rose to power. Using his monetary base in Belgium and the rest of Western Europe, Baran had fashioned an insurance empire that was larger than any other in the world. It was now a household name in industries ranging from energy and petroleum to airlines and defense—through a series of sheltered interlocking subsidiaries that effectively disguised his role in their management.

And Baran had pledged that once Operation Prometheus was accomplished, his power would be passed on to his associate, making the banker essentially the chief executive officer of the world. Upon Baran's death, his financial and corporate empire would be placed in trust in Carothers's hands. Along with the financial power, there was political power the likes of which the world had never seen.

When the car halted in front of the mansion, Carothers thanked the chauffeur, climbed from the limo, and walked up the tiered steps, casting a quick appreciative glance at the immaculate, beautiful grounds.

"Good evening, Mr. Carothers." The butler spoke clearly, deeply, with no trace of an accent. "Mr. Baran will receive you in his study. May I have your coat?" Carothers turned to face away from the butler, unbuttoned his cashmere topcoat, and allowed the butler to remove it from his shoulders. "Please follow me."

"Kincaid, it's always nice to see you." Baran's voice conveyed an enthusiasm that he reserved for those few he considered his equal. Baran did not get up from his Eames chair. Carothers knew this was more from the man's arthritic condition than any lack of respect.

"Come in. Sit down. I'm sorry you couldn't be present at the Virginia meeting." Was there a tiny bit of scolding in that last phrase?

"Of course, I too regret my absence," Kincaid said. "But as you know, business emergencies do sometimes materialize that simply cannot be handled by anyone but myself." Carothers walked to a chair facing Baran, a Spartan chrome and leather contraption that looked like a fugitive from the Spanish inquisition, but which had been designed for the ultimate in comfort by Baran's personal orthopedic surgeon.

"It wasn't easy," Baran said abruptly. Carothers knew he referred to the proposal to escalate the Sino-Vietnamese conflict. "But I got a consensus to proceed." Carothers nodded. "However, they want a fail-safe go/no-go on it 24 hours before the strike is scheduled."

"That's really no problem."

"Yes, I told them that. You know, Kincaid, it seems so impossible that we're this close. We're this close to making the dream happen, our dream. I don't know

175

what drives people like us, like your father and his before him. It's not wealth—"

"The desire to organize, to control," Carothers interrupted.

"Yes, that and more! For those imply power. But it's greater, more majestic. Just think, *we* are the first in the history of mankind to have any hope of fulfilling the dream. And we're close now to that fulfillment. For once, for the very first time, the world will run as it's *supposed* to. Huxley *knew* how things were supposed to work, and in many ways he was prophetic. But when he wrote *Brave New World* his mind was poisoned by such superficial matters as patriotism, and that elusive concept of self-determination. People have never really cared about those; they have simply been manipulated by those who could use them.

"Well, that's about to stop. We'll give the masses what they really want: food, shelter, security, freedom from war. And we'll do it and make a profit too!"

"Yes, Alec," Kincaid Carothers said, "You know I agree with you. But—"

"But could we get on to the matters at hand?" Baran completed a bit sadly. "You never do let yourself dream a bit, do you?"

"Of course, but—"

"But nothing more," Baran said. "You're quite right. We need to get on with things. Proceed."

"Yes. Well, there are two matters: First, the elimination of Adam's little concubine and her latest paramour; and then, the disabling of Simon and his tin soldiers."

"Why don't we eliminate Simon first?" Baran suggested. "Not the man, of course," he added hastily. "But him as a problem. Now of course it's a mistake to underestimate the enemy, but Simon appears harmless. Although he and his cadre are sprinkled throughout the government, I don't think they're resourceful enough to cause us serious problems. It should be sufficient to simply tie them up until Prometheus is over. Eliminating Simon would be counterproductive; it might cause his followers to take some monkey-wrench actions that could delay or inconvenience us."

"Uhmmm . . . I tend to think they have a bit more power than that," ventured Carothers. "But I'll defer to your judgment. Now, as to the dossier . . ."

"Yes, the dossier," Baran said quickly, shifting as he did to relieve the pressure on his knees.

"We need to recover it at all costs."

"Why is that so urgent? It can't stop Prometheus," Kincaid ventured. "All it contains is an outline of the program, and a file full of dirt that's ten or twenty years old. I can see making an effort to recover it, but I don't believe the possessors have the ability to use it in a manner that could be a threat to us." He waved his hand in the air, dismissing any notion of a threat.

"Do you know what's in the 'file full of dirt'?"

"Not precisely," Carothers said dropping his hand to his side.

"Nor do I," Baran said. "You know, Kincaid, you always underestimate your brother. I consider your judgment to be as good as mine in every matter save that. I—"

"But . . ." Carothers leaned forward.

"Wait. Let me finish. Your judgment is immaculate. But—quite simply—you hate your brother. You've eliminated his body, but he still lives in your mind, in your hatred of him. That, I believe, impairs your judgment. Remember, genetically and culturally and in the areas of intelligence and education, he was your equal. Only your ambition made you triumph. But you've underestimated his resourcefulness. I'd suggest that until we know what it is, the contents of that little file of dirt should be treated as a serious threat. Trust me."

"Perhaps you're right," Carothers sighed. "At any

177

rate, we'll recover the dossier and determine if we really did need to be so concerned."

"Are there plans?"

"I've informed Sherbok that I have taken a personal interest in the matter, and instructed him to provide me with a daily progress sheet. It's a matter of keeping track of Simon until we have all of them together. The girl and Snow we'll eliminate. Simon—as per your suggestion—will not be eliminated."

"Things, then, seem to be going rather well. I'm pleased for you, my old friend." Baran's face grew long, his voice distant and sad. "My only regret is that I will not be around longer. If I were your age, I'd have so many more years to enjoy the progress we are going to be responsible for."

"It's not that bad, is it?" Carothers said with alarm in his voice.

"Something seems to be," Baran said, looking down at his wasted legs. "It's goddamned frustrating. The best doctors money can buy, the best in all of history, and they can't find out what's wrong with me. It's gone beyond what can be called arthritis. They've tested and prodded and inspected me, and can't seem to put a name on it. I personally think it means I don't have a helluva lot of time left."

"I'm sorry to hear that," Carothers sympathized.

"Don't be." Baran grinned. "Life, my friend, is the one thing even you and I can't beat."

Carothers nodded; it was best, he decided, not to dwell on it. They talked, briefly touching on the elimination of Isaac Roth; the joys of sailing; how nice it would be in a couple of months to get the ketch out of storage down in Essex, and have what for Baran might be a last season of cruising on the Sound, Block Island, Narragansett.

Neither of the men was aware—any more than such men usually are of hired help—of a man named Peter

178

Gilbert; of his fondness for Isaac Roth; his guilt and doubts over his role in intimidating a White House aide named Leslie Lewis; or of his subsequent suspicious behavior. But they would know him soon, and both would wish they didn't.

Chapter Sixteen

Beckett Snow looked over his shoulder; no one threatened. He scanned passing faces for a sign of hostility, and studied autos as they cruised past looking for parking spaces. He felt for the bulk of the Ingram stashed inside a padded cardboard envelope. He felt reassured. The sun directly overhead was warm on his shoulders.

He continued along C Street, S.E. toward the park at Fourth Street, and halfway there he saw the panhandlers and derelicts stretched out in the unseasonably warm Washington weather. Snow froze and leaned against a black Mercedes at the curb. The derelict! The bum at the beach! His stomach tightened. He crouched at the curb, looking at the men through the window glass of the Mercedes. He closed his eyes. When he reopened them, the bums were just derelicts; they were always in the park, he knew it now. This was no time for an attack of nerves.

None of the derelicts seemed to take notice of Beckett Snow as he rounded the corner of Fourth and C Streets, trod cautiously through the gasoline station lot, and turned left on Pennsylvania Avenue and went through the door of the Dew Drop Inn.

Snow took a booth in the rear and sat facing the door to wait for Steve Drachler. The waitress came and took his order for a Pabst with a snarl, then tramped back to the bar, annoyed that a single tipper was sitting at a booth for four.

Snow scanned the walls of the bar that never failed to amuse him, deer heads and old guns, beer company lights, clocks and gadgets, the only menu—a sign on white posterboard—and a dozen pieces of kitsch. His eyes went again to the restrooms: over each door was the mounted rear end of a deer. Snow smiled.

The waitress brought his bottle of Pabst and a glass, her scowl softening slightly when he declined the glass and drank from the bottle. After that beer he ordered another. The lunch crowd was getting thicker now. He looked at his watch: 12:38. Drachler was nearly half an hour late now, and that was uncharacteristic. Snow tried to put it out of his mind.

Lunchtime diners came and went. Snow ordered a bowl of chili and another beer, and consumed them desultorily. No Drachler. At 1:09, Snow slid out of the booth. At the pay phone by the restrooms, he dialed Drachler's office. He was told that Drachler had left for lunch at 12:10. The newsman's office was only four blocks away.

Growing more and more anxious Snow plugged another 15 cents into the phone and dialed Drachler's home number. An unfamiliar voice answered.

"Hello, Steve?" Snow asked, thinking that he'd somehow mistaken his friend's voice.

"No. This isn't Mr. Drachler." The voice replied. It was official, suspicious. "Who is *this*?"

"A friend," Snow replied. "Is Steve there?"

"No. Well, yes, but why do you want to know?" the voice questioned. "Who are you?"

"I told you, I'm a friend. Now tell me why you're in my friend's apartment."

"And I asked you what your name is, buddy. I don't have time to play games." The voice bristled with hostility.

181

Snow placed his right hand over the disconnect lever, and slowly brought it to its fully depressed position.

Despite the coolness of the room, Snow felt perspiration trickling from his armpits down his ribs to make cool wet streaks in his shirt. Suddenly he realized: He was frightened. For an instant he fought panic, then he replaced the receiver, dropped a five dollar bill on the table, and walked out.

Snow walked down Pennsylvania Avenue through the lunchtime crowds. He stopped at the end of the block at a pay phone to give Tracy a call, and cursed when he discovered he had no more change save pennies. Snow slammed the receiver into its cradle and charged across Third Street, barely making the light.

Just past the old theatre, he saw a man on a motorcycle staring at him. Their eyes met. He'd seen the man somewhere before, and recently—but where? His pulse quickened. Quickly averting his eyes, Snow kept walking, holding the man in his peripheral vision.

"Excuse me, sir." The man on the motorcycle spoke. As he turned to face the man, Snow slid his hand inside the brown envelope. Safety off, finger on the trigger. It would be no trouble to fire through the envelope. They looked at each other neither moved.

The motorcycle was a beat-up Harley with battered panniers and a radio with a whip antenna and looked normal enough. Just another motorcycle delivery service vehicle like thousands in Washington.

Nor was the man on the bike exceptional looking. Snow figured him to be over six feet tall and in his middle twenties. Unkempt black hair formed banks in greasy strings; his blue jeans were nearly green at the thighs from constant hand wiping; a faded blue tee-shirt looked out from under a cracked and peeling black leather jacket.

The man smiled maliciously. His grin revealed two

rows of yellow, uncleaned teeth. The muddy stubble on his chin looked to be four or five days old.

"What do you want?" Snow demanded anxiously.

"Come here." Beckett made no move. Lunchtime crowds threaded their paths around him. "Come on, man. You want everybody passing by to hear our conversation?"

"No." Snow moved forward slowly. "I don't suppose so." He approached the motorcycle cautiously and stopped at arm's length away.

"Get your hand out of the envelope, Snow, you look ridiculous."

His name! The man knew his name! Snow grabbed him by the lapel of the leather jacket.

"How do you know my name? Who are you? What are you doing here? Tell me or I'll—"

"You'll do what?" The man asked and slowly drew himself up to his full height, which was greater than Snow expected. "Well, what are you going to do?" The tone was defiant. "Shoot me here on the sidewalk? In front of a hundred witnesses? Or maybe we want to get into a fistfight? That'd be nice, right? Get arrested— and you such a brutal murderer." The smile was gloating now; he had won.

Snow suddenly saw the ludicrous scene: his left hand reaching upward like Mutt threatening Jeff, his right hand swallowed by a large brown envelope, holding a gun. He slowly relaxed his grip on the man's jacket and sheepishly withdrew his hand from the envelope. He watched as the man, still smiling, sat down again on the motorcycle.

"Okay. Okay, you've got me. So what're you doing? You could've killed me by now, you seem to know my movements pretty well." Snow spoke calmly in measured tones that hid his fear; but the man failed to acknowledge.

"I have a delivery for you, Mr. Snow" the man said, but made no move to give him anything. Instead, he reached behind him and snatched his helmet and stuck it on his head and secured it. After he'd opened the visor, he turned the ignition of the motorcycle. The starter whined briefly and the cylinders fired. He goosed it twice.

"Oh yeah," he said as an afterthought, opening the right pannier and withdrawing from it a medium-sized box wrapped in brown paper. "Here . . ." He tossed the box at Snow and then accelerated into traffic. From habit, Snow's eyes leapt to get the license number; but the bike had none.

Snow's heart stopped. He felt like running after the man, but he knew immediately it was hopeless, as the man maneuvered expertly between lanes of traffic stopped at the light at Second Street, and then disappeared.

Snow strolled anxiously toward the house on C Street where Tracy was waiting for him. He fumbled nervously with the brown paper covering the package. He looked at it and saw it bore no markings, no writing of any kind. He examined both sides of the paper carefully, hoping it might contain a clue to the sender's identity, but he could find none. He wadded it into a ball and tossed it into a sidewalk refuse container.

Underneath the brown paper was a metal cracker box, the kind that contains four columns of soda crackers, each wrapped in wax paper.

Beckett Snow turned left at Second Street and passed Pete's Diner, he thought briefly of the superb barbecue the man served, and walked on, amazed that he could think of food in his current state of mind. He was going crazy. Who had been following him? Or had anyone followed him at all? Steve! They'd somehow learned of the lunch from Steve and then staked out the restaurant. Jesus! he thought, and here I am leading someone back to Tracy! He stopped abruptly in front of a red brick townhouse that was being gutted for restoration. He looked around, scanned faces, looked in the distance, behind him, across the street. If someone was following him, it was a pro.

Snow continued. He turned right on C Street, but instead of going into the house, he continued past it, crossed First Street, and took the escalator down into the Capitol South subway station.

The basic subway trick probably wouldn't work completely here, he thought. They probably worked in pairs. Even if he leapt off the train as the doors closed, leaving one trailer on the train, there might still be a partner left on the platform to pick him up. But on the other hand, it would eliminate one agent.

As he reached the bottom of the escalator, Snow paused deliberately to look at the people behind him. He could pick out no one who looked as if he were following him.

After getting through the gates and down the escalator to the platform, Snow paused by a trash container. He continued to pick at the tape that held the cracker box together.

A Blue Line train headed for downtown pulled into the station and disgorged its passengers. Most of the passengers waiting on the platform boarded, and the train glided from the station. He looked around. There were four people still waiting on the track with him: a fat woman with four shabby shopping bags; a tall man in a dark blue three-piece suit, and two girls who looked like high school students.

If one of them was the tail, he thought, it had to be the man with the suit, although it could conceivably be the old woman, in makeup and disguise.

Snow's fingers worked at the box, which was wrapped in layer after layer of reinforced strapping tape. He rummaged in his pocket for his Swiss Army knife, but decided to wait, as lights announced the arrival of a train toward the Stadium Armory Station.

Snow got on, carefully noting that all of the people waiting with him boarded the train, along with two other men, both in their forties, casually dressed, who had just arrived.

The doorbell chime sounded, and as the doors started to close, Snow leaped out through the narrow gap. As the doors slid shut, Snow saw a man spring toward the door and attempt to pry it open. He was a nondescript man, about 40 years old, with greasy, thinning hair, and a polyester plaid sportcoat.

Snow saw the man struggling with the door and watched as it started to open.

Snow ran for the escalator, taking the moving steps two at a time. He sprinted for the gates. He could hear the train's driver shouting angrily at someone; the man had succeeded in getting out of the train.

At the top of the escalator Snow paused for only a second to gain his bearings. He still held the cracker box, cradled between the crook of his arm and his hand like a football. Behind him he heard shouts and loud footsteps. Run! But where? He couldn't risk the house.

He ran east to D Street and turned right. He saw the man emerge from the Metro entrance. Snow also noticed another man run from the shelter of a tree to join him. At New Jersey Avenue, Snow crossed against the light, vaulted a low wire fence, and began scrambling down an embankment to the railway tunnel which led under the Capitol to Union Station. It was a twin tunnel that had received a great deal of use before passenger trains had started to die. Today, he knew, only one tunnel was in use.

In the darkness of the tunnel he stumbled, fell, and got up again running. The surface was uneven, the ties spaced too wide for easy running, and the tracks were littered with rocks and garbage. About 50 yards into the tunnel, a utility closet protruded from the rock wall; he pressed his back against the wall behind it. He could see the man with the sportcoat slide down the embankment and peer into the darkness. He disappeared for a moment, Snow figured to peer into the other tunnel, and then rematerialized in the hemicircle of light of the tunnel mouth. Shortly, another man dressed in overalls joined the man in the brown pants. They conferred. And then the man in the brown pants started walking cautiously down the tunnel, his arm bent at the elbow, hand in front of him. He was carrying a gun.

Without allowing his body to break the profile of the utility closet, Snow slid the cracker box to the ground. He reached into the brown envelope and withdrew the Ingram. But seconds later, he crammed it back in the envelope. His second thought was risky but potentially more fruitful, he wanted information from the man.

He unbuckled his belt, withdrew his knife, and unfolded its longest blade. Even though it was only three inches long, it would feel like a dagger in the dark.

The man in the brown pants was getting closer. Snow didn't dare to chance a peek, but he could hear the cautious steps, the quiet tread of a man who was listening for other steps.

Snow fed the end of his belt through the buckle to make a noose. The man's steps grew louder. Snow could now hear heavy breathing. A pebble clattered. When it came to a rest, there was no sound at all. Snow breathed through his mouth, assuring silence even though he was gulping air in fear. Blood rushed through his ears, sounding his own pulse in the stillness.

Nothing.

Had the man in the brown pants spotted him? Was he creeping up on him at this very moment? Snow considered the gun again. No. The noise would surely give him away now.

Snow waited tensely, thoughts flashing through his mind. If the man had wanted to kill him, he could have done it on the street. No, he was probably working with the man on the motorcycle. But that didn't answer any questions, for who was the man on the motorcycle working for, and what about the man who joined the man in the brown pants? Shit! People were coming out of the woodwork and he had no idea what they wanted.

If only he could get the man in the brown pants to talk. As he thought it through, Snow felt confident the man wouldn't try to kill him unless his own life was threatened.

Time passed with a limp. Snow grew edgier and edgier. Something *had* to happen. He thought of confronting the man.

Then there was the grinding of grit beneath a shoe, a tentative step. Then a genuine step. The man was moving again.

Snow positioned himself. He held the looped belt in his left hand, knife in the right. As a shadow dimly slid past, he caught his breath. As the man drew near, Snow threw the loop over his neck, pulled the loose end with his right hand, and threw his weight against the man's body. They both fell to the tracks, Snow's knee in the small of the man's back. The man's gun clattered to the tracks.

"One word, and I'll cut your throat," Snow hissed. He couldn't be sure if the other man had waited at the entrance or had taken the other tunnel. Brown pants clutched his neck when the belt tightened against it. The tight grip strangled every sound the man could make save for feeble gagging.

Brown pants lay still and Snow eased up on the belt. "Now, I'm going to slack up some more because I want some answers," Snow told him. "But if you make any impolite moves, you're not going to walk out of this tunnel. Understand?" The man nodded. With one swift motion, Snow released the belt and snatched the gun from the ground. It was a Ruger .357 magnum with an unwieldly sausage-shaped silencer attached to the muzzle.

The man slowly pushed himself from his prone position and sat upright, rubbing his neck. He uncollared himself and tossed the belt at Snow's feet.

"You can't stop us," the man snarled insolently.

"Who's 'we'?" Snow asked. "The Delphi Commission?"

"Those shits! Double-crossing scumbags! No, Mr. Snow, we're people who believe, not in corporations for the sake of corporations, we believe in people and we all believe in a great one. To tell you would be to endanger our cause. You can help us. If you choose to help us then you'll know, but once you know, you're in for life."

"Like the Mafia?" Snow was amused by the theatrics of the man, the drama in his voice.

"No, not like the Mafia, damnit!" The man had a short fuse. "More like . . . like . . . it's not like anything else. It has its own code."

"Well, that may be so, but you're not going anywhere until I get some answers from you. Like who was the man on the motorcycle? Does he work for you?"

There was no response.

"Have you killed Steve Drachler?"

There was still no response.

"Are you part of the Consortium?"

The man gave no response, but Snow thought there was a flicker of recognition, faint and hard to discern in the twilight of the tunnel.

"Look, Mr. Snow, you're not going to get answers

from me, and you're not going to get out of this tunnel without us knowing."

"What do you want? Do you want to kill me? You . . ."

"We could have done that a number of times."

"That's what I was about to say. So what is it you want? What?"

"I think you know."

"The box?"

"Yes, and your cooperation."

"What sort of cooperation?"

"You'll find out when the time comes."

"And what if I decide the time won't come? What if I don't like being pushed around? What if I decide to kill you and walk out of here."

"I'll take the last question. You see, there are two men with radios outside on both ends. I followed you down this tunnel, and another man is in the other one. They won't hurt you. No, they'll only confront you with the same problems I'm presenting to you."

Snow was fascinated by the man's obtuseness. But he was mad, frustrated, boxed in. He had to know what was happening.

"You filthy shit," Snow kicked brown pants in the testicles. He doubled in pain and wallowed on the floor of the tunnel. "Tell me, or you're going to crawl out of this a fucking soprano." The man was in a fetal position. Snow moved closer, intending a kick to the man's kidney when there was a muffled explosion. The man's body jerked to its full length like every muscle had tetanused at once. The back of the man's head was missing and though the light was dim, Snow could see the red-stained white of the man's brain staring from the gaping wound and splattered on his sleeve.

Snow rolled him over and a single shot derringer fell from the man's mouth.

Revolted, Snow turned from the man, picked up the

soda cracker box, and sat down on the rail to think. He couldn't walk out of the tunnel.

He looked at his watch: 3:50 PM. Snow knew there were Amtrak trains that still used the track, but he wasn't sure of the times. No matter; he would wait. He had to. It would be his only way out. He'd hop aboard one and ride it into the station. The train would give him a cover, and with that he might be able to lose their man at the other end.

Snow slowly raised himself from his sitting position and walked over to look at the dead man. So many people hurt, and for what? The man had killed himself rather than give information. What had the man said . . . *we believe in people and we all believe in a great one*? But who, and what organization could inspire people to a willing death? *It has its own code.*

This was too much! Snow's training as a copy had provided him with experience to tread in a dangerous forest, but there he dealt with people who had motives —profit, greed, revenge—and seldom with fanatics. And never this! Snow sat back on the tracks, his eyes on the corpse. So many . . . To escape from the tunnel, get Tracy, and disappear; run away from the whole thing. Run, run!

Snow sat for ten minutes, fifteen. He felt vibrations. A train! Snow's head snapped up, but no train was visible yet. He scrambled to the body and dragged it behind the utility closet. He had to hide the body. If it were spotted by the engineer, the train might stop and Snow would be discovered.

The body, still limp, refused to stay in the cramped space, sprawling over the track each time Snow released it. Now he could clearly hear the train. He looked up and saw it framed in the half circle of light at the tunnel's end. Panting from exertion and fear, Snow remembered his belt, which the man had tossed at him. He bent over and snatched it from the ground.

Snow peered into the dankness of the utility closet wall and spied an electrical conduit emerging about six feet up on the wall.

With the belt looped over the dead man's neck, Snow hauled the free end to the conduit and looped it over, keeping the body pinned against the wall with his own. The sweet smell of blood and the aroma of interior organs nauseated him. One overhand knot and then another was twisted in place. He had to strain on his tiptoes to complete the task.

The body slumped, looking like the aftermath of a lynching. But, Snow noted, it was out of the train engineer's line of sight.

The light from the train's nose illuminated the tunnel and soon it lumbered by at a crawl, the red, white, and blue Amtrak cars passing sluggishly. Snow left the man's hand gun in the tunnel, grabbed the cracker box and brown envelope, and leapt at the brakeman's station on the rear of the last car. He thought his shoulder would be pulled from its socket, and he knew he'd be sore later, but he hung on.

Linking his left arm through the handhold, Snow transferred his packages to his left hand and tinkered with the train's rear door. The latch moved freely; in seconds, he was inside. He closed the door carefully and walked into the restroom.

His hair was thrown in a dozen directions, and his jacket was splattered with blood. A red-grey glob of the man's brain clung tenaciously to his lapel, Snow's face was smudged with soot from the tunnel and his hands were black with greasy dirt.

He removed his jacket and discarded it, scrubbed his hands and face and ran his fingers through his hair to smooth it. Snow surveyed the results and thought himself presentable enough to escape undue attention at the station.

As the train slowed, Snow exited the restroom, and

strolled with a practiced nonchalance toward the front of the train. He was looking for a crowd of people to exit with, and he found them in the next car.

The crowd held cohesively together along the platform, and Snow succeeded in hiding in their midst. At the vast high-ceilinged waiting room, everyone dispersed, and Snow headed east to the cab station.

"Fourth and E, Southeast," he told the driver and settled into the rear seat. Snow loosed a long sigh of relief, and relaxed as the cab circled around the statuary in front of Union Station and headed up Massachusetts Avenue.

The brown envelope with its deadly contents was settled securely on the seat beside him. Snow leaned back and straightened as he fumbled for his Swiss Army knife, and, failing to retrieve it, remembered that it lay somewhere on the floor of a railroad tunnel near a dead man. A pang of separation hit him as he remembered how many years he'd possessed the knife, genuine Swiss Army, purchased in Geneva.

Oh hell, he thought, if that were only the worst thing that had occurred.

Hampered without a cutting blade, Snow nevertheless attacked the tape-bound cracker box he had received from the mysterious man on a motorcycle. He found an end to a strip of tape and unwound it, and then another, and finally enough was unbound to allow him to open the other end.

He removed the end and pulled out a plastic bag.

Beckett Snow stared transfixed at a human hand.

The hand had been crudely amputated at the wrist, and the tendons and nerves and blood vessels dangled from the cut stump in a mass of gelatinous blood. The hand was gnarled in a grotesque spastic shape. On it was a ring he recognized! It belonged to Steve Drachler.

Shocked, Snow slid the hand under the seat of the cab and retained the box.

193

Snow blankly paid the driver and tipped him.

The former federal prosecutor strode toward the house on C Street, and to Tracy. He wouldn't tell her about Steve, yet. And he also wouldn't witness the screams of terror shrieked by a middle-aged schoolteacher who would discover the hand while returning by taxi from a PTA meeting later that night. He wouldn't hear her, but he had already shared her horror.

The newspaper story acclaimed Isaac Roth as one of the great unseen powers of American government, mentioned the sacrifices he had made for 40 years, and ran a picture of him on the front page (dressed in a poplin windbreaker at Camp David, 1963). It was a fitting tribute, Peter Gilbert thought as he angrily rammed the Capital final edition of the *Star* into a refuse bin at the northeast corner of Lafayette Park.

He was gone. Isaac Roth was really gone.

Peter had held out hope, after the call from Roth's sister, hope that she was just addled. But less than an hour later he got a call from the assistant security chief of the National Security Council to tell him that Roth's body had been found, drowned, on a sunken sailboat.

Now, four hours later, after wandering over half of northwest Washington, Peter Gilbert still carried the undiminished pain, the bewilderment, the . . . what was he feeling: alone?

He paused at a pay phone, intending to call his office and tell them he was sick. Fuck 'em! he thought as he slammed down the receiver. They weren't worth the 15 cents. The whole lot of them weren't worth half of what Isaac Roth had meant to him.

Gilbert wandered across Lafayette Park, the President's Park, and sat on an empty bench that faced the White House. Isaac had been more important to him than any other human being in the world ever had. And now he was gone.

Something had to be done, Gilbert thought. But what? Nothing in his experience or his training had prepared him to defend someone or seek revenge. He'd been bred to lead. But now he knew he must decide whether a deep friendship was worth risking his career, his carefully plotted future.

And as he sat with the White House transfixed in his mind, with its too-green lawns and too-perfect trees, and the limos gliding through the wrought-iron gates, Peter Gilbert knew he would—knew he must—find out who killed Isaac Roth. And then he'd kill them.

"I think he's coming along fine, just fine," Eric Simon said to the man in the scruffy black leather jacket. "You've done an outstanding job. Pretty soon, he'll do anything we tell him. The man's got good judgment. But I think we've got the means to bend that judgment to our good. Got a make on the professor?" The man nodded. "Good. You've got your instructions. I'll meet with you afterwards." The man in the leather jacket smiled and left. Simon turned to papers on his desk.

"Well, it's clear that the first thing we've got to do is get the hell out of here," Tracy said. "We can't stay here."

Snow nodded. They were reclining across the bed in the borrowed apartment. He'd told her of the man on the motorcycle, discovering the tail on the subway, the chase, and finally discovering Drachler's hand in the box.

"I'm not *sure* they know the place," Snow said. "After all, Steve might not have told them. We—"

"We can't be sure."

"True, but look—they didn't hurt me. They're not Commission people."

"They could be. Maybe they just wanted to keep you alive so you could lead them to the files."

"No," said Beckett. "You didn't see the man's eyes. There was a genuine hatred there when I mentioned the Commission. He wasn't lying about that. But you're right about them wanting the dossier. And you could very well be right about getting away from here. But it seems like a waste of time. Just about everything we've been able to do to hide has been thwarted."

"It's scary," Tracy said. "We've been able to elude the Commission, but not this group of people, whoever they are."

"What's really scary to me," Snow said, "is how easy it's getting to kill. It's just too easy, too easy." He turned to look at her.

"But it's us or them," Tracy said. Snow nodded.

"Wouldn't it be nice to just take the money you've got and run away?" Snow asked.

"Sure, but only if you like running," Tracy said. "You think they wouldn't find us eventually? It's like escaped convicts who eventually turn themselves in: They get tired of running." She leaned over and kissed him lightly on the forehead.

"I know you're right, but it's handy to have a fantasy. Besides, I owe Drachler. That alone would keep me from running away. He was a good person, a rare one.

"I owe him. And Nelson too," Snow mumbled, remembering the dead LAPD inspector.

"But who owes us?" Tracy asked sadly. Snow's face trembled, then hardened.

"A lot of people we don't know yet."

The connection was crisp and clear, but the scrambler delay gave the conversation a slightly disjointed quality.

"Stefan, the old man's pissed."

"Jesus, didn't you tell him I was opposed to using that goddamned amateur daughter of his?"

"It doesn't make any difference, Stefan. The man's mad. I tried to cool him down, but the only thing that's going to satisfy him is the return of the dossier. There's no other alternative." Carothers's voice was authoritative, unyielding.

"Yes sir," Sherbok replied, "I understand."

"Good. I'm glad. On a brighter note, I see by the papers you have done an admirable job with that old curmudgeon."

"Thank you."

"It was necessary. The man's been a pain in the ass for four decades, a traitor to his legacy. By the way, how's the fellow Gilbert you told me about doing?"

"I don't think we've got any problems. He's alert and he's dedicated. In fact, he's one of the hardest people I've ever met. I can't ever remember him making a decision on the basis of an emotion. . . . No, he's a hard cold operator and he knows where his interests lie. . . . He took off the day, but I think it's for appearances. He knows he'd offend people if he didn't appear saddened. Is there anything else?"

"No, Stefan, that's all. Get the dossier, understand?"

"Yes sir."

"Goodbye."

"Goodbye."

Chapter Seventeen

"What do you make of it?"

"It's a curious conglomeration," Snow replied. "But what does it mean? It's a riddle."

They had returned to the townhouse on Capitol Hill from a visit with Snow's professorial friend who had succeeded in opening the strange grey box. The man had been apologetic, for the contents were a single piece of Carothers's stationery with notations in the former vice president's handwriting; a tiny, torn photograph of Carothers's that looked as if it belonged in a locket; and a tattered Star of David, fashioned from a coarse yellow cloth. The items were spread out on the sofa between them.

"I think that question is easier to answer than what the meaning is," Tracy began.

"First of all, this isn't an end. It leads somewhere, to something he's hidden."

"I feel that too."

"But you said earlier that Carothers wanted you to get this to the President. He's on the Commission too. Wouldn't it have made more sense for him to just have given the stuff to the President himself?"

"I don't know. Maybe it wouldn't have carried the same meaning then as after Adam's death," Tracy replied.

"Yeah, maybe," Snow mumbled. "There are just too many maybes in all this." He was silent.

"Well, okay, so what have we got here?" He picked up the stationery. "Two words: *'het Achterhuis.'* Two lousy words and they're not even in English."

"They sound German," Tracy offered.

"Or Dutch. Yes, Dutch, I think. Somehow, those two words are familiar, though I don't know why. But I'm going to find out."

He reached for the telephone and dialed. "CRS, please," he told the operator. "Yes, this is Anthony Bevilacqua in Congressman Savrona's office, 5-2842, could you translate a couple of words for me, I think they're Dutch . . . yes. Yes, well I'm in the middle of a piece of correspondence and need it in a hurry, could you look it up and just give me the dictionary meanings? Yes . . . thank you. The first word is *het*, H-E-T . . . right. The second one is a long one. You'll probably have to look up two words. The word is *Achterhuis.*" He spelled it out. "Why don't you look under *achter* and *huis*, okay? Thank you."

Snow smiled while he was put on hold.

"What did you do?"

"The Library of Congress has a special research service for members of Congress. I just picked out one I knew, used the name of a friend of mine who works for him—hello, yes, I'm still here. Thank you. The first word means 'the', okay . . . *achter* means 'behind, or in back of', and *huis* is 'house.' Thank you very much. Goodbye." Snow hung up.

"The behind house," he repeated.

"Outhouse?" Tracy suggested.

"Did he have one?"

"Not that I know of."

"Maybe at one of his mountain properties? Could he have hidden something in the outhouse?"

"I doubt it." Tracy said. "The people from the Commission searched everything pretty thoroughly. I don't think Adam would have hidden anything there."

"Okay, let's take things together: There's a picture of him. And the Star of David, like something from a concentration camp. So, maybe we can presume that *het Achterhuis* has some Jewish connection. But what?"

They sat in silence, thinking.

"The behind house, *het Achterhuis;* Dutch, Jewish, concentration camps," Tracy said, her voice near a murmur.

Snow leaped from his seat. "Shit, I know it. . . . I *know* it! Wait. You said it . . . Dutch and Jewish: Anne Frank. They lived in a secret compartment. It was a little house behind a house: *het Achterhuis.* And the star, it's like the Jews had to wear in Europe. What a great place for someone like Adam to hide his secret: in Anne Frank's house in Amsterdam!"

They looked at each other in silent awe. Things had fit together too well to be coincidence. There was something waiting in Amsterdam.

"I've been there," Snow began. "It was an eerie place, like . . ."

Snow's sentence was truncated by the sound of shattering glass coming from the bedroom.

"Get down on the floor!" he yelled and scrambled for the Ingram.

Snow moved on his hands and knees to the bedroom door. Beside the door, he stood up, his back flattened against the wall. He listened and heard nothing besides the rasping of his own breath. No sound came from the room. Snow threw open the door. There was no response. Slowly he peered around the jamb.

Nothing in his life could prepare him for the scene which confronted him. It was horrible beyond nightmares and real beyond life itself. Bathed in the late afternoon light was a human head—the object which had been hurtled through the window, putted like a shot from somewhere below. The head was that of the professor who greeted them with such warmth only two hours before.

Snow rushed to the shattered window and stood transfixed as the man in the black leather jacket waved at him and gunned the motorcycle out of the alley and into traffic.

"Beck, what is it? What happened?" Tracy had been squatting behind an overstuffed armchair. She straightened up and started for the room.

"Don't. Don't go in there." Something in his voice made her stop. Her face turned ashen when he told her.

"Tracy, you're right. Let's get the hell out of here."

A plan was coming into focus. Snow ordered her: "Don't pack. Just grab anything that has your name on it, anything the police could use in identifying us, and whatever you need for survival. Leave the rest. We may have to do some running."

In less than 15 minutes they were waiting by the door, ready to move. Snow had outlined his plan. "It's risky, but I think we have to take the chance," he said. Tracy nodded.

"Okay, let's go!" They ran the half block to the Metro. A train headed downtown was decelerating beside the platform. Snow thought he recognized one of the passengers that boarded with them, but he couldn't remember if it was a face he'd seen in the last week of running, or from the time he was legitimate. Legitimate! The irony, Snow thought. He and Tracy were the ones who *were* legitimate, and the others *weren't*. But they were fugitives—not from justice, but from injustice and death.

The train gathered speed and glided toward the dark gaping mouth of the tunnel. Snow was looking up toward the escalators when suddenly he spotted the man in the black leather jacket.

"There!" Snow pointed his finger and twisted in his seat, pressing his face against the glass of the car window. "That's the man!" They watched as the man receded into the distance and the car was swallowed by darkness. Soon all that was visible was a mirror-like image of themselves in the glass.

They disembarked at Metro Center, entered the Washington Hotel through a side entrance, and grabbed a cab in front.

"Capitol Hilton," he told the driver.

"This may thin them out," he whispered to Tracy. "But it won't throw them off our tracks entirely, not yet."

Five minutes later they walked into the convention-eer-jammed lobby of the Hilton at Sixteenth and K Streets, two blocks from the White House.

Who are they? thought Snow, looking around. Which ones? That man in the grey slacks and blue blazer? The woman with the slim attache case? A busboy? Who? They had shown themselves in the past days as more organized than any surveillance team he had ever dealt with.

Snow touched Tracy's elbow. "This is where it gets tricky."

The pair threaded their way through the crowds, hampered only by airline shoulder bags.

"Head for the elevators," Snow directed.

They boarded with a mob of conventioneers. Tracy and Beckett sighed when they all got off on the same floor, thankful that hotels tend to put conventioneers in blocks by themselves when possible.

Snow pushed the button for the top floor and while they rode examined the ceiling panels. The maintenance access panel was visible, half-hidden in the shadows.

"Okay, when we get to the top, pull the red stop button," Snow said. "It probably won't ring a bell. Bellhops in hotels like this use them too frequently, so the bells have usually been disconnected. Let's hope." The elevator decelerated to a halt. "Now!" Tracy pulled the button. There was not a sound. "Hurry, up on my shoulders, we haven't got much time. I'm sure they must have sent someone up the stairs."

Snow squatted and Tracy looped her legs over his shoulders. He stood up to bring her to ceiling level. She manipulated the maintenance hatch.

"There!" She had the panel open.

"Okay, stand up on my shoulders and climb up. Stay away from cables and machinery, but not so close you'll hit part of the shaft."

He helped her onto the roof of the elevator cab and handed up their flight bags. He could hear a stairwell door close. Snow released the stop button, and the elevator door shut immediately.

As the elevator plunged swiftly, Snow used the downward acceleration to advantage, leaping to grab the edge of the open hatch. Slowly he pulled himself to a position beside Tracy. The walls of the shaft moved by now with a dizzying regularity and speed.

After a careful search, Snow managed to locate the control bypass box. It was unmarked.

"Well, here goes nothing," he whispered. He flipped one lever and the car shot up. Another switch stopped the car, a third made it move downward. He tried them all, one by one, to determine the function of each.

"I guess that'll do us," Snow remarked. "We'd better make our moves before the repairman comes. He's gonna be surprised." He flicked the switch that sent them hurtling downward. The car automatically slowed to a halt. A flip of the switch immobilized the elevator cab. They were at the bottom of the shaft in the lowest parking garage level.

"This one opens the doors," Snow told Tracy and briefly touched the switch with his index finger. "Don't throw it until I tell you. Okay?"

With that, he opened the hatch to the elevator cab, withdrew the Ingram, and wedged it into the front of his pants.

Tracy grinned ruefully. "Careful, you could hurt yourself like that," she whispered as he lowered himself through the opening. When his feet were about two feet from the floor, he dropped, bending his knees to absorb the shock and make as little noise as possible.

Somewhere outside, there would be a man watching the elevators. Just as there would be someone keeping an eye on the parking garage and all other exits of the hotel.

With the Ingram gripped firmly, safety in the "off" position, Snow whispered for Tracy to open the door. It rumbled open. Snow stayed wedged into the corner.

At first he heard nothing, and then a low sliding sound, from the corridor. It *had* to be surveillance.

Snow sprang into the corridor and squeezed the Ingram's trigger as the man's hand flew to his pocket. Snow's hand was steady, but his insides winced as the slugs slap-thudded into the man's chest.

The man fell, his grey flannel suit ripped in the front, the club tie severed by the crude hacking of bullets. Snow had aimed for the chest, the heart, because the sooner it stopped bleeding, the less blood would be spread on the corridor floor. Snow had seen people stabbed or shot in the heart who had left no blood at all when they fell. Snow looked at the floor indicator above the other two elevators, and saw one was descending.

"Tracy, Tracy!" There was a muffled response. "Throw down the bags and get out here. We've got to hurry."

As Snow bent over the limp form of the man, he heard first one bag thump to the elevator floor, then a second. As he reached into the man's breast pocket, he heard a heavier thud which he assumed was Tracy.

The man had been reaching for a silenced .357 magnum revolver strapped in a shoulder holster.

Snow decided to leave the man's belongings intact. The revolver might identify him as a hit man, and make police less likely to come looking for private citizens. Tracy arrived.

"Oh, God! Isn't this ever going to stop?"

"Soon, I hope. Soon. Help me move him into the garage. Someone's coming." Snow glanced at the floor indicator. Another elevator was about to stop on the garage level. Hastily, they lugged the man's body out of the corridor and into the parking garage. Snow noted with satisfaction that there was but a tiny puddle of blood on the floor. Something, he figured, that wouldn't attract a great deal of attention.

They heard the elevator doors open.

"There, against the wall," Tracy said. "The trash can." Snow spotted it, a 55-gallon oil drum with the top cut out. They scurried toward it, but before they could reach it, the door to the elevator corridor started to open. They heard voices.

"Quick, beside the pillar." They tossed the body on the pavement and lay down beside it, hidden from the gaze of the people who had just entered the garage. Snow fingered the Ingram, and prayed the people would go in the opposite direction. From this point on, their escape was dependent on being observed by no one, not even innocent bystanders.

The group chattered as they headed toward Beckett and Tracy. Snow tightened his grip on the gun and flicked the safety off. The group got closer. From their voices they sounded elderly, and there were at least three of them.

Their footsteps grew louder. The conversation became intelligible. It was about grandchildren and a son who had done so well in Washington.

Snow brought the gun in front of him. Tracy put a hand on his arm. "Beck, no." Snow shoved her hand away. Survive. Survive. Survive.

Just as Snow thought they would come into sight, the group reached their auto. There were sounds of doors being unlocked, opened, slammed shut. A balky engine fired, and the automatic transmission—reverse —slowly, drive. The sound of the car diminished.

Snow flicked the safety of the machine pistol on again, and rested his head in the crook of his arm.

"Thank God. Thank God!" He muttered. "Oh, Jesus, I'm glad." His hands were shaking.

"Yes," Tracy echoed. "Thank God."

But as suddenly as the shakes had begun, they disappeared.

"Okay, let's finish this." Beckett looked at the dead man. "Go over to the barrel and remove the trash from it. Put it on the ground beside the can."

Tracy obeyed while Snow half-carried, half-dragged the lifeless form, and with her assistance, dumped it unceremoniously into the can, head first, and then arranged arms and legs to make it fit. Finally, they covered the corpse with the litter that Tracy had removed.

"That should give us a little time," Snow said. "All right, let's find a way out of here. Check the cars with stickers like this," he said fingering a cardboard chit wedged under the windshield wiper of an auto. "These are for people who aren't guests here—means they're likely to leave sooner than guests. Okay? Then let's find one with the keys in it."

"The keys? I can't believe people still do that."

"Believe it. The insurance companies do, cops too."

It took them fewer than 10 minutes to find a car with the door unlocked and keys in the ignition. Snow removed the keys and unlocked the trunk of the car, a four-year-old Chrysler. Snow climbed into the trunk.

"I want to make sure I can open the lid from inside," he explained. "Shut it, okay?" Tracy complied.

Fearful the car's owner might return at any minute, Tracy looked around her anxiously, listening for the sounds of the elevator door opening, thinking about the almost endless string of killings. How could it get so easy to accept? One by one, the body's sensibilities were harder and harder to offend.

She heard the metallic thunks of Snow tinkering with the trunk latch with his new Swiss Army knife. Snow cursed, his exact profanity muffled by the closed lid, and finally it opened.

"No sweat."

They left the lid opened, replaced the keys, and closed the door. Snow then sprinted into the elevator lobby, snatched their bags, ran back to the car, and threw them into the trunk. He plucked a pop-top ring from the garage floor, bent it until it broke, and inserted the broken pieces into the trunk lock, to make it impossible to open from the outside.

Climbing into the backseat, Snow tugged at the top of the seat back, and handily loosened it to allow a tiny bit of air to circulate into the trunk.

"After you, Mademoiselle," with exaggerated courtesy Snow motioned Tracy toward the trunk, and then climbed in after her.

"Ouch! Your elbow." Tracy complained as Snow attempted to close the trunk lid in the cramped space.

"Sorry," Snow said after he'd closed the trunk and settled down in the stale darkness, "I tried to get first-class tickets but they were overbooked."

Tracy squirmed until she was face-to-face with Beckett.

"I forgive you . . . this time," she said as she kissed him lightly on his cheek.

They lay in the trunk for what seemed like ages. The air grew stale and thick, and Beckett began to worry about what might happen if someone sat on the rear seat and shoved the cushion back into place.

They fretted in the darkness for more than two hours when finally they felt the car shake as the doors opened and closed and finally the auto bumped and jolted out of the garage and onto city streets. Shortly the seismic bouncing calmed as they entered what Beckett thought must be a highway. Expansion joints beating faster and faster beneath the tires told him they were probably on one of the freeways leading out of the city.

The air got stuffier as it got hotter from the exhaust pipe that led under the trunk. Tracy and Beckett sweated and resisted the urge to cough. Dust was stirring in the heat and just as the two fugitives believed it was unbearable, the car began to slow and then came to a stop. After several turns, the engine died and the occupants of the auto left.

It was an almost intolerable five minutes, but they waited until they were sure the car's occupants were gone. Snow fiddled with the trunk lock; it released on the second try and they both climbed out cautiously, shut the trunk, and walked casually away.

"Where . . . where are we?" Tracy asked as she looked around her at the mammoth parking lot and huge brick structure.

"Springfield Mall," Snow said as he slapped dust off his trousers. "We're in Virginia, about 12 miles south of Washington."

Tracy said nothing and they walked in silence to the mall, where Beckett called for a taxi.

In the cab on the silent drive back into Washington, they held hands letting touch be their communication.

As they passed the Pentagon and entered that twisted section of freeway known as the Mixing Bowl, Snow looked at Tracy. Why were they going back? he wondered. Were they going back to the destruction of the enemy or of themselves? Perhaps it might just be better to run.

Chapter Eighteen

The waiter parted the curtains. Peter Gilbert rose from his seat.

"Hello, Peter." Leslie Lewis's voice was polite, but all business.

"I'm glad you could come, especially on such short notice."

"My curiosity wouldn't let me stay away," she said coolly.

"Yes. Yes, I'm sure."

She sat down, surveyed the surroundings. The booth was completely enclosed, curtains blocking its interior from the eyes of passersby.

"The . . . the events of the past couple of days have made . . . have had an effect on me," he said. "That's why I had to call you."

"Why me?"

"Why? Yes. I'm sure that seems strange to you. It seems strange to me also, but it's because . . . because I couldn't . . . that is, there isn't anyone else . . . that I could call on."

"I see."

"No, you don't see yet," Gilbert continued. "I was quite upset after our last meeting and then I got a telephone call the next morning. It was from Isaac Roth's sister."

"Tragic accident. He was such a kind old man, I thought, charming in his own way."

"Yes. In his own way he was a lot to a lot of people. I thought of him as a father. But the point was, the telephone call from his sister . . . she said he was murdered!"

"Murdered? By whom? Who'd want him dead?"

Gilbert then told her about the discussions he and Roth had had, their arguments, their differing positions on the Delphi Commission.

"But come on, Peter. Corporate executives don't go around bumping people off, especially ones like Roth. They're—"

"They do go around threatening and coercing people," Peter said.

"Yes," Leslie responded. "They do, don't they?"

They stopped as the waiter eased through the curtains to take their drink order. When he'd left, Gilbert continued.

"Anyway, I started checking through the computer files and there were missing segments, missing data that should have been in the file. I got codes that indicated that some information was being kept in hard copy—on paper—in Sherbok's office."

"What's so unusual about that?"

"You don't understand. *I* set up the system. Everything pertaining to the Commission, from the money it spends on paper clips, to the blood types of its members, to their decisions on international matters, is supposed to be in the computer.

"But there are two missing files—not missing, incomplete—that are kept in Sherbok's office, and damn it, they're not supposed to be!"

"What files were missing?" Leslie asked.

"There was a notation for Project Prometheus. *Some* information was there, but the computer said 'map by NSA', which I assume means that the full plan for it is in Sherbok's office."

"What's Project Prometheus?"

"It's—" Gilbert looked at her, watched as she sensed his reluctance. "You know I'm going to get my ass in trouble if you repeat this?"

"Did you think that both our asses might already be in trouble?"

"Yes. Yes, you're probably right." He took a deep breath. "Uh . . . I, ah, suppose the best way to begin is to tell you what I do.

"My part in Prometheus is strictly logistics. I keep track of the locations of all our members and their alternates and agents and staff members wherever they are in the world. And I also keep track of the locations and the amounts of their assets and investments— deposits of foreign currency and what bank they're in and the names of the bank officers, stocks and bonds and what exchange they're traded on and where they're kept and their precise market value from moment to moment when the exchanges are open. All that sort of thing. There's more, but for the most part, I know where the members and their assets are."

Leslie leaned forward, fascinated.

"Why do you need to know?"

"I honestly don't know. Like most big corporate structures, things are done on a 'need to know' basis. So I don't know."

"Guess?"

"Maybe they just need the information; maybe they want to know everything in case they have to bring pressure to bear somewhere; maybe for investments; maybe to back up a push for a country to develop a certain program the Commission members want."

"How would they do that?"

Peter sighed, tilted his head back and then began: "Easy. Suppose a country is setting monetary policy that's going to hurt a Commission member. They tell the country that unless the government sets a more sympathetic policy, then the Commission is going to pull their deposits out of all the banks."

"So?"

"So," Peter hesitated, overcome momentarily by anxiety, doubt at trusting her. He recovered. "The 'so' is that the Commission members control so much currency, that a shifting of even four or five percent is enough to send the currency of a government spiralling. If they wanted to, they could make the currency of a country worthless overnight."

"No shit?"

"No shit. They could do the same thing with stocks and bonds. They could bankrupt companies, blow entire countries right out of the economic water."

The curtains parted, and the waiter returned to take their order, the third time he'd come for that purpose. After the waiter left, they resumed.

"Do you really think that Isaac Roth was murdered?"

"I can't say he wasn't, and that bothers me," Peter said. "You see, the second computer file that the computer said was stored in Sherbok's office was one on personnel. It was called alterations and sanctions."

"Is that unusual?"

"Beyond the fact that the file was missing? Yes. Does the word 'sanction' mean anything to you?"

"I remember a spy book or something with that in the title."

"Right. That's it. Sanction is spy terminology means a murder, an assassination, an elimination of an enemy agent."

"And you think that's what it means in the file?"

"It could. Look, all the other personnel files are there—everything, every detail, personal foibles, sexual tastes, the whole picture of a person, not only on the Commission members, but on hundreds of thousands of people worldwide that dossiers have been compiled on. What's more sensitive than that; what has to be kept even more secure?" He looked at her, waiting for her reaction.

"Uhmmm, I can't think of anything."

"Neither have I," Peter said. "That doesn't mean it fails to exist, but it makes me suspicious as hell."

"That they killed Isaac Roth?"

"That they killed Isaac Roth."

It was all the busboy needed to hear. He'd been lingering near the set-up table most of the evening, eavesdropping on the couple in the booth. He quietly replaced the glasses he had been carrying, draped the washcloth over the chrome rack next to the napkins, and walked out of the restaurant to his car.

"So what do you intend to do about it?"

"Because I didn't . . . don't know. I suppose I'm considering the unthinkable."

"Which is?"

"Breaking into Sherbok's office and stealing the files missing from the computer."

"You really know how to pick 'em, Beck."

"True, it's not the Claridge."

They both laughed. Tracy's was a nervous laughter. She'd never seen the inside of a place like this before. In the most generous terms possible, it was a flophouse.

"Look, people here don't ask questions. They don't talk to strangers, and they stay away from cops."

"I really feel sleazy though," Tracy said, surveying herself in the smudged and cracked mirror with mottled images from a peeling silver coat. They had stopped at a cheap clothing store before arriving and outfitted her to look like a hooker.

After alighting from their taxi on K Street near Farragut Square they'd walked east toward 13th Street, the nucleus of the Washington sin trade. It was a crumbling strip of peep shows and strip joints with teenage hookers from Dubuque. Snow found the hotel he wanted facing a park full of pigeons and prostitutes.

The hallway reeked of urine and vomit, and a derelict huddled in the corner by the radiator, either dead or passed out.

The room was worse: the ubiquitous naked light bulb, a double bed that sagged in the middle. The window was cracked and repaired with masking tape. What little wasn't obscured with tape was matte-dirty with the accumulated filth of chronic nonwashing. Snow drew the draperies by hand—the mechanism was broken—and a subtle cloud of dust crawled slowly toward the floor.

"Creepy."

"Yeah. I agree," Snow said. "But we won't have to stay here forever."

"I'd kill myself first."

"Okay, help me?" Snow stripped the bed of its linens, and noted they were dotted with the stiff brownish-yellow stains of aged semen. "Yeecch!" He dumped them in the corner. "Hand me the bag, please." Tracy handed him a large loud crackling brown bag containing a shaker of dust insecticide, a plastic sheet, mattress pad, and bed clothes. He proceeded—with Tracy's helping hand, to put them on the bed.

"We'll have to do without pillows," he said. "Unless you want these?"

Tracy shivered.

"Cold?" Snow said, walking over to embrace her.

"No," she said. "Just a sort of chill of the soul. It's so inhuman, so base. Humans shouldn't be required to live in places like this."

"I know. We won't for long. But we're safe now." Snow said. "We're in a filthy little world with bedbugs and slime and the detritus of humanity, but we're safe.

It's ironic. Our world of clean sheets and courtesy wants to kill us. This one just takes our eight dollars and leaves us alone."

"We've got a load of trouble."

"What do you mean, 'we'? Please explain."

"Fifteen minutes ago I received a surveillance report on Gilbert."

"And?"

"My man was covered as a busboy and picked up the entire conversation."

"For God's sake, get to the point. *Why* is there trouble?"

"He was having dinner with the woman who was snooping."

"Yes, yes. I don't want to pry things out sentence by sentence. Please just start at the beginning and tell me what you've found."

"He suspects we killed Roth. Roth's sister reached him before we got her. I think he's been messing with the computer files."

"Well, he won't find anything there. So tell me why it's *we* who have trouble. As my security director, it's *your* problem."

"He's *your* assistant."

"Peter? He'll be no trouble. He's got too much invested. We'll talk to him very sternly."

"Why take so much trouble with him? Why not just line him up for mandatory sanction?"

"Because we need him. He can run that system better than anyone else in the world; he's a brilliant mind. That's why. Because things are happening too fast for us to bring in a substitute. Let's enter him as a post-execution sanction, with the others."

"And the Lewis woman?"

"Immediate transfer, no sanction. That *would* make Gilbert suspicious. Get with the President, she was *his* appointment. See if he can't think of some good place to send her, somewhere away from Washington."

"Done. Anything else?"

"Only one. I'd like the transcripts as soon as possible of your tapes of the Carothers-Baran meeting. The quality, I presume, was acceptable?"

"The best. The transcripts will be ready tomorrow. There isn't anything surprising, though."

"That's okay. I still want to go over them."

"Will do."

"Goodbye."

"Goodbye."

Eric Simon was *not* worried about relocating Beckett Snow and his sidekick Tracy Reynolds. They would, he knew, respond to the advertisement he had placed that afternoon for Monday's Washington *Post*.

What Simon *was* worried about, was how they could have escaped from the best-coordinated surveillance in the world. It was a mystery, and he hated not knowing. If he only *knew*, he'd know how to prevent it from happening again.

"I suppose I miscalculated his resources." Simon was talking once again to the Assistant Director of the CIA in charge of covert operations. They were huddled in a darkened booth at a Chinese restaurant in a shopping mall in Northern Virginia, a short drive from the Langley headquarters of the CIA.

Lowell, as usual, was wolfing down food while he listened to Simon.

"What kind of resources?" Lowell asked and immediately wadded a massive forkful of hot shredded beef into his mouth and washed it down with a long gulp of Kirin beer.

Simon looked away in distaste. "His emotional resources. We've struck at him from just about every angle. We've isolated him, killed his friends, left him

217

without people to call on, thrown dismembered pieces of bodies at him, chased him down dark train tunnels, and tied him up in a tangle of inconsistencies that would have sent most other people into a screaming nosedive.

"But this man Snow has taken it. He's not only taken it, but he's been able to function, think, plan, strike back."

"Sounds like somebody we ought to get hold of." Lowell's speech was muffled by the half-masticated mushi pork he'd just ingested. Simon was grateful he'd chosen a restaurant that was so dark it masked enough so even he couldn't see the man's atrocious manners.

"You're right," Simon agreed. "He's the type of person we could use a lot of. But I'm worried about controlling him. He's been able to resist and survive. We've got to do something that will break him, make him have to lean on us."

"You don't want to lose him though," Lowell managed. "Guys like that are like carbon steel. They'll take more abuse than you think is possible, but just the right amount will make them snap. You don't want that."

"We're going to have to risk it."

"What are you suggesting?"

"The girl."

"Kill her?"

"No, something more subtle."

The glutton from the CIA looked at Simon, and even in the dark, Simon could see him smile, flecks of beef caught between his front teeth.

218

Chapter Nineteen

"You're shameless." Tracy laughed and wriggled in Snow's grasp.

"Are you complaining?"

"Bitterly." Turning her head, she bit him on the side of his neck.

"Hey! You're not exactly behaving yourself either."

"I know. . . . Isn't it fun?"

"Yeah, it's fun. But I'm getting tired. Four times since dawn . . ." Snow smiled and then began to sing words to a calypso tune. "All day, all night Mary Ann, who do you think I am, superman?"

"Oh, you!"

It was 9:51 AM, Sunday. Outside the weepy grey sky drizzled on downtown Washington. Dark raindrop lines crept across the opaque matte of the window's grime, crisscrossing the dingy yellow light that filtered through.

They had gone to bed early the previous night, emotionally and physically exhausted from the day's ordeal, and from the ordeals of the past two weeks.

They had grown insular together. What had happened was more than anything in their lives could have ever prepared them for, and the strain was taking its toll. The justice that their country stood for, the security from physical harm they thought they'd always had, were—now—only elusive fantasies they had almost lost hope of finding. Yet the fantasy was what sustained and drove them both. That and knowing that stopping or failing meant death. The vision of the woman in the motel room haunted them.

Sleep had been a struggle the night before, but finally they'd both dropped into a deep, druglike unconsciousness.

And awakening the next morning, they found that their hunger for each other had been renewed, that the defenses had softened enough to let them into each other's lives—at least for the morning.

Now, relaxed and drained, refreshed and invigorated by lovemaking, they lay listening to each other breathe, to the sounds of Washington, D.C. waking up outside their room.

Snow held Tracy close, inhaling the sweet musky fragrance of her, a scent of love. She shivered as he moved his hand lightly across the small of her back, across the dimples where her buttocks began, along the cleavage between the cheeks. It was, he thought, an instant that should be captured, and yet it was beautiful only when allowed to live untrammeled.

It was Tracy who broke the trance.

"I hate to sound like I'm not enjoying this—because I love it—but you've got to get moving if you're going to visit that person this morning. It's ten o'clock."

"Shit."

"I agree. But you do."

"I know it. I know it. I just feel like being lazy."

"Tell the Commission that." Snow made no comment. "Beck, what do you expect to learn?" Tracy finished her question as she rolled on her left side and propped up her head on her hand. The sheet slid down, exposing her breasts.

"I don't know what I hope to find. It's like any sort of investigation—police, newspaper, what have you. You've got to follow every lead you get, no matter

220

how slight its chances seem for success. Dead-ends and more dead-ends. But sometimes you strike pay dirt, and that's what makes all the frustration worthwhile.

"It's also for a sense of completeness," Snow continued. "For the sake of no 'if onlys'. Also," he eyed her mischievously, "because we ain't got much else to go on."

They dressed quickly and walked down the creaking stairs of the hotel to a fast-food hamburger joint which served various amorphous deep-fried things and pronounced them breakfast. Before leaving the room, Snow had removed an electrical outlet and cached the contents of the box—the torn photograph, the yellow cloth Star of David, and the note in Carothers's handwriting—in the hole and replaced the junction box.

After breakfast Snow walked Tracy back to the room, and left her with instructions not to let anyone, *anyone* in the room, and that anyone who tried to get in should be shot. He left her with one of the Ingrams and several spare clips of ammunition. He also left with a password, an act that would have seemed ridiculous and melodramatic only a week ago, and which, after their ordeal, seemed only natural. It was a line from a Sandburg poem: "Tell us again, nothing is impossible."

Like most top and midlevel officials in Washington, Leslie Lewis's home address was no secret. It was contained in a number of directories. Snow had memorized the address and noted the neighborhood. He knew it was a solid, safe collection of apartment buildings occupied mostly by single women who worked either on Capitol Hill or at the White House.

As he walked toward her home the events of the past two weeks played back: the murders in Los Angeles, the tortured woman in Santa Monica, the massacre at the sidewalk cafe, the fright, the running— all part of a world that he was getting too familiar with.

Snow paused several times to look around, but he spotted no signs of a tail. But why should there be, he thought, he'd thrown them completely the day before—whoever "they" were—and it had cost them the life of one of their agents.

Snow walked on, slowing occasionally to check the house numbers. Soon he came to the yellow brick building in which Leslie Lewis lived. Casually he strolled past. It was a security building, complete with desk clerk inside, telephone outside.

Quickly, not wanting to be spotted for the prowler that he was, Snow walked to the rear of the building. There he saw what he was looking for: a service door through which the garbage was brought to be picked up. The double wooden doors were not deadbolted.

The large flat blade of Snow's knife easily jimmied the door latch and he was inside. In the dim light, Snow combed his hair, straightened his clothes, and walked to the front of the building. A section of the hallway was lined with mailboxes. He quickly located one which read L. Lewis and noted the number: 410.

The hallway was deserted. The elevator was waiting at the first-floor landing. The door to apartment 410 was three down from the elevator. The Sunday *Washington Post* lay scattered against the door.

The third time he pushed the bell, a voice responded with a predictable, "Who is it?"

"My name is Beckett Snow. I want to talk to you." Snow thought surely he must be waking people in other apartments.

"About what?"

"Your job." Snow yelled. There was a noticeable pause.

"At 10:30 on Sunday morning? Go away. I don't want to talk about it. Come to my office tomorrow."

"I can't."

"Then call me on the telephone."

"I *must* talk to you now," Snow said. "People's lives could depend on it. It's very important."

The doorbell had reached her through the mist of a dream she didn't remember. When she looked at the clock beside the bed, reality began to penetrate. The digital display told her it was 10:29. The doorbell rang again, insistently.

The face she saw through the peephole in the dimly lit hall was unfamiliar. It was a handsome face though, she noted. But the sight of a strange man's face at her door at 10:29 on a Sunday morning left her with more than a vague anxiety. Without a word, she returned to the bedroom, pulled open the top drawer of her bureau, and from under a pile of scarves, pulled the .44 magnum.

She went back to the door this time, pistol in hand. Since the dinner with Peter Gilbert, since listening to his suspicions that Isaac Roth had been murdered, she had become increasingly edgy. Paranoid, she thought. She hoped this person was someone harmless.

She'd asked the caller what he wanted. Jesus Christ! Her job! Was he from Sherbok's office? Was he here to threaten her? But she'd never seen him before. What did this stranger know about her job?

Then his reply. He couldn't come to her office? She just wanted him to go away, wanted the whole mess to go away. But at that moment, things seemed to coalesce. Something told her it was going to be a long time before anything like this "went away."

"I *must* talk to you now," came the voice through the door. It sounded pleading, honest, perhaps even desperate. A good con job? She couldn't tell. "People's lives could depend on it. It's very important."

"People's lives." The words struck home. Whose lives? Hers? Others? His, whoever *he* was? He was pleading now, earnestly. She looked through the peephole again at his face. He didn't *sound* like he was there to threaten her, and he didn't *look* like someone from Sherbok's group.

Snow meanwhile, looked up and down the hall. If his voice had disturbed anyone, they hadn't come into the hall to investigate.

Leslie put her back to the door and leaned on it for support. Her heart was pounding now. She wondered if the man on the other side of the door could feel its vibrations. *What* was she going to do? On the one hand, he might be a spy, some sort of henchman. If they had killed a man of Roth's stature, how much hesitation would they have in doing away with her? On the other hand, maybe she was just being paranoid. Maybe, maybe . . . No matter how you added it up, the answer was equivocal. She looked once again through the peephole. "You, out there!"

"Yes?"

"I'm not going to let you in."

Snow's stomach turned to mud.

"I want to meet you somewhere, okay?"

"Sure." He was elated.

"Clydes?"

"Too public. How about someplace your employers won't see us?" Snow said.

"Fine with me. Uh . . . How about the . . . there's a Chock Full O' Nuts on Eighteenth Street, just east of Pennsylvania Avenue. That okay?"

That, Snow thought, was close to the Executive Office Building. Was she leading him into a trap.

"That's pretty close to where you work."

"Okay, okay. Have *you* got a better idea?" Leslie was exasperated. Although she admitted, he *was* right about the location. But was she letting him choose the place, letting him set up a trap?

"Okay, how about the dining room at the Stouffers in Crystal City. Is that safe enough for you?"

Leslie thought. It *did* seem innocuous enough. What the hell.

"Okay. I'll meet you by the hostess stand. . . ." She looked at her watch. "11:15. That enough time?"

Snow replied affirmatively.

Snow exited the building the same way he'd entered and jogged down to Virginia Avenue and caught a cab in front of the Watergate. The cabbie was delighted, the trip was at least a five-dollar fare.

"I don't believe it!" Leslie released an audible sigh and leaned back against the back of the booth. "And yet . . ."

"I know it sounds preposterous," Snow said. "But *please*, you have to believe me. It's true. All of it."

"I know. I believe it. I believe," Leslie said.

"You do?" Snow was bewildered. He didn't expect this woman to understand. The meeting had been cold, strained at the beginning.

They bantered, parried, and thrust. Each was suspicious, yet a trust born of mutual necessity had begun. Snow concluded that he'd found a sympathetic ear in a sensitive place. Unilaterally he decided to take a risk and tell her the entire story—all save his fake identity.

And he told it all, beginning with the accident on the Pasadena Freeway and ending with the escape on Friday night.

"You seem surprised that I believe you," Leslie said.

"I am. Frankly, there are times I'm not sure I didn't dream it myself. It's too fantastic; things like this just don't happen."

"They do," Leslie looked at him sadly. "They actually do." She inhaled deeply, held it for a minute as if she were deciding something important—which she was—and then let it out quickly.

"Okay. You've told me your story. That doesn't obligate me to reciprocate. But I'm going to tell you anyway.

"I believe you because of what's happened to me in the past two weeks. I've been threatened. I think, rather an associate of mine thinks, a fine, kind old man was killed by these people. I know something strange is happening.

"I'd noticed that I was no longer receiving information from the Delphi Commission and started poking around. Then, several days later, I received an anonymous threat in my office. By accident, I discovered the person who had threatened me." And so it went, Leslie detailing the chain of events of the past couple of weeks concluding with the mysterious dinner with Peter Gilbert in Georgetown. It was Snow's turn now to play the enraptured audience. Once again, the feeling of nonbelief.

"Roth . . ." Snow whispered. "I met him once when I had just started work at the Justice Department. He was the grand old man, the Brahmin, and . . . yes, he was a good man. A really *good* man—and you can't say that about too many people here, at least not the ones who spent as much time in the circles of power as he did. They killed him. . . ."

"You don't know that for sure."

"No, but I have a hunch. Every good detective develops a sense of intuition. And I've got that about Roth. I had it about calling on you. There was no other reason for me to hold the hope of finding an ally by pulling a name out of a directory—"

"I was wondering how you got my name. . . . I never asked."

"Well, I just had a good feeling," Snow said. "Not that I didn't have doubts, but . . ."

"I know what you mean."

"So what do we do?"

"That, my new friend, is a damn good question."

Chapter Twenty

"You're sure he'll be there?"

"He won't miss it. The ad is clear."

"And the girl?"

"Doesn't matter. Either we'll have our fun then, or follow him back to wherever she's staying. You *won't* lose them this time, will you?"

"I hope not."

"You'd *better* not," Eric Simon said, and hung up.

Peter Gilbert shook his head slowly as Beckett Snow and Tracy Reynolds recounted their two weeks of violence at the hands of the Commission.

His earlier misgivings were replaced with sadness and anger. He had been reluctant to meet with them, the newspaper accounts of their misdeeds described them as an opportunistic whore traveling with a sadistic murderer who disemboweled people.

And there were the implications of someone at the Commission finding out about the meeting.

For their parts, Beckett and Tracy had been reluctant to meet with someone so high ranking in the Commission; they feared a double-cross.

It had taken Leslie's relentless persuasion to get them together—that plus the fact that each side might have the information the other was seeking.

As they talked in Peter Gilbert's brick Georgetown townhouse, the death of Isaac Roth and the activities of the Commission took on new and horrifying proportions that seemed to leave Peter no alternative but to commit himself to helping these two people. Isaac would have wanted that, he thought.

For more than three hours, broken only by a silent supper somberly consumed, Beckett and Tracy recounted their tale. Now there was silence, the room filled with the emptiness of four scared people: breathing, thinking.

Leslie broke the silence.

"Peter, tell them what you found—or rather didn't find—in the computer."

"There are files missing," he began and proceeded to describe the missing dossiers.

When he'd finished, Snow spoke softly, half in thought.

"That's what was in the microfilm."

"What was?" Peter asked.

"Of course!" Tracy said. "The microfilm. The plans for Prometheus! That's why they want them back so badly."

"And maybe even the details about the Commission's sanctions of Carothers, Roth, and God only knows who else," Leslie added.

No one spoke as the gravity of what they said weighed on them.

"But of course that's just conjecture," Gilbert said.

"You may be right," said Snow. "But I don't think so, and I don't even think *you* believe it. Do you?"

"No, no, you're right," Gilbert said. "I wish I thought differently, but I don't."

"I guess that pretty well dictates what we're going to have to do." It was Leslie who spoke now. They all looked at her quizzically.

"Well, come on," Leslie said. "Doesn't that mean just one thing?"

"What?" Peter asked.

"We've got to break into Sherbok's office and steal the missing files."

Chapter Twenty-one

A Cezanne sky smiled on Middleburg, Virginia. Brush-stroke clouds chased each other from mountain to mountain across a sky colored a blue only seen the day after it's rained for a week.

The inn was an old one—stone and rough-hewn timbers—that had been serving visitors for 250 years. Beckett Snow pulled to a stop at the curb in front. As well as providing them with a place to stay, Peter Gilbert had loaned Beckett and Tracy his Fiat for the day.

It was not crowded, this first day following the weekend. The advertisement in the *Washington Post*—Simon's signal—had been clear about the meeting place, and it was well timed for privacy.

The host seated them in the rear tavern at a trestle table next to the huge fireplace.

It all seemed like a holiday save for the deadly errand they were performing.

"How do you feel, kid?" Snow asked.

"Good. Better than in a long time. It's been nice to get some rest the past couple of days. I'd almost forgotten what eight hours' sleep could do for me." They sipped Mimosas made with the inn's freshly squeezed orange juice and a respectable domestic champagne and talked, staring into the fire and at each other. There were moments in that half hour when the grotesque world of guns and dead people and hired killers and conspiracies vanished completely. It was a relief; it was blessedly welcome.

At precisely noon, the silhouette of a very large man loomed in the doorway of the tavern.

The man was Simon.

But something was wrong.

Even in the dim light they could see his face was pale. His left shoulder was hunched, and he held his elbow tight to his ribs.

"What happened?" Snow scrambled from behind the table, and pulled out a chair for him.

"The Commission . . . an ambush near the beltway." Simon's voice radiated pain. "My escorts got us out. . . . They may be on their way. My men are outside. If anything happens, head for the men's room; there's a service door that leads to the kitchen. Let's hurry . . . not much time." Simon grimaced as he endured a bolt of pain, then relaxed as it passed.

"You brought the microfilm?" asked Snow. Simon nodded. "Good. Tracy, give him the Xeroxes."

"You got the box open, then?"

"We did. It cost the lives of two good friends," Snow said. "I want to know something about your organization. What's the name of it? The Consortium?"

Simon's eyes widened. The surprise was apparent. "You're stepping out of bounds, Mr. Snow. You've gotten into areas that don't concern you."

"Have I? Really? How do I know you didn't kill Steve Drachler?" Snow looked for recognition in Simon's eyes, but found none. No matter, Snow thought, it could be the light, or it could be the veneer of pain that masked all else. Whatever the reason, it was no proof the man didn't kill Drachler.

"I read about Mr. Drachler—a newspaper reporter, I believe? I had no idea he was a friend of yours," Simon said politely. Snow decided to let it pass.

"Okay, you've got the contents of the box," Snow said. "Where are the microfilms?"

Simon reached down for the attache case he had carried in with him.

"Oh yeah, I forgot to tell you," Snow began. "Besides the note from Carothers, the box—" It was all he had time to say. An object looking remarkably like an aerosol shaving cream can smashed through the narrow, basement-like window above and behind Snow's head. Snow saw Simon take his left arm from its protective position against his ribs, and give the object a backhand slap.

"Cover your face," Simon yelled. The object exploded. The bright flash faded instantly into the black mists of unconsciousness. Snow reached for Tracy, gathering instead an armload of emptiness.

"Goddamnit!" Peter smashed his fist against the surface of his desk, littered as it was with paper cups of coffee, notes, files, and phone messages. Gilbert had been trying all morning to reach Sherbok. He'd also placed calls to the President himself and to Kincaid Carothers's office.

Gilbert paced the floor. He ran a check on the missing files through the computer again, hoping there has been some malfunction that caused the situation as he discovered it. But the results were the same.

While waiting for the calls, he started to make a file, methodically committing to paper everything he knew about the case, the missing computer files, Roth's death—murder?—the stories told the night before by Tracy Reynolds and Beckett Snow.

Hoping that a pattern would emerge, he categorized the information by time; by place; by the people involved; and by possible motive. Everything pointed to a high-level involvement of people managing Project Prometheus. But how high? And the spurious attacks on Snow and the people who aided him: that certainly looked like psychological warfare. Somebody wanted Snow rattled. For what?

As he read through his notes for the fifth time, he was struck by the only person it could possibly be: Simon. Yes, Gilbert thought, Simon *was* saving Snow and Reynolds for something.

The telephone rang. Peter noticed that his hand was shaking as he brought the receiver to his ear and wondered briefly what had happened to the control he had cultivated all his life.

"Peter Gilbert here."

"Peter, are you free to come to my office and visit a little?" The voice turned breakfast into a lump of cold concrete in his gut. It was the President himself!

He was in trouble and he knew it.

"Of course, sir, when would you like me?"

"Now."

"Certainly. I'll be right up."

There was only electronic disconnection clicks to serve as parting courtesy.

Impending doom, that was the feeling. The world was coming to an end. Did they know about Beckett Snow and Tracy Reynolds or about his conversations with Leslie Lewis? It was the not knowing that got to Peter.

The elevator arrived. The President's chief of staff smiled at him when the doors had opened.

"Hi, Peter. He would like to speak to you on the East Lawn. He thought you two might take a walk and discuss whatever it is you must."

The East Lawn? Maybe it was worse than he thought. The President surely wasn't taking him there to discuss the rhododendrons.

Gilbert was met at the east steps by Secret Service. They checked him against his ID and waved him through.

The President who had been sitting on the bottom step, now rose and extended his hand. Peter took it, fearing the touch, as if it might be waiting to electrocute him.

"It's been quite a while since I've seen you." The smile was genuine.

The President started walking toward the Ellipse. Peter followed.

"I wanted to make sure we weren't disturbed," the older man said. "What you intimated is pretty serious."

"Yes, sir," Peter began. "I've stumbled on some things that are absolutely amazing. I'm astounded at what seems to be happening." Peter started to open a file folder he'd brought.

"Put that away, Peter. We won't need it."

"But there's . . ."

"We don't *need* it." The President's voice was firm. "I already know."

"You . . . know?" Peter forced out the words in a daze.

The President nodded, and as they walked described in detail the killings of Roth, of Carothers, and more.

They reached the end of the East Lawn. Tourists poked cameras and hands through the wrought-iron fence, and Secret Service officers moved in to protect the President, who signed autographs on proffered pieces of paper.

They moved on, and the Secret Service agents faded back to where they had been before. Gilbert felt as if he were being led through a room of mirrors. What the President had told him was too much to believe.

"Why are you telling me all this?" Gilbert asked. "You're saying that the National Security Advisor has some kind of secret police to protect Project Prometheus, and he's gone around killing people, and that *you* knew about it all along? Aren't you afraid—isn't Sherbok afraid, I'll go out and spill my guts to the press?"

234

"It wouldn't make any difference."

"What do you mean?"

"They wouldn't believe you. They'd think you were crazy. And believe me, Sherbok's people would make sure you ended up in a strait jacket."

"Jesus, that's what they do in Russia!"

"It works. There's a lot to be said for things that work."

"But you. What . . . how could you . . . I mean, you're a decent, honest man. You've . . ."

"Why, Peter?" The President's voice was soft, sympathetic. "Because I don't have a choice."

"*You!* You're the most powerful man in the world! You're the leader of the most powerful, the richest nation on earth! You—"

"No, Peter. I am not. And the United States is not. Look, you're intimately familiar with the assets of the members of the Delphi Commission. What's their annual gross?"

"Uh . . . reported to public or actual?" Gilbert's mind found some familiar ground to latch onto.

"Actual."

"Something over 12 trillion dollars."

"And how much was the GNP of the United States last year?"

"Something over one trillion."

"Does that say something to you?"

"But that doesn't count," Gilbert argued. "The members are in dozens of countries, they are not unified like the GNP. You're lumping a whole bunch of entities that aren't coordinated to act as a unit. You—"

"You've just hit the essential," the President said. "They're not coordinated as a unit now, but they will be. *That* is the goal of the Delphi Commission.

"Peter." The voice was stern now. "You're acting naive. You knew this was what everything was heading toward. You surely must have followed the trends of

235

corporations, the way they set up their accounting where no country can honestly tell what their profits or revenues are; how they're insulated from government regulations; how they've slowly grown into a ruling class of bigness that is impossible even for the U.S. government to challenge. So that's why I don't challenge it. I have no choice."

"And neither do I, is that what you are trying to tell me?"

"I think that's plain."

"But why don't they just kill me, get me out of the way?"

"Because you are very valuable. Apparently they're going to need your expertise."

"But after that, they'll get rid of me. Right?"

"I don't know. Perhaps they'll get rid of all of us. There's no way of telling. But whatever it is, is better than dying now or spending the rest of your life in a mental hospital. Remember, Peter, nobody is going to believe you. You have no proof. You might make a big splash: 'Administration Official Claims Plot in White House to Take Over the World.' Sure. You'll get that much, and then they'll lock you away for good. People simply aren't going to believe you. It's too far-fetched."

"But the others, the others who were killed. Why weren't they just put in a strait jacket too?"

"There is one difference between them and you, Peter: power. They had power. *And* I suppose, they might have had some proof.

"You know," the President said as they walked back to the White House. "The rhododendrons are dying. It's a shame; they're such beautiful plants."

Peter looked at him as if he were crazy. And then realized that perhaps the President was the only sane one in the White House.

236

Chapter Twenty-two

Peter Gilbert trudged slowly toward his house, keys jangling in one hand, a stack of file folders in the other. Following his conversation with the President, Gilbert had returned to his office and twice resisted the impulse to phone Leslie Lewis. He figured that his telephones might be intercepted.

He was cut off now; the President had told him that much. Upon returning to his office, Peter called Sherbok and this time the National Security Advisor spoke to him.

"I lost my head," Gilbert remembered saying. "I've acted unreasonably and exceeded my authority. I apologize."

The appeal to Sherbok's ego seemed to work, Peter thought now as he rounded the corner toward his house. Perhaps, he thought, it would give him the time to decide on a plan of action.

Gilbert turned off the alarm, released the deadbolt, then worked the door key, and pushed open the door.

In the middle of the foyer floor was a body.

The pile of file folders spilled from Gilbert's hand and fluttered to the floor.

Gilbert slammed the door quickly behind him.

The rasps of difficult breathing were audible in the foyer. Gilbert caught his own breath and determined that the sounds came from the body.

The man was alive.

In the twilight of the entrance way, Peter Gilbert stood transfixed. Where had the body come from? Then he remembered that the alarm had not been triggered. It was on, in an undisturbed state, when he'd arrived. Somebody had defeated the alarm, delivered the body, and departed, taking care to rearm the alarm. It was no mean feat. Gilbert had purchased one of the most effective and sophisticated alarm systems available.

Gilbert kneeled beside the crumpled prone figure and rolled him over.

It was Beckett Snow.

He was alive and seemed to be uninjured, save for smears of soot on his face.

Gilbert read a note pinned to Snow's shirt. "This man mumbled your address and thus you find him in your home. Take care of him. Though injured saving this man's life, our commander will be in touch with him. We were unable to rescue the woman."

The note was not signed.

Peter Gilbert picked up the injured Beckett Snow and carried him a dozen paces into the front bedroom where Gilbert placed him in his own bed. He arranged Snow in what seemed to be a comfortable position and walked to the dry bar in his living room to pour himself a glass of Tanqueray. He poured the drink, fetched lime and ice from the kitchen refrigerator, and returned to the bed and sat beside Snow and waited.

Somewhere there were pinpricks of lights, mostly blue. And somewhere behind them there was action; Snow couldn't see it at first. The activity—was it a dream?—focused and blurred. His head hurt.

The dark had disappeared and somewhere before it there was light. The light, the darkness, now the light again. The first light. . . . What had happened? His mind tried to splice the fragments into a whole. Brunch.

Yes! They were having brunch. They? Tracy and he. And . . .

"Tracy! Tracy!" Snow bolted upright, ignoring the screaming nerves in his head. He looked side to side, and then up at the ceiling, then side to side once again, dazed, the surroundings unfamiliar. Then he saw Gilbert.

"Where is she?" Snow asked. Gilbert looked at him dumbly; the words wouldn't come out. "Where *is* she? Where's Tracy?"

The words rested in Gilbert's throat, glued somewhere between his mind and his throat. He reached for the note that had been attached to Snow's back and thrust it into Snow's hands.

Gilbert watched as Snow read the note once. And not comprehending its full import, a second, and yet a third time. Snow sat on the bed, legs askew. A tear traced a shining streak across his cheek.

"They got her. After all of this, they got her, and I was no help." He drew his knees up and encircled them with his arms.

"They got her," Snow cried, and laid his cheek against his knees.

Peter Gilbert sat there, helpless, frustrated in his helplessness. He wanted to offer words of solace, but none would come. He wanted to help, but he couldn't. He sat, absorbed in the man's sorrow, and the sorrow became his own. And he knew he could never return to the world of the men who had created it.

"Judas Priest, I don't see how they can continue doing this!" Eric Simon was in pain and every word was a dagger's bite, but he continued the tirade. "We're the best fucking people the goddamned government has and we're fucking letting those fucking incompetents run our asses over with their fucking surveillance." He started to pound the hospital feeding table with his right arm when he realized it was strapped. "Sh-i-i-i-i-t!" Simon bellowed. He sat upright, gulping air, drained from the anger and the frustration.

He was in a private hospital in Northern Virginia which asked no questions. It was an ultra-secure medical treatment center for personnel of the Central Intelligence Agency.

Hospital personnel didn't know that Eric Simon no longer worked for the CIA, not that they cared. They hadn't been hired to ask questions. The only thing that mattered was that Simon's entrance had been authorized by the Assistant Director of the CIA, and that Simon was to be placed in the most secure section of this most secure hospital.

The room was empty save for the corpulent presence of the CIA's Assistant Director who had personally overseen the admittance of Simon. The Assistant Director listened to Simon's tirade while he silently stuffed chocolate-covered caramel pecan candies in his mouth.

"Well, it wasn't so bad," the fat man said, his teeth stained brown by the last piece of candy. "We got the girl and we got the contents of the box."

Simon looked at Lowell as if he were crazy.

"That's fucking easy for you to say. I'm sitting here on my ass with the skin burned off of one arm, a fucking knife wound, and a concussion, and you want me to smile and agree that things weren't so fucking bad?"

Simon looked at the man and hated the way the fat made little rolls at the back of the man's neck. The man popped another candy in his mouth.

"You're alive," the man commented matter-of-factly through the sticky goo of the candy in his mouth.

Simon looked at him, shook his head from side to side slowly, and looked away.

"What . . ." Lowell swallowed. "What do we do with the girl? We've got what we must. Why not just kill her and cut the guy loose?"

"I'll answer the last question first," said Simon. "*Because* the guy happens to be hiding out with a White House aide named Peter Gilbert who also happens to be a top Commission whiz-kid. I don't know what the deal is, but I'll wager another box of those candies you're eating that we can use Snow to gather information from Gilbert, or use him somehow. Understand?"

The fat man nodded.

"And as to the first question, we take her out of strategy. And in such a way as to force both Gilbert and Snow into our laps."

"How?"

"A stage four interrogation. I want her brought up, cut down, and delivered—signed and *Commission* sealed—to their doorstep."

Simon watched the fat man's eyes light up. There was only one thing in the world Lowell loved better than eating—and it wasn't sex. Unless, of course, the sex hurt.

It was twenty after seven and twilight when Leslie Lewis unlocked her apartment door. Her mood matched the hour of night: light fading fast. Her emotions had been lifted so high with the prospect of activity, of progress, and now dropped so low with the absence of both the action and any communication from Gilbert.

What had happened with Gilbert, she wondered as she picked at a hastily cooked supper. Why hadn't he called? She was tempted to call him, but the night before he had left specific instructions for her not to. He had been adamant about it.

But it depressed her. She was ready to do something. She needed, she wanted to participate. She believed in what those two people—Beckett Snow and Tracy Reynolds—had said.

And all the motivation was sitting inside her, going nowhere, doing nothing.

Then, in the moment of daydreaming, she was bothered by the living room. It seemed somehow different than it had been when she left that morning. Nothing specific, just . . . small things she couldn't place, the room was a hair at odds with the image she had in her mind when she'd left for work.

Or was it?

Was she getting paranoid? The emotional stress might be getting to her. Still . . . She wondered if someone had entered her apartment during the day.

Leslie left her supper and went to the bedroom to check on the .44 magnum. The gun lay in the drawer just as she had left it. She grasped the handgrip and examined the cylinder; it was still loaded. She checked the other drawer of the bedside table and noted that the extra ammunition for the firearm seemed undisturbed.

She looked around. Was this room just a little off too? Or was that a product of an overstimulated imagination?

The telephone rang.

The jangle of the phone startled her and brought prickles to her arms and legs.

"Yes?" she answered. It was Peter. Relief flooded through her.

"Leslie, can you come over?" he asked. "It's very important and I don't want to discuss it over the telephone." The statement was a plea.

"Of course. . . . Sure, Peter. I'll be right over . . . just as soon as I clear up a couple of things here."

"Thank you . . . very much," Peter said and they rang off.

Leslie looked at herself in the full-length mirror on her closet door and judged the jeans as inappropriate. She started a search for something more suitable, remembered the emotions, the—what was it she heard?—desperation in Peter's voice and decided to wear what she had on. She grabbed a sweater and hurried toward the front door. For a reason she didn't understand—after all, one hardly understands emotions or hunches—she returned to the bedroom, removed the .44 magnum from the drawer, and placed it and the extra ammunition in a Garfinckel's shopping bag, covered them with clothes that had been lying around, and headed for the door.

"He's been like that for more than two hours now," Gilbert said, pointing at Beckett Snow, who was currently sitting up in Gilbert's bed, arms wrapped around his knees, staring at the opposite wall. His eyes were glazed, unfocused.

"Shock," Leslie said. "He loves her very much, it was apparent the other night."

"So much that he's a zombie?"

"He'll get over that, I'm sure. What happens to Tracy will determine how he gets over it, maybe what he does." She walked to the bed and sat down.

"Beckett?" Leslie placed her arm around Snow's shoulders. He looked at her. "Can you go to sleep? Can you rest? You're going to need that, you know. Need that to help Tracy, to have the strength to get her back . . . to deal with the people who got her."

Snow continued to look at her. He glanced first at her, then at Peter Gilbert, and finally back to Leslie.

"Yes," Snow said and sniffled. "Yes, you're right. I should . . . I should do that. Tracy . . . Tracy will . . ." He wept again. Leslie dipped into her handbag and withdrew a wad of tissues which she pressed into his hand.

"We'll be right out here if you need us," she said. "Go to sleep. Sleep." She rose and motioned to Peter and they both left, closing the door behind them.

"It's hard to believe," Peter Gilbert said when they'd settled down in the living room with a couple of beers. "He was Mr. Rock Hard yesterday—resourceful, tough. Now look at him. It's unbelievable. He seemed like the sort who'd be racing through the door like the cavalry to the rescue."

"Where would he rush?"

There was a long pause.

"That's true," Gilbert conceded. "Very true."

They sat for a long time without talking. The only movement to disturb the silence was Beckett getting out of bed to extinguish the bedroom light.

Finally Leslie broke the silence.

"I'm worried that someone's entered my apartment."

"Why? Is something missing?"

"No, not that. It just seems like everything is just a little bit out of place. You know, like somebody searched it very carefully, but just as carefully replaced everything so that it wouldn't be noticed."

Peter Gilbert nodded.

"Do you want to stay here tonight?" he offered.

"Thank you for saving me the awkwardness of asking."

"Well, it looked as if you came prepared," he said, looking at the dark purple-blue and white shopping bag.

"Oh, that." Leslie got up and retrieved the bag and returned to her seat. She stuck in her hand and rummaged around the bag's bottom, retrieving—to Peter's amazement—the .44 magnum.

"This was my overnight baggage. The rest of this stuff was to hide it."

"You know how to *use* that thing?" a wide-eyed Peter Gilbert asked.

"Well enough."

"I feel safer already. . . . Uhmmmm, isn't that sort of thing kinda, you know, illegal here?"

"Yep. But I picked up a good saying from the good-ole-Virginia boys I bought it from, several sayings, in fact. The one that comes to mind is 'It's better to be tried by 12 than carried by six.' Which is a glib answer that nevertheless has some merit."

"You know, I never took you for a gun nut," Gilbert said.

"Nor I either. And I'm not now. But I'm through taking shit from people."

"I see. Well," Peter began. "You take the other bedroom, and I'll make the sofa into a bed and sleep here."

Leslie fell asleep quickly, but woke up periodically all night, always after the same awful dream. In the dream she was with friends at night. It was a cool night, and the windows were open to let in the breezes. Suddenly she was alone in a silence that seemed to absorb her cries before the sound reached even her own ears. The lights went out. She rushed to the switch and found it inoperable. Then the night darkness would turn into a void and the physical confines of the room would disappear. And she'd find herself sucked into the void, a nasty angry silence that laughed laughs that she could not hear, could only feel, and the laughs had teeth that snarled and ripped at her mind and the intensity overwhelmed her. But with a great effort, she woke up.

Chapter Twenty-three

The tap-tap tapping echoed across a gulf of misty gray thought. Peter Gilbert hoped it would go away. It didn't. It turned first into a loose shutter banging in a thunderstorm and then into a faulty piston in a tugboat diesel. Peter Gilbert did not want to wake up. The tapping stopped.

He woke up.

The room was still mostly dark, but the first light shades of day had started to filter in through the living-room windows.

At first it sounded like a squeak. Peter held his breath. There it was again. From the front door? He got up, slowly releasing his gathered breath, and walked to the front door. Nothing was visible through the peephole. Peter Gilbert unchained, undeadbolted, and unlocked the front door, turned off the alarm, and opened the door.

Even once in the entire life of a person is too much for someone to view the sight that greeted Peter Gilbert. For lying on the front steps, barely discernible in the gathering light of the dawn of a beautiful day was Tracy Reynolds.

It took Peter several stunned, paralyzed moments to recognize the creature as Tracy. It was a sight that transcended hideousness. He knelt down. The squeaks

246

he had heard were the only sound she could make through swollen, cracked bleeding lips.

She was naked.

And visible were the cuts, some of which still oozed amber fluid, and massive discolored bruises and swellings. Her scalp bore the marks of instruments, sharp and blunt. There were abrasions on the insides of her thighs and teeth marks, some of which had drawn blood, on her breasts and stomach. Dried semen matted her pubic hair.

Though one eye was swollen shut, with a gaping wound bleeding below it, the other eye was wide, filled with fear, and glazed. Peter thought she looked drugged, but perhaps she was simply in shock.

Peter was rooted to the steps. Suddenly he heard an unmuffled engine start. Two houses down, a motorcycle! The man Snow had described waved at him, and accelerated up the street toward the university in a blast of noise that reverberated from house to house.

"Peter, I heard the door knocker." It was Leslie, coming from the hallway. "And that motorcycle just now woke me up completely." Her voice was husky with sleep. She was walking toward the front door where Gilbert stood. "What's happened?"

"Don't come any closer. Don't—"

"Oh, dear God!" Leslie gasped. "Oh, God, oh, God! *What* did they do to her?"

"The man on the motorcycle." He turned to her. "The man on the motorcycle that she and Snow mentioned . . . he was here."

"Oh, God! Oh, God! Oh, God!" She leaned against the doorjamb and looked at Gilbert. "What are we going to do? What are we going to do?"

"We have got to get her help."

"But we—" Leslie stopped short. They both turned toward the front door. Beckett Snow was awake, they heard him thump out of bed.

247

"We can't let him see her like this," Leslie said.

Beckett Snow appeared in the doorway of the bedroom, clad in jeans and a half-buttoned shirt.

"Hey, guys, what's all the commotion?" He walked toward the front door. Gilbert met him just as he entered the living room.

"Let's go over here," Gilbert said, taking Snow's arm and directing him toward an armchair by the hallway wall. Leslie stepped outside and started to close the front door.

"No!" Snow wrenched his arm from Gilbert's grasp. "What's going *on?* What's outside?" He stood there, face to face with Peter Gilbert, who stood a head taller than he. "Well?" And Snow started to the front door.

Gilbert grabbed Snow by the shoulders and attempted to use his superior size to manhandle Snow into the chair. Gilbert quickly found himself face-down on the floor.

"No-o-o-o-o-o. No!" Snow screamed. "Bastards!" And suddenly he was calm as he knelt beside Tracy on both his knees. "Hey, babe, it's going to be all right. You're gonna be okay. Can you hear?" It was then Snow noticed the fluid running from her ears. They had punctured her eardrums. She was deaf! God why? Why? Goddamn! Goddamn! Goddamn!

Leslie and Peter watched helplessly, knowing they couldn't help him in this sorrow. They watched the rage build. It was passion. Passion born of love. And when passion of love is injured, it creates a passion of hate. Both Leslie and Peter were frightened when Snow became suddenly calm, steady, cold.

Snow scooped up Tracy's body and gently placed her in the bed from which he had just risen.

"We've got to call a doctor, an ambulance," Leslie insisted.

"No," was Beckett Snow's terse reply. Leslie and

Peter looked at each other anxiously, surprised, as Snow walked to the phone.

"Yes, I'd like the telephone number for Duane Monroe, please. . . . "Yes, that's right, Potomac, Maryland. Good, thank you, operator. Goodbye."

Snow's courtesy to the operator stunned them. "Please" and "thank you" were hardly the language of the bereaved. But they were just beginning to realize the psychological limits that this man Beckett could reach.

Leslie got hand towels from the hall linen closet and took them to Tracy's bedside along with a basin of warm water. While Snow made telephone calls, she gently sponged Tracy's wounds.

"Duane? Sorry to wake you. . . . It's Beck Snow. What? Yeah, it *has* been a long time. . . . Well, you might have guessed that I didn't call up to have a friendly chat this early in the morning. . . . Uhmmm, right . . . right." Snow nodded as if the man were sitting in front of him.

"Well, I didn't think there'd come the time I'd have to take you up on that offer, but I need a favor . . . a big favor. I can pay. . . . Sure I understand, but I've got the money if you want to reconsider.

"Right," Snow continued. "Look, I want to shoot straight with you. I'm a fugitive from justice. Right . . . you knew? Okay, yeah, that's a real kick. Sure, I understand *your* past predicaments better now. Uh-huh. Okay, look, I have a friend, a *very* special friend who looks like she's been worked over by experts. What? The worst, whatever class interrogation that is. . . . I'm not very conversant with the terms you guys use. But she needs medical help. No, no, no, more than a safe doctor. She needs institutional care."

Snow listened. "You think you can swing it? I know it's a big favor, but you think it's possible? Okay, where

249

do we meet you? Yep, okay. I've got you. . . . Thanks, I *do* appreciate it. Bye."

"Okay, Peter, Leslie—can I get some help from you?"

"What're we doing?"

"Well, you can't just call the hospital for someone who's hurt like she is. There'll be cops crawling all over."

"But she's *got* to get to a hospital," Leslie protested.

"You think I don't realize that?" Snow said sharply. "I certainly want to get her to a doctor. But it has to be the right doctor and the right hospital. Putting her anywhere else is to deliver her into the hands of the people who want to kill her." He took a breath.

"I've called in an IOU, a big IOU, with a fellow who recruits mercenary soldiers. I had him by the balls once and didn't prosecute."

"Why?" asked Peter.

"Reasons," Snow said. "Because it was necessary. Anyway, he's got pull with the CIA hospital in Northern Virginia . . . says he's worked for them in the past and they owe him big. He's going to get Tracy in. We're supposed to meet him at Tysons Corners, and go to the hospital with him. Okay? Let's go. Just help me get Tracy into Leslie's car and then I can handle it from there."

Duane Monroe had made a good living killing people. He had—he thought this morning as he drove through the paddocks and gazed at his horses—made a *very* good living for himself.

Ex-Green Beret, Ex-Navy SEAL, Ex-CIA (covertly), Monroe was a big man—he towered a head over people who were only six feet tall or so—and was built like a fireplug. His sandy-brown hair was still cropped in a bushcut through which the healed scars of wars in a dozen countries were visible.

Monroe wheeled his Corvette onto River Road and

wound through the gears in quick succession. When Vietnam had ended, Monroe, and thousands like him, all expertly trained by the armed forces, made a poor reentry into society. They simply loved violence too much. So they enlisted in the services of African countries—Angola, Rhodesia, Yemen, Ethiopia—the names were familiar. They were paid well, and they killed well. And they enjoyed it.

Modern buccaneers they were, and the image satisfied them. The CIA used them; the United States depended on them, supplied them with arms; the Pope hired them to guard missionaries from the atrocities of guerrillas.

But no one claimed to understand them. No one could claim to understand a person who could enter the jungle in the morning on horseback, armed with an M-16, track down men—human beings—as if they were big-horned rams, kill them, and then return to camp in the evenings, listen to and appreciate Bach's Brandenburg concertos, and debate the bouquet of the latest arrival from Bordeaux.

But that's the way they were: educated, cultured, expert killers, and proud of it. Soldiers of fortune with hospitalization plans and life insurance underwritten by Lloyds of London.

But now Monroe made most of his money recruiting former Vietnam vets for mercenary service. It paid better and he didn't have to get shot at—physically. That was where he had run into Snow. Recruiting mercenaries is against federal laws, and Snow had caught him redhanded at it. But the government relies too heavily on mercenaries to allow someone to prosecute them. The CIA, the military intelligence heads, among others, had "reasoned" with Beckett Snow, and as far as he could tell, Monroe figured it was the only time Snow had dropped a prosecution.

Monroe pulled off the Beltway onto Route 123,

caught the green light and turned right into the parking lot of Tysons Corners regional shopping center.

Snow had already arrived. He was alone, save for the figure stretched out in back. The back seat of the auto was folded forward, making plenty of room for Tracy. Monroe stopped the Corvette behind the orange subcompact. He leapt out, agile and fast for a man his size and age; he had just turned 58.

"Snow, good buddie, you look a little different than the last time I saw ya; little something to throw your colleagues, uh, former colleagues, off yer trail?"

Snow got out of the car. He offered his hand and the huge man took it immediately.

"Yeah, guess so," Snow said, his voice somber. "Hadda do something. Uh . . . the hospital okay?"

"Hey, I wouldn't have told ya so if it wasn't sure."

They both got in their cars, and Snow prepared to follow Monroe out of the parking lot.

"Duane?"

The window of the Corvette rolled down. "Huh?"

"Thank you."

"You in love?"

"Yeah."

"No thanks needed."

An hour later, Snow and Monroe sat silently, facing each other over two cups of stale vending-machine coffee. The doctor walked toward them.

"Gentlemen," the doctor began. Names were never used in the hospital. People in deep cover seldom knew each other's names, rarely saw their faces. Patients in this hospital wore hoods when outside the rooms and while being serviced by any of the hospital's personnel. One leak could wipe out the deepest cover.

"Gentlemen, I'd like to report the young lady is resting well in her room. The . . . interrogation was done thoroughly and expertly. There is no internal bleeding and the tympanic membrane—eardrums—

252

were easily repaired. I've given her antibiotics to combat the threat of infection, which is severe with the number of fouled injuries she has—"

"Can I see her, doctor?"

"Of course, I'll escort both of you to her room. But I'll caution you, she's had a shock. The emotional shock will take far longer to heal than the physical ones. I've given her a sedative, and instructions to keep her heavily sedated for the next four days. She won't be very coherent before the end of the week. I hope you understand."

Snow nodded. Monroe made no comment.

"Gentlemen, please place these over your heads and draw the strings tight. Security, you understand."

Snow and Monroe were handed heavy black cloth bags, which they placed over their heads and drew shut as the doctor had prescribed. They followed the doctor into Tracy's room.

"You can take off your hoods."

An orderly in a white coat, holding an Uzi machine gun greeted them.

"Stevie, how's tricks?"

The doctor left.

"Fine, Duane. I'm surprised to see you here."

"So am I, especially this early in the morning."

"Yeah, so's he. . . . Meet Steve Goldstein . . . sometimes CIA, sometimes Mossad, sometimes freelance."

"Mossad?"

"Israeli CIA." Monroe noticed the frown on Goldstein's face. "Only better." Goldstein smiled.

"Can I have a minute or so?" Snow interrupted their banter. "Alone?"

"Sure," Monroe said and went into the bathroom with the guard.

"Tracy?" Snow walked to the edge of the bed. "Can you hear me, babe?" He walked closer. She was swaddled in gauze and tape. She looked so helpless, Snow

253

thought. Oh, God! Why did this have to happen? Could he have prevented it by being more on his guard that day?

"Hey, babe, can you hear me?" Then Snow remembered the eardrums. Of course she couldn't hear him. She was deaf for the time being. A tear dribbled down Snow's cheek. With the knuckle of his index finger, Snow slowly stroked the bare spot on Tracy's cheek. One eye fluttered, opened, tried to focus on Snow's face. Was it recognition that he saw?

He stroked her cheek again. "I love you," he whispered moving his mouth slowly, praying she could read his lips. "I love you." And there was the most imperceptible of nods, underneath the bandages, she was telling him she understood; that she loved him too. Then she closed her eye and returned to the world of drugged rest.

"It's going to be all right, babe. It's going to be all right." He said aloud, more for himself than for Tracy. But somehow, something inside of him knew it wouldn't be all right.

"Duane," Snow called out. "I'm ready to leave."

Chapter Twenty-four

"You're going to do *what?*" Leslie was incredulous.

"Look, there's nothing I can do here anyway, not right now," Snow explained. "The doctors said she'd be sedated for at least four days. She's in another world and she's not going to miss me or anyone else when she's in that state."

"But she's going to need you when she comes out of it," Leslie protested.

"I'll be back by then. Anyway I've left your name and Gilbert's name with Duane Monroe."

Snow looked at his watch. "We've got to get moving. It's nearly seven and my plane leaves from Dulles at eight-thirty. Can you drive me or should I catch a cab?"

"Suit yourself. I'll be happy to drive."

"Let's do that, I can fill you in on everything else during the drive."

Snow grabbed the handles of the soft-sided luggage he'd borrowed from Peter Gilbert and slung the carry bag over his shoulder.

"Let's go."

After leaving Tracy at the CIA medical complex, Snow and Duane Monroe had headed for Alexandria.

Among the trendy shops, restaurants, and boutiques of the Old Town section lies a remnant of the times before the old harbor area was restored and renovated.

A long series of windowless warehouses stretches for four blocks parallel to the Potomac and bears the cryptic name of Interarms.

Interarms was once owned by the CIA. It was a company, a wholly-owned subsidiary. This had been the Sears, Roebuck of the American-approved terrorist. Through here went arms for Israeli freedom fighters; for the Bay of Pigs; for a dozen uprisings—some successful, others not—in countries the U.S. wanted to destabilize.

And so half an hour after leaving the hospital that afternoon, Snow and Monroe arrived at the white brick warehouse of Interarms.

They walked to the front door, an impressive dark-stained walnut entrance—incongruous, given the warehouse setting.

"Walnut veneer," said Monroe. "With an inch and a half of armor plate behind it."

The door clicked and buzzed. An intercom voice asked them to step in.

As the door closed behind them, they heard it click locked again. They found themselves in a cramped anteroom, facing a battery of lights and a camera, as well as a mirror, which Snow assumed was a one-way window with someone on the other side scrutinizing them.

"Please face the camera and look at the red dot, gentlemen," the voice commanded. They obeyed. The camera whirred, the brighter of the set of lights dimmed.

"Thank you," the intercom said. "Mr. Monroe, I believe. And who is your companion?"

"I'll have to insist on talking to Porter about this."

"As you wish. You realize it entails complications. You don't have an appointment." The voice was disapproving.

"Cut the bullshit and buzz us through to Porter. This box is getting too fucking hot."

And so it had gone for the better part of three hours. It had been an expensive three hours, Snow observed now as Leslie drove him up the George Washington Parkway toward Dulles Airport, and toward a solution to the riddle.

Yes, it was an expensive solution. By the time the security officers at Interarms had buzzed them out that afternoon, Snow was minus $30,000.

For that sum, Snow now had two fake passports: one for his current altered identity, and one for a disguise they had supplied him. He also had credit cards: American Express, VISA, and a dozen others, in each name, as well as a driver's license for his second fake identity.

In addition to the passports and the cards, Snow carried a variety of shaving cream, toothpaste, and other containers inside of which were the component parts of an Ingram automatic machine pistol. The firm offered a variety of such weapons tooled and modified to fit ordinary items, all so perfectly disguised as to pass even the most rigorous customs inspections.

Snow leaped from Leslie's car when it arrived at the ramp at Dulles and grabbed his bags from the rear seat. He started to close the door.

"Beckett?"

He leaned into the car. "Huh?"

"Be careful." She patted his cheek. Snow closed the door and watched as the car made its way through traffic, back to the access highway.

The customary check was perfunctory; the bag with the concealed weapons was checked, and Snow took his shoulder bag through the X-ray inspection with no trouble. His KLM flight to Amsterdam was called soon after he'd checked in at the counter.

When the seatbelt sign blinked out, Snow pulled his shoulder bag from underneath the seat in front of him and withdrew a paperback book.

"In spite of everything I still believe that people are good at heart," Snow read. "If I look up into the heavens, I think that it will all come right, that this cruelty too will end and that peace and tranquillity will return again."

The power and energy of the passage was overwhelming. Snow closed his paperback copy of *The Diary of Anne Frank* and laid it on the seat beside him. And he wished it were so. It hadn't been for Anne Frank, and he wondered if it would be for him.

Chapter Twenty-five

It was a brilliant blue day when Snow arrived in downtown Amsterdam, and people were walking around with their coats unbuttoned. Snow watched the steady stream of people getting on and off the bright yellow trams and the buses, trying to hail the few taxis that plied the main train station, catching rides with friends in their autos, and the bicycles, everywhere the bicycles.

Snow finally obtained a city map, walked inside the station and bought $100 worth of Guilders, and headed right, out of the station, on foot.

Northwest along the Prins Hendrikkade, Snow threaded his path through crowds of people and across the cobblestoned main drag. He turned southwest when he realized the Singel Canal and the traffic thinned, the noise dissolved, and save for the infrequent motor vehicle, Snow imagined he could be in almost any century since these buildings were constructed, some of them, five and six hundred years ago.

The buildings echoed the architecture of the train station: fancy brickwork, gables, white stone, and white trim for windows. Most were three stories tall with a basement half above, half below ground. To go deeper was to invite the invasion of the sea that was the Amsterdammers' constant companion.

The water in the canal moved more rapidly than

Snow had remembered. It must have rained recently, he thought, for the levels of the canals were regulated very carefully.

The sun spilled into the canal and made its waters roil with gold. Streams of Amsterdammers, headed to work, walked self-absorbed, and Snow wondered if they ever looked up to appreciate the beauty of their city.

Snow walked into the street to circumvent a car parked on the brick sidewalk, and then back on the walk as one of the funny little cars that Amsterdammers drove—the ones that look like a cross between a Volkswagen Beetle and a bloated toad—came racing down the street, its driver oblivious to the traffic hazards.

The street sign Snow noted was the Raad Huisstraat. He pulled out his maps and checked it. He looked right and saw the church tower from which Toren (Tower) Hotel took its name. It was, Snow knew from his last visit, the bell tower whose chimes were mentioned in Anne Frank's diary. He'd gone too far; but not by very much.

A quick block west to the Keisergracht, the Emperor's Canal, and a block and a half north along the canal brought him to the hotel.

It hadn't changed. The concierge was in the breakfast room chatting with a guest, and, to Snow's surprise, remembered him from his previous visit. He recalled warmly Snow's enthusiasm for learning some basic words of Dutch. And yes, the single room on the second floor with its private bath and the view of the yard behind was available.

A shower washed away some of the emotional grime of the transAtlantic flight, and Snow went downstairs to have breakfast. The Anne Frank house didn't open until 9:00 AM, which meant he had almost an hour to kill.

What would he say? Snow wondered as he walked down to breakfast. It seemed ridiculous to spill his story to the first person he approached.

Snow decided he would take every opportunity to chat with the museum personnel, dropping hints along the way. Someone would pick up on them and they'd proceed from there. Here he was, Snow thought, wandering around Amsterdam on the faith of a handful of facts and a boxful of tattered artifacts.

But there *had* to be an answer, because the answer was the only route to justice. Justice for Tracy. The thought of her made him want to cry. And there were all the others, all important, but none so much as she.

He finished the meal and hurried up the narrow stairs to his room where he opened the fake toiletries and assembled the Ingram. He slammed a full magazine into the pistol, and slipped a spare into his jacket pocket.

In the other pocket went the contents of the box.

With the Ingram securely secreted in the pocket of his Burberry overcoat, Snow stepped into the crisp Amsterdam weather. The Anne Frank House was only two blocks away, one up, and over one canal at 263 Prinsengracht, Prince's Canal. He noted that his watch read 9:17 AM, plenty of time for even a late opening.

He almost passed the slightly shabby, nondescript canal house. The brickwork was pedestrian when compared with some of the better examples of architecture, and missing was any pretension of ornament.

Snow stopped in front of the door and realized with alarm that the house was still closed. He knocked.

"Hello?" He waited for a response that didn't come. "Hello, is anybody here?"

There was still no response. Snow started to walk back toward the hotel but pounded on the door again instead.

Finally, the door opened a crack.

"The museum is closed." A voice issued from the dark crack in the door. No face was visible.

"When will it open, sir?" Snow asked.

"Not today."

"Tomorrow?" Snow asked.

"Perhaps then, maybe not. I don't know."

"Please, I must talk to . . ." Snow stopped. "I've just come from the United States," he explained. "I haven't come here for pleasure. I've . . . I've come because I have business here."

"What sort of business?" The voice was wary.

"Well, I . . . I don't want to talk. . . . That is, can't I just come in and talk to you a bit. It's very important. It's the only reason I flew all the way from America. Please don't make my trip fruitless."

"No. Tell me your business first," the voice continued. "What could be so urgent here that you must come all the way from America? Who are you?"

He was on the spot. To give his real name, especially to someone he didn't trust, could be to be turned over to the authorities. In addition to which, he had no identification on him with his real name.

On the other hand, what sort of credibility would he have when he admitted he was traveling—and illegally at that—under a fake passport?

"My name, sir, is Beckett Snow. I am a scholar, from Cornell University." Snow lied, using his alma mater as cover. "I've come to do research."

"You lie." The voice was harsh. "We have no appointment, no record for a request to do research."

"I didn't realize you needed that."

"Either you are a liar or a careless scholar," the voice said.

"All right. All right. I've come because of *this*." Snow reached in his pocket and withdrew the yellow Star of David.

"So?" The voice mocked him. "If you were a

scholar, you'd know that there are millions of those. That cloth star has haunted us since the Middle Ages. That one appears to date from 1942. I can't imagine that you travelled 3,000 miles to study that."

"This was given to me by Adam Carothers," Snow said.

"Wait right there," the voice commanded. The door slammed.

Fifteen minutes passed, and then half an hour. Snow watched merchants and the delivery men and school children and tourists pass. He watched as several tourists approached the house, read the sign, some even tried the door, and walked away. Snow was about to knock again when two men walked up to him coming from the direction of the tower. One moved with a distinct, painful limp.

"Beckett Snow?"

Snow panicked. Were these policemen? Had the man inside the house called the authorities? He started to put his hand in his coat pocket to grab the Ingram.

"I wouldn't do that if you want to stay alive." The man with the limp was already pointing a gun at him. "Are you Snow?"

"Yes."

"If you're not what you say you are, you're dead. Understand?"

Snow nodded.

"Good, now follow us."

Chapter Twenty-six

The two men who escorted Snow were dressed in a shapeless fashion. Their clothes were identical; only the colors and patterns differed: baggy woolen pants that were too long and slumped at their shoe tops, held up with a belt that was too tight; a cardigan sweater covering a plain white shirt; a faded black overcoat that had turned gray at the elbows.

Both men appeared to be in their late fifties and both were unmistakably Semitic.

They walked around the corner of Prinsengracht and Raad Huisstraat to a house on the Keisersgracht and were admitted by a gray-haired housekeeper. She promptly conducted them out the rear of her home across the courtyard and through the rear entrance of 263 Prinsengracht, the Anne Frank House.

They entered the basement and as Snow's eyes adjusted to the dim light, his mind exploded.

The man on the motorcycle sat in a chair facing the door. He smiled at Snow.

"You! You fucking bastard . . . killer!" Snow screamed and lunged for the man. Before the two young guards could get control of Snow he had managed to kick the man in his crotch and pound his head against the rough stone basement walls.

In the end it took the two young men and the older ones who had brought Snow to the basement to gain control. The man who had ridden a motorcycle in Washington now lay unconscious, bleeding from one eye and from the back of his head. But it was doubtful, Snow would learn later, that he had felt any of the blows.

"Please, please let me up," Snow pleaded. Tears of frustration and anger coursed down both cheeks. He strained at the four men who pinned him to the damp basement floor.

"You don't *understand*, he killed my friends. He tortured the woman I *love*," he tried to explain. Please, please . . . please." He closed his eyes and wept. He felt a needle prick the skin of his thigh, and remembered seeing a softness in the eyes of one of the older men just before the world went gooey.

The dose was a light one. Snow awoke two hours later, stripped to his shorts, lying in his room at the Hotel Toren. Leaning over his bed were the two older men.

Snow slowly opened his eyelids and focused his eyes.

"Easy, my friend," the man with the limp said. "We will not hurt you."

"But the man . . ." Snow groggily propped himself up on one elbow. "The man in the basement . . . Where is he now? How did he get here?"

"He got here yesterday," the other man said, "and demanded information. And when we wouldn't give it to him he attacked Aaron," he said, indicating the man who limped, "and threatened to kill me. I am Joseph."

"But how?" Snow was still reeling from the tranquilizer. "I want him. . . . He's got some answers I *have* to have."

"Easy," said the man called Aaron. Snow couldn't place the accent. It was perfect English, colored by no accent Snow had ever heard before. "We tried to get answers. This man was a professional. We've never seen anything like it. He refused to break—drugs, electronics, pain—nothing worked. He's a zombie and you wouldn't have had any better luck than we."

"But give me a chance."

"It's too late," the man called Joseph said. "He's dead."

"Dead?"

"Yes. We would have killed him sooner, but we wondered if he was working alone; wondering if he'd be missed."

"Jesus, you must've thought I worked with him."

"Indeed," Aaron said. "But your response, and the contents of your pockets, were your witness."

"Then you know why I've come?"

"No, I'm afraid we don't."

"But you see, I'm looking for something, something that is very important, something I . . ."

"We know that. We've been carefully briefed on the arrival of *someone* bearing the . . . artifacts you have.

"But we don't know what it is you're looking for. We're gatekeepers, screens, part of a network. We can only tell you what step to take next."

"Which is?"

"Before we tell you that," Joseph countered, "please explain your relationship to the man."

Snow did. Starting with Steve Drachler's hand, the man's presence when the professor's head crashed through the bedroom window—events that seemed years past—and his presence when Tracy had been delivered to Peter Gilbert's home. As he told the story, the man called Aaron seemed to withdraw. His eyes grew transparent, and his mouth long, sad. At the end he placed his hand on Snow's.

"It never ends," Aaron said softly. "Things change and evil remains. It's sad. We work, we pour our all into making things change; making sure, or trying, that

266

history won't, can't repeat itself, and yet it does. It does."

Snow was puzzled. "And who are you?" Snow asked.

"We," Aaron looked at the man called Joseph, "are survivors." He reached down and pushed the cardigan sleeve up past his elbow. He slowly unbuttoned the cuff and rolled it back, revealing a bluish-black tattoo whose origin in a concentration camp was unmistakable.

"We work," Aaron said. His voice was sad, no, Snow thought, not sad but despairing. "We work against the minds that drive the people who must destroy others. We only hope you are successful in finding the people who sent that man."

Aaron got up and Joseph followed his lead.

"Tomorrow at precisely 3:30 PM you will visit the Van Gogh Museum. You will check your bag, as required at the door. You will then walk into the main area and turn right, toward the artists' workshop. You will go to the entrance to the workshop and tell the person who meets you, 'I'd like to inquire about entering your course of instruction'."

"And?" Snow asked.

"That's it," Aaron said. "That's all we know."

"But what's supposed to happen?" Snow persisted.

"I've told you all. You must have faith."

Aaron and his companion walked to the door. Aaron turned around.

"In your shoulder bag, you will find your weapon and reproductions of everything identifiable we took from the man who attacked me. May God be by your side."

While Beckett Snow slept off the after effects of the tranquilizer, Peter Gilbert stood just outside Stefan Sherbok's inner office and pretended not to notice the activity at a keyboard where one of Sherbok's other assistants was punching in an elaborate alphanumeric code.

A casual observer would have no way of knowing that the same activity was taking place at an identical console in Sherbok's office. But Peter Gilbert was no casual observer. He knew that each person had half the required combination to Sherbok's safe, and that the dual keyboard system—similar to those used in nuclear missile silos—was used to make sure that the safe could not be opened by a single person.

Technically, Gilbert should not have been in the anteroom during the process. But rules, in most bureaucracies, are rarely followed to the letter, and this one was no exception. Bending this rule would give Peter both halves of the code.

When the time came to open Sherbok's document safe, Peter politely moved away from the keyboard, pretending to show no interest in the activity.

The codes and clearances and the sequences made Sherbok's files one of two such super-secure repositories in the White House. There *were* better devices extant, but the White House, with a need for easy access to its information, settled on a level it felt sufficient, particularly since the personnel were subject to checks and investigations as rigorous as those for intelligence branch personnel, at least that was the case for people like Gilbert.

Quietly repeating the code to himself, Peter kibbitzed with the office occupants and busied himself at a table on the other side of the office on paperwork he had invented. After a respectable time, he politely said his regards and left. In his breast pocket was a scrap of paper with the code penciled on it.

The outer door to the National Security Advisor's office clicked slowly shut behind him as he made his way toward the elevator. Perspiration trickled down his ribs.

Resisting the urge to turn around and look behind him, Gilbert punched the elevator call button and waited impatiently for the doors to open.

At the bottom, the elevator occupied the dead-end of a corridor leading to Gilbert's office. There was no one present. He checked his watch. It was 9:53 AM, Wednesday.

In Amsterdam, Beckett Snow groggily rolled over and fumbled on the nightstand for his watch. He heard his map and several coins hit the floor. When he saw the time he sat up hastily. It was 3:53 PM. He had to get to the post-telegraph office to make a phone call to check on Tracy and he wanted to visit the American Express office to pick up any messages for him.

The second shower of the day had a better effect than the first. Despite the sedative, most of the jet lag seemed to be gone, and he felt normal. Gone was the fishbowl, spaced-out feeling he had had when he first arrived. But in its place was a nagging anxiety about Tracy, lying unconscious halfway around the world. How was she, he wondered? What would she be like when he got back? God! How he loved her. Why, he thought, why did he have to meet her like this?

Snow tried to put thoughts of her out of his mind as he strode over the cobbled sidewalk along the Keisergracht. Behind him the bellwork of the Wester-kerk chimed a baroque melody that was familiar, secure, and reassuring. He walked on.

The Dam, the old square on which the national palace sat, was jammed with college students, sitting, standing, milling about, listening to a protest speech. Judging from the signs the demonstrators carried, it was an antinuclear rally.

The post-telegraph office, Snow's memory told him, was in the vicinity of the National Palace. After wandering for a couple of blocks, he found it.

Snow made his way up the half-flight of steps into a fluorescent-lighted room that could have been any bureaucracy in any country. He filled out the forms, giving as the requested telephone a number left by Duane Monroe. The number, the mercenary had told him, was a sterile exchange box that would automatically redispatch the caller to whatever number Monroe chose.

This afternoon the exchange directed Snow's call to the hospital room in which Tracy still lay unconscious. A male voice which answered informed him of her condition. The man, who identified himself as an associate of Duane's, said the doctor's report indicated a slight infection, but nothing serious.

Snow breathed a sigh of relief. "Do they, does the doctor, have any idea when she might wake up?" he asked.

"Well, she's still sedated and sleeping pretty deeply," the other replied. Then he added, "They got a head man for her when she wakes up, you know, a shrink."

The tension flooded back. "Yeah . . . yeah, she's gonna need that," Snow managed. "Good."

There were no other messages, the man told him, from Duane or anyone else. He invited Snow to call back any time; the call would be directed to whatever location Monroe had prearranged.

Snow hung up and headed for the American Express office. They had no messages for him. Snow supposed any messages from Leslie or Peter would go through Monroe's system now. But he'd, just to be sure, check again tomorrow before visiting the Van Gogh Museum.

So he had nearly 24 hours to kill. Amsterdam, Snow knew was a live-wire city. Anything, literally anything, was available. Perhaps he'd visit the Zeedijk that night to try and take his mind off things. But for now, he decided to take his stomach's mind off being hungry.

Brilliant sunshine lit up the Damrak as Snow walked

toward the train station. The yellow masts of barges glowed in the sun; the reds were fire and the blue electric. Shadows seemed to have no bottom.

Snow finally arrived at the little Indonesian restaurant he had remembered from half a decade before. He took a table by the window where he could watch the people pass.

And he thought.

The half decade since he'd been here seemed more like half a century. He had been young and restless and bold then; now he was restless, a little older, and a lot bolder. His daydreams took him back to the Anne Frank house. Was that really this morning?

And the men who greeted him, Joseph and Aaron. What drove them? Who were they, that they had been entrusted with this part of the path, and, Snow's heart caught up with itself, he *was* on the path! The gamble had paid off. Funny, with the excitement of the morning, the realization that he was indeed on the trail, on the right trail, had not hit him until now.

But someone had gotten there before him. The man on the motorcycle. How? How could the man have learned, and why now, just a day ahead of Snow?

Snow gazed at the people waltzing in the sunlight with their shadows and he wondered, what motivated Aaron and Joseph. Was it love for the future, or hate of the past, anger over those who had tortured and abused them? And the man on the motorcycle, what of his motivations—ideology, greed? And as he wondered about their motivations, his thoughts turned inward.

What was it for him? What drove him on, plunged him relentlessly through this insanity that would not stop? It was love for Tracy, he reflected; that certainly was his prime mover. But it was more than that. It was frustration. And rage, yes, rage, at the unfairness, at the disorder. The power these people possessed was

271

intolerable, unthinkable. And it was evil. That was clear and simple, as few things these days were.

He had to go on. He had to sort out the chaos. Keep on fighting. There were still so many pieces of this puzzle that did not fit.

The man on the motorcycle. A carrion bird in Washington, a mysterious visitor to Amsterdam. He had gotten to Snow's contacts here even before Snow had managed to. How could he have known? That bothered Snow the most. Yet somehow he felt he had the answer, lodged somewhere in his unconscious mind. He had the missing piece; if only he could put it into place.

Snow brooded and ordered more beer, one after the other. His thoughts chased each other in endless circles: Tracy, the man on the motorcycle, Aaron, Joseph, Steve, the professor, and always, always Tracy. Snow realized after his fifth glass of Amstel that what he really needed, what he really wanted to do while killing time was to get roaring drunk. At 7:09 PM, fortified with a good buzz, he set off for the Zeedijk, Amsterdam's wide-open red-light district.

"You can't mean that." Leslie was talking through a mouthful of hamburger. "I mean, it's so soon and all."

"We have to," Peter Gilbert explained. He'd spent the morning checking and rechecking. He and Leslie were having a late lunch at the Old Ebbit Grill on F Street, N.W., about three blocks from the White House. He looked down blankly at his untouched food as he spoke. "You know, we don't have much of a choice."

Leslie swallowed. "It's just . . . It seems like what you're talking about could be so . . . final."

"*That* is why it took me so long to make the decision," Peter said quietly. "I realized from the beginning how final it might be."

Leslie was silent. Peter went on. "You know," he said. "I've always been keen at knowing which way

272

things were going, and then going with them as far as they would take me, getting out when I had made a big enough profit. I never really cared which way it went or what had to happen to other people when I took my profit. I never did something just because it 'felt right'. I've never trusted feelings." He was looking at her intently now.

"But this is *it*," Gilbert continued. "I *feel* this is the right thing to do. I have got to do it."

"Peter, you make me feel better about it," Leslie said. "You're a very inspiring person, you know. A leader. I can't turn back either for my own reasons. So show me the way."

"Well, since the safe codes are changed after tomorrow, we'll go in early, like 5 AM. That's early enough to beat Sherbok's people, but not so early that it'll raise too much suspicion from the guards."

He continued. They would both enter the White House complex through their usual gates and meet in his office. He gave her the code to the inner office terminal. As a top assistant to Sherbok, Gilbert had a key to the inner office door. He would, that afternoon, steal the secretary's key to the outer door.

"Take whatever you can't live without to my apartment tonight," he told her. "We'll contact this Monroe tonight and see if he can find some place for us to stay."

"You're really committed." Leslie was in awe.

"I have to be, don't I. It means the end of my life as I know it. And you'd better know it means the same for you."

"What will you do?" she asked.

"I can start over. Plastic surgery, forged diplomas and credentials. It'll have to be a life in Europe, maybe in one of the capitals of the more developed African countries that still tolerate whites. I have plenty of money. I called my broker today, told him I was buying some real estate. I'll have about $300,000 by tonight."

Leslie looked at him numbly.

"And you?" Peter asked.

"Survive," Leslie said. "I'll survive."

Chapter Twenty-seven

Somebody was using a staple gun to nail pieces of rotten beef jerky to the sides of his head, and somebody else was stuffing his mouth with cotton and peanut butter.

Beckett Snow had a hangover.

After one attempt at getting up, which made the man with the staple gun go berserk, Snow settled for opening his eyes slowly. It was the first time he could remember sunlight making a sound—but it did—loud enough to make his head hurt. He settled for lying quietly watching the red of the back of his eyelids. He wanted to move his head out of the sun but was afraid of the motion.

The realization that he was in Amsterdam came quickly. The events of the previous day were recalled with comparative ease: the phone call, American Express, the Indonesian cafe, and the walk to the Zeedijk.

Then things started to get fuzzy.

First there was the sleazy bar on the Oude Zijds Achterburgwal where the pitchers of beer were but a thin front for hashish users and the air hung in parallel layers, grey with the pungent fragrance. Snow vaguely remembered a spotlight shining on a scruffy rock band that sounded like fourteen miles of tin cans strung together with high C piano wire. After a while he didn't notice.

Things started to get lost totally about the time he entered a club on the Oude Zijds Voorburgwal that featured a variety of live sexual perversions involving groups of people, champagne bottles, snakes, Christmas tree lights, and a terrier.

His fifth round of strong, and expensive, drinks was the last thing he remembered before this morning.

Or was it morning? Fear that he might be missing his Van Gogh Museum rendezvous overcame the little man with the staple gun, and Snow opened his eyes to fumble for his watch.

It was gone. Snow thought and bolted upright, which sent fits of righteous indignation into his head. Snow started to panic but then he realized his watch was on his wrist: 12:17. He had a little more than three hours.

Snow contemplated sleeping for several more hours and decided against it; he might not wake up. Slowly, he dragged his legs over the side of the bed facing away from the sunny window and slumped up.

Stumbling into the bathroom, he was thankful for having taken a room with its own shower. He turned on the hot water and faced the mirror to survey his face. A shower would help.

A half hour later, Snow had packed and carried his bags down the stairs to check out. Regardless of what occurred that afternoon at the museum, Snow felt he would be leaving Amsterdam.

It was 1:15 when he finally settled his bill and headed toward the train station. There he'd retrieve his shoulder bag, leave his suitcase, and take the yellow tram that ran from the Grand Central Station to a point only a few blocks from the Rijksmuseum and the Van Gogh.

Several tablets of aspirin purchased from a drugstore on the Damrak served to dull the pain of Snow's ravaged head. Not trusting his constitution to foreign food, Snow scarfed down two Big Macs and two large cups of coffee at the McDonald's he'd passed the day before.

The tram clanged to a halt at the stop. Snow boarded the tram and sat suffering in silence until it reached the Weteringschans. There he disembarked.

It was 3:11 when he reached the Van Gogh Museum. He had nineteen minutes to kill, so he sat on the grass and gazed nervously at the passersby.

At precisely 3:30 PM, Snow traded his shoulder bag for a receipt, paid another three guilders to enter, and found the artists' studio.

He was met at the door by a gaunt man who looked emaciated to the point of danger.

"I'd like to inquire about entering your course of instruction," Snow told the man.

There was no recognition in the thin man's eyes. Instead, he held up his hand, indicating that Snow was to wait where he was. Soon, the emaciated man's opposite—a jolly, well-nourished burgomaster type—approached.

"Yes, my friend. What can I do for you?"

Snow repeated his sentence, word for word, as he'd been instructed by the men from the Anne Frank House.

"I'm sorry, there must be a mistake." The smile had vanished from the man's jovial face. "One must be referred here, and we take only the most highly recommended pupils."

"No, listen." Snow drew closer, lowering his voice. "I'm here because of Aaron and Joseph."

The man's face did not change. "I know of many people with those names; can you be more precise?"

"Yes, damnit!" Snow's voice rose, panic welling up just below his skin. "You *know* who I'm talking about. Aaron and Joseph from the Anne Frank House."

"I see," the man said. "And I suppose you have these men's last names?"

Snow felt sheepish. No. He didn't have the names.

"Well, I suppose you have made a mistake, my friend."

"No!" Snow was yelling now. He hadn't come this far to be turned back by some uniformed fool. Heads turned and politely looked away. "*You've* made a mistake. You have something for me. Give it to me *now*!"

"My friend," the man said, speaking in a voice so quiet that Snow had to strain to listen. "It's you who have made a mistake." Then, suddenly louder, "And if you don't leave immediately, I shall have to call security." With that the man turned on his heel and strode back to the midst of his class.

All eyes were on Snow now. A uniformed guard took a step toward him, waiting for his next move. "Damn!" Snow muttered under his breath.

Snow turned and walked angrily back to the check stand, retrieved his shoulder bag, and stalked out the front door. He had gotten about four strides down the sidewalk when he realized the tiny padlock he had used to secure the zipper to the main compartment was missing. He turned and found it on the sidewalk, about halfway to the building.

"Dirty bastards!" Snow was about to storm back through the museum doors, when he stopped. What was he doing? He couldn't afford to lose control of himself now. He couldn't just barge in there and demand things. He didn't speak the language, he was traveling under an illegal passport, was wanted for murder in the States, had a gun in his bag, and had just verbally accosted a museum employee. No, it wouldn't fare well.

Cursing to himself, Snow sat on a bench in front of the museum and unzipped his bag. Nothing was missing. The pistol was there, as was the additional ammunition, and the Star of David, the photograph, and the rest.

He started to calm down. Perhaps it was his own fault, perhaps he had not closed the lock himself. Then he saw something at the bottom of the main compartment.

It was a receipt for an item stored at the Left Luggage counter at the Hauptbahnhof, Munich.

It was *there*. The link. He had *not* been mistaken. But the man's reaction to him was puzzling. Why was he so hostile? Why did he react as if Snow had made a mistake?

Snow shouldered his bag and walked toward a tram stop. Why? He was utterly confused. Was it possible, then, that the man was not a part of it at all? Perhaps the errand had just been a subterfuge by the men at the Anne Frank House to get him to leave his bag? That way, if Snow were followed, their contact would not be identified. But *who* would be following him? Would the mysteries never end?

Perhaps, maybe, possibly, it might be, it could be, chance, uncertainty, fate, kismet, predestination, random chance, divine intervention. Shit! Snow thought as he sat in the Amsterdam Central Station's restaurant waiting for his 7:45 PM train to Munich, what he might give for just a little certainty.

Roughly an hour before Snow had awakened in Amsterdam, Peter Gilbert passed through the gate between the White House and the Old Executive Office Building adjacent to the East Lawn. Investigative records would later show him entering at 5:07 AM. Those same investigative records would show that a Leslie Lewis entered at her usual place of business at the old Executive Office Building's 17th Street entrance near the corner of Pennsylvania Avenue, at 5:11 AM Thursday.

"Jesus Christmas," Larry Murchison greeted Leslie as she signed in. "What in the hell are *you* doing in here so early?"

Leslie quivered inside. She hadn't expected Larry to be on watch. He had, as previously expected, been transferred to better duty, and had accompanied the President to the economic summit meeting in Japan, a meeting sponsored by the Fulcrum Commission. His presence disrupted the carefully built frame of mind she had worked so hard to construct through the remainder of yesterday and most of a sleepless night.

"Larry!" Leslie said enthusiastically, hoping she sounded natural. "The question is, what are *you* doing here, and on such a dog shift? I thought the Service had been good to you."

"I got into a couple of arguments with the management," the young man replied, shrugging his shoulders.

"Why didn't you tell me, Larry?" Leslie said. "You *know* I'd try to help you out."

"Oh, I was embarrassed. I mean, you were mainly responsible for my getting the job in the first place, and I . . . Well, you know what I mean."

"Sure I do. Well, listen, I've got to go, The Man demands." They laughed and Leslie walked on, ashamed at having to deceive such a genuinely nice person. He was, she decided, too gentle to live among the wolves that inhabited this world.

The sounds of her heels clicking on the marble floors echoed off the marble walls and back again.

At three checkpoints on her journey into the White House and down to Peter's office, Leslie presented her credentials. At 5:23 AM she walked into Peter's outer office.

"Good morning," Peter said.

"How about just 'Morning'?"

"Suit yourself. You got the code down? And everything is in your car?"

"Yep. Parked behind yours."

Peter nodded. He fumbled around in his desk drawer and stood up. "You ready?"

Together they walked out of Peter Gilbert's office. He paused by the door and took one last look behind him. Leslie read it in his eyes: it was a last glimpse at three decades of training, education, ambition, motivation, struggling, fighting, achievement.

The elevator hummed upward. Neither spoke.

"You've got the code?" he asked again, seeking to reassure himself.

"Yes. I told you that before. I've *got* it."

"Okay."

The elevator door slid open and they walked soundlessly out toward Sherbok's office. There was no one in the hallway. Peter sighed with relief.

The key slid into the lock and it opened. Once the door was closed, Peter turned on the lights.

"Okay, here goes," came Peter's strained voice from the other room, and immediately lights blinked on the console in front of Leslie. She punched in a nine in response. Moments later another light flashed; again she responded. And so it went for six steps until the green light reilluminated.

"Come on, hurry," Peter called. "Get your ID out."

She had it out by the time she reached Peter's side.

"In here, like this," he said, and they shoved their cards in. The faceless machine whirred and clicked; the two vault doors slid open. Inside were row after row of file drawers.

"Shit. It could be anywhere in here."

"Well, let's not waste time," Leslie said. "You take that row and I'll take this one."

They sorted through the files, watching the minute hands on their watches move as they did. Leslie's heart started hammering, beads of cold sweat lined her upper lip.

"I got the personnel file," she called out.

Peter grunted but didn't stop his task. It was nearly 6 AM. Shivers passed between his shoulder blades, and for just an instant his hands shook.

They sweated and kept sorting. 6:15 crept upon them. It wasn't unusual for National Security Agency people to come into work at that hour.

The floor was littered with files examined and discarded, the settling of papers the only sound louder than the two breathless intruders.

At 6:22 they had finished going through the files and they still had not found the plan for Project Prometheus.

"Come on." Peter's voice cracked. "Let's get out of here before someone comes."

"But we don't have what we came for," Leslie protested, anxiety in her voice. "I want to get out of here as much as you do, but we've *got* to find that file." She grimaced. "If you're going to fuck up your life, don't you want to have something to show for it?"

"Damnit, Leslie, you can see for yourself that they're not *here*!" Gilbert started to get up.

"No." Leslie's voice was suddenly cold. "Let's just look this thing over one more time," she said carefully. "Could we have missed something?"

"It doesn't *matter*. Let's *go!*"

Leslie smacked a file down on the table. "Wait a fucking minute, will you?" she barked. And then more softly, "Give me five minutes, okay?"

"All right, but no more."

Leslie stood back, wiped the sweat from her upper lip and surveyed the safe.

"Close all the drawers," she snapped. Peter complied.

"There." She pointed to an area inside the closet and just above the top row of file drawers. "That strip of wood. See if it moves."

Peter reached up and felt the wooden panel. To his surprise, it was hinged and moved outward with ease. A catch on each end facilitated access to the shallow drawers that ran across the top. Peter snatched the drawers from their alcoves.

"Fucking-A, they're here!" Gilbert cried.

But what he pulled out was not paper, as the other files had been, but rolls of microfilm. "This is it. *Now* let's go."

"Wait," Leslie said. "Let's put things back together. That might give us the few extra moments we need."

"Just a little too late, lady!" a voice from the door to the outer office. "Now, unless you can do some better explaining than I think you can, you're in trouble."

Leslie and Peter both whirled to face the man. He was dressed in the uniform of the Executive Protection Service and not, to Peter's relief, one of Sherbok's elite agents.

"Look, mister," Peter said, feigning confidence. "We have urgent business here for the National Security advisor." Gilbert shoved his identification badge at the guard. "Check my ID and you'll find the clearances for here are valid.

"I've got no time at all for your little police games," Peter continued. "And unless you clear out and let us get this done, you and your entire future are going to be in a helluva tight place. Do you hear me?"

"I've got to check this out." The man sounded more conciliatory now. Gilbert's act of indignation and outrage had worked. There was no one in the White House or its protection services, with the exception of Sherbok's corps, that didn't always have his eye on the monumental egos that could give him a break, or break his career.

"Okay, Mr. . . . ." Gilbert leaned close to scrutinize the man's name plate. "Mr. Erickson. You call your supervisor, and you call him in a hurry, and you give him our names, because we've got to close up here and move. Do you understand?"

"Yes, sir," Erickson said. "But you have to understand, I'm just doing my job. If I hadn't checked out a light burning . . ."

"*Mister* Erickson," Gilbert interrupted. "*I* am the top advisor to the National Security Advisor. *This* is the National Security Advisor's office, and I am here at his instructions and engaged in activities for which I possess *all* the proper security clearances. I *don't* have to understand anything other than that an urgent task I have been assigned to has been interrupted by someone who is now exceeding his authority. *That* is the only thing I understand right now, and you can be damned sure *that* is what the National Security Advisor will understand."

The guard was resting his hand on the telephone, barely two feet from Gilbert. He hesitated.

"I suggest, Mr. Erickson," Peter continued haughtily, "that since you've checked my ID and its security classification, you now check Ms. Lewis's here, and if it matches, get the fucking hell out of here!"

The guard nodded, mollified. He moved toward Leslie, who had been standing speechless throughout the entire exchange. Peter had seemed to be handling things, and she had almost begun to breathe freely again. But Peter's last statement sent her into a new paroxysm of terror.

What are you doing?! Leslie thought. *Are you crazy, Peter?* For she knew, and he must know also, that she didn't have the proper identification and it would be apparent as soon as the man looked at the back of her credentials. She was *not* cleared for this high a security classification. Dear Jesus, she thought as the guard approached her, *what* is going to happen? She tried to swallow, but her mouth was dry, pasty.

Peter Gilbert had a plan. He was now behind the guard, out of his eyesight. Like most who were in the business of guarding the White House and its contents, the guard was a big man, broad shoulders and half a head taller than Gilbert.

Gilbert briefly considered trying for the guard's service revolver. But even if he succeeded in obtaining it, the resulting gunshot would alert reinforcements.

Calmly surveying his immediate surroundings, Peter spotted only books and papers.

The guard had moved another step. One more, and he'd be within arm's reach of Leslie's credentials, which hung from her neck on a beaded metal chain. The fear was gone for Peter. Now was only a time for thinking, acting—not feeling.

What? Where? Something? There was a set of fireplace tools by the office fireplace. But that was across the room.

There! Just inches from his hands, on the front of Sherbok's desk: a pewter replica of the Statue of Liberty, presented by some freedom group or another just three days before.

Gilbert watched the man extend his arm for Leslie's badge. He hesitated, since the plastic credentials badge rested at the end of its support against Leslie's left breast. She saw the guard hesitate, looked briefly at Peter, and then reached down to hand it to the guard.

The pewter statue was heavy. The engraved plaque pronounced Sherbok as a hero for freedom.

With the statue in his right hand, Gilbert twisted in a quarter arc, his right arm extended. The guard now had Leslie's ID in his hand and was turning it over to look at its security clearances.

Without thought, without hesitation, Peter Gilbert heaved from the waist. The strain of his shoulder and chest muscle pulling at their maximum distorted his face into a grotesque mask.

The corner of the pewter statue smashed the guard's third cervical vertebra. The guard felt the stab of pain, and suddenly felt nothing at all.

Peter Gilbert was amazed that there were but a few drops of blood.

Leslie was stunned.

"Grab the files, let's go!" he ordered. "Let's split up at the elevator. If I'm not at the car when you get there, I'll meet you at Monroe's meeting point." Leslie nodded. "Okay, let's go. But avoid running, that'll be sure to draw suspicion."

One fact that Peter had been unaware of was that the security system of the National Security Advisor's personal safe contained a time limit on the length of time the safe could remain open. Had Leslie and Peter closed the safe when they'd finished, the alarm would not have sounded. But the interruption by the security guard, and the subsequent confrontation, prevented them from doing so. As it was, a silent alarm had roused the NSA security.

They had passed one checkpoint and were heading through the basement of the Old Executive Office Building when they saw a guard approaching, a guard armed with an automatic rifle.

"You! Stop!" The guard yelled as he raised his weapon.

"Quick, in here." Gilbert shoved Leslie into a doorway recess. "Flatten out!"

"Peter." Leslie dug into her purse and handed him the .44 magnum she was carrying. "Here."

She saw Peter lift the weapon and pull back the hammer. The gun exploded and almost as quickly as it did, she saw Peter Gilbert twist and grimace as his body was lifted clear off the marble floor by a burst of machine-gun fire. Gilbert pitched backwards and landed almost perfectly supine. She watched horrified as the back of his head thudded resonantly against the stone floor like a ripe melon. Though she would never know it, Peter Gilbert was dead before his body had come to rest.

Leslie surprised herself by not crying out, perhaps in an unconscious instinct to survive. She stood rigid at attention in the doorway for an instant, expecting to hear footsteps. But she heard nothing.

The sight that greeted her as she peered beyond the door recess was at once horrifying and relieving. There were two bodies in the hallway: Peter's and the man with the automatic weapon. There was a growing pool of blood around the other man. Gilbert's first shot had nicked the edge of the man's aorta. The aorta is the main, and only, artery running from the heart to the lower part of the body. It contains blood pressure sufficient to raise a fountain of blood more than three feet high. The nick that the slug made in the aorta wall quickly enlarged as the intense blood pressure literally blew a hole in the wall. The man had been able to loose a solitary volley from his machine gun at Gilbert before his blood pressure dropped to zero and he lost consciousness.

He was now dead.

Grasping the files, Leslie prepared to flee. She stepped carefully to avoid treading in the blood of either man. Before she left she kneeled over Gilbert's body and whispered quickly, "Thank you." Then she ran.

The corridors were frantic with guards and Secret Servicemen pounding echoes off the walls. Confusion reigned and Leslie ran. Not to run in such circumstances would be suspect.

She cleared the next-to-last guard post by convincing the more than slightly sexist guard that she was a woman and how could she be involved? And she only wanted to get to her office where it was safe, and she started to cry and the guard passed her through.

Though it had been less than five minutes since they had left Sherbok's office, the efficient alarm system of the White House compound had roused all security personnel. Doors were ordered sealed, and automatic weapons were being issued. A general alarm was issued that required all nonsecurity personnel to take refuge in their offices. In less than ten minutes the streets outside would be crawling with a combination of personnel from the Secret Service, the Executive Protection Service, the Washington Metropolitan Police Department, the FBI, and Park Police. It was the first time the procedure had been used since the military had threatened a coup during the final days of Watergate.

Leslie ran, breathlessly, toward the entrance she had used this morning. Standing there, blocking the doorway, was Larry Murchison, long a friend, an honest, earnest young man, and the last barrier to her freedom.

"Leslie, get back to your office," Murchison said. "I should arrest you, but I won't. Go back, I'll forget I saw you."

She stopped.

"Leslie, please. *Please* go back. This is serious business. My reinforcement will be here any minute and he'll arrest you. *Please* don't let that happen."

"Larry, I've got to get out of here." As she spoke, Leslie saw the expression in his eyes change.

"You're part of this, aren't you?" he mumbled incredulously. "You're part of whatever's going on. Oh, God! Leslie. I . . . I can't believe . . . What?"

"Larry, I've *got* to get out of here. Let me by."

"I can't do that, Leslie. Not even for you. There must be some mistake; just wait, everything will be all right. You *couldn't* have done something all that wrong, could you?"

"Larry," demanded Leslie. "Let me pass."

Meanwhile, her mind was racing, tortured. Oh, God, why Larry? Why did it have to be *him*? Why not somebody else? It would have been so easy; but not *him*! Leslie reached into the pocket of the blazer she wore and withdrew from it the other gun she carried, a derringer. She pointed it at her friend, her acquaintance, Larry Murchison.

"What are you doing?" Larry said.

"Don't move. Keep your hands away from your gun, Larry," Leslie said. Survival was all. They'd kill her. There would be no investigation, justice would be swift and deliberate. Larry Murchison was the instrument of her own destruction, the last barrier to her escape.

Larry Murchison walked toward her, his arms outstretched.

"Leslie," he said. "Give me the gun. You don't want to do this."

"Stop! Stop, please!" Leslie cried. But Larry Murchison wouldn't stop. And she noted with a mixture of revulsion and fascination the expression of curious amazement on his face as the slug from the derringer passed through his neck, severing as it did the carotid artery.

She stumbled over his slumped form, clutching the files, and ran through the exit. She tripped on the steps and the files flew across the sidewalk. She heard someone yell. Leslie Lewis calmly gathered the files, tucked them neatly under her arm and sprinted toward the cars. Peter's sports car was behind hers, both cars, she was aware, with the keys in them. She realized now that Peter's Fiat was smaller and handled better than her own; it was into his that she lunged, threw the files, and turned the ignition.

The engine wouldn't catch. The starter ground, and still it wouldn't catch. Then she realized it had a manual choke, pulled it and the engine sputtered to life immediately. The car leapt away from the curb just as a slug from somewhere behind her passed through the rear window and embedded itself in the dashboard.

Chapter Twenty-eight

Darkness soon overtook the long TEE train as it sped southeast from Amsterdam toward Munich.

Snow had ruled out traveling to Munich by air because antiterrorist measures in effect at the airports would be certain to discover the Ingram machine pistol.

The *International Herald Tribune* held no interest for Snow and merely decorated his lap as a convenient place to rest his eyes when they strayed from the window.

The train seemed symbolic for him. He wondered now, as he hurtled through the darkness, whether or not it was carrying him toward some greater infinite darkness from which he could never extricate himself. He thought that maybe, just perhaps, it had gone that far. For, in this attempt to create order from the disorder that had engulfed him three short weeks before, he had finally sunk in over his head.

If there was, indeed, a path to the world of light, he wondered if it started in Munich.

As the train carrying Beckett Snow and hundreds of other people sped into the night, a shorter journey was coming to a halt.

The momentary confusion that reigned at the White House for less than ten minutes was the margin by which Leslie Lewis escaped. One shot had been fired at her as she drove away from the old Executive Office Building. She forgot, for the time being, that there were three dead men lying on the floors of the building and that all that the old Leslie Lewis had come to love and appreciate was gone just as irrevocably as if she too lay on a floor of cold marble surrounded by a crimson pool of blood.

She abandoned Peter's car in an alley near George Washington University and scurried the half block to the GWU-Foggy Bottom Metro Station. There she boarded a train that dropped her off at McPherson Square. She emerged at 14th and I Streets, made her way the three blocks to the Greyhound Bus Station and purchased a one-way ticket to Warrentown, Virginia, to meet Duane Monroe.

Chapter Twenty-nine

Daylight streamed through the cracks between the casement and the shades of the train compartment and cast a long warm strip of light across Beckett Snow's right shoulder. The stripe moved from side to side as the train curved and the sun rose. The dream that had absorbed Snow for the previous ten minutes gradually blended itself into reality.

Snow groggily wiped the sleep from the corners of his eyes and sat up.

Ten minutes later the train jerked to a halt underneath the Hauptbahnhof Munich, Bavaria, home of lederhosen, Hofbrau beer, glockenspiels, and, in his adult life, Adolf Hitler.

Snow grabbed his luggage and bumped through the narrow passageway to the end of the car.

It was 7:47 AM and the coffee shop was smoky and crowded with travelers. Snow had found an empty table for two at the rear of the restaurant. Nearby people were drinking beer. After pancakes and three cups of coffee, it was 8:30 and Snow decided to try and call Tracy before redeeming the baggage chit.

Snow had no German currency, but the clerk had apparently had a good morning thus far and agreed to accept American dollars, albeit at a rate that would guarantee a nice profit.

More than 25 minutes passed before Snow was connected to Duane Monroe.

"Hello?" Snow said. "Hello, is anybody there?"

"Holy Mother of Jesus, Beck, it's after two in the fucking morning. Where the fuck are you?"

"Munich, Duane," Snow said. "Where are *you*?"

"In goddamned bed where I ought to be, motherfucker!"

"No, I mean . . . The last time I called I got the hospital room."

"Well, my little exchange works very well. You got my goddamned bedroom and you fucking woke me up! No offense, good buddy, it just takes me a while to wake up."

"How's Tracy?" Snow asked expectantly.

"Not as good as expected."

Snow's stomach turned to putty.

"What does that mean?"

"It means she has a serious infection. The doctors are trying a whole shitload of antibiotics trying to knock it out, but so many of the cuts she got are infected that it's not doing so good."

There was silence. Snow could think of nothing to say.

"Beck?"

"Uh . . . Yeah, I'm here, Duane. It's just that . . . she means a lot to me. A whole helluva lot."

"I understand."

More silence.

"You wanna call me back when you feel better?"

"No," Snow said. "I might as well get business taken care of now. Have you had any contact with Leslie Lewis and Peter Gilbert?"

"Yeah. As a matter of fact, Leslie's staying in the guest house here."

Snow knew that Monroe's guest house was an underground bomb shelter with all the trimmings.

294

"What about Peter Gilbert?"

"He's dead."

"What happened?"

"Why don't I let Leslie tell you," Monroe said.

The phone clicked as Monroe transferred the call to Leslie's room.

"Beckett?"

"Leslie, is that you?"

"Yes, I'm fine but Peter's . . . dead." Her voice faltered.

"Hold up the tears," Snow pleaded. "What happened?"

The story gushed forth. Leslie hoped to hell she would never have to tell it again.

"Maybe Peter didn't die for nothing," Snow said grimly. "Have you got the materials you escaped with?"

"Yes, they're here with me now. But I can't read the microfilm without a machine."

"That's okay. We'll get access to one when I get back."

"When will that be?"

"I don't know. I guess I'll know later today."

"What are you . . . Where are you?"

"Munich. I've got a baggage slip to redeem. But I wanted to call first. Look, go back to sleep. I'll call again either tonight or tomorrow. Okay?"

"Sure."

"Leslie, can you get them to let you visit Tracy? I'd like you to be there if she comes to, someone familiar."

"Sure," Leslie said. "That shouldn't be too much trouble; after all, a friend of Duane's is there also. Eric Simon."

An observer looking at Beckett Snow as he conversed in the plate-glass telephone booth at the main post office in Munich would have seen him stagger a bit, and lean against the wall for support.

295

"Beckett?" Leslie said to break the silence. "Are you there? Are you all right?"

"Yes." Snow took a deep breath. "Yes, I'm all right. Look, I'll try to call tonight," he said and hung up abruptly.

Snow hurried back to the train station. Simon! Of course, it *had* to be Simon, the only other person to have known about the Anne Frank House, the only other person in the world to have access to the materials in Carothers's box! Of course, it was so plain!

Snow returned to the train station coffee shop and then reached for his shoulder bag. Somewhere was the material lifted from the man in the Anne Frank House, the man who had been present when Steve, when the professor, and . . . Tracy—oh God, Tracy!—had been abused.

Snow sifted through the contents of the main compartment, and found the envelope that Aaron had given him in Amsterdam.

This is what he *knew* instinctively in Amsterdam but couldn't coax to consciousness. But the night of rest had allowed his mind to work on the problem. Today it had taken only the mention of Simon's name to conjure up the answers.

Out of the envelope tumbled a variety of papers, copies of the labels of the man's clothing, a photograph of the man who Snow first saw on a motorcycle on Pennsylvania Avenue in Washington, D.C., and—and what Snow *knew* had to be there—a photocopy of the letter from the box. The man on the motorcycle *had* to work for Simon. There was no other explanation.

That meant that Simon had to be responsible for the torturing of Tracy Reynolds.

The waitress arrived at that moment to ask if Snow wanted more coffee, but she decided not to disturb the man—his eyes were the eyes of something not human. They frightened her, and she hurried away.

Snow continued to stare at the photocopy. His hand shook as he deliberately, slowly crumpled the photocopy into a tiny wad. Nothing in the world, nothing, mattered more than returning to Washington, D.C. to find Eric Simon and kill him.

Chapter Thirty

The poplars, yellow-green with the promise of spring, stood in ranks at attention across the tarmacadam from Dachau: the hope of a new season.

Snow shivered as he got off the L-3 bus with two other passengers. It was a warm day; he pulled his coat tighter. The chill grew as his eyes drew in the stark lines of the whitewashed stone walls and tangled barbed wire.

The two other passengers crossed the road. Snow stood transfixed on the shoulder, watching as they seemed to shrink and finally disappear, swallowed by the camp's gate. Beyond them, the long wall receded toward the horizon.

A passing truck shook Snow out of his reverie, and he crossed the highway and entered the camp.

Snow hung back as the other two visitors entered the museum building and bought guidebooks. When they had walked out of sight, Snow unlatched the tarnished buckles on the battered leather briefcase he'd received at the Hauptbahnhof in Munich and retrieved a tattered and worthless Weimar Republic banknote.

The instructions in the briefcase were clear, concise. Snow approached the old man at the front counter. The man appeared to be in his seventies, and the wrinkles in his face mirrored each of his three score and ten. His grey hair was brushcut.

"Guten Tag," Snow greeted him when the others had moved on. *"Sprechen Sie Englisch?"*

"But of course, my friend," the man replied, his voice firm and resonant, his blue eyes twinkling. "What can I do for you?"

"I'd like a copy of the deluxe guidebook," Snow said. "In Dutch, of course," he said, following the instructions.

The man regarded him cautiously. "Of course." He reached under the desk and produced a grey-covered book with a Star of David on the cover, a star identical to the one Snow carried in the leather satchel. The man took Snow's money and gave him his change. He waited, his face openly curious. Now Snow reached into the briefcase.

"Pardon me, but I was wondering if you could make change for this." Snow handed him the worthless banknote. The man's eyes now reflected respect.

"But of course, *mein Herr,*" the man said. "Perhaps after you've had an opportunity to inspect our testament here." His eyes then said, "Go now."

"Thank you," Snow said, and made straight for the showing of the film: "K2, Dachau." He took a seat on the aisle, two rows from the back, and prominently displayed the briefcase and guidebook on the seat next to him. He had followed all his instructions to the letter. Now it was out of his hands.

The lights dimmed and the film began with scenes that duplicated many of the photographs in the exhibit. About five minutes into the showing, the attendant tugged at his sleeve.

"Your change is ready, *mein Herr,*" the man said. "Please come with me."

Snow gathered the book and briefcase and followed the man from the darkened theater. Outside, the bright light stabbed at his eyes. But his eyes could not miss a man standing next to a glass display case, pointing a gun at him.

"Look out!" Snow yelled and slammed his shoulder into the old man's ribs, knocking both of them to the floor just as two slugs pockmarked the wall.

Then Snow saw the man reaim the gun with its cylindrical silencer and rolled out of position as the man fired again. Two more pockmarks appeared.

Snow scrambled for the cover of a display case as he saw the man crouch and aim again. Then he saw an incredible sight: the old man with the short gray hair and blue eyes had produced a pistol from his baggy pants and proceeded to expertly pump three rounds into the assailant. The old man's first round straightened up the assailant from his crouch; the second shot slammed into his right shoulder and spun him around, and the third blasted into the rib cage just below the man's armpit. Snow marveled at the reflexes the shooting required, for each shot was precise and calculated; the second two had been made at a moving target. The report of the old man's Luger—probably 9mm, Snow thought—resounded in the room.

A woman screamed and excited shouts echoed through the exhibit hall. Snow snatched open his briefcase and withdrew his Ingram, checked to see that the safety was in the "fire" position and that the mode indicator was on "full auto."

"This way, quickly." The old man now seemed much younger. "We haven't much time." The last syllable was barely uttered when a burst of automatic weapons fire snatched at the old man's body.

The screams from the museum visitors grew louder now. Snow saw a man herding two small children out a fire exit. The man who had killed the old German man was not in sight. Snow squeezed himself into the corner between the wall and the black metal base of the exhibit he was now using for cover, hoping to make the best of it.

More automatic weapons fire, but this one a deeper rattle, coming from a different weapon from the one that killed the old man. The rattle was answered by the first weapon. Loud angry bursts. The muzzle of a weapon shattered through the panes of a door directly in Snow's line of fire and fired. Snow heard a scream and a thump.

Snow could guess only by the sounds of the weapons who was friend and who was foe. The higher pitched weapons, one of which killed the old man, had to be enemies. The deeper rattling weapons must be allies.

The crouched figure spotted Snow and brought the gun to bear. Suddenly someone rushed out of the theater to the man's right and the man wheeled and fired. A boy of no more than 16 years screamed a high-pitched squeal of agony and lurched forward. Snow fired. The silent passage of the Ingram's slugs chipped at the wall beside the man and then skidded across the man's chest, knocking him backward on his heels, and left him lying across the door sill, half in and half out of the building.

The room was silent. Layers of pungent cordite hung lazily in the morning sunlight. Outside, people were shouting and crying. But in the room there was no noise at all, no hint of assailants in hiding.

Perspiration crawled slow, tickling snail treads down his ribs. Beads formed on Snow's upper lip as fast as he could wipe them away with the back of his left hand.

Everyone waiting. Waiting for someone to make the first move. But who? Himself, certainly, and most probably an associate of the old man. But who was in the third group? Commission henchmen? Members of the Consortium?

Suddenly he heard the trochaic rise and fall of European sirens whining in the distance.

More shots rang out. A man screamed in a strange language and Snow heard a weapon rattle on the museum floor.

From around the edge of the metal exhibit base a young man in a business suit beckoned to him.

"Come on. It's safe, but we haven't much time before the police arrive."

Beckett clutched his leather briefcase and scrambled after the young man, through the movie theater, and out the rear exit. An old Mercedes taxi waited at the bottom of the rear steps, its engine idling, the driver and one other man waiting. They got in.

"Where's Chaim?" the driver asked.

"Dead," said the young man in the business suit.

The car sped off.

"What happened?" asked the driver. "Who?"

"Fucking Palestinians," the young man in the suit said.

"Do they know?" the driver said, indicating Snow with a sweep of his hand.

"No way of telling. They're fucking crazy. Maybe they knew, maybe they're just fucking crazy. You can never tell what the hell they're going to do."

"Is Chaim clean?"

"Yes. I brought his Uzi. His papers identify him as an Israeli tourist. But you know something?"

"What's that?"

"They killed Heini!"

"Shit," the driver muttered. "The bastards. What a beautiful old man he was."

The third man said nothing, but fingered his Uzi machine gun anxiously as the battered and beaten car made its way deftly out a narrow rear gate and then picked up speed.

The occupants of the car ignored Snow. Once out in the street, they rode in silence.

The taxi took a crazy-quilt trip through the town of Dachau and along a lonely straight section of highway, finally turning down a dead-end street that terminated at the camp's perimeter.

At the last house on the left, the taxi veered suddenly into a driveway and on into the garage.

Six male sentries were waiting, their ammunition belts and Uzi machine guns incongruous against their casual sports clothes. Snow heard bolts clattering as an old woman, relying on a metal cane, approached his door. He did not move.

The man in the business suit got out of the car first and approached the woman. They spoke in what sounded to Snow like Hebrew. The old woman grimaced and shook her head as the young man spoke. Then she turned to Snow. Her eyes were transparent and sad.

"So it is come," she said in English. "Welcome and may God have mercy on us all."

"Yes," Snow began. "I am—"

"Beckett Snow, traveling under an illegal passport. We know who you are. Our associates in Amsterdam are quite competent."

"And you?" Snow asked.

"It makes no difference," the woman said. "But now, before we go further, please let me have the star and the photograph."

Snow withdrew a manila envelope from his briefcase and gave her the yellow Star of David. One of the sentries returned from the house with a sack-like dress fashioned from the coarsest cloth imaginable. The breast bore the outline of a star of David, darker than the rest of the material, a spot protected from washings *by the star Snow had been carrying*. The old woman

303

mated the star with the dark area on the dress and they matched perfectly.

"Mine," she said absently. "Something I will never forget."

"And the photograph?"

Like a worshipper approaching the altar, Snow passed the photo fragment of Carothers's image to her. She seemed to mumble a prayer as she pulled a locket from around her neck and opened it. Inside was half a photograph: the old woman's image from decades ago.

The ragged edges of both photograph fragments mated exactly. The woman closed the locket on both halves and replaced it around her neck.

"To be separated never again," the woman intoned. "It is done. Follow me."

Chapter Thirty-one

The twin obelisks of the World Trade Towers came into view through Beckett Snow's window for the ninth time. Dear God, Snow thought, squirming in his seat to watch Manhattan as it disappeared again, Tracy may be dying and I can't *get* to her.

He considered buzzing the flight attendant again to ask when they'd land, and then thought better of it. She was getting annoyed at his persistence.

He counted the weeks since he'd met Tracy and was amazed that it had been barely a month. But that month had taken him a lifetime to live.

Her eyes, so bright and full of life, and that blend of soft and hard, compassion and determination, that was so typical of Tracy—he longed to see her again. But Tracy was desperately ill. Even if she survived . . . And there was nothing he could do to help her, not now. He'd called the hospital before his flight left Heathrow, and the prognosis was growing worse.

Beckett slammed his fist down on his armrest, drawing a startled glance from his seatmate.

"Sorry," Snow apologized. "Sorry, I'm just a bit nervous, that's all," he mumbled.

It was odd how everything could change so fast. A month ago, he was at the top of his profession; now he was a wanted man.

But two days ago—had it only been two days since

his arrival in Munich?—he was a powerless fugitive; and on this Sunday, he figured he might just be the most powerful man on earth.

A fat lot of good it would do Tracy, he thought bitterly.

But it had been there: information, dossiers in a dank tunnel under a concentration camp. Power. He could devastate twenty-seven of the world's most powerful men. But why? He still didn't know. *That* information lay in microfilm, in the hands of Leslie Lewis. And in the hands of a man Snow had to kill.

It all seemed too overwhelming. No matter what he did, no matter what the dossiers could do, they couldn't make Tracy whole again. And their survival itself was in jeopardy; could they survive without Simon's help? For surely as he loved Tracy, Snow was going to kill the man.

All this power, and none to do what he wanted most: go somewhere they could never find him and spend the rest of his life with Tracy. The more powerful he became, the more impotent he felt.

Half an hour later the 707 finally touched down at JFK. It was two hours before Snow climbed off the shuttle at Washington's National Airport. By the time he'd made it to the main waiting room of the airport, Beckett Snow had decided what he was going to do with the materials from Dachau.

He had to make copies of all the materials and get them into the hands of people who could deal with it in the event that he failed. What he was going to do was to take the documents to the best known investigative reporter in the world, John Christiansen, a man whose name was synonymous with the craft. Snow decided that he would do it Monday, tomorrow.

He had to do it alone, since he couldn't be sure how closely Monroe was cooperating with Eric Simon, and how closely they were keeping tabs on Leslie.

306

The disclosure of the Dachau notes to Leslie and what they contained would have to wait until they were absolutely assured of privacy. No one, including Leslie, knew of his arrival plans. He had been careful to make them as vague as possible.

Snow's taxi cruised across the Key Bridge and into the mobs of traffic that choked Georgetown on weekends. He got out at a quick copy shop on Wisconsin Avenue that stayed open on Sundays and made two copies of everything in his bag: the Dachau notes, his handwritten account of the past three weeks beginning with the accident on the Pasadena Freeway, the notes from Carothers's box.

It was a complete chronicle of his ordeal, and enough to start a serious inquiry if something happened to him.

He mailed one of the sets of copies to his lawyer from an automated kiosk with instructions that if anything happened to Snow, copies of the packet should be mailed to three Supreme Court justices whom Snow had met, respected, and prayed were beyond the reach of either the Commission or the Consortium.

The entire task had taken him less than half an hour. It was 12:35 P.M. Snow located a pay phone to call Duane Monroe.

"Hello, Duane."

"Beck, is that you?"

"Yes. I've just returned. How's Tracy?"

"Yeah . . . Hold on a minute."

Snow waited, confused at Monroe's response. Then Leslie picked up the receiver."

"Beck . . ."

"Yes, Leslie," Snow interrupted. "What's going on? What's happening there? I want to see Tracy and Duane—"

"Beck . . . Tracy died two hours ago."

307

Chapter Thirty-two

Beckett lay back on the bed in his room at the Georgetown Inn and stared at the ceiling. Every light in the room was burning, as if they could chase away the darkness that had engulfed his life.

The pain stabbed and bit and pounded him.

How could it be so? Tracy was dead? No, it couldn't be. . . . He had not had a chance to say goodbye.

A chance to say goodbye, a chance to make amends, to ask for forgiveness, to praise an act gone unnoticed—to say goodbye.

While Duane, Leslie, and Eric Simon, who had recently been discharged from the hospital, all searched frantically for Beckett Snow, the object of their search had finally turned out the lights and cried himself to sleep.

He slept because he knew he had to be keen and refreshed if his revenge—Tracy's revenge—was to become a reality.

At 7 AM the telephone jarred him awake and took his order for breakfast and to hire a car. Thank God, Snow thought as he hung up, that Tracy had given him the money from her expense account. Tracy! Damn, it was always Tracy. He pushed the thought from his mind. He had to have his concentration, and that meant exorcising emotions. He could do it. The albatross that made him quit police work was now his biggest asset.

He checked out of the hotel and threw his bags into the Mercedes 450 SL the inn had arranged for him and drove off for his 9 AM meeting with John Christiansen. Snow got hung up in traffic at the intersection of Wisconsin and Massachusetts. The frustration of sitting in traffic with no alternative dried his throat and made him angry. He started to curse aloud at the other drivers when he realized how emotional he was getting.

He fought back the emotions, cleared his mind. Emotions were the last thing he needed now. Function, achieve, thwart, use, kill. Those were all that mattered now.

He needed a weapon, he thought as he waited. He couldn't return the Ingram to its original containers since they had been destroyed removing the parts and so he hadn't brought it through the airline security checks. A gun, a gun for Simon, was the first priority after the meeting wtih Christiansen.

Snow arrived at Christiansen's at 9:19 AM. Instead of parking several blocks away, he circled the block looking for anything suspicious.

He saw nothing, and returned to park in the employees' lot behind Christiansen's building.

If he had not been late, he might have noticed the tiny viewing port in the robin's-egg blue panel truck parked on 16th Street. And had he been on foot, he might have spotted the black sedan with the heavily tinted windows as a government vehicle. Or he might have noticed the man sitting patiently in the back of a limo on Riggs Road on the opposite side of 16th Street. Of course, if he had been on foot, he might not have made it to Christiansen's building.

But as things happened he did make it. Snow walked around to the front of the white marble building and leaned into the dark walnut door with its shiny brass fittings. The door whispered shut behind him.

It was twenty-four minutes after nine when Snow pushed open the door to Christiansen's office. He introduced himself and was immediately ushered into the columnist's working quarters which overlooked the gravel parking lot at the rear.

"Have a seat. Sit down. We've got some talking to do."

Snow selected a wooden chair that faced the windows, and sat down in front of the reporter. The man was legend, his name *was* investigative reporting. Christiansen was a distinguished man of about 55, his thick gray hair was stylishly trimmed, with not a single hair out of place. The signs of middle age tugged at the waistline of his gray-pinstriped suit.

Snow looked at him coolly, dispassionately, the epitome of the cop he'd once been.

"It's been a long time since I've seen you," Christiansen began. "I've always admired your work."

Snow was not flattered. There was no Beckett Snow to flatter, just a cold man with a tough job to do.

"But it looks as if your career has taken a . . ." Christiansen's face reflected concern, "a certain downswing."

"Yes, well, I think much of that is explained by this." Snow handed the second copy of the Dachau notes to him.

"Perhaps you'd care to read this, and then we'll talk some more. There *is* more."

"Very well," Christiansen said. He opened the manila envelope and began to read.

During the course of the next quarter hour, Christiansen muttered several dozen "Oh mys" and twice that many "Goodnesses" and only at the end—for he was devoutly religious and refrained from blasphemy—

310

he opened his mouth and said, "Oh, my dear God in Heaven!" and looked up at Snow.

"You know what all of this means?" he asked Snow as if Snow really didn't. "Do you know what an incredible shock it would be to the world if this information were released?"

Snow leaned forward, his nails dug into the arms of the chair. "You're not thinking of suppressing it, are you?"

"Of course not," Christiansen said. "It's just . . . This is a staggering revelation. The twenty-seven most powerful men in the world, damned by the record of their own deeds. . . . But you said there's more?"

"Yes. There are nearly 100 smaller envelopes, sealed with a special compound on which is imprinted Carothers's fingerprint—readily identifiable and irrefutable," Snow said. "Those envelopes labeled with the names of the powerful people you've read about. I surmise that for the records we've read to have credibility with the victims or intended victims, there must be something in each envelope that Carothers knew would be incontrovertible."

"Do you know what that is?" Christiansen asked.

"No," Snow replied. "The answer to that must be in each envelope and I haven't opened any of them."

Christiansen frowned and leaned back in his chair.

"I believe each envelope must be presented to the person it is addressed to," said Snow, "with Carothers's seal unbroken."

"Yes," Christiansen assented. "Yes, that makes good sense." He leaned toward Snow again. "*If* you are correct, and *if* this is genuine," he pointed to the materials Snow had given him, "this could be the single most important event in this century's history."

Snow nodded. Christiansen turned his attention to the papers.

"But this . . ." Christiansen pointed to a line of Snow's handwriting. "What does this mean?"

Snow got out of his chair and leaned over to examine the line Christiansen referred to. As he did, he glanced out the window and saw a blue van parked behind his Mercedes, blocking its exit. Men wtih machine guns were walking away from the van toward the building.

"John." Snow was mute. The blood had drained from his head. His heart pounded. He started to shake, and suddenly the paralysis transmuted into anger.

"Goddamn you! You tricked me!" Snow grabbed the reporter by his lapels. "You called the fucking cops. No . . . no! They're not cops; you're a goddamned member of the Commission."

"Don't . . . don't!" The reporter threw up his hands to protect himself. "I don't know what you're talking about!"

"Sure you do, you filthy scumbag. Look," Snow pointed to the parking lot. "Look down there and see the people you called."

"I didn't!" Christiansen protested. "Honest, I di—" and his words were interrupted when Snow's fist slammed into the side of Christiansen's cheek.

Suddenly the door opened.

"You shouldn't have struck him." A well-dressed man stepped in accompanied by an armed bodyguard who shut the door.

"We have surveillance on every major reporter and newspaper in the country," the man said. "Certainly you don't think we'd miss a phone call to Mr. Christiansen here."

"I know you," Snow said. "I've seen your photograph."

"I'm hardly surprised. My picture has accompanied thousands of newspaper stories."

"Kincaid Carothers." Snow's pronouncement was a whisper.

"Yes. Now, I want those papers. Any sudden moves, and I'm afraid this man may have to kill you."

"Search them," Carothers said to the guard, who proceeded to frisk both Christiansen and Snow. "Don't think of trying to escape. There is another man like him outside the door, and ten more in and around the building. They are the *best*."

"Why?" Snow said.

"Why what, dear fellow?" Carothers's voice was condescending. "Certainly they taught you better than that in school; or did they?"

"Why you? Here?"

"Because this is the dead-end of my weak brother's treachery. That's why. I wanted to see its end personally. He's caused me a great deal of anguish in his lifetime, and I intend to see the end of his feeble efforts to defeat me."

"I had no idea you hated each other."

"Yes. Oh, yes, we did. He failed to use his wealth and his power as he should. He was weak. And the fact that his greatest weapon is in the hands of people like you is the best evidence I can think of for the frailty of his thoughts and actions.

"Now," Carothers continued. "I want the papers. Please hand them to me, *now!*" Christiansen complied. "These are copies. I want the originals." He turned to Snow. "Where are they?"

"Mr. Carothers, that's not going to do you any good," Snow said evenly. "I've made another copy and left it with a trusted person who will mail copies to selected people if I'm not heard from in three weeks."

Carothers smiled benignly. "Your little mind *has* been busy, hasn't it? Mr. Snow, all we need to do is start eliminating everyone you know—and we have quite a file on you. We'd begin, naturally, with your attorney—a logical choice to send documents to. So do you want to give us the original and tell us to whom you mailed the copy? Or would you rather have us keep you captive? We'd be happy to bring them to you one by one and take care of them before your eyes—as they *beg* you to give us what we want."

Snow sank into the chair, sapped of strength. It was over. He couldn't have those deaths on his conscience, too. Weeks of running and hiding and killing and seeing his friends and loved ones killed, but now it was all over. He'd walked into a trap. It was his own fault. Perhaps Carothers was right. Perhaps he *was* a lightweight with no business trying to play in the leagues of players like Carothers.

He sat there, silent, hearing only the passage of his own breath in and out of his open mouth. He was tired. The prospect of turning over the Dachau notes and facing a clean quick death was seductive. The rest, the rest.

Suddenly Christiansen sprang from his chair. "You vile, revolting monster!" he cried, and grabbed the millionaire's throat. Carothers began to gag as he tried to free himself, but the guard stepped quickly to the side and fired at Christiansen. The reporter slumped to the floor.

Back to his feet in an instant, Snow lunged at Carothers and sent him crashing into the guard.

While the older man rolled helplessly on the floor, Snow and the guard struggled for possession of the silenced Uzi machine gun.

Snow slammed his knee into the guard's groin and the man momentarily released his grip on the gun. Snow snatched at it but the gun flew out of both men's hands, clattering uselessly on the opposite side of the room.

Snow was on top and leaped for the gun, but the guard was too quick. He grabbed Snow's foot and tripped him. Beckett fell face first on the floor, his outstretched hand inches from the weapon.

The guard was all over Snow, his arm around Beckett's neck, choking him, cutting off the circulation to his brain. The room started to spin, colors paled. With his last reserve of strength, Beckett grabbed the man's elbow and jerked it to the left, moving it so Snow's neck was now in the crook of the elbow, letting some blood and air through.

Snow then reached behind the man and searched for his head, found it and immediately plunged his thumbs into both of the man's eyes.

Snow's assailant screamed, released his grip on Snow's neck. Beckett grabbed the Uzi and pulled the trigger of the unfamiliar weapon. Nothing happened. What! The safety was off, Beckett quickly deduced; he squeezed the trigger.

Still nothing happened. The guard got up now, his face a hideous mask of blood and rage. He stepped closer as Snow struggled with the Uzi.

Then Beckett Snow remembered a sound; the sound of an Uzi machine gun in the old woman's garage at Dachau. What was it? A clank, the clank of a bolt sliding home!

As the guard lunged at him, Snow yanked the bolt back and fired.

Only seconds had passed since Christiansen had been shot, and by the time Carothers's men in the hall had broken into the room, Snow had pulled Carothers to his feet and was using him as a shield.

"Don't come any closer, or I'll kill Mr. Carothers."

"Do as he says," Carothers ordered.

The guard stopped.

"Okay," Snow said. "Get out of the room and close the door. Anybody who comes in without my permission is responsible for this man's death. Got it?"

The man glared at Snow, looked at the body of the dead guard, turned back to Carothers.

"Go," Carothers said. The man obeyed.

When the door shut, Snow released his grip.

"Sit down," Snow told the millionaire. The man did not move. "I said, *sit down*. Now!" Snow slapped him with the back of his hand, and Carothers sat down hard.

"So, little man, you've aroused your creativity, have you?" Carothers's eyes held the fury of a man not used to being treated any way except his own. "You know you can't get away with this, don't you?" Snow did not reply. "You realize that at this very moment my people are calling for reinforcements. And *you*, my public school friend, are no match. Why don't you just quit this silly little charade and let me go?" Carothers smiled. "We will win, you know."

"Silly charade?" Snow snarled. "Do you know how many people have been killed? Do you know what people who worked for *you* have done? They've tortured and maimed and coerced and terrorized people."

"My dear boy," Carothers smiled. "Those people deserved to die. They—"

"What!"

"They were weak. They were ineffectual. They didn't deserve to exist."

"Like your brother, I suppose?"

"Like my brother."

"And who has the right to decide whether or not they should live, or be tortured or threatened for your amusement?"

"Ah, not for amusement. We do things only because they are necessary."

"That's irrelevant. Who has the right to decide? You and your nouveau-Nazi friends?"

"Yes. I believe we do. Now let's get on with this. See here," Carothers said. "You—"

Snow hit the man again across the mouth and followed with another and yet another, all punishing.

Carothers brought his hands up to shield his face.

Now Snow grabbed the fingers of the millionaire's right hand and bent them backwards until one popped, dislocated. Carothers wailed in pain.

The door to the office started to open. Snow whirled, raking it with a short burst from the Uzi. "If anyone comes through the door," he shouted, "the next round is going into Carothers's head. Got it?"

"Stay away," Carothers called. "He's crazy! He means it. Stay out!"

Snow regarded the millionaire who now crouched, examining his well-manicured and rapidly swelling fingers. When he finally looked up at Snow, there was fear in his eyes.

"Look, Mr. Snow," Carothers began. "I control billions. Surely we can work something out here, something that is . . . mutually satisfactory to both our goals. I—"

"Shut the fuck up, would you!" Snow interrupted. "You stink and your fucking money stinks. You're a rotten slimy bag of pig shit!" Snow raised his hand to strike Carothers again, but stopped as the man cringed. "So how does it feel, Mr. Millionaire? Scared? Frightened? Frustrated and powerless? Welcome to the world that you and your fucking big banks and greedy global corporations have made for the rest of us. Now you know how it feels. You haven't got your cashmere-lined life and an army to wipe the shit off your ass anymore. You're a *man*, Carothers, not a god. You bleed. See! Look how your beautiful tailored shirt is getting all bloody, look at the blood caked under your nicely manicured fingernails. Look at it, because it's the blood of the people you've killed and maimed and abused. It's your world now, and you're going to live in it."

"And you're going to die," Carothers said simply.

Snow's anger passed as quickly as it had come. For an instant there had been Tracy and Steve Drachler

317

and the way this man had destroyed his world. Now there was a cool resolve, the emotionless machinations of a human machine that had no time to feel. There was also disgust, but it was quantitative, not passionate.

"Maybe," Snow said, and started rummaging through the drawer of the desk behind him. He knew that the success of his escape would depend on acting quickly.

"Ah . . . just what I needed." Carothers regarded him with both curiosity and alarm. Snow had withdrawn from the drawer a roll of nylon reinforced strapping tape. "Turn around and face the wall."

Snow strapped Carothers's hands together behind his back. The nylon strands would not break. "Take it easy, Carothers," Snow said. "The more you struggle, the more those nylon strands are going to cut into your wrists. Okay, turn back and sit down."

Snow placed the muzzle of the Uzi against the left side of Carothers's head and carefully wound a loop of tape around the muzzle, then passed it around Carothers's neck and looped it around the muzzle again. He repeated the motions four more times from different angles, securely fastening the machine gun against the millionaire's head.

"There. Now just one more thing," Snow smiled as he cut several strips of tape and taped his trigger finger to the trigger of the machine gun.

"Okay, Mr. Millionaire. If they shoot me, I fall and this gun blows your head into a billion little pieces. Are you ready for that?" Carothers was silent. "Are you *ready*, I said?" Snow jammed the muzzled against Carothers's mastoid.

"No." Carothers's voice was weak. The man was scared, Snow thought.

"Okay," Snow said. "Let's walk to the door. Carefully, slowly. You make a sudden move and you're going to blow your own head off. Got it?"

"Yes."

"Okay. Also tell your men what the situation is. Tell them not to do anything that might surprise *either* one of us, because if that happens you're a dead man—"

"And so are you," Carothers pointed out.

"Thanks, I needed that reminder." Snow gave him a shove.

As directed, Carothers called his instructions to the guards outside. When Snow opened the door, none made a move. The guards regarded Snow and Carothers with a mixture of awe, hostility, and curiosity as Snow and Carothers made their way along the hallway, down the steps, and out of the building.

"Have the personnel outside been told of this situation?" Snow asked.

"They're professionals," Carothers replied. "I'd stake my life on it."

"Good," Snow said. "You have."

The Mercedes had been brought around to the front door of the building as instructed. A guard held the door open as first Snow and then Carothers gingerly entered through the passenger's side door.

"You know that following us is going to get the gentleman killed, don't you?" Snow said to the guard. "Good. And, goodbye."

Snow clicked the safety to "on," shoved the transmission into drive, and accelerated rapidly up 16th Street.

"What are you going to do with me? You know my organization has ways of tracking this car and that they'll get you if you either kill me or let me go. You know that, don't you?"

"Maybe," Snow said. "Maybe not."

Chapter Thirty-three

"Don't ask me any questions and don't hesitate, Leslie. I need your help if you're ever going to see me alive again."

Snow was talking into the receiver of a pay phone beside a narrow winding road in Prince George's County.

"No, you *can't* meet me. The Commission has me in their sights right now. You'd only fall into their hands. Look, just get a pencil and paper and take all this down," Snow said. "Go to a large sporting goods store . . ."

Three hours later, Snow pulled into a small roadside picnic area. Snow got out of the car, wondered where Carothers's men were. Certainly they were watching, certainly they had means of tracking them. The thought didn't ruffle Snow's tempered composure. The only thing that mattered was the plan.

Ten minutes later, Snow and Carothers sped out of the turnoff. Snow now wore a crash helmet, and behind the seat were the other items Leslie had hidden for him: a double scuba tank, regulator, fins, mask, and weight belt, and water-tight plastic for the Dachau notes.

Carothers glowered at Snow.

"What's it like being on the receiving end, old man?"

Snow taunted him. "Worried that your henchmen haven't rescued you by now?"

Carothers didn't answer.

"Fuck you," Snow said, and pressed harder on the accelerator.

Soon they were cruising south on the Beltway heading down hill toward the Woodrow Wilson Bridge.

Snow pulled to the shoulder of the road before getting to the bridge.

"What are we doing here?" Carothers asked.

"Shut the fuck up, asshole," Snow said and rammed the gun barrel into Carothers's head. Nerves. Things were getting too tense even for *his* nerve. Beckett Snow found himself clutching the armrest with his left hand. They couldn't wait long, or the road might be blockaded.

But less than 15 minutes later, he saw what he'd been waiting for: a small shallow draft freighter was making its way up the Potomac toward Alexandria.

Soon the warning lights to the bridge started to blink, and shortly thereafter, the gates waved down, cutting off traffic as the two huge spans of the bridge began to tilt open.

Snow unwound the tape from the trigger of the Uzi and smashed his right fist into the side of Carothers's left temple, dazing him, but not quite rendering him unconscious. He started the engine of the Mercedes and slammed it into gear. It leaped into traffic and quickly overtook the traffic that was slowing for the bridge signal. When the Mercedes reached the end of the line, Snow twisted the wheel left, and the vehicle leaped over the low median divider into the opposite lanes. Snow was all concentration now. It was no time to be timid.

As the Mercedes climbed the rapidly inclining pavement, he heard a siren somewhere. He also heard the blood rushing in his ears. Crash helmet in place, shoulder and seat belts secure, Snow closed his eyes, and felt the rush of the G-forces as the Mercedes ran out of pavement, tilted nose down, and plunged into the Potomac River.

Chapter Thirty-four

They fished Beckett Snow out of the Potomac River at midnight.

Monday night.

That Monday night was a time of pain and gladness. Fear and the joy of escape. It had been nearly dark when the Mercedes plunged over the edge of the drawbridge. Snow had planned it that way, so that any surveillance would be unable to spot the scuba bubbles in the dark. It all seemed so preposterous, the plunge off the bridge and escape under water. But Snow remembered newspaper accounts of traffic accidents where cars had run off various Potomac bridges, and rarely were the drivers killed. So he knew it was possible.

When the Mercedes headed nose down into the river, Snow had braced the crash helmet against the steering wheel, which obligingly collapsed on impact, just as it was designed to do. The rush of cold water brought Carothers back to his senses. He screamed at Snow as the car slowly sank.

Ignoring him, Snow wrestled the scuba tanks from behind the seat.

He slid the gear into the water, strapped on the tanks, adjusted his mask, snorkle, and fins. Then he headed downstream with the current, hoping he wouldn't get some sort of fatal disease from the filth in the river.

The tanks gave Snow two hours' time. For the first hour, he stayed totally under water, not wanting to risk being spotted, either by police or by Carothers's people.

At the end of the hour, though, his sprains and bruises had begun to hurt, the adrenalin and nerve hype that had sustained him were wearing off. Snow surfaced and was surprised to find that he had gone past Mount Vernon, much farther than he had originally imagined.

An hour later, he spotted a small sluggish creek, wrapped the weight belt around the tanks and ditched them, making do with a quiet, slow dog paddle.

Two hours later, a beaten and bedraggled Beckett Snow was met in the parking lot of a 7-11, twelve miles south of Occoquan, by Leslie and Duane Monroe.

They helped the exhausted Beckett to bed, where he lapsed into comalike sleep, the Dachau notes still strapped to his chest in their watertight plastic. Duane and Leslie wanted to take that off too, but Snow had protested.

Beckett dreamed dreams that he would never remember. The pain would be too great. He cried in his sleep, and he cried in his dreams. And when he awoke eighteen hours later, he had crawled back into the armor he had made for himself. Feelings were something he couldn't afford, not this close to killing Eric Simon.

"It's too much. Too much. I thought I had seen as much as there was to see when I read the notes from Dachau, but this just tops it all off." Snow had been leaning over the viewing glass of the microfilm reader for more than four hours. "It's easy to see, now, that is, why Adam Carothers would have prepared the notes for Dachau. After all, he *knew* that something like this could get out of hand. He knew his brother too well."

"Speaking of Carothers," Leslie said. "I wonder how they kept it all from getting into the newspapers? I mean there were hundreds of people on the bridge, and the people from the freighter who rescued him and—"

"Power," Snow said. "More fucking power than we can imagine. No, I don't imagine that people will ever read about it all."

He turned back to the microfilm reader and winced as he did.

"How's your shoulder?" Leslie asked sympathetically.

"Not too bad. I'm just sore all over. But the doctor said I didn't really do anything to myself other than sprain just about every ligament in my body. I hurt in places I didn't even know were places.

"By the way, Leslie, where did Duane get the microfilm reader?"

"Beats me. I asked him and he said, 'Don't ask.' I decided not to argue with him."

"Good thing."

"Yeah. But you know, I'm beginning to like him," she added in a strange voice. "Sure there's a bizarre side, but he's somebody who's got *control* of his life, somebody who refuses to take shit from anybody. I could learn from a person like that."

Snow looked at her curiously. "Yeah?" he smiled. "You fallin' in love or something?"

"No, but I'm gaining some respect for the man."

Snow grunted his agreement and turned back to the microfilm. Four hours at the viewer and he was barely into the second roll. Yes, he thought, Duane Monroe was a man to be respected, but how far could he be *trusted*? Snow was still unsure what Duane's involvement was with Simon. How much did he know about Simon's terror tactics against him and Tracy. Tracy!

325

Shit, he thought, she meant so much. But he couldn't think about her now. He'd have time to cry later. His face-to-face with Simon was less than two hours away, and there could be no room in his thoughts for her. Only the will to kill.

Snow glanced at his watch. It was 6 P.M.

He had hoped to get a chance to talk with Leslie before the meeting, but he resisted for fear that the house might be bugged. She had changed, somehow. Or maybe, he mused, it was *he* who had changed. He knew only that he no longer felt totally comfortable with her. Comfortable! What a strange word to be thinking of now. At a time like this.

He returned to the microfilm.

"Operation Indochina." Snow read it aloud, and then caught his breath and held it. He was looking at the birth of a war. The Commission had actually started a war between China and Vietnam to prod China into quicker dependence on Western aid!

"Leslie!" Snow called. "Come here. Look at this."

"Yeah. Ingenious, no?" Leslie commented.

"Is that all you can say? 'Ingenious'?"

"Well, you have to admit it *is*," she countered. "But if you think that part's something, wait until you get to the end of the last tape where they have the most recent stuff."

"What's there?"

"Well, as you know, the Chinese showed a lot more intelligence about invading Vietnam than we did, and pulled out," Leslie said. "Well, that set the manipulators on the Commission into a rage and they decided to reignite the conflict with a very hot object."

"Like what?"

"Like a nuke from some of the weapons captured by the Vietnamese during the debacle of our last few days there."

326

"You've got to be joking." Snow was incredulous. "*Nobody tries* to start a nuclear war."

"Not a war. China might retaliate with one," Leslie said. "But they're more worried about the Russians, and they'd save the big ones for them."

"You sound like an expert."

"I've been listening to Duane."

"And how does he know so much about it all?"

"It seems that some buddies of his were involved in the war's initial provocation."

"Duane?"

"Uh-huh. He said he was offered it—he didn't know then that the people worked for the Commission—but he turned it down."

"Jesus." It was too much for anybody to absorb. Too much to comprehend. Snow's head spun and the sprains and bruises all seemed to throb at once. No sense in it all, Snow thought. No sense, this isn't my world. It was like being transported to an alien planet that was a carbon copy of earth, but none of the rules he knew applied. But he knew it was his world, he was just realizing that the rulebook he'd been issued didn't contain the plays that the big boys called.

"I think I'm going to lie down," Snow told Leslie. "Things hurt and I want to be in good form for tonight. I think it's going to be a very heavy-duty evening."

"Why do you say that?"

"Just a feeling," he answered. "Just a feeling."

Leslie woke Snow gently at 7:30 PM to ask if he wanted something to eat before the meeting. Yes, he replied, he'd be down after he'd showered.

As he lay there in the semidark room, sunshine behind draperies, Snow thought about the evening. He knew what he had to do.

The blood rushed through his head; Beckett could feel his pulse speed up, throb more deeply as he lay there thinking about Simon—and Tracy. The anger and the sorrow, the frustration and the hatred boiled together. He threw back the covers and took a scalding shower, as if he could burn away the fire of hate. To survive that night, he had to purge himself of emotion, streamline his cunning. Snow knew that survival meant being colder and more calculating than the cold and calculating killer he had to kill. Snow was prepared to die, for he knew it would be impossible to live knowing that somewhere Eric Simon was still alive, and those he held dear were not.

"I represent an extraordinary group of men and women from all over the United States, and the world, for that matter."

The speaker was a slight man named Alexander Hamilton. A man who dressed like a politician and spoke like one. Slick, charming, untrustworthy. Snow knew his type well.

"These men and women have given their sweat, blood, and dollars to our organization. They work for us—often forty hours or more a week—after completing their regular hours of employment. Most of these people are presently employed by the federal government, though we do have some members in private industry. We're known within our own circles as the Consortium."

Hamilton leaned back in his wingback chair, crossed his right leg over the left, and glanced at Eric Simon, with whom he had entered fifteen minutes before. The weasely Hamilton seemed to have something over Simon. Rank? Snow wondered. Certainly it seemed as though the little man was the power politician and Simon was the man who carried out rather than originated the orders.

Snow checked his watch: It was 8:15. Hamilton continued, unperturbed, and droned on.

Leslie and Duane were also listening, with only half an ear. It seemed to Snow that they had heard all this before. Snow felt an elation and a strange curiosity. Tonight, he knew, the mystery would finally unravel; tonight the pieces would all fall into place.

Beckett's heart raced. As casually as he could, he reached down beside the cushion of the chair he sat in, seeking the reassurance of the Ingram he had taken from Duane's armory earlier that afternoon and placed there. His entire body tensed and shook imperceptibly as he listened to the weasel talk. His taut muscles screamed for a call to action. His breath came faster; he breathed through his mouth to avoid making noise. How long could this go on? He wanted to kill! *Now!*

Snow looked at Leslie. Her face belied no emotion. In fact she seemed to be more intent on staring at a Matisse print than on listening to Hamilton. Duane, too, sat impassively and sipped at his scotch. Christ! he thought. How can they be so fucking calm?

Suddenly Simon's voice overrode Hamilton's snide drone.

"This group of people is not widely known. Its existence would cause some alarm to its enemies—the foremost of which is the Commission—and to a number of other people as well, who would be likely to misunderstand us. That is primarily because the news media have distorted and twisted everything about the man to whom we have pledged our allegiance. I expect they'd try to destroy us just as they did him."

His voice grew bitter. "They *think* they've destroyed him—the liberal-dominated news media and the Jews. But they have *not!* My presence in this room, and the existence of thousands of us, bears witness to the fact. Just as he was, we too are patriotic. We don't wish to see America destroyed.

"You have read the files on Operation Prometheus. You know what the Commission plans to do and how they plan to destroy America." Simon was fervent, captivating. Even Snow was intent on what the giant man had to say.

"*We* can use the Commission's plan to our own good," Simon said. "With the microfilm information you have, and—" he looked straight at Beckett, "with the material you have, Mr. Snow, we can force the Commission to accept our voice in the execution of their plan. By gaining a niche for ourselves, we may prevent the destruction of this great nation."

Snow choked. Anger was bitter and vile in his mouth. "And you want it to make a power base for this man you follow, correct?"

Simon nodded.

"And who might that man be?" Snow asked, struggling to keep the hostility out of his voice. Trying not to tip his hand before its time.

"That goes without saying, Mr. Snow."

"Does it? Try me; I want to be sure."

Eric Simon straightened his spine and leaned forward. "Who is the only president in history to be hounded from the presidency by a pack of lying, cheating thugs and Commies?" he asked.

Snow had stopped feeling the blows of surprise, but this one nearly threw him. Certainly he had heard rumors that people still loyal to this disgraced president hung on in government, feeding him information, urging him to unite them and march again to power. They threw fundraisers for him, had their sad little get-togethers to honor him. True, many powerful leaders still sought his advice, and he was even invited to the White House on honorary occasions.

"You've got to be out of your mind!" Snow said quietly, leaning forward. Hamilton's hand moved quickly to his coat as if going for a gun, when Snow leaned back, he relaxed again. Snow stared at him, disbelieving. "You want *me* to join you in helping put that fascist back in power?"

"You shouldn't talk like that, Mr. Snow." Simon's voice was threatening. Snow felt his anger rise dangerously.

"Easy, Eric," Monroe intervened. "It's quite a shock to hear, and I think you ought to give Snow a better chance."

Simon acquiesced with a nod and an impatient gesture. "Mr. Snow, we are everywhere," he continued. "We are at the highest levels in the military, in police departments, in the intelligence communities—in every important government branch, from the IRS to the Justice Department. We are powerful. And we will prevail."

"That's fine," Snow declared icily. "But I don't choose to join you. In fact, I don't think I want to hear any more of this." Snow started to get up, reaching as he did for the Ingram. He'd end it now.

"Sit down, Mr. Snow!" With stunning speed, Hamilton had pulled a revolver from his armpit holster. Snow slowly sat down. His moment could wait; the story would play itself out.

"I don't think you understand what I am saying, Mr. Snow," Simon continued. "You don't have a choice in that matter. You can either join us or we kill you. It's that simple."

"Now wait a minute, Eric." Monroe was on his feet. "That's going a little too far, and I'm not going to have that kind of shit happening in *my* house." Hamilton looked nervously from him to Beckett, his weapon at the ready.

"Please sit down, Mr. Monroe," said Hamilton.

"Sit down?" Monroe's voice grew louder. "You're

telling *me* to sit down? This is my fucking house," he roared, "and I will do as I fucking well please. Do you understand?"

"Please, Duane," Simon said. "Please sit down."

"Eric, I've gone along with a lot of the things you've done." Monroe's face twisted into a frown. "I've helped you to some extent. But I had a choice, and I think Beckett here deserves the same choice."

"He *does* have the same choice," Simon told him. "Only you didn't know it was a nonchoice. Luckily, you took the correct course."

"You filthy bastard, get out of my house!"

Monroe had moved less than half a step toward Simon when Hamilton shot him.

The big mercenary soldier stiffened, and then like a monster hemlock deciding whether or not to succumb to the logger's axe, toppled to the floor.

It was all the distraction Snow needed. He whipped the Ingram from the cushion beside him and shot Alexander Hamilton in the head. The slick little man's face and head were now unrecognizable.

"You!" Snow pointed the Ingram at Simon. "Sit still."

"Snow, don't be a fool," Simon pleaded. "What better option do you have? You're going to be tracked down and killed by the Commission. Do you want to spend your entire life running until some day when you're a little too tired of running and they come for you. Join *us*. *We* can give you the chance."

Snow listened. Christ, the man was persuasive!

"No, Mr. Simon. Your band of marauders and terrorists aren't where I cast my lot."

"Terrorists?"

"I know about you, Mr. Simon. I *know* about you."

"I don't know what you mean," Simon replied, seemingly perplexed.

"Have you talked to your buddy on the motorcycle lately?"

Simon's eyes grew wide.

"Come on, Mr. Simon, your man on the motorcycle. What's wrong, cat got your tongue?" Snow moved closer. "Well, maybe we ought to cut it out."

"I . . . I can't imagine what you're talking about," Simon said. "I don't know of any such person."

"Liar!" Snow kicked him on the shins. When the giant bent over in pain, he smashed the barrel of the Ingram down on Simon's head. Blood rushed out of the gash. "You're not only a fucking murderer," Beckett shouted. "You're a liar, to boot.

"I found you out, Simon . . . in Amsterdam. Your man arrived at the Anne Frank House the day before me. They killed him. I've got his papers, Simon. All of them. And the Xeroxes I turned over to you at the inn were among them.

"You killed Steve Drachler, and the professor, and—" Snow's voice choked wtih rage. "And Tracy!"

Leslie's face was white with horror, amazement.

"Why did you *do* it?" Snow cried. "Why? You pile of shit!"

Simon did not answer, his face an inhuman mask. "Why!" Snow screamed again and loosed a single shot from the Ingram. Simon's bloodcurdling scream was one of anguish. His right kneecap was shattered.

"Why? Tell me or I'll blow the other one off too!"

"A mistake," Simon grunted through clenched teeth. "It was a mistake. It was unauthorized, the man used to work for me. He was a defector, he was working for the Commisshu-u-uu-u-n." Simon's words faded into a plaid of screams as Snow put a bullet into the other knee. Simon clutched himself in agony. "For Christ's sake," he wailed. "Have pity! Show some mercy!"

"Like you showed Tracy? You filthy sack of shit!"

Snow walked over to Simon and slapped him up the side of his head. Simon's face was turning ashen. He was losing blood, and he would be in shock soon.

"Call a doctor, for Christ's sake." It was a high-pitched whine now.

"Sure, Mr. Simon. Just as soon as you tell me why. Why the hand, the head, and why, for God's sake, Tracy?"

"Because we . . ." Simon's voice was weaker. "Because we needed you. We wanted you to do things. We . . . uhhhn, oh mother of Christ, it hurts, call a doctor."

"Okay, just finish."

"Because we could manipulate *you* better if we isolated you. We were trying to drive you crazy. We wanted to use you against the Commission. Uhhhh fuck! Fuck, it hurts! That's it! That's all! Call the doctor!"

"Why me? Why did you need to manipulate me?"

"You were our ace in the hole," Simon muttered. "You had the box. We knew what was in it, and we wanted to use it. I really didn't think they'd give it to any of my people; they're too well known to Mossad. You—you they'd trust."

"Thank you, Simon," Snow said. "You don't know how I've waited for this. I'll take care of things now. The pain'll be over soon."

Snow walked over to Simon and looked at the twisted mass of exposed tissue and tendons. He put the muzzle of the Ingram to Simon's temple and squeezed the trigger. Simon fell back limply in his chair.

Snow felt the tension ooze from his own body. He was emptied, released. It was over.

"Come on, Leslie, let's get out of here." Beckett turned to Leslie and the sight that greeted him was a hammer blow to his gut: She was pointing a monstrous handgun at him.

"I'm not going anywhere with you, Beck. Drop your gun." Leslie's voice was calm but determined. "I'll blow your guts out before you can raise it." His Ingram clattered to the floor. "Now sit . . . there." She pointed to a chair next to her.

"I don't believe this," Snow said. "You, Leslie, of all people. You? What are you *doing?*"

"Simon was right, you know," she began. "What kind of life would it be to run from place to place. Never being your own person, never being yourself. Always having to be the name on your false ID. Huh? What kind of life is that?"

Snow was silent. She had bought Simon's arguments.

"I've changed in the past weeks," Leslie continued. "They've been changes I always wanted to make. If I went back to running away from people, I'd be going back to reacting, responding, instead of taking my life in my own hands. I've lived like that before, Beck, and nobody is going to take my life away from me again— ever—until I die. I want control and the Consortium is my only protection."

Snow took a deep breath.

"I hadn't mentioned anything too specific about the Dachau notes," Snow began. "But there is something that can screw up the Commission's Operation Prometheus for good. That can give you the protection you want."

"Oh, come on. You saw what happened when you went to the press. Do you think you're going to have better luck next time?"

"No, it's not that way. You know I mentioned that the notes contained dossiers on twenty-seven members of the Commission. Well, one of them is proof that Kincaid Carothers and three other top Commission members, including a man named Alec Baran who is known as 'Prometheus,' were behind assassination attempts on Mao and top Chinese leaders."

"That's past history. Mao's dead."

"One of the people that the group tried to have assassinated is now China's premier," Snow continued, pleading. He felt the hair stand up on the back of his neck.

"Don't you understand?" he asked. "All we have to do is get that information, that and the Operation Indochina materials, and they'll pull out. That will destroy Operation Prometheus forever."

"So what does that accomplish," Leslie asked sarcastically. "The Commission will just find another way. Don't you see that by using the Dachau notes to your own end, you can have a big hand in shaping a future for yourself?"

"If it means dealing with people like him, Leslie, I don't want to." Snow nodded toward the hulk of Simon's body. "And what, you ask, would getting the materials to Peking do? Well, the stopping of Operation Prometheus would buy time. Time to use the rest of the Dachau notes to blow the Delphi Commission apart. Time to dismantle it.

"Look, the Commission is evil. That much power in that small a group of hands cannot *help* but be abused, as long as people are human and have human urges to possess and control. Something that big is inevitably evil."

"I don't know that I agree," Leslie said. "But it's a moot question, for you, at least."

"Why?"

"Because I'm going to use the materials the way *I* see fit. Simon isn't alone, you know. I have the names of others. I will use the material just as Simon envisioned."

"You're mad!"

"You're mistaken," Leslie said. "I'm sane. For me to do anything else would be insane."

"No. Look, come with me. The Chinese will be

grateful. We won't have to run. They'll take care of us."

"Maybe," Leslie said. "But first you've got to get there, and those odds aren't too good. Everything is going to be doubly watched. And if you *do* get there, what makes you think you'll get an audience with the premier? Why would anybody believe you? Or if they did, what's to prevent them from just taking the notes, getting rid of you, and using them for their own power purposes? Those notes could be a real handy weapon for international negotiations. No, Beck. I'm sorry, but there's too much left to chance. I can't buy it."

Snow was shaken. She could be right. What kind of hero *would* he be?

"Can I think about it?" Snow asked.

"No. You've thought it out very well, thank you, and I don't think it's going to do any good. All it might do is give you a chance to escape. I've seen your treachery, and I can't risk that. I hate to do this, Beck." She pulled the hammer back. "But it's either you or me."

Snow faced sure and sudden death. But a soft purring filled the room, and for years to come Snow would remember its sweet notes. Duane Monroe emptied an entire clip of the Ingram's ammunition into Leslie Lewis, who twitched and jerked under their impact. Her huge revolver's single report sailed harmlessly through the ceiling.

"Help me up, will you, Beck?" Monroe said. "Well, come on, you look like you've seen a ghost, boy!"

Snow helped wrestle the giant into a chair. A massive circle of red stained the side of his shirt and pants.

"I don't think it hit anything vital; it's just a graze," Monroe said.

Snow was unable to speak.

"Call a doctor, Beckett, would you? The number's above the phone."

"But, but . . ."

"Look, it's the first thing a professional learns. If

you're outgunned, take the first shot like it was a ringer and play dead. If you're lucky, you won't stop any more rounds. I'd say it worked."

"Jesus . . . Jesus."

"Right. Quit mumbling. This hurts like fucking bloody hell. Call the medic, okay?"

Beckett and Duane sipped on drinks while they waited for the doctor.

"So, Beck. What're you going to do?" Monroe asked.

"Go to Peking."

"What if you don't make it?"

"I have to."

MORE
BEST-SELLING FICTION
FROM PINNACLE

More Best-Selling Fiction from Pinnacle

More Best-Selling Fiction from Pinnacle